To Face the Sun

Frances Patton Statham

TO FACE THE SUN

BOCAGE BOOKS

ISBN: 978-0-9895007-2-2
(Previous ISBN: 0-449-90140-8)

Library of Congress Control Number: 2013917667

Cover Design by Steve McAfee

First Edition: May 1986 by Ballantine Books,
                a division of Random House
Second Edition: April 2014 by Bocage Books

10 9 8 7 6 5 4 3 2

www.bocagebooks.com
bocagebooks@mindspring.com

To the valiant Allied men and women
who fought for freedom in the Pacific
during World War II

Chapter 1

WITH ENGINES AT FULL THROTTLE, THE U.S. NAVY hospital ship *Good Hope* sliced through the deceptively tranquil waters of the Pacific.

Amanda "Sunny" Fitzpatrick stood at the railing and watched the foaming waves as they parted in the wake of the moving ship. She had come on deck to escape the heat and to hide her tears from the others. Navy nurses were supposed to be tough, but the death of the nineteen-year-old marine corporal in her care had devastated her.

Now, in the setting sun that cast a sepia glow over the seascape and gave an unearthly, eerie quality to the distant coral islands rising out of the sea, Sunny fought for composure before returning belowdecks. Hungrily, she gulped the clean, pure air and felt the cooling breeze, like a comforting whisper, touching her face.

From his vantage point on the bridge, Lt. Commander Kirk Singleton watched the young nurse. At first, she was indistinguishable from any other white-uniformed woman aboard ship. But then she moved, and an aureole of light encircled her, setting fire to the pale blond hair. Sunny Fitzpatrick. It could be no other.

"Take over for me, Mister Brogdon," Kirk requested, and immediately left the bridge.

As the sandy-haired officer traversed the hospital ship

that had once been the luxury liner *Lelani,* he was aware that no trace of the ship's ancestry was apparent. Her elegant staterooms had been turned into sick bays, her chandeliered dining rooms into blacked-out mess halls. And her passenger lists, once boasting the privileged scions of society, now contained only name, rank, and serial number of the wounded being transported to the base hospital in Auckland, New Zealand.

The war in the Pacific was not going well. Wake Island had fallen to the Japanese; the Dutch East Indies had been invaded; the British surrender of Singapore was imminent. And MacArthur was being pushed to the very edge of starvation as the siege against the Bataan Peninsula continued.

The roar of the ocean disguised Kirk's footsteps on deck. "Here, I thought you might need a mug-up, Fitzpatrick," he said in a gruff manner as he held out a coffee mug for Sunny.

At the sound of the familiar voice, she quickly brushed a lingering tear from her cheek and faced the ship's officer.

"Thank you, Singleton." She accepted the mug and cradled it in both hands before taking a sip.

Seeing the remnants of tears marring her almost flawless complexion, and her topaz eyes unable to hide the vast sadness, Kirk guessed the cause of her distress. Losing a patient was always hard for the men and women charged with the care of the wounded. But losing Hurdy, the little guy who had cheered the entire ship, despite his grievous wounds, had been especially difficult to reconcile.

"It wasn't your fault. Don't take it so..."

The lift of her chin warned him that she wanted no sympathy. "Isn't it strange," she interrupted, "that it's the middle of winter at home, and yet summer in this part of the world."

He took his cue from her words and responded in kind. "Not so strange, actually, when you realize we're upside down on the globe." With a sudden , teasing grin he warned,

"But enjoy this luxury sea voyage, Fitzpatrick, because it's going to be hotter than Texas chili once we reach land."

She smiled in gratitude at his feeble attempt at lightness for her sake.

The drone of a plane and the clanging of bells cut through the stillness of twilight. "Enemy approaching at five o'clock. All hands take cover."

The voice from the loudspeaker came too late. With coffee mugs flying, Kirk Singleton pushed Sunny to the deck just as the Japanese Zero dived for attack.

To the Japanese pilot, the red cross of mercy painted on the deck of the undefended hospital ship *Good Hope* merely served as a practice target, until a U.S. destroyer, escorting the vessel through Japanese infested waters, retaliated, opened fire and drove the plane away.

Getting up from his protective position, Kirk said, "That was close."

Sunny pushed herself up from the deck also, until she was almost at eye level with Kirk. "You knocked the breath out of me," she accused.

"What are you complaining about, Fitzpatrick? I saved your life, didn't I? What more do you want me to do?"

"You can recommend me for a Purple Heart."

His laughter stopped when he saw blood marring the knee of her white stocking. "Were you hit?" he demanded.

"Don't look so frightened. It was the broken coffee mug—not the Zero—that did it."

The relieved naval officer chided, "And you want a medal for your altercation with a cup of coffee?"

"No. Just warn me, Singleton. That's all I ask before you attempt to save my life another time."

Lt. Commander Kirk Singleton suddenly grinned. Sunny Fitzpatrick was braver than he thought. Yes, she was going to be all right after all.

Chapter 2

IN A PRIVATE COMPARTMENT OF SINGAPORE'S RED Dragon Restaurant, Alex Ramsay, marquess of Dalhousie, sat oriental-style before a lacquered table and watched Chuang San Chu finish his cup of tea.

Born in India, Alex was the fourth generation of Dalhousies to serve as British diplomats in the East. He had returned to England with his parents only on the brief leaves awarded to all His Majesty's foreign servants every few years, and then later to attend Oxford. Now, his parents were dead. And the ancestral home in Scotland that he had inherited seemed more alien to him than the government compound in New Delhi; for his heart had remained in the East.

"The guns sound closer," Alex commented, his clipped, British voice giving no hint of the urgency of the moment.

"Yes. The Japanese will be here soon," Chuang San Chu agreed, equally unhurried in his reply.

When Chuang placed his empty cup on the table, Alex uncrossed his legs and rose to his feet. Silently he gripped Chuang's hand in friendship. A priceless ruby suddenly weighted the sleeve of Chuang's coat. The transaction between the two men was so swift that not even the white-bearded man at the peephole was aware of the change in ownership.

Without looking back, Alex parted the bamboo curtain to the next compartment where MaFleur was hiding. He nodded in her direction and proceeded to follow her out the back exit into the alleyway.

Chuang, the young Chinese general, waited for an additional five minutes. Then, he too left the Red Dragon and headed east.

Shapes and silhouettes came alive in the dark, and a terrible sense of time running out gripped the city. As the lion beaters once flushed their prey from the savannahs for the hunter, so the steady din of guns in the distance announced the approach of the Japanese to the city of lions, jewel in the British crown, and royal gateway to China—Singapore.

Towering over the oriental woman at his side, Alex Ramsay traveled south toward the canal. He glanced at the February sky blazing with fire. The air, perfumed for so long with the scents of musk and opium, now bombarded Alex's nose with the scent of death.

The British naval fleet was destroyed. The great battery of guns, set in immovable concrete on the bluffs, faced hopelessly out to sea, while the conquerors, coming by land, moved steadily down the Malay Peninsula and crossed the Straits of Johore to the north. Soon, Singapore would be in the hands of the enemy.

Alex did not plan to be among the 130,000 British prisoners of war handed over to the Japanese in the official surrender ceremony. But he had cut it too close, waiting for Chuang to arrive. The airdrome was destroyed, the last flying boat had left two weeks previously. Now, he had to rely on MaFleur for his escape. Even though Abdul, his Indian valet, had given her name to him, Alex was still uneasy. For in war-torn Singapore, loyalty was governed by the amount of money put into the hand. Nothing else.

A pile of rubble from the recent bombing blocked their way as Alex and MaFleur emerged from a side street. The woman stopped. "We will go back to the Buddhist temple and pass through the grounds."

Alex had no recourse but to follow. As they retraced their steps to the narrow street that intersected the alleyway, Alex saw no one. Yet, he had a distinct feeling that they were not alone. He slowed just long enough to peer over his shoulder. Shadows paused as he paused and then sped up again as he moved. His jaw tightened, but he said nothing to MaFleur.

Like a bizarre apparition, the temple came into view. Carved in white stone, the temple resembled a slain Goliath's head, with the entrance through a huge, cavernous mouth. Its walkway formed a zigzag pattern, to circumvent evil spirits from entering. Before Alex reached the entrance, he suddenly forced MaFleur off the bridge.

"Keep quiet," he whispered, and with his gun aimed at her head to insure her silence, he crouched and waited.

Two men passed within a few feet and Alex gritted his teeth to keep from swearing aloud. He recognized Ah Min, the gardener he had fired at Government House in New Delhi. And he knew the man was up to no good.

The other man with him wore gauze over his face, but with the stench of the debris in the open irrigation ditches and the threat of cholera, the mask might have been a health precaution and not a disguise. There was something about the man's walk that reminded him of Abdul. But that was impossible. His personal valet was still in India.

Regardless of the identity of the second man, Alex was almost certain that he was being led into a trap. He waited until the two men disappeared into the temple. Again, Alex spoke to MaFleur. "It's up to you, woman, whether you want to live or not." He clicked the trigger in her ear and she shuddered. "You understand?"

"Yes."

"Well then, let's go. In another direction."

A cautious Alex stood, and MaFleur, clad in a brightly flowered sarong and jacket, half-trotted through the maze of streets, for her own life depended upon Alex Ramsay's reaching the canal.

In the jungled botanical gardens in the heart of the city, a soft rain peppered the leaves of trees where wild monkeys screeched at the sudden invasion by humans. The two passed a greenhouse where exotic flowers waited to replenish the gardens. And in a shed at the back, a hidden cache of bicycles, sent ahead the previous week, also waited — for the Japanese foot soldiers crossing the strait.

On into the night, MaFleur and Alex traveled by foot, until they finally reached the old canal teeming with Chinese and Malayans preparing to leave the city before the invaders arrived. A steady pitch of voices bargaining for last minute goods greeted Alex. MaFleur quickly led him through the mass of milling boat people toward the sampan that he had contracted for, sight unseen.

Creaking against the rising wind, the boat, with its orange sail lowered, looked as if it were in danger of sinking before it left harbor. Smoke and cooking odors indicated that the boatman was preparing his evening meal.

MaFleur stopped and pointed to the boat. While she remained on shore, Alex, balancing himself on the swaying plank, negotiated the space between the riverbank and the sampan.

Standing before the old man who sat before his cooking pot, Alex said, "You are the owner of this boat? Li-Chen?"

The old man nodded.

Alex knelt before the man, pulled a leather pouch from about his neck, and handed it to Li-Chen to seal the bargain. And when he turned toward shore to dismiss MaFleur, she had already disappeared.

With a small lantern flickering over the dark waters, Alex retrieved his pipe and sat in silence while the old man dished up his stew.

There was no need to be in a hurry, for it was low tide. They would not be moving from the harbor until early morning. Finally, when Li-Chen had finished his meal, he hauled up the wooden gangplank at Alex's insistence, to prevent anyone from boarding the boat in the night.

Along the walkway of the temple, Abdul paced up and down and searched for some sign of MaFleur. After an hour, he had given up trying to track her and had returned to the temple grounds. Why had he not waited for Sir Alex by the canal? He knew the answer even as he asked himself the question. There were too many witnesses about the canal in the early part of the evening.

The empty temple had been the right place. But something had gone wrong to arouse the Englishman's suspicion. If that had not happened, Abdul would now be the possessor of the priceless ruby.

But it was still not too late. That is, if MaFleur returned in time to lead him to Sir Alex before he left Singapore. There was no way he could escape by water before the tide came in. Abdul looked in disgust at Ah Min, his accomplice, picking his teeth with his dagger.

MaFleur suddenly emerged from the darkness. "Your master is more cautious than you led me to believe," she admonished Abdul.

His look of relief was tempered by anger at waiting for MaFleur. "What did you do to make the sahib suspicious?" Abdul demanded.

"It was your fault, not mine," she countered. "Why couldn't you have stayed farther back, or even waited for him inside the temple?"

He did not honor her question with a reply. Instead he said, "Did you deliver him to the sampan?"

"Yes."

"And you can point it out from all the others?"

"Yes. It has a dragon painted on its prow."

"Fifty boats have dragons on their prows," he spat out.

"But this one is green and gold. If I found it the first time, I should have no trouble finding it a second," she scolded.

Motioning for Ah Min to follow him, Abdul set out toward the canal with MaFleur. He would wait until the boat people had gone to sleep before making his move.

The petite MaFleur walked again through the ravaged streets of Singapore. The route was much shorter this time, for she had taken Alex Ramsay out of the way in the hope that Abdul would catch up with them.

"Why didn't you steal the ruby in India?" MaFleur asked Abdul as they walked.

"Because the sahib didn't have it there. The gem was hidden with an old priest beyond the mountains. And he left the compound before I could follow."

"You think he still has the ruby?"

"Of course. It's part of his inheritance from his father. He would never give it up willingly."

With Ah Min trailing them, MaFleur led Abdul to the canal. "That's it," she said, pointing to the familiar shape of the sampan tied to the wooden piling. "I'll wait for you at the Red Dragon."

One by one, the lights on the boats went out, and soon a soft snoring, magnified over the expanse of water, reached the bank to tell Abdul and Ah Min that the boat people were asleep.

Andul gave the signal to Ah Min. They crept silently onto the pier and seeing the plank taken up for the night, they slipped into the water and swam to the sampan with the dragon barely visible on the prow.

In the fine mist that surrounded the boat, the metal of the dagger blade held between Ah Min's teeth was dull, with no reflection. A slight movement of the boat, a more urgent lapping of water against its hull were the only indications that the sampan had been boarded.

Used to working in the dark, Ah Min pointed to the two sleeping figures. One was in full view on deck—the old man who owned the boat. The other was partially hidden by the woven rattan mat cover at the stern, and the tarpaulin thrown over his body to ward off the dampness of the monsoon season.

With a last-minute aversion to taking his master's life,

Abdul motioned for Ah Min to kill the man in the cabin of the boat while he attended to the other in full view.

As Abdul made short work of the figure on deck, he heard a slight gurgle from the stern of the boat. Disappointed that Alex Ramsay had not even put up a struggle against Ah Min, Abdul walked to the stern. He removed the tarpaulin and looked down.

The man, with short dark hair, still looked asleep, even though the blood from his throat was rapidly forming a stain on the quilted pallet beneath him. But something was wrong. The man was not a Caucasian, but an Oriental. Swiftly, Abdul ran to the prow and examined the dragon head. It was not green and gold, but silvery blue. A furious Abdul realized he was on the wrong boat. He and Ah Min had killed the wrong man, while the marquess of Dalhousie, somewhere on the canal, still possessed the coveted ruby.

An angry Abdul placed the gangplank onto the riverbank. And signaling for Ah Min to follow him, he raced back and forth along the canal, but the green and gold dragon eluded him. Finally, in frustration, he gave up and returned to the Red Dragon to settle his score with MaFleur.

Farther down the canal, Alex, with only an occasional light from shore to guide him, dug the strong wooden pole into the deep mud bottom and leaned hard against it. At first, the boat moved little, but it wasn't long before he got the hang of it and was able to use his energy more wisely.

He only wished Parliament had been a little wiser. And then, perhaps, Singapore could have been saved. The government should have accepted Chiang Kai-shek's offer of Chinese troops to help defend Malaya. But the M.P's had never been able to tell the Chinese from the Japanese, or friend from foe. To them, they were all Orientals, to be distrusted equally. Even Chuang San Chu had not been able to convince the authorities to arm the Chinese against their common enemy. But now that the primary source of tin and rubber had been taken over by the Japanese, the men who'd previously had their heads in the sand would be forced to deal with the situation.

The military brass in the Far East had been equally unseeing. Too busy sending optimistic messages to London to negate the dismal predictions of many of the foreign correspondents, they had made no provisions whatever to defend the peninsula against invasion from the north. It never occurred to them that the flooded rice fields could be breached by small tanks and gun carriers.

Ordered to leave the East for Australia, Alex was glad that he had waited for Chuang to arrive in Singapore. The Dalhousie ruby he had turned over to the young general would buy many guns to use against the Japanese. That's why it was so necessary for all the caution he had taken that night, even to moving the sampan from its mooring place at the pier. He wanted no one to discover the priceless ruby had changed hands in the Red Dragon. For if China collapsed, then the invasion of India would be certain.

Close to the mouth of the harbor, Alex, unable to use the pole because of the depth of the water, weighed anchor and, in the creaking, lapping motion of the boat, he walked toward the woven rattan cover indicating the sampan's sleeping quarters.

Like other men all along the canal, he wrapped a gray tarpaulin around him and went to sleep.

Chapter 3

AS THE SUN BURNED ITS WAY ACROSS THE WATER WITH a glare bringing tears to the eyes, Alex Ramsay awoke. He reached inside his shirt, felt his passport, and then turned to make sure his survival kit was beside him. A box of fishhooks, twine, matches in a waterproof can, a flare, a knife, tablets of quinine were the main ingredients, with a small packet of biscuits to stave off hunger—no item priceless in itself, yet each capable of saving his life if need be.

Feeling the movement of the boat, Alex knew that Li-Chen had already unfurled the orange sail to catch the quartering wind. As the tide pushed them from the harbor, Alex stood, stretched, and looked back at the vast armada of fishing boats and sampans trailing behind them.

The boats were crowded with far too many people for safety, and sat low in the water. There were Chinese in most of them, for they faced certain massacre if they remained in Singapore. They preferred to take their chances on the open sea, even though they were unsure of reaching another island.

Alex walked past the cooking pot, where the cold fish stew from the previous evening waited to be eaten for breakfast. With no appetite for it, Alex left the stew untouched. Far more important to him was the half-filled rain barrel lashed to the stern. The water supply to Singapore had been cut off by the Japanese; so Alex had drunk little liquid for the past few days beyond the occasional cup of tea, such as the one shared with Chuang at the Red Dragon.

Once he had satisfied his thirst from the rain barrel, Alex greeted the old boatman, who had put on his coolie hat as protection against the sun.

"Good morning, Uncle. I'll take over for a while, if you'd like."

"You have eaten breakfast?" Li-Chen questioned.

"I'll eat later. I'm not hungry yet. You go ahead."

Accepting Alex's offer, Li-Chen gave up the oars. He watched as Alex settled into the routine and, satisfied that the sampan would be safe, he started in the direction of the cooking pot.

Alex's championship sculling became an asset. Only the sound of the oars in the water disturbed the sea's stillness as the sampan moved steadily along the curve of the emerald green island with its palm fronds leaning against the breeze.

With his bowl in his hands, Li-Chen left the stern and crouched beyond the oarlocks. "There is little cloud cover this morning," he remarked to Alex.

His uneasiness transferred itself to Alex. "Perhaps the Japanese will be too busy to bother with boats trying to leave—especially today."

"Perhaps," the old man repeated. But his voice held no confidence.

A few minutes later, a slight drone, barely perceptible at first, grew steadily louder, diminishing the peace and serenity of the early morning. Out of the soft white cumulus clouds to the north, a Japanese Zero headed for the armada.

"Take cover, Li-Chen. Here it comes," Alex warned, and began to row in double time.

Geysers of water flew up where machine gun shells searched for prey. Alex didn't look back, but he could hear the cries of the frightened, the wounded, as masts, like broken matchsticks, splintered in the wind from the strafing attack.

"Li-Chen?" Alex shouted, and waited for the man to affirm that he was all right.

When there was no answer, Alex turned his head to look. The boatman, still gripping the wooden bowl in his hand, lay on the riddled deck. Beside him, water from the damaged rain barrel rushed toward the bow and carried his coolie hat in its stream.

Leaving the oars to go to Li-Chen, Alex heard the plane returning for a second run. And this time, another plane joined it. With the rising sun visible on its fuselage, the second plane dive-bombed for the lead sampan, with its orange sail flapping furiously.

Alex sat down, grabbed the oars again to maneuver the boat out of the way. But this time, Alex Ramsay's luck ran out. A piece of shrapnel hit his arm, the force knocking him against the deck. The oar to his portside splintered, and the boat, as if twisted by a giant hand, spun helplessly in the water and finally foundered against the coral rocks.

Time and again the planes flew into the clouds, banked, and returned to produce further devastation upon the armada. Bits of wreckage, pulled by the tide, floated out to sea. But the marquess of Dalhousie, servant to His Majesty King George, lay where he had fallen, with the sun beating down upon his head while the boat remained caught on the rocks.

Two planes had effectively riddled the armada, with no help from the Japanese battle guns farther out to sea.

Alex's first awareness that he had survived came with the slow, steady throbbing pain in his arm and the stiffness of his neck. He lay in a cramped position in the boat rapidly filling with water.

He didn't know how long he'd lain there, with the boat buffeted by the wind. As he raised his head, he saw that somehow the boat had worked its way free from the rocks, but the damage to the sampan was grave. It wasn't seaworthy enough even to get back to shore, much less to reach an island in the West Indies chain.

Alex looked at the debris still floating in the blue-green sea. Telltale fins of sharks were visible above the waterline — a special danger to any man with the smell of blood upon him.

He removed his shirt, tore it into strips, and wrapped his wounded left arm. He had not received the full force of the shrapnel missile, else the bone in his arm would have been broken, as well.

The boat began to list badly. Alex had only a few minutes before it sank. Crawling carefully along the boat to the stern, dragging the one remaining oar, he passed the body of Li-Chen. The old man was dead, and there was no help for him. As Alex shifted his weight to reach under the matted cover for the military survival kit, the boat groaned. Quickly he brought the bundle out from under the tarpaulin and removed the deflated rubber raft. He pushed the cord and waited for the one-man raft to fill with air. He held his breath for the hissing that would indicate a hole. But the sinking sampan was now the vocal one.

Without knowing whether the raft was still intact after the Zero had riddled the deck, Alex threw the raft free of the sinking boat. In desperation, he grabbed the tarpaulin, the oar, and the kit containing the fishhooks and the flare, and slipping into the water, he swam toward the raft as two sharks, only a hundred feet away, responded to the noise in the water.

Hoisting himself onto the raft, Alex raised the oar to defend himself against the shark heading straight for him. A second before impact, he turned the oar into a javelin, deflecting the blow of the shark. On impact, Alex was thrown into the water, along with his survival kit. But using his last remaining source of strength, he managed to scramble back onto the raft.

Helpless now without the oar, he waited for the second attack while his survival kit floated from his reach. But the shark, unlike the Japanese Zero, did not return. And Alex Ramsay, in the flimsy raft, floated out to sea on the whim of the current.

Refueling at Surabaya, the American destroyer, *Viscount*, under the command of Matt Willoughby, headed out in the middle of the night to seek and intercept the Japanese fleet bound for the northern section of the five-hundred-mile island of Java.

They traveled in convoy — the flagship, with two light cruisers bringing up the rear. Protecting the starboard and port wings of the convoy were eight destroyers besides the *Viscount.*

Twice before, Matt had taken his destroyer into battle under the Dutch admiral, Helfrich. The first time, the Dutch had received credit for his hit; the second time, the British. The Allied joint command did not want the Japanese to know the whereabouts of the American ships.

Once they were under way, with the clouds and mist making visibility impossible, Matt stood on the deck alone until his executive officer, Pearson, joined him.

Commander Matt Willoughby was tall, golden-tanned from the Pacific sun, with eyes to match the blue-green lagoons beyond the coral reefs. Yet his good looks had long ago been discounted by his men, except for an occasional teasing at his effect on the female population of the islands.

As Pearson gazed out into the waters, he spoke. "Tokyo Rose just sent us a message, Commander. Looks like we'll be changing our Dutch guilders for Aussie money by the end of the week."

"Did she say anything about Singapore?"

"Yeah. They're celebrating the surrender in Tokyo right now. Seems Hirohito has ordered *sake* for every adult, and candy for the children, to honor the heroes of the rising sun." The bitterness showed as Pearson spoke. "Oh, and they've changed the Raffles Hotel to some Nip name."

"What about the civilian population? Did she say what's

happened to them?"

"I think they've slaughtered most of the Chinese. Even the ones trying to escape in sampans didn't get beyond the harbor. And they've put all the European women and children in Changi Jail. I swear I got so mad, Commander, that I had to stop listening to her and come on deck for some fresh air. They act like they've never heard of the Geneva Convention."

Matt nodded. "They operate under another code, Pearson. *Bushido.* 'Save the last bullet for yourself.' They consider anybody who surrenders a coward, to be treated worse than a dog."

"Evidently that's what they're doing."

"Well, something has to give soon, Pearson. The Japanese can't keep overextending themselves forever."

"If Washington would just send us some air reconnaissance."

Matt didn't respond, for the lack of air support was a sore subject with him. The Japanese had the command of the skies. And because of it, the movements of the Allied fleet could be monitored, while the Allies had no idea where or when they might run into the entire Japanese fleet. For all Matt knew, the enemy could be directly in front of them at that moment.

They had been lucky so far. And despite the dismal news on two fronts, morale on his ship was high. They had survived the conflagration at Pearl Harbor, the battle of Makassar Strait, and the skirmish near Bali prior to this run.

Pearl Harbor had been lucky for Matt in more ways than one. It was on his shore leave there that he had met Sunny, the daughter of Brigadier General Fitzpatrick, a brilliant retread from World War I. The hospital ship on which she was stationed was due in Auckland in March. And if his luck held out, she would be there by the time he arrived.

A parachute flare, dropped from a plane overhead, suddenly lit up the sea surrounding the Allied convoy.

Dark, heavy hulks of ships loomed on both the port and

starboard sides —ships that were not a part of the Allied convoy.

A startled Matt Willoughby said, "My God, we're in the middle of the whole damned Japanese navy. Sound the alarm, Mr. Pearson."

"General quarters. All men man your battle stations."

Guns in the distance roared and their salvos tunneled through the air to seek out the Allied ships, while the gunners on the *Viscount* took up their positions.

There was now no need for flares. The sea was lit up with the firing of guns, their star shells outlining the enemy ships, until a hit amidships in the Allied convoy caused a huge explosion.

The *Viscount*, part of the fast Jaguar fleet of destroyers designed to protect the slower-moving vessels, had her hands full. Spent shells lay on the deck as gunners fired at the enemy, even as sailors from the abandoned cruiser off port bow swam rapidly to avoid being taken down by the vacuum of their sinking ship. On the *Viscount*, with fires raging on the bridge, the fire brigade attempted to put out the conflagration before it reached the ammunition supplies on deck.

A second deafening explosion pierced the air as another Allied ship was hit. The battle continued, salvos exchanged unremittingly, ships passing from view and then re-appearing while a sudden rain squall diminished all visibility as it helped to contain the flames sweeping along the deck of the *Viscount*.

On into the night, the battle raged. For some, it was an initiation. Raw, young recruits sent straight from basic training stations at Great Lakes, Orlando, and San Diego got their first taste of battle alongside more seasoned veterans.

Their dunking upon passing the equator had been mere horseplay. Now, they were in a baptism of fire, in a deadly game where the survivors of the fire had another gauntlet to run. The Japanese gunners, seeing the sailors bobbing in the water, turned their guns to pick them off, sailor by sailor.

When early morning came, the sea was silent. The battle was over, with the Japanese convoy undeterred in its destination for the Java coast.

Remaining behind, the *Viscount* prowled the waters to search for survivors. Eleven men were picked up—most of them badly burned from the explosions on ship or the fiery oil upon the waters. Some were half-naked. The shape and severity of their wounds followed the lines of their clothing. For the gunners, who regularly removed their shirts, the burns were more widespread. But regardless of their clothes, all were covered by the thick, black oil that floated on the once-beautiful sea.

"Raft sighted off starboard bow," sang the voice of the lookout overhead.

A weary Matt Willoughby, with the sound of guns still ringing in his ears, lifted his binoculars. Amid the oil slicks and debris, an orange raft floated upon the waves. And on the raft was a body. There was no movement, and from that distance, Matt couldn't tell if the body were dead or alive.

"Prepare for rescue," Matt ordered for the twelfth time within the past six hours.

Alex Ramsay was delirious. He had no knowledge of his rescue by the American destroyer *Viscount*. He lay in sick bay with the others, his body badly burned by the sun rather than in battle.

As a corpsman packed his body in ice-cold saline solution to lower his raging fever and soothe his burns, Commander Willoughby walked in.

"Has he said anything yet?" Matt asked.

"Nothing intelligible, sir. He's got heatstroke. I pumped him full of penicillin for his arm, but there's not much you can do about heatstroke—except try to get the fever down. No telling how long he was on the raft."

"He wasn't wearing dog tags?"

"No, sir."

"Any other identification?"

The corpsman shook his head. He didn't mention the small tattoo hidden under the man's left arm. Like hundreds of sailors, he'd probably had it done in some foreign port, but there was no way of knowing where.

Matt left the unknown man's side to speak to the other survivors. Seeing one man in great pain, he said, "We're going to rendezvous with a hospital ship tomorrow, sailor. Think you can hold out until then?"

"I'll have to, sir," the man asserted, and then coughed.

The corpsman turned his head for the owner of the cough. Pneumonia was the complication that sounded the death knell for burn patients. He left Alex Ramsay and went to attend the other patient, while Matt finished his rounds and then went topside.

Chapter 4

THE HOSPITAL SHIP GOOD HOPE RODE AT ANCHOR AS Sunny Fitzpatrick and eleven other nurses stood on deck to watch the *Viscount* link up for the transfer of patients.

Standing beside Sunny was the gray-haired Benita Barksdale, now a veteran of two world wars, for she had served in a naval hospital in Edinburgh in 1918 and after that transferred to the Pacific. There was almost no tour of duty, no Pacific island that she had not already seen or served on.

"Listen to that crew," Benita remarked. "They act as if they haven't seen a woman for twenty years. How disgusting."

Enthusiastic whistles and smart remarks carried over the water as the sailors from the *Viscount* voiced their appreciation of the nurses, dressed in fresh white uniforms.

On board the *Good Hope*, the medical corpsmen, like Benita, bristled at the familiarity of the sailors on the *Viscount*. The corpsmen were not above whistling at others themselves, but they resented it when the nurses on their own ship were treated the same way.

Sunny looked at Benita and laughed. "Don't be such a man-hater, Barksdale. I think they're kinda cute—especially their commander."

"You know him?"

"Yes. His name's Matt Willoughby. I dated him at Pearl. In fact, I think he's just come on deck."

The sailors quieted immediately as their commander appeared and the signal was given for the transfer to begin. Like a cat's cradle seesawing back and forth, the *Good Hope's* Stokes stretcher swung over the expanse between the two ships. As soon as the first patient was safely strapped to the stretcher, the corpsman on board the destroyer gave a sign for it to be hoisted back to the hospital ship. Once the patient was removed, the procedure began all over again, until eleven men had been transferred.

Each nurse, accompanied by a corpsman, left the deck with her charge, until one nurse, Sunny Fitzpatrick, remained to await the last patient.

Matt Willoughby, watching Sunny through his binoculars, made up his mind. He would request permission to board the *Good Hope* for a few minutes, even though only one of the injured had been a member of his crew.

When the last man had arrived on board, Matt's message was received. "Request permission to come aboard."

"Permission granted."

When Sunny saw the cat's cradle swing into action once more, she was elated. Matt was coming aboard.

How frustrating it had been to know that they were close, yet not able to say a word to each other. But then she stared down at her patient and knew she couldn't stay on deck until Matt arrived. Her patient had priority over her heart.

Walking beside the man on the wheeled stretcher, she glanced at his chart. Name: Unknown. Ship: Unknown. Picked up at sea. Diagnosis: Heatstroke, dehydration, second-degree burns, shrapnel wound in left arm, comatose. Treatment: ice baths, intravenous saline solution. Last dosage: 0800.

The man briefly opened his eyes and then closed them again, as if he had seen nothing. "You're going to be all right, sailor," Sunny assured him. "You're on a hospital ship. We'll be in port soon, and then we'll let your family know you're safe."

She spoke, not knowing whether he could hear her or not. But it didn't hurt to try. Many patients in a comatose condition could nevertheless understand what was being said, even though they couldn't respond. How embarrassing for families, sometimes, to be told later every word spoken in a hospital room.

The ship, equipped with enough medical supplies to last a year, had taken on food to last for six months. Huge freezers and refrigerators held meat, vegetables, and fruits, and the greatest delicacy of all in that hot, humid climate — ice cream.

When Sunny reached the ward assigned to her patient, she heard one of the recently transferred men say, "Please, may I have some ice cream?"

A nurse responded, "Sure, good-looking. Just as soon as the doctor finishes with you."

Staring down at the still form of her own patient, Sunny said, "Would you like some ice cream, too, sailor?" But the man did not respond.

Removed from the stretcher to a lower berth usually reserved for the severely burned, the unidentified man waited his turn with the doctor.

"Hello, Sunny."

"Matt."

So happy to see him. Sunny didn't care that Matt Willoughby swept her off her feet and, in front of the entire ward, kissed her. But for propriety's sake, she protested. "Matt, please. Put me down. My patients…"

"Oh, go ahead, Commander. Give her a kiss for me, too," the marine on the second bunk encouraged him, with the ratification of all the men in the ward who could speak.

"I've got two weeks in March," he whispered. "Can you come to Sydney then?"

"I don't know. I'll try."

"I'll write you," he said, and then was gone.

The doctor of the bay appeared and Sunny became a professional again, attending to her patients.

"Has this man spoken?" the doctor asked, looking at the last one brought aboard.

"No, Commander. Not a word. He opened his eyes briefly, but that's all. The chart says he was picked up at sea."

"His burns don't seem to be too severe. See that he gets an ice bath, Miss Fitzpatrick, and then sprinkle him liberally with sulfanilamide powder. I'll wait until he regains consciousness before I send him to surgery to remove the shrapnel."

"Yes, Commander."

The man, far too large for Sunny to handle alone, became the charge of one of the corpsmen. It was after his bath that Sunny, in redressing and sprinkling the powder on his wound, happened to see the small tattoo, the only mark upon his body beyond the ravages of shipwreck and the shrapnel wound.

Puzzled by the unusual mark, Sunny called to Benita, who was attending another patient. "When you get a minute, Benita, would you see if you can identify the foreign mark on this man's body?"

When Benita approached the berth, Sunny lifted the man's arm. "Have you ever seen anything like it?"

Benita frowned. "Yes, but not for a long time. It looks like a mark the Indians put on their babies to ward off the evil eye."

"The American kind?" Sunny asked.

"No. Eastern."

"But he's supposed to be an American."

Benita looked at his chart. "He could also be Dutch, or British. Colonial, maybe. Born in India, with an amah who wanted to keep him from harm."

"If that's true, then we can't evacuate him back to the States."

"We won't have to worry about that for a while. If he regains consciousness, he can tell us who he is. And if he doesn't, it won't really matter, will it?"

"Except for his family," Sunny replied, saddened to think of anyone in an unmarked grave, with a mother and a father not knowing. But if the man could survive twenty-four to forty-eight hours without going into renal failure, then he would stand an excellent chance of recovery.

Although Sunny went off duty late that afternoon, she visited her ward before turning in for the night. "Hey, gorgeous, your mystery man has started talking," the patient on the second berth informed her. "But Hatfield here says he's speaking in some heathen tongue."

The man's breathing was shallow and rapid. Sunny quickly took his blood pressure. The systolic was elevated and, alarmed at the deterioration of his condition, Sunny raced to find the doctor on duty.

"I'll take over, Fitzpatrick," the duty nurse said, coming to aid the doctor. With nothing else to do, Sunny left the ward and walked back to her own quarters for the night.

Sunny prepared for bed in a cubicle smaller than her own dressing room at home in Macon, Georgia. Shared with three other nurses, the cabin had two double berths on each side that took up most of the room, with just enough locker space for their uniforms and a few personal possessions. Alone, Sunny removed her uniform and, in her underwear, she turned on the small electric fan.

How different even from the spaciousness of the nurses' quarters at Pearl, with its lanai surrounded by flowering bougainvillea and hibiscus, and the small, tropical banyan trees on which the wild orchids grew.

She had deliberately requested assignment on the hospital ship stationed at Pearl Harbor. Her father, Brigadier General Fitzpatrick, had been recalled to active service, and her mother, Kenna, had been living on the island for over six months. Neither parent had been enthusiastic about her joining the Navy Nurse Corps. But her mother, of all people, had no logical argument against it. Hadn't she done the

same thing in World War I—turning her back on the debu-
tante world in Atlanta for nurse's training and service in
France? Besides, her mother had been in more danger than
she ever would, for Pearl was considered the safest harbor in
the Pacific. That is, until the seventh of December. What a
fool's paradise she had been in, those first six days of
December.

The door opened and Wendy Johnson walked in. "Hi.
You're not asleep, are you?"

"No. It's too hot to sleep," Sunny complained.

"I know. I just finished a walk up on deck with Brogdon.
There's not a breeze around, except the one you stirred up
this afternoon."

"What are you talking about, Wendy?" Sunny looked at
the small brunette who had joined the *Good Hope* the same
time as she.

"Brogdon repeated the ship's scuttlebut about you and
Matt Willoughby smooching in sick bay. Lt. Commander
Singleton's quite unhappy."

"It wasn't my fault, Wendy. Matt came up from behind
me. If he feels my professional ethics have been
compromised, I guess I'll hear from the review board."

"Oh, I don't think you'll be put on report. He's only upset
that *you* might be compromised. Somebody overheard Matt
asking you to share his leave in Sydney."

"That's ridiculous. You know what he meant. We both
want to be together on shore leave, not share a bed, for
heaven's sake."

"Speak for yourself, Sunny. I'm not so sure Matt doesn't
intend that, too. I remember how taken he was with you at
Pearl."

Sunny's defensive attitude vanished as she smiled. "It
was a lot of fun, wasn't it? That is, before the Japanese attack.
You remember how excited we were when we left San
Francisco?"

"Yes. All that shopping we did—and how loaded down
we were. I'll never forget that pilot's face when he saw us

standing on the dock while we waited to board the PBY."

Sunny deepened her voice to imitate the pilot. "And just where do you think you're going to store all that loot?"

"Why, Ensign, we shipped most everything ahead. You can't be talking about these tiny little shopping bags, can you?" Wendy imitated Sunny's Southern accent that had turned the pilot to instant putty.

"Well, at least we wore the clothes for six terrific days," Sunny countered, her face losing its sparkle.

The two nurses became silent while each remembered the frantic, hectic week at Pearl Harbor, as casualties were brought to the hospital ship—over two thousand dead, many more injured, military and civilian alike; the bandages and morphine running out; the operating rooms, with teams of doctors going twenty-four hours a day, until no one could stand or even remember when they had last slept or eaten.

"I was proud of my mother," Sunny said. "You know, when the base hospital was bombed, she pitched right in to help. My father told me later that she rounded up all the kitchen boys who were hiding and made them come back to the kitchen. And she saw to it that they kept the coffee hot night and day, for the doctors and nurses, as well as the patients."

"You think she'll stay at Pearl Harbor, even if your father is reassigned?"

"I think she'll try to be with him wherever he goes. General MacArthur's wife is with him in the Philippines." In a confidential manner, Sunny said, "I overheard her use that argument one night when they were discussing her going back to Georgia. She absolutely refused."

Again the door opened, and a tired Benita Barksdale came in to claim her own berth for the night. She was later than usual.

"What happened to you, Benita? Were you on deck, too?"

"No. The medical chief of staff sent for me. He wanted to see if I could translate what our delirious patient was trying to say, since I understand a little Mandarin Chinese."

"Did you?"

"Only a little."

"Well?"

"I'm under orders not to repeat it."

Both Sunny Fitzpatrick and Wendy Johnson knew that was the end of the conversation. Nothing would make Benita breach a confidence or an order.

Once the lights were out, Sunny opened the porthole. A few drops of rain blew inside, carried on the slight breeze. But no one cared. The mildew had already spoiled their shoes. Luckily, they were too far out to sea to be bothered by mosquitoes.

That night, Sunny dreamed of the last dance she had attended with Matt at the Naval Officers' Club. But when she woke the next morning, she realized the face in her dream had not been Matt's after all, but that of her patient — the one with no name.

Chapter 5

BY THE TIME SUNNY REPORTED FOR DUTY, THE MAN picked up by the destroyer *Viscount* had regained consciousness. Delighted to see him awake, Sunny smiled and said, "Would you like some ice cream now?"

"I would prefer a cup of tea," he responded in a weak voice.

"Righto. Hot, I presume, with cream?" She had recognized the British accent. None of her other patients requested anything but iced tea in the hot climate, and she knew she would have to prepare it herself.

"Yes, thank you."

As she left the ward for the galley, she motioned for a corpsman to shave the patient's light-colored beard and give him a cool bath while she was gone.

Upon her return, she hardly recognized the man. With his beard gone, his square, determined jaw was very much in evidence—at odds with the soft blue of his eyes. But as she looked at him, the blue eyes became flint to match his jaw.

"I'm not a freak in one of your Western sideshows, to be stared at, Miss Fitzpatrick."

"Sorry, I didn't mean to. Only, you look so much better than you did yesterday when they brought you on board.

Here. I'll help you with your tea."

Sunny put her right arm under his head and lifted him so that he could manage to take a few sips from the cup she held. He was extremely weak, and she let him take his time. When she moved her arm from under him, so that he could lean back on the pillow for a moment, his face inadvertently touched her breast. He drew in his breath, but Sunny didn't seem to notice.

"Are you ready for another sip?"

"Just leave the cup on the tray. I can manage alone, thank you."

Sunny smiled. "I'll come back later to check on you." She left his side to attend to the other patients. She dismissed his irritability as merely a residue of damage from the heatstroke.

"Hey, beautiful, may I have a cup of tea, too?" a voice down the aisle begged.

"You know you've never drunk tea in your life, Andrews," she teased.

"You're right about that, Fitzpatrick," his berthmate overhead agreed. "Wouldn't mix with his ninety-proof blood."

"A little frangipani red is all he's going to get today. Ain't that right, nurse?" another man piped up as he pointed to the plasma dripping from the IV.

"Oh, we'll give him something else, too, to keep him happy. What do you want, Andrews?"

Before the man could answer, another man spoke. "It sure as hell ain't in the kitchen."

Sunny ignored the comment. "How about a Coca-Cola float?"

"Yeah. I think I'd like that."

Up and down the ward she went, taking blood pressures and temperatures, giving medication, and checking on the IVs to see that the drip had not stopped. The floor was slippery from the tannic acid liberally doused on the bandages of the burn patients.

At one end of the aisle, separated from the others, a special hammock had been set up. With a hole cut into the canvas, it allowed for the drainage of a patient's abdominal wound—a more comfortable arrangement than lying on his side in a bunk.

Shortly before lunchtime, the doctor on duty made second rounds. Sunny walked with him and stood by each patient's berth while he gave new orders. When they approached Alex Ramsay, the doctor requested Sunny to stay behind and update his chart.

"Your name?"

"Alex Ramsay."

"Nationality?"

"British."

"Your ship?"

"I'm a civilian."

"Would you like the Red Cross to send a message to your nearest relative that you're safe?"

"No. I'll attend to that when I leave this ship."

Her topaz eyes stared at him in distress. "But your family will be worrying about you."

"That's my concern, Miss Fitzpatrick—not yours. Just as the mark on my arm is my concern and not yours."

Sunny opened her mouth, but she had no appropriate response. No wonder he had been so distant with her. He had overheard her conversation with Benita, even while he was comatose. "I'm not a freak to be stared at." Remembering his words, she became embarrassed. She placed his chart at the foot of the bunk.

"Do you wish anything else?"

"No, thank you."

Sunny left him to his solitude. She would not invade his privacy again unless it was absolutely necessary.

The marquess of Dalhousie was not proud of his behavior. He had never been that sharp with anyone before, especially a woman. He had watched the young nurse making her rounds—with a sunny disposition and not taking offense at the crudeness of her patients. She had joked with them and not cringed at all, even as she attended the poor fellow down the aisle who had both legs gone.

Yet Alex had hurt her. He'd seen it in those magnificent eyes of liquid amber that had darkened with his biting words — all because of his own pride.

How could he tell her there was no family to contact? Only a male cousin, Malcolm, who would be disappointed that Alex was still alive and he would not yet inherit the title and lands of the Dalhousies.

But the woman was a danger to him, with her softness, her beauty. He could not afford to be distracted from his duty. No, he would have to maintain his distance from her. For beauty with compassion represented a powerful force that affected all men.

By the next day, the doctor felt that Alex Ramsay was strong enough to be scheduled for surgery. The X-rays indicated that several small pieces of shrapnel were still embedded in his upper left arm.

After midnight, he was given nothing to eat or drink, in preparation for the operation. At 0700 the next morning, Sunny administered a mild shot as ordered, and within a few minutes a corpsman had come to wheel him to the operating room where the surgical team waited. The last thing he saw before going under was the anesthetist leaning over him.

"Mr. Ramsay? Mr. Ramsay?" the soft voice called to him. "The operation is over. Everything went fine."

Alex struggled to open his eyes. It was not the anesthetist who leaned over him but the white-clad nurse with the pale golden hair. His vision was slightly blurred and the light hurt his eyes. Closing them again, he wanted to return to that comfortable slumber that had enveloped him when he was on the raft, when it didn't seem necessary to remain awake any longer. But the nurse would not let him sleep. He felt her hand upon his face as she stroked his jaw.

"You'll have to wake up, you know. You've slept long

enough." Her hand became more insistent, like a worrisome mosquito, demanding attention. "Speak to me, Mr. Ramsay. Are you awake?"

"Yes, I'm awake," he croaked, his throat feeling strangely sore and dry.

"Good. Now can I get you anything?"

Alex began to shiver. "I'm cold."

"Quick, Heinman. Get me a warm blanket, on the double. He's having a chill." Sunny wrapped the blood pressure cuff around his good arm. His blood pressure was falling—not a good sign at all.

As soon as the corpsman returned, Sunny wrapped the warm blanket around Alex Ramsay. With the blanket sealing in the heat, he soon began to recover. His teeth stopped chattering as his blood pressure came back up to near normal.

Now, he was fully awake, alert to his surroundings and to the nurse attending him. Sunny Fitzpatrick. She smiled with a gentle compassion that caused his stomach to knot. His only recourse was to close his eyes again.

"It's all right," she assured him. "You can go to sleep again, Alex Ramsay. I'll come back later."

As the hospital ship plied its way through the tropical waters on the Lollipop Run, so named by the patients because of the sweets and ice cream aboard, the Japanese landed on New Guinea; the British army in Burma lost Rangoon, and Bataan surrendered.

Periodically, the hospital ship anchored outside the harbor of a little-known island and waited for new casualties. They were flown from the combat areas to the island's mobile hospital, and then transferred to the ship.

The nurses did not go ashore at any of these islands until they reached Pago Pago in the Samoas, where they dropped anchor.

Untouched by the fighting in the Pacific, the island had a festive air about it. And for the first time, the crew of the *Good Hope* had something to celebrate—Doolittle's successful raid on Japan.

That Sunday afternoon, as Sunny, Benita, and Wendy went ashore in the small launch, they could hear the police band playing music in the center of the village.

"I want to see where that hussy, Sadie Thompson, stayed. The one the minister tried to convert," Wendy commented.

"And I'd like to put a flower on Robert Louis Stevenson's grave," Sunny added. "I was scared out of my wits by his *Treasure Island.* My brother used to read it to me when I was little. I expected a pirate to kidnap me any day."

Sunny turned to Benita, who had remained silent. "And what do you want to do, Benita?"

The gray-haired nurse smiled. "I want to visit the native hospital."

"There she goes again—a regular busman's holiday," Wendy remarked.

"You must remember, I helped to train some of the native nurses. Naturally, I want to see if they're still here, and how they're coping."

"What do you want to do, Heinman?" Wendy asked the corpsman sitting beside her. "Or need I ask?"

With a straight face, Heinman said, "Why I'm planning a very scientific study of all the flora and fauna on the island."

"Especially Flora in the grass skirt, I bet. Men!" Wendy added in mock disgust.

Ignoring the exchange, Benita said, "There used to be a little Mormon church on the island. They might be having services right now."

Heinman sighed. "If they're all Mormons, I guess I won't find anything stronger to drink than a Papuan milkshake. I hear they preach teetotalism."

"Is there such a word in the dictionary?" Wendy inquired.

"If there isn't, there should be," Heinman retorted.

Sunny laughed. "I know what you're talking about, Heinman. The Mormons in the Carolinas converted the

Catawba Indians to their faith some time in the 1800s. The local bootleggers became so angry when their chief market for liquor dried up that they chased the two Mormon missionaries and horsewhipped them."

"How terrible," Benita commented.

"I know."

The music grew louder as the launch reached shore. Standing on the dock to greet them were beautiful, brown-skinned women dressed in colorful sarongs, with large flower blossoms pinned into their glistening black hair that hung down to their waists.

"I think I see Flora," Heinman announced with a wide grin, and parted company with the three nurses.

Alex Ramsay stood on the deck of the *Good Hope* and watched the launch until it disappeared into the harbor. He had no desire to leave the ship until she reached a port of the British Commonwealth with an embassy.

Since he had no identification, no passport, and no money, he would be hard pressed to establish who he was. And he didn't relish parading around in borrowed clothes donated by the crew—his only other outfit besides the brightly striped pajamas that Sunny Fitzpatrick had brought him in the misguided assumption that he needed cheering up. He would have preferred the more conservative pajamas worn by most of the men in his ward.

"You're sure you won't change your mind about going ashore?" Kirk Singleton stopped to inquire as the empty launch came in sight again.

"I'm sure, Mr. Singleton. Thank you."

"There'll be a native feast, with hula girls…"

Alex shook his head. "I've seen it all before."

He walked back to the shaded seat on deck and, with the breeze ruffling his hair, he picked up the book from the ship's library and attempted, in reading it, to understand the strange customs of the Americans.

* * *

Loaded down with coconuts, sarongs, and taro leaves for their own luau later, the nurses, with that part of the crew who'd gone ashore, returned to ship. By late evening, when the sea had changed to a shimmering purple, and the harbor of Pago Pago had become invisible, like a tropical flower closing for the night, the *Good Hope* cast anchor and set her course for Tonga, a small island protectorate under the British crown. Overhearing their next destination, Alex Ramsay was particularly pleased.

"I guess once you've seen one tropical island, you've seen them all," an exhausted Wendy commented to her bunkmates late that night.

Benita laughed. "Don't expect Tonga to look like Pago Pago, Wendy."

"Why? Is it so different?"

"Completely. You won't see any thatched huts, or *fales*, in the heart of town. Tonga looks more like Gloucester, Massachusetts, or any of a dozen fishing villages up and down the Northeast coast."

"Hey, Sunny, did you hear that??" Wendy called out in the dark. But Sunny was already asleep.

"She's had a hard day," Benita cautioned, "trying to stay on good terms with Lt. Commander Singleton, who absolutely adores her."

"While *she* adores Matt Willoughby. Wish I had that trouble. Even Brogdon treats me like one of the boys," Wendy complained.

"It's far easier that way. Keeps your mind on the patients, where it belongs."

"Yes, ma'am," Wendy replied meekly, knowing how irked the older nurse became when anyone called her 'ma'am.'

"Go to sleep, Wendy," Sunny ordered as she rolled over on her side.

"I'm going," Wendy promised.

Chapter 6

THE QUEEN OF TONGA LIVED IN A BEAUTIFUL WHITE clapboard house in the heart of the capital, Nukua ᐧbfa. Called a palace, the house with its widow's walk around the roof looked as if it might have been built for a sea captain rather than a queen.

The black woman, six feet tall and weighing over three hundred pounds, dressed for official occasions in her gold crown and cape of dubonnet velvet that partially hid a white silk peau de soie Parisian gown.

As the *Good Hope* anchored in the harbor, Alex Ramsay became interested in his whereabouts for the first time since rescue. He hurriedly wrote a message and gave it to one of the natives who'd rowed out to meet the ship in an outrigger canoe. Loaded down with cigarettes and sweets that had been dropped overboard to all the natives, this particular boatman took Alex's message and headed for shore, while Alex returned belowdecks.

An hour later, when Sunny and Wendy had come off duty, they stood on deck and watched a barge approaching the ship from the lagoon.

"Look at that fancy boat, Sunny. I don't think I've seen anything more regal since Cleopatra sailed down the Nile."

"It must belong to Queen Salote herself," Sunny speculated. "There's a flag of state flying at her helm."

The barge, with twelve rowers dressed in brightly colored loin skirts, or *lap-laps*, contained only one passenger—a black man in white uniform with a red fez on his head. He signaled to come aboard and the officer on watch granted him permission. When he returned from the captain's quarters, the protocol officer of the queen was accompanied by Alex Ramsay.

Sunny, still on deck, watched as her taciturn patient left the *Good Hope* and set sail in the royal barge toward the lagoon. Neither she nor Wendy, at her side, had time to conjecture why. The broadcast message that Salote, queen of Tonga, had invited the entire ship's crew and passengers to a feast that evening created a buzz of excitement and activity. Racing back to their quarters to get ready, Sunny said, "What a shame that Madeleine is on duty."

"Andy is the only thing she really cares about," Wendy answered.

Sunny knew that Wendy was right. They almost never saw their fourth roommate, for she had requested night duty to be with her fiancé, whom the ship had picked up from the battle in the Java Sea. Her special care of the man she loved had made a difference. Severely burned on his chest, he was healing well, with the burned skin already sloughing off to show the new, healthy pink skin underneath.

"Dare we wear the sarongs we bought in Pago Pago?" Sunny and Wendy looked at each other.

Benita put a quick stop to that idea. "You'll wear your uniforms, you two. Ship's orders."

The three, barely having room to dress in the small cubicle at the same time, put on fresh uniforms, a little lipstick, and quickly brushed their hair. By the time they reached the deck, the first group had already left by launch.

Sunny was unusually restless and she walked away from the group of chattering nurses who waited for the launch to return. The *Good Hope* had been at sea too long, and Sunny was anxious to get to Auckland where she could have a few days to herself. Once their patients were taken to the base hospital, where the less severely injured would be reassigned to duty, and the others would be flown back to the United States, the nurses were free while the ship was being cleaned and readied for another 'lollipop run" through the islands off the coasts of Australia and New Zealand.

Sunny had taken a dislike to one of her patients, Alex Ramsay, and it bothered her. His eyes seemed to condemn her at every turn as she smiled and cajoled her patients from their melancholy. Yet, in calling them "handsome" and "good-looking," and not flinching in her care of them, she'd tried to give back—especially to the paraplegics—the self-esteem they'd lost and would need again when they faced their families and loved ones.

"Sunny, you're going to miss the last boat if you don't come on," Wendy called.

"Coming." Sunny hurried to catch up with the others.

In the twilight, as the sun sank below the spire of the white church in the square of Nukua ʻlofa, the familiar scene of a new England seaside town was at odds with the lush, tropical vegetation surrounding it.

Sunny was aware of the dichotomy, of the civilized juxtaposed against the primitive, as the natives pushed to gain a better place on the dock to watch the launch coming again into the lagoon. But she was not prepared for the coming reception of the nurses, with their white skin, eyes the color of the sky, and hair lighter than most of the natives had ever seen.

Shortly before reaching the dock, the skipper cut the launch's motor and drifted until he was close enough to cast his bow line.

"Well, there's lover boy," Wendy announced to Sunny, pointing to Lt. Commander Kirk Singleton, who waited in the crowd. "I knew he wouldn't go far without you."

"And I see Brogdon waving to you, Wendy."

Wendy sighed. "At least Kirk is a few inches taller than you are, Sunny. Brogdon is such a shrimp, even *I* have to look down on him."

"Character is not measured in inches, Wendy," Benita scolded.

"Well, he's a character, all right," she admitted. "You haven't seen his latest invention, have you?"

"Move on, Johnson. You two are holding up the rest of the boat."

After climbing out of the launch, Sunny began to walk down the pier that jutted from the water. But her progress was hampered by hands that reached out to touch her hair. She gasped as a sudden jerk told her that someone had stolen a few strands for himself.

"Hold on there," Kirk called out, and brushed his way past the natives to rescue Sunny. "No touch," he commanded, sternly shaking his head.

The men from the launch closed in to protect the other nurses from being touched by the curious natives.

"Did he hurt you?" Kirk asked Sunny.

"Not much. It was just a surprise. What in the world does he want with a few strands of my hair?"

"He probably thinks he's captured part of the sun, or maybe a moonbeam." Kirk grinned. "It's not often a man gets to save a woman from being snatched bald. You'll have to be extra nice to me tonight because of it, Fitzpatrick. And remember, this is the second time I've saved you."

"And you'd better be careful, Singleton," she teased. "In the East, if you save a person three times, you're responsible for her the rest of your life."

"I wouldn't mind that at all."

They followed the flares into the tropical forest, to a clearing where large tables were set up in every direction. Turtle and octopus roasted on spits, and the tables, covered by pandamus leaves, held gourd bowls and coconuts filled with a mixture of milk and rum flavored by spices that tantalized the nose, while dripping fat spewed into the fire with a hiss and sudden flame to awaken the tastebuds. Fruits, some exotic, some familiar—papaya, avocado, breadfruit—lined the tables as far as the eye could see.

The head table was dressed more lavishly, with cushions instead of the soft woven mats of the other tables. Motioned to find a place, Kirk, Sunny, Wendy, and Brogdon, with Benita and "Sleepy Joe" Tyler, the anesthetist, sank down onto the mats that protected their white uniforms from the evening dew.

As the queen and her retinue approached the clearing in the jungled forest, they all stood. The black woman, with a golden crown on her head, appeared regal, formidable. Her dress of white was only slightly less formal than her official parliament regalia, and rather than the velvet robe, a blue and white cotton batik cape rested on her wide shoulders.

"Isn't she magnificent?" Wendy whispered.

"Ssh!" a voice in her ear commanded.

Sunny's gaze went from the queen to her four male escorts. It was no surprise to see the *Good Hope's* captain, Elmer Moriarty, the ship's medical chief, or even the queen's protocol officer, who had appeared on the ship earlier that day. The real surprise lay in seeing Alex Ramsay at her right.

He was no longer dressed in borrowed clothes, but in white tropical shirt and trousers like the protocol officer. But there was also a difference. Across his broad chest was draped a blue ribbon with medal, appropriate for a visiting dignitary or guest of honor.

Flanked by torches against the approaching night, the queen smiled at the crowd and, in her British accent, said, "Ladies and gentlemen, welcome to the island of Tonga. It is my pleasure to have you and your captain here this evening to rejoice with me in the rescue of my dear friend, Alex Ramsay, marquess of Dalhousie, late of India and servant to His Most Gracious Majesty." She picked up her cup and, raising it, said, "A toast to His Majesty, King George."

Quickly, the men and women at the long tables picked up their cups and feeling slightly foolish, drank. Then, Alex stepped forward and picked up a second small cup.

"As a representative of the king-emperor, may I propose a toast to Her Grace, queen of Tonga. May she prosper on this island, and be kept safe from harm in the ensuing days."

Again, they lifted their cups. Then, the president of the United States was toasted. And when that was done, the protocol officer gave a signal for everyone to be seated.

"I don't believe it," Wendy said, breaking the silence surrounding the small group that included Sunny. "You mean the man I gave a bath to just a few days ago is one of those British lords, or something?"

"I don't believe it either," Sunny said, taking a surreptitious glance toward the man seated at the head table. No wonder he'd been so distant on the ship. And he looked even more so now, smiling and laughing with the queen. His manner was completely different, a self-confidence apparent, an ease that spoke of another world filled with ambassadors, royalty, and state dinners. And Sunny, looking at him, decided she liked him even less than the day before.

"I just thought of something," Wendy said. "What do we call him when we get back to the ship tonight. Sir? My lord?"

Brogdon, feeling slightly off stride, said, "Didn't we fight a previous war so we wouldn't have to say 'Yes, my lord?' Personally, I'm going to continue calling him Mr. Ramsay."

"What about you, Sunny?" Kirk Singleton inquired.

"I have a few choice names I'd rather call him," Sunny declared. "But I can't say them aloud in front of Benita."

They all laughed. The tension was broken and they turned to the food in front of them. Serving girls replenished the rum punch and brought large dishes of turtle, octopus and *akule* fish.

In the background, music began—the soft, hypnotic rhythm of the islands. Other native girls in their sarongs appeared and, using their hands and hips, they began to sway and dance their sensuous island dance, until some of the crew members, fortified by the punch, rose to join them.

After it was all over, Sunny could barely remember how it happened. Somehow the musicians of the ship took over the native instruments, and the soft, indolent beat turned to a more insistent rhythm of boogie-woogie.

"Come on, Fitzpatrick," Kirk urged. "Let's show them an American dance." He grabbed Sunny's hand and pulled her to the center of festivities. And the young nurse, feeling strangely rebellious, did not protest.

It wasn't long before the jitterbug steps caught on, with other couples joining in. But then, two by two, they dropped out to the sidelines to watch. A self-consciousness caused Sunny to falter. She didn't want to be in the limelight. But as she looked toward Alex Ramsay, she saw a frown on his face. And that changed her mind.

She smiled at Kirk, and the two, encouraged by the crowd, broke into different steps, marked by the experience that had won them the ship's title the night of the first party aboard the *Good Hope.* Finally, Sunny was out of breath. "Enough, enough," she begged, and laughingly fell into Kirk's arms while the crowd roared with approval.

The native instruments were returned to their owners; the music changed back to the soft and sensuous. Sunny found her place again, but this time she did not look in Alex Ramsay's direction. She quietly sipped her punch and pushed back the tendrils of her hair that had come loose while she danced.

Soon an announcement was made for the group to return to the pier. Sunny began to walk with Kirk, but before she reached the edge of the clearing, a voice called out to her.

"Miss Fitzpatrick. Will you wait a moment, please?"

Sunny recognized Alex Ramsay's voice. She turned around. "Yes?"

"The queen wishes to speak with you."

"I'll wait for you, Sunny," Kirk said.

"That's not necessary, Mr. Singleton. You'll miss your boat. I'll see that Miss Fitzpatrick gets back to the ship," Alex replied.

Sunny looked from one man to the other. Alex's face was impassive, while Kirk's showed his frustration. Reaching out to Kirk, Sunny said, "You go on. Don't worry about me."

Reluctantly, the man left the clearing and hurried to catch up with the others. Their flashlights, covered with blue paper, made only enough light to keep them from stumbling along the path leading back to the pier. They had been safe in the dense green of the forest, but lights along the beach were forbidden.

"Your Grace, may I present Miss Fitzpatrick."

Sunny made a slight curtsy and waited for the woman to speak.

The black queen smiled, and Sunny saw her even white teeth. "I wanted to see you up close, my dear," she said frankly. "Your exuberance is matched only by your beauty."

Sunny also smiled. "I hope that's a compliment, Your Grace."

"I assure you it is."

She turned again to Alex. "My dear Dalhousie, what a pleasure it has been. Take care of yourself, and Godspeed."

After a few parting words, the queen left. And Sunny, now forced to walk back toward the pier with the marquess of Dalhousie, said, "I hope we can get a ride on the second boat."

"That's not necessary, Miss Fitzpatrick. The queen's boat is still at my disposal. You will ride with me."

The royal barge, made from *te itai* wood, rested on the sandy beach in a cove not far from the pier. Seeing Alex arrive, the twelve rowers took their places, six men on each side, and once the two passengers were seated, they pushed the boat into the water.

Sunny had nothing to say. Finally, an angry Alex broke the silence. "You had better be more careful in the future, Miss Fitzpatrick. It is not in your best interest to make such an exhibition of yourself."

"I was only having a little fun," she countered.

"Aided by the rum punch, no doubt. I suggest you leave that off, as well, on any future stopover."

"Why are you so angry? I did no harm to you or to anyone else."

"How can you be so sure of that?"

Sunny sank back onto the cushions and yawned. "Our worlds are completely different, Alex Ramsay, marquess of Dalhousie. And I suggest we make a pact until we reach Auckland. I won't attempt to understand you if you won't attempt to understand me. Agreed?"

"There's little chance of either happening, Miss Fitzpatrick, I assure you."

"Good. Then we can both enjoy the lagoon in silence."

Alex began to rub his arm, and Sunny, the nurse once more, admonished, "Leave your bandage alone."

Alex laughed. "You've broken your vow of silence already."

"I have to speak out when I see a patient worrying his sutures. If they're beginning to itch, I'll get you something from the pharmacy once we reach the ship."

"Thank you."

"Not at all."

Chapter 7

THE SHIP HAD SET SAIL FROM TONGA WITH ONE MORE stopover to take on casualties. Now that the five-hundred-bed floating hospital was filled to capacity, the captain's orders were to head south for Auckland, New Zealand.

On the day the *Good Hope* arrived in port, Sunny and Wendy stood on deck with the patients who were ambulatory. On shore, flags and banners flew; a band played "Roll Out the Barrel"; the mayor waited to give official greetings. And lined up for blocks were the ambulances to take the severely wounded to the newly constructed naval hospital, while buses and cars waited to give transportation to the others.

"Have you heard, Wendy?" Sunny asked her roommate. "Singleton just told me that we're to be guests of the city while the ship's in port."

"How lovely."

They had no time for further conversation. Immersed in seeing to their patients, the medical staff's evacuation from ship to shore was coordinated with an expertise that would have made any general proud.

At last, when all the patients had been removed and the only persons remaining aboard were crew and medical personnel, the four nurses— Sunny, Wendy, Benita, and Madeleine—packed their gear and went on deck, ready to leave the ship.

Sunny had not seen Alex Ramsay get into the car waiting for him. For a moment, she wondered about him. Then she dismissed him from her mind.

Feeling slightly worn from her long sea voyage, Madeleine looked down at her uniform. "You think it would be all right to dress in civilian clothes again, while we're ashore?"

"I don't see why not," Wendy answered.

"There's only one catch," Sunny reminded them. "We don't have any other clothes, except the sarongs."

"If we're to be guests of the city," Benita cautioned, "it would be more appropriate to remain in uniform."

"Sunny! Over here," a woman called, waving her hand to attract Sunny's attention.

The woman was middle-aged, still stunningly beautiful. Her hair, cut in a short, sophisticated style, was almost identical in color to Sunny's, with the exception of a few gray strands that a person would have to look hard to find. Fresh and dainty in a lavender voile dress, with white gloves, she gave the appearance of being much younger than she actually was.

"Mother!" Sunny called out. "What are you doing here?"

Sunny Fitzpatrick left the group and ran to greet her mother. "Is anything wrong? Has Dad—"

"He's fine, darling." Then lowering her voice so that she would not be overheard, Kenna said, "Your father has just joined General MacArthur's staff. We left Pearl in such a hurry that I decided to meet your ship rather than risk missing you. I've arranged for you to spend your few day's leave with us."

But Sunny was not reassured. "Something's happened to Jack, and you came to tell me in person."

Kenna shook her head. "No, Sunny. Your brother's fine, too. He's been reassigned to the aircraft carrier *Lexington*. We had a letter from him only ten days ago."

Sunny breathed easily again. Assured now that her

family was all right, she looked back to the three nurses waiting for her. "I want you to meet my friends," she said, and led her mother over to the edge of the gangplank. "Mother, may I present my dearest friends—Benita, Madeleine, and Wendy. My mother, Kenna Fitzpatrick."

"How do you do, Mrs. Fitzpatrick," Benita said, smiling at the woman. "I can tell that you and Sunny are related."

"How do you do," Kenna replied. And then looking at Wendy, she said, "I remember you from Pearl Harbor."

"Yes, ma'am. It's a pleasure to see you again."

"Listen, gang," Sunny interrupted. "I'm going off with my mother. Guess I won't be seeing you until we board ship again. So, have fun."

"You, too, Sunny," they chimed in and, with their transportation waiting for them, the three nurses joined the rest of the group.

"I have a taxi waiting," Kenna informed her daughter. "There's a PBY Catalina leaving in two hours.

"We're not staying in Auckland?"

"No. We're flying back to Sydney."

"Oh, super!" Sunny exclaimed, hoping that Matt Willoughby would be there, as well.

Kenna stared down at Sunny's uniform, slightly yellow from the mineral deposits of the water on board ship. "I packed several of your nice dresses you left in Pearl. They're at the hotel in Sydney."

"What a relief. You must have known I didn't have anything decent to wear."

Kenna smiled. "I remember the last war, and what a hard time we had finding something to wear. There was one dress I took with me all through the war. It was pink and beaded. I'll never forget it." She stopped in front of the taxi. "Well, here we are."

Sunny stared at the strange contraption that waited on the pier. With little gasoline for civilian use, the taxi had a large charcoal burner mounted on top, with pipes running from it to the engine.

Sunny laughed. "I haven't seen such a monstrosity since Annie Lyn back home had her station wagon top designed to carry her harp.""

"It's quite handy, though," Kenna explained. "And it gets you to where you're going. That's the important thing, isn't it?"

"I guess so."

The nurse stowed her gear in the front of the taxi and, seated beside her mother in the back, she looked around her at the festive activities. Friendly civilians were everywhere, determined to make the Americans feel at home. Australia and New Zealand now realized that their closest ally was the United States, with her ships and her fighting forces in the Pacific. With the fall of Singapore, Britain's strength in the East was diminished. She was fighting for her very life against Germany, an enemy far closer than the Japanese.

"I'm so glad President Roosevelt ordered MacArthur out of the Philippines," Sunny commented. "It would have been such a disaster to have him die with his troops, as he'd vowed to do.""

"But he's received a lot of criticism in the newspapers because of it," Kenna replied. "All of it undeserved."

"Well, not everybody has criticized him. Did you read that funny comment quoted in *Time* magazine? What the insurance salesman from Kansas said about him?"

"No. What was the comment?"

"That 'MacArthur was the greatest general since *Sergeant York.*' "

"That is amusing," Kenna agreed, "He has his rank slightly confused, doesn't he?" After a few moments of silence, Kenna continued, "Did I ever tell you that I met Sergeant York in France?"

Sunny shook her head.

"He was a very mild-mannered man, not at all the type you might think a hero would be."

"He and Dad were in the same outfit, weren't they?"

"Yes. The 82nd." Kenna's eyes softened, as if she were

lost in the past. "Now, your father was the one who looked like a hero. Acted like one, too. He didn't capture as many Germans as Sergeant York, but he saved his entire platoon from annihilation... Well, enough of that. World War I is old news."

They passed a poster that read, "Be careful. The enemy is listening." Sunny, glancing toward the taxi driver reverted to a whisper. "Did you-know-who specifically ask for Dad to join his staff?"

"Yes. You remember, we knew Dougie and his first wife, Louise, when they were stationed in Atlanta in 1925. He was impressed with the way your father ran the family mills." In a confidential manner, Kenna said, "There was an awful lot of dead wood in the top echelons of the army when this war began. It's taken a little time to clear it out and put in men with modern experience."

"Like Dad," Sunny added, trying to stifle a yawn even as she talked.

A sympathetic Kenna said, "I suppose you're rather exhausted."

"Nothing that a little food and a little sleep won't fix."

"We have several hours to waste before the plane leaves. How about some tea and sandwiches?"

"Sounds good to me."

Kenna tapped on the window. "Driver, can you let us out at the nearest tearoom, please?'

By early afternoon, with their light meal behind them, Kenna and her daughter, Sunny, waited to board the PBY, known more familiarly as "The Cat." A flying boat with a hull similar to a boat, it was one of the earlier models that only landed on water. Holding twenty passengers besides the crew, the plane was equipped with a blister on each side—bubble-shaped picture windows to house the guns and provide a lookout.

The passengers waited in a loosely formed queue along the left side of the pier. Sunny, farther back in line with her mother, recognized a familiar figure ahead. As he turned around, she suddenly found the riotous bouquet of flowers in the wooden flower box to be extremely absorbing.

"Good afternoon, Miss Fitzpatrick. Are you going to Sydney, also?" Alex Ramsay's inquiry forced her attention from the flower box. Standing directly in front of her, the man waited for an answer.

Glancing at her mother, she acknowledged him in a subdued, monotone voice. "Yes, I am." And turning to her mother, she said, "May I present one of my former patients, Alex Ramsay, marquess of Dalhousie. My mother, Mrs. Fitzpatrick."

"How do you do?" Kenna replied. Noticing his bandaged arm, she was polite enough not to inquire as to his health.

With Alex Ramsay's clipped response, Kenna's gray eyes came alive with interest as she watched her daughter's reaction to the man.

The names of the passengers were called, and Alex, nodding to the two , took his place in line again.

"You could have been a little nicer to him, Sunny," Kenna admonished gently.

"No, Mother. *You* can be nice to him. I don't ever want to see him again."

"Was he that difficult a patient?"

"Yes. Difficult, cold, condescending, and snobbish."

"You father was a difficult patient, too."

A surprised Sunny looked at her mother and saw the amused expression. Sunny laughed. "Men are a pain, sometimes, aren't they, Mother?"

"Indeed they are, Sunny."

Seated far enough away from Alex Ramsay to make conversation with him impossible, Sunny and her mother watched through the glass bubble as they took off from the harbor. Azure blue water reflected the azure blue of the sky.

The city of Auckland rapidly receded from their view. Then, flying over the Tasman Sea, Sunny looked down at the boats and ships and searched for a gray destroyer on her way to the naval repair base on Cockatoo Island, in the

Sydney harbor.

But then a rain squall spoiled her view. And the PBY, caught in the bumpy updrafts , began to resemble one of the rides at a county fair. A passenger behind Sunny became ill. Without thinking, Sunny went to her.

"I'm feeling faint," the woman complained. "I'm pregnant, you know," she confided in a lower voice. "Three months."

"Lower your head," Sunny instructed. "Take your fingers and press hard between your eyes."

The woman did so, and after a few minutes, when she began to feel better, Sunny slipped back to her seat.

The weather started to clear, with the aftermath of the storm visible only in the mountain of clouds ahead, and in the choppy water below that had changed from its beautiful azure to a raw, faded hue.

By the time the mammoth span of the Sydney Bridge became visible, the PBY was ready for descent. Circling like a great bird coming in for a landing on a mountain lake already filled with other migrants, the PBY searched for the buoy assigned to her for tie-up in the harbor.

The woman behind Sunny groaned, and she felt sorry for her. The woman would not get better until they reached shore.

Once the plane had landed, the passengers began to crawl from the wing to the dinghy waiting below. The usually calm waters of the harbor churned the small boat and washed over the occupants. Sunny was drenched, as was the gear that she also carried.

Looking slightly green, Kenna murmured, "How can you manage to stay on a ship for weeks at the time, darling?" She mopped the salt spray from her face, and pushed back the wet tendrils of her hair. "I so desperately need to feel the ground beneath my feet."

"You're not getting seasick, are you, Mother?"

"Of course not. But I'll be happy to reach land as soon as possible."

Sunny smiled in sympathy. She would never get her mother to admit to any weakness. She should have known better.

When the tug pulling the dinghy finally reached the dock, the wet, bedraggled passengers climbed out. This time, a bus waited at the dock to take the men and women into the center of town. The same contraption of charcoal burner with pipes that Sunny had seen in Auckland decorated the Australian bus.

Incredibly beautiful at twilight, the city was getting ready for night. Submarine nets were secured against enemy subs slipping into the harbor, and the people of the once-free metropolis, subdued by the news that Darwin had been bombed and their best Aussie soldiers sacrificed in Malaya, prepared for the possibility of their country being invaded by the enemy.

Brigadier General Irish Fitzpatrick waited impatiently for his wife and daughter to arrive at the Carleton Hotel. With only a sprinkling of gray in his dark hair and a few wrinkles on the brow to indicate the hazards of time, the man still looked magnificent. The West Point-designed wool uniform of World War I, with its neck-choking collar and tight breeches that cut off leg circulation, had been replaced by summer khaki, much more comfortable for a more modern war. Irish paced up and down outside the hotel, while he watched for the bus to arrive.

"Good evening, General," a man greeted as he walked up the steps to the lobby.

"Good evening, Mr. Prime Minister," Irish replied, turning his head to see the man, Curtin, in town for the upcoming conference.

The noise of the approaching bus drew Irish's attention, and by the time it stopped, he stood only a few feet from the vehicle.

"There he is," Sunny said, catching a glimpse of her father from the bus window. Without waiting for her mother, she danced off the bus and rushed toward him. "Dad," she called.

"Angel," Irish responded. The reunion of father and daughter caused smiles as Sunny dropped her gear and hurled herself into his arms. "Oh, I've missed you so much."

"Not half so much as we've missed you." Irish searched for Kenna, and when she reached the two, he put his arms around both and ushered them into the hotel. "Looks like you two got a little wet," he commented.

Witnessing the family reunion, Alex frowned. He was not used to public displays of affection. In her exuberance, the young nurse had even forgotten her seabag. All at once, the words of the queen of Tonga came back to him. "I wanted to see if your beauty matched your exuberance, Miss Fitzpatrick." Alex, himself, could vouch for that. The damp uniform clung to Sunny's body, leaving little to the imagination. The seawater bath had merely heightened her beauty, giving her the appearance of a small, blond hoyden, a younger replica of her beautiful, but more reserved mother. But perhaps with time she might become more like her mother.

Alex suddenly shrugged. Why should he be concerned with how the American nurse turned out in years to come? He walked to the registration desk. "You have a reservation for Alex Ramsay?"

The young desk clerk straightened immediately. "Yes, my lord. And you have a message waiting—from the governor-general. Also, your campaign trunk arrived this afternoon. Any other luggage, sir?"

"No. Only my kit. But the young woman, Miss Fitzpatrick, left her seabag on the pavement."

"I'll get someone to take it up to her at once. Thank you, sir."

Alex, with his key in hand, walked to the elevator. Once he reached the hotel room, he saw the personal trunk he'd shipped more than a month ago from Calcutta. He was glad to have some of his own clothes again. After removing his travel-stained shirt and trousers, he turned on the water in the bath and contemplated a nice, leisurely soak.

As he lathered himself, he thought of the Raffles Hotel in Singapore. Only at that moment did he acknowledge how lucky he'd been in the past weeks.

Chapter 8

COMMANDER MATT WILLOUGHBY MISSED THE *GOOD Hope's* docking in Auckland by only a few hours. Boarding the ship, he fumed as he questioned Kirk Singleton.

"You don't have any idea where Sunny might be staying?"

An equally unhappy Kirk, forced to remain aboard, shook his head. "She left the ship with the other nurses. That's all I know."

"What rotten luck," Matt lamented. "I'm in port for only a day."

Kirk knew exactly how he felt. But he was actually better off than the commander of the destroyer. For Sunny would return to the hospital ship within two days, while Matt might not see her for another six months.

Neither officer discussed the top secret orders their ships had both received—to join a task force headed for the Coral Sea. A major naval battle was about to get underway. That was the reason for the *Good Hope's* crew to be denied liberty, and her officers forced to remain aboard. The hospital ship was a necessary part of the task force, and nothing was to deter the ship from keeping its rendezvous with the cruisers and destroyers assigned to the sea battle.

"You might find her at the Red Cross canteen," Kirk suggested. "I understand the city's throwing a big party for the medical personnel tonight."

"Thanks, Singleton," Matt replied, brightening immediately.

He left the ship and headed for the canteen. The sound of the gala party just getting underway greeted him a block away. Matt grinned as he heard the noise. Thousands of miles from home, Matt already felt at ease with the people from down under. They were just as friendly as Americans, and their zest for life was equally matched.

Seeing Madeleine and Wendy in the crowd, Matt was certain that Sunny was with them. He walked to the table where the two were sitting. "Where's Sunny?"

Wendy looked up and regret darkened her brown eyes. "She's not here, Commander."

"Where can I find her?"

Madeleine, who'd bumped into Sunny in the tearoom that afternoon, spoke up. "In Sydney. Her mother was waiting for her at the dock and she flew to Sydney with her."

"Sydney?" He formed the name as if it were suddenly offensive to him.

"She won't be back until late tomorrow," Wendy added. "I'm sorry."

"Not half as sorry as I am." He turned to leave the canteen.

"Would you like to join us?" Wendy invited.

"Are officers allowed?"

"This party is for all of us—you, included, if you want."

For a moment, Matt was silent. Then he shrugged. "Sure. Why not?" He took a chair from another table and the people rearranged themselves to make room for the unhappy commander of the destroyer *Viscount*.

At the Carleton Hotel, Sunny awoke from her nap at the insistence of her mother.

"You'll miss the party if you don't get up now, Sunny."

She stretched and yawned. "You two go ahead. I think I'll have dinner in my room tonight."

"Darling, you don't renege on a dinner invitation from the governor-general. Now get up and take your bath."

"I don't have anything decent to wear."

"Yes, you do. Your apricot silk. Didn't I tell you I brought your party dress with me? The shoes, too. Now be a love and step on it, darling. We can't have your father late for the party. It wouldn't look good on his record."

Sunny sat up on the side of the bed. "And just when did they start giving him points for attending boring dinners?"

"Long before he was recalled to the service."

Sunny Fitzpatrick laughed; for one of her memories as a child of ten, was of her mother cajoling her father to attend the opera benefit in their hometown. As strong as her father was in dealing with the business world, he could never refuse Kenna anything she really wanted. And she'd wanted to go to that dinner.

"I don't relish hearing Mrs. Pruitt mutilating the 'Bell Song' like she did last year," he'd protested. "It gave me indigestion then, and it'll give me indigestion tonight."

"Mrs. Pruitt retired from singing last season, Irish. And *Lakme* is out this year. You'll be hearing excerpts from *Madame Butterfly*, instead."

"And who's performing that?" a wary Irish had questioned.

"Anna Grace Langley."

"Wasn't she the soprano who cracked the chandelier in church several weeks ago?"

Kenna smiled. And in a low, sultry voice that the ten-year-old could hardly hear, she said, "We don't have to stay for the entire evening. We can have our own little party later."

Irish laughed as he put his arms around Kenna. "You're terrible — promising an old dog a bone, once he's jumped through the hoop. All right. I'll get dressed. But you'd better hurry and get dressed, too, or the old dog will claim his bone first."

Standing in the hallway, the young Sunny saw her father

reach out and pat her mother on her derrière. Kenna giggled and hurried to her dressing table as Irish disappeared into the bath. And it was in that hallway that the ten-year-old had made up her mind as to the kind of husband she wanted when she grew up.

"You're miles away, Sunny," her mother reprimanded.

She looked up. The hallway had disappeared and she was once again in the hotel room of the Carleton. "I know. I was thinking of something that happened a long time ago." She stood up and hurried to her own bath.

Twenty minutes later, Sunny was putting the finishing touches to her appearance. Smoothing the apricot dress to her hips, she peered into the mirror to make sure her slip was not showing.

Seeing her mother in the beautiful aqua silk Chinese dress, Sunny let out a low whistle, similar to the ones with which she'd been plagued whenever the sailors in port had spotted her.

"Sunny! How unladylike," her mother scolded. "I hope you don't make a practice of behaving this way."

"Take it as the compliment it's meant to be," Irish teased as he joined them. "You two could pass for sisters, instead of mother and daughter—not only in looks, but stubbornness, too. Well, if you're both ready, let's go."

They took the elevator to the lobby and within a few minutes were on their way. In the darkness, with the windows of the taxi rolled down, Sunny could smell the exotic odor of eucalyptus leaves and see the outline of wattle—great bouquets of yellow on the bushes lining the park. Seated beside her mother and father, she felt marvelously happy and secure.

"If Jack were with us," Sunny commented aloud, "tonight would be absolutely perfect."

Sunny saw her father reach out and touch her mother's hand. "We'll all be back together again one day," Irish assured them both.

"Will you be staying in Sydney long, Dad?"

He glanced toward the taxi driver. "As long as there's a reason to," he answered. "In other words, darling daughter, button your lip."

Sunny laughed. "I get the message, Dad."

She should have known better than to ask. Any information, however trivial, concerning one of MacArthur's staff might be picked up by the Japanese. Tokyo Rose had thrived on careless remarks that she twisted to her own advantage each night. And Sunny was certain the Japanese High Command did the same, only they didn't boast about it over the radio.

From the outside of the official residence of His Majesty's representative, little could be seen of the lights within. Since it was far enough away from the actual war zones, the city maintained only a brownout, sufficient to give the residents a cat's-eye view of the dark, with shapes of buildings outlined against the blue-black of the sky.

The taxi, with only its parking lights on, drew up to the castle-like structure, and a smartly dressed guard holding a flashlight downward escorted Sunny and her parents to the door.

Inside the magnificent residence, the three were announced. "Brigadier General and Mrs. John Ireland Fitzpatrick, and Miss Amanda Fitzpatrick."

Feeling on display, Sunny looked out over the crowds milling about prior to the dinner. Uniforms were prevalent, with the insignia of the ANZACs in prominent display, for the celebration was in honor of the Australian-New Zealand Army Corps, who had won heroic but tragic fame in the Battle of Gallipoli in the First World War, as the memorial in Sydney attested.

Now, the sons of those first troops were giving their lives in far-off places like Crete, Africa, and Greece, while their homeland was being threatened. Curtin, the Australian prime minister, had recalled a division headed for Rangoon, and the situation between England and Australia was extremely delicate. That night, the representative of the king was doing his diplomatic best to repair the damage to that relationship.

"Irish, old chap, what enormous luck to see you." The English officer nodded to Kenna and Sunny, and then took Irish aside.

Holding a fruit juice concoction in her hand, Sunny looked at her mother. "I don't want to appear ungrateful at being invited to the castle, Mother, but I have a feeling I'm going to be extremely bored tonight. The stuffiness is in the air."

"Would that have anything to do with the fact that the median age of the men here is about sixty-two?"

"How did you know?"

An attractive, matronly woman, seeing Kenna and Sunny alone, immediately rushed up, took their hand and led them through the assembly, with introductions to other women and some of the men who were at their wives' sides.

"And what is your impression of Australia, Miss Fitzpatrick?"

"What I've seen of it is quite beautiful."

"Are you here for long?"

"No. I'm visiting my mother and father."

"Ah yes, how lovely."

The same conversation was recycled several times. Sunny was propelled through the rooms. With the various introductions, she was separated from her mother and, when the signal was given that dinner was being served, she began to look for Kenna and Irish.

A familiar voice at her elbow said, "I believe we have been paired as dinner companions, Miss Fitzpatrick. Are you ready to go in?"

Sunny gazed unbelievingly at the man before her. One of the few civilians attending the dinner, the man, attired in Scottish kilt and plaid, dominated the room.

Despite the kilted skirt, he was disturbingly masculine, with his square-cut jaw and his sandy hair with a touch of red threatening to escape its rigid combing, while his eyes, the color of blue azurite, seemed to mock her even as he stood waiting for her to accept. A slight bulge of his left sleeve indicated the bandage he wore.

"I have to find my mother and father," she hedged.

"They have already gone in with the prime minister."

Sunny was aware of the woman next to her, listening to their conversation. With a graciousness she didn't feel, she finally acceded. "Thank you, my lord."

Offering his arm, he remonstrated, "My name is Alex."

"I wouldn't presume such familiarity, my lord," Sunny said archly, her topaz eyes equally mocking. "Especially toward someone dressed in all that splendor."

"For a woman who's familiar with every inch of a man's body, I find that lack of presumption to be a little late, Miss Fitzpatrick."

The woman beside them gasped. And Sunny, realizing she'd overheard, deliberately stepped on Alex's foot with the heel of her sandal.

"And how is your wound, my lord?" Sunny inquired loudly enough for the woman to hear, also.

"Which one?" he replied, grimacing from the sudden pain in his foot.

They sat above the salt, in a carefully planned orchestration of rank and title. Seeing the beautiful young woman, small and fragile, dutifully exchanging pleasantries right and left, Alex realized that no one asked her anything but the politest of questions. It probably never occurred to them that the daughter of a general was equally involved in the war beyond the bandage rolling of the Red Cross volunteers, or a simple afternoon a week reading and writing letters for soldiers unable to do so.

At one point, Alex leaned over and in a low, confidential voice said, "Fifteen minutes more, Amanda, and you'll be free."

"Is my restlessness that obvious, my lord?"

"Only to me."

Later, as they left the table, the governor-general spoke

to Alex. "You must go to the races with me this week, Dalhousie. They're not like your Christmas races at Dacca, but all the same, you'll see some examples of fine horseflesh."

"That would be most pleasant, sir," Alex responded.

"I'll call you tomorrow. Is ten o'clock convenient?"

"Quite."

Sunny didn't know why the mention of the races should incense her. True, it was a national sport, but it didn't seem appropriate for men not in uniform to be enjoying themselves while others were getting their arms and legs shot off in battle. She had no way of knowing that the governor-general had just received a direct order from the War Office in London to be relayed in private to one Alex Ramsay, in His Majesty's service.

As Sunny attempted to leave him, Alex said, "The evening is not yet over, Amanda. There's to be dancing, too. Perhaps you waltz as well as you jitterbug?"

"You'll have to find another Waltzing Matilda, my lord. I'm ready to leave."

"That will be hard to do, since no carriages will arrive for another hour."

"Carriages? What happened to the taxis?"

"They're out of service until morning."

"Then, excuse me, please. I think I'll find the powder room."

She began to walk up the winding stairs to another floor, while Alex, with a frown on his face, stood at the base and watched her.

When she reached the upstairs, Sunny saw a maid in attendance. "Please," she said, "do you happen to have an aspirin?"

"I'll get one for you, miss."

Every bit as stubborn as her mother, Sunny was determined not to admit to any weakness, especially in front of Alex Ramsay. But she should never have eaten the shrimp. The shellfish always gave her a headache because of her allergy. And she usually steered clear for that reason. But somehow, tonight it had seemed impolite to refuse a course at the governor-general's table. Now she was to pay for her indiscretion and her politeness. She remained upstairs as long as she dared, hoping that the time would pass quickly and she could return to the hotel room.

When Sunny came downstairs again, Alex Ramsay quietly walked to her side. "I have a carriage waiting," he announced. "I've said our good-byes." He ushered her toward the entrance, even as she protested. "There's no need to play the martyr, Amanda. I've spoken with your mother. So, let's hurry on."

The evening air, with a hint of fall, felt good to Sunny. The fresh air, combined with the aspirin, made her feel much better.

Watching her inhale deeply, Alex said, "You're a little fool to have eaten the shrimp, knowing that you're allergic to them."

"Thank you for pointing that out to me, my lord."

Alex's patience with her ran out. "You're a reverse snob, Amanda. And I'm growing a little weary of your charade. No one asks to be born into a certain titled family. No one has a choice even as to countries or nationalities."

"And most men don't have a choice, either, when it comes to serving in their country's army or navy during wartime. Just how is it, my lord, that you've remained a civilian, when almost everyone else is serving in the military?"

A thunderous look passed over Alex's face as he swore softly under his breath. Gritting his teeth to keep from saying words he would regret, Alex, in a cold voice, replied,"If you can't be civil, then I see no reason for further conversation."

They rode through the streets of Sydney in silence, until a general siren went off, alerting the city to danger.

"Take cover, mate," a voice called out. "An enemy sub has been spotted in the harbor."

Guns in the distance fired, and Sunny couldn't tell if they were the shore batteries, or enemy fire directed at the Allied ships anchored in the harbor. The disaster that was Pearl Harbor encroached upon her memory as the carriage stopped to oust the passengers.

Unwilling to leave his horses in the open, the driver rushed back to the stables with lightning speed, while Alex and Sunny sought cover.

Chapter 9

HUDDLED TOGETHER IN THE BASEMENT OF A DARKENED stone building, Sunny and Alex were the only two in the shelter. A small gaslight flickered overhead, with just enough light to throw shadows on the wall whenever they moved.

Ever since she had spoken in anger, Sunny knew that an apology to Alex was in order. Civilians were needed for the war effort just as desperately as soldiers. And because a man was not wearing a uniform did not necessarily mean he was a coward.

"I'm sorry, Alex. I had no business speaking to you the way I did."

"What's the matter, Amanda? Making your peace with your fellow man in case a bomb hits you?"

Sorry now that she had offered an apology, she remonstrated, "A submarine is little danger to me. Only the ships in the harbor."

"You might be in more danger than you know."

"Are you suggesting I might be in danger from you? I rather doubt that."

Again, he gritted his teeth. "You have been a pain in my side from the moment I laid eyes on you."

"Not half so—"

She had no opportunity to finish the sentence. Alex's

mouth captured hers, cutting off any further argument. With all the passion of a Scottish chieftain taking what he wanted by might, Alex was oblivious to Sunny's struggle against him. He explored the taste of her lips, the curve of her body crushed to his own.

"Please…"

"Be quiet."

Little by little, Sunny's resistance disappeared. She became aware of a spreading warmth and the strange feeling that made her yearn for something more, beyond her realm of knowledge, that even Matt had not been able to summon from her inner being.

Losing all sense of time and place, she strained against Alex's body as his hand sought the softness of her breast. In mortal danger of betraying her own standards, she was brought back to reality by the sound of the all-clear from the street above.

The warden, with his light, walked into the opening. "All clear now. You can leave the shelter."

Sunny smoothed her silk dress as she stood. Her face revealed nothing, but her breathing was far too rapid. Without looking at the man by her side, she walked onto the deserted street.

There were no vehicles for hire. Forced to converse, Alex said, "Looks like we'll have to walk the rest of the way to the hotel. Are your shoes up to it?"

"Why should you be concerned with the state of my feet? You haven't cared for my comfort for the past twenty minutes."

"Damn it, woman. Then take your shoes off and walk in your bare feet."

"Will that not spoil your sense of propriety, my lord? Or do you expect me to walk ten paces behind you?"

"One day, Amanda Fitzpatrick…"

"Are you threatening me, sir?"

In an instant she was seated on a park bench. Reaching down, he removed both sandals and pitched them into the shrubbery. She had never seen a man so angry. She gazed toward the shrubbery, and with what dignity she had left, Sunny rose from the bench and began to walk barefooted. Conversation between the two was now impossible.

A few blocks later, Sunny walked into the lobby of the Carleton Hotel. She secured the key to her room and, ignoring the interested glances of the people in the lobby, she walked regally to the elevator. The last person she saw as the doors closed was Alex Ramsay, standing in the middle of the lobby. With his hands behind his back, he looked thoroughly miserable. And Sunny was glad.

By the time Irish and Kenna arrived back at the hotel, Sunny was sound asleep. By morning, when the clock indicated it was time to leave Sydney for the return trip to Auckland, the sun had not yet come up. With a few stars still visible in the sky, Sunny left the hotel and arrived at the harbor to board the PBY. Folded in her seabag was the apricot silk dress. But the shoes to match remained in the wattle bushes, to be retrieved by some passerby.

The return trip to Auckland was uneventful. The scare of the Japanese submarine was over and, for the time being, there was little fear of Japanese planes that far south.

Two days later, the Burma Road was no longer in the hands of the Allies. As Stillwell, the American general, loaned to Chiang Kai-shek as his army commander, set out for the Indian border by way of the Irawaddy River, Alex Ramsay set out for the Sydney racetrack in the company of the governor-general.

"My wife tells me that you left early from the party, Dalhousie," the governor-general remonstrated. "Was anything wrong?"

"General Fitzpatrick's daughter was not feeling well, my lord. I escorted her back to her hotel."

"A pity," the man responded. "We had a most engaging evening—once the lights came back on. That was rather a scare, what, with the submarine slipping into the harbor. But I must say it put a different slant on the conference yesterday. Everyone seemed quite willing to cooperate."

The small talk continued as the chauffeur drove onto the racetrack grounds, stopped the car, and then held the door for the two occupants.

Following the older man with silver hair, Alex walked toward the crowd that had already gathered for the first race of the day. As the governor-general put his binoculars to his eyes to watch the starting gate, he seemed more interested in the horses than in Alex Ramsay, or his reason for inviting the younger diplomat.

"If I were a betting man, I'd put a pound or two down on number three—Waltzing Matilda."

Alex raised his own binoculars and looked toward the starting gate. "A little skittish, isn't she?" he asked, seeing the horse protest the enclosure.

"Nothing but what a little time and experience won't improve. Stunning, simply stunning," he remarked after a while. Then, he laughed. "I'm afraid my mind isn't on the horse. Actually, my mind wandered to that gorgeous creature that is General Fitzpatrick's wife. I must say, I was quite smitten with her. In a paternal way, of course," he added quickly.

"Of course, " Alex agreed. It was strange how they were both thinking of two women in the same family—mother and daughter.

In a confidential voice, the governor-general returned the conversation to the subject of horses. "Some jockeys, you know, refuse to ride a filly—too high-strung, they say. But Dingo Farms has had fantastic luck with its fillies. And they have big plans for their two-year-old, Waltzing Matilda."

There was the name again. And Alex, as if he were standing in front of Sunny, remembered her remark. "You'll have to find another Waltzing Matilda, my lord."

The gates were opened; the race began, and Alex watched the horse's progress. As the crowd pressed closer to the fence, Alex was alone with the governor-general.

Without lowering his binoculars, the king's representative said, "I have special orders for you, Dalhousie. When you get back to my office this afternoon, you can pick up your new passport. Edwards will add to your wardrobe if you need anything else. By this time tomorrow, you will be on your way to Port T, in the Addu Atoll."

"And the reason?"

"A strategic defense planning session with the best brains of the Eastern Fleet—and some Chinese and American chaps. If the Japanese invade India, then there's nothing to stop them this side of the Bay of Bengal."

"And our sea lanes to the Middle East will be lost," Alex added.

"Exactly. We can't rely on the Vichy government to defend Madagascar. We'd be pushed all the way to the eastern coast of Africa."

"The Allies will *have* to reinforce India and arm China. That's all there is to it," Alex offered with a particular grimness.

A spectator moved within hearing distance and their attention turned once more to the race. The voice from the loudspeaker boomed, "Waltzing Matilda leading on the inside. Edging up from the outside—Maitland's Jack, number six, with Seaweed, number eight in third position. Maitland's Jack and Waltzing Matilda, neck and neck, with Seaweed gaining on the two—a three-way race. Maitland's Jack, now in the lead with Waltzing Matilda dropping to second place. Seaweed falters.

"Ladies and gentlemen," the excited voice announced, "it's Maitland's Jack by a nose. Maitland's Jack the winner, with Waltzing Matilda second and Rob Roy, number five, out of Lennox Farms, placing third."

The spectator moved away to follow the crowd, and the governor-general spoke again. "I say, Maitland's Jack was certainly a dark horse." Then as if he had been interrupted by the race, he continued, "Your diplomatic expertise in India will be invaluable at the conference, Dalhousie. The War Office is counting on you to be persuasive in India's defense. You think the Hindu Congress will give us trouble?"

"Yes. Ghandi is a pacifist," Alex reminded the man. "If it were left up to him, he'd allow the Japanese to invade without a shot fired. But there are others, such as Nehru, who know firsthand what the Japanese do to a subjected people. If internal differences in India, as well as China, can be put off until after the war, we have a chance of stopping the Japanese."

"Oh, by the by, one of your Chinese friends will be at the conference."

"Chuang San Chu?"

"Yes."

Alex smiled when he heard the news, for it was the first substantiation that the Chinese general had also escaped Singapore. "And after the conference, what then? Has my request come through?"

The governor-general acted reluctant to answer. "Unfortunately, yes. But I must warn you, Dalhousie. All those islands will soon be overrun by the Japanese. You'll either wind up as a prisoner, or if you're extremely lucky, you'll be hiding out in the hills for the rest of the war."

Alex looked down at his binoculars. "I'll take my chances."

The next morning, armed with passport, tropical clothes, and quinine, Alex Ramsay left Sydney.

Six hundred miles below the island of Ceylon, off the coast of India, a group of jungled coral islands known as the Maldives rose from the floor of the Indian Ocean.

Out of the commercial shipping lanes, the islands had a secluded lagoon, reachable by four channels through the barrier reef. The port, designated only as Port T by the War Office, had been set up as a possible base to be used eventually in strikes against the Japanese mainland. An airfield had been built on the largest island, while the harbor sheltered a store ship, a hospital ship, and a repair base for

His Majesty's navy.

Surrounding the main island, like small stones decorating a larger stone, were the auxiliary islands containing shore batteries and searchlights, ready to spot any Japanese ships that might stumble onto the secret base.

It was at this secluded island that Alex Ramsay landed in a PBY similar to the one in which Sunny Fitzpatrick had flown back to Auckland.

As Sunny left the New Zealand port on the *Good Hope,* Alex debarked at Port T for the high-level conference of military and civilian minds intent on developing a strategy of saving India from the Japanese.

Aboard the *Good Hope,* Sunny and Wendy, seeking shade from the late afternoon sun, lay on the afterdeck that had been declared off limits to the crew.

"I heard Heinman say we were joining a task force for a major battle, " Wendy confided. "In the Coral Sea. Do you think he's right?"

"If he is, it's about time for some action," Sunny responded. Shielding her eyes, she stood up and gazed over the ocean. "The *Viscount's* out there, somewhere."

Wendy came to stand beside her. "You should have seen Matt in Auckland when he found out you'd flown to Sydney."

"Wendy, I have this awful feeling that I'm going to keep passing him all through the war, without ever being in port at the same time.

"Did you know that when I boarded the PBY from Sydney, there was a guy coming in who'd missed his ship in three different ports? Every time he got a ride to the next stop, his ship had sailed. And he was too late in Sydney, too. His ship had pulled out that morning."

"Will they court-martial him if he doesn't catch up with the ship eventually?"

"I don't know. He's in the merchant marine, not the regular navy."

"Well, to get back to Matt, I expect he'll arrange some

way of finding you, even to becoming a patient on the *Good Hope*."

"Don't say that, Wendy. Even in jest. That's unlucky."

"Sorry. I talk too much, especially when there's nothing to do. But it *is* rather nice to have an empty ship, isn't it?"

"It won't be empty for long," Sunny predicted.

Benita and Madeleine appeared, and Madeleine, pulling out her deck of cards, said, "Anyone for bridge?"

"How about a game of blackjack, instead?" Wendy inquired.

"You've been associating with Brogdon too long," Madeleine accused.

"Well, it's either that or being a guinea pig for one of his inventions."

"What's he working on now?" Benita inquired as she shuffled the cards.

"A wheelchair that can be converted to a dental chair, so the patient won't have to be moved."

Benita looked down at her hand. "Pass."

"Two hearts," Sunny replied.

"Two hearts! That's not fair. You're supposed to be unlucky at cards," Wendy pouted.

"My luck has turned," Sunny explained. "I'm no longer lucky in love."

Madeleine sniffed. "The girl danced all night with the prince at the ball, and she's complaining."

"I didn't dance one step with Alex Ramsay. So stop teasing me."

"Three clubs," Wendy called out.

"Four hearts," Madeleine answered.

"Double."

"It's not your turn again, Wendy," Madeleine scolded. "Do you want to double, Benita?"

"No. Pass."

"Pass."

"Double," Wendy persisted.

Madeleine sighed as she waited for Wendy to lead. If she

were ever on a desert island, she hoped Wendy wouldn't be with her to drive her mad.

Sunny forgot both Alex Ramsay and Matt Willoughby and turned her attention, for Madeleine's sake, to winning the hand of bridge.

Chapter 10

NOT FAR FROM THE PIER AT PORT T, CHUANG SAN Chu stood and watched the PBY circle the lagoon and then touch water. Only one passenger emerged — a man so distinctive in his appearance that there was no mistaking who he was — Alex Ramsay, the man he'd last seen in the Red Dragon Restaurant in Singapore.

Alex was dressed in khaki, with a bush helmet upon his head and a pair of binoculars around his neck, while the Chinese general wore the dull green uniform with mandarin collar that the generalissimo, his superior, had made famous.

Chuang waited for Alex to negotiate the long wooden pier, and then he stepped into the clearing. Seeing the slender, tall Chinese, Alex accelerated his pace until he was standing face-to-face with Chuang.

Ceremoniously, Chuang bowed three times and Alex, with no smile upon his face, returned the bows. "My friend," Alex said in Chinese, reaching out to grip the man's arm in friendship.

Still, Chuang displayed no emotion. "I thought you had gone to the tomb of your ancestors."

"The moon was wrong. T'ien would not accept me. And you?"

"Shang Ti had no need of me, as well."

With their formal greeting over, Alex broke into a huge

grin. And Chuang, allowing himself the slightest hint of a smile also, began to walk with Alex to the headquarters hidden from the view of an enemy scout plane by tropical trees.

Off and on, other men arrived and, by late afternoon, twelve men gathered around a table and examined a map of the Bay of Bengal.

Alex, the career diplomat, was the only one not in military uniform. Twice he had tried to resign from the diplomatic service to join the British army, but had been refused. As a salve, he had been attached to intelligence, but he was still a civilian. For this reason, he was acutely aware of the high-ranking officers surrounding him—five British, three Americans, and two Australians, in addition to Chuang.

"Gentlemen, the news is not good," one of the British naval officers began. "Ever since Pearl Harbor, Admiral Nagumo has ranged his carrier force throughout the Pacific, without the slightest check. Everywhere we turn, British ships have been sunk. The island of Ceylon is now lost to us. And I have no hope that Port T will remain a secret much longer. Mr. Churchill has petitioned Mr. Roosevelt to intervene with a diversionary tactic to give us some relief. But he has been slow to respond. Captain Wentwood, can you speak to this problem?" The British officer looked toward the American navy captain, propped comfortably in a bamboo chair.

Ignoring the rather overbearing tone of his questioner, Teddy Wentwood replied in a slow, unhurried drawl. "Nagumo isn't the only Japanese admiral roaming the Pacific at the moment. Admiral Nimitz intercepted a radio code between Goto and Takagi. Seems they're cooking up a little diversion of their own, prior to invading Papua New Guinea.

"They're planning to destroy the American fleet in a pincerlike movement somewhere in the Coral Sea. Two task forces have been placed on alert. I assume this naval battle will take precedence over anything else for the next few weeks."

"But if that's true," a pleased voice spoke up, "isn't it the very diversionary tactic that Churchill would like to see?"

"If it's successful."

Alex remained quiet while the naval discussion took place. But once the talk concerning India and China began, he was called upon to give historical background of the East. No one at the table knew India so well. And like a patient teacher, Alex brought them up to date.

"Gentlemen, forget the newsreels you've seen lately about the Raj and the Indians fighting side by side against the Japanese. That's for home consumption in England, and not to be taken seriously by the military.

"The truth of the matter is that India is at war with herself along two religious fronts—unchangeable and irreconcilable. On the one hand, you have the Moslems, worshipers of the One God. On the other hand, you have the Hindus, a polytheistic religious group , with numerous gods and numerous social castes. The Moslems and the Hindus hate each other.

"The Moslem might fight for his country, whereas the Hindu is concerned only with his immediate family, his caste, and himself—not necessarily in that order. So we cannot expect any defense of India from the Hindus."

"Aren't those rather harsh words, Sir Alex?" another British naval officer questioned. "Are you certain your recent set-to has not colored your judgment of the Hindus?"

Before Alex could answer, the ranking British army officer spoke up in his defense. "Dalhousie saved a thirteen-year-old widow from being burned alive with her dead husband. For his efforts, he was set upon by Thugs hired by the greedy relatives, who wanted the widow's share of her husband's estate, as well."

"Good Lord! Are you talking about *suttee*? I thought that went out of style a hundred years ago."

Alex turned to the American. "Unfortunately, it's still

practiced, but in a more clandestine way. A widow is drugged; her house mysteriously burns down. But to get back to the question.

"The assassination attempt on me and the reason behind it, far from coloring my judgment, only show how deep the roots of religious fervor go in the Indian culture. The high command would do well to understand it."

"And what about the Chinese culture, General Chuang?" the Australian officer asked. "If the Allies arm China, is there anything in her background that will keep her from fighting, also?"

"My friend, the marquess of Dalhousie, understands well the oriental mind. The same lack of concern for the welfare of soldiers not of their own village plagues the Chinese army, too. But you must remember that Chinese soldiers do not have the same proud tradition of the British Commonwealth. Their wounded are left by the wayside to fend for themselves; officers are shot for losing their troops in battle, and no commander trusts another commander over him. One platoon, waiting for battle, suddenly finds its right flank undefended because the other officer has withdrawn his troops, his guns, from the battle line."

"Vinegar Joe Stillwell certainly has himself an army," one of the Americans voiced.

Chuang continued. "Everywhere there is the *kumshaw,* or 'squeeze,' up and down the power structure, from Madame herself down to the lowliest. And I fear that many of the supplies have already gone to warehouses behind the lines to be used by the generalissimo later against Mao."

"Will Mao be a problem for the generalissimo?" the naval commander asked Chuang San Chu.

"After the war, yes. But the generalissimo will accept his help for now. That is why he has released him from prison."

The man turned to Alex. "And Nehru?"

"Naturally, he presses for India's independence after the war. But also for now he has indicated a willingness to fight against the Japanese. The Ghurkas are fine soldiers, as you know. And there are a few others willing to bear arms, despite Ghandi."

The twelve men looked across the table from each other. "The missionaries have certainly painted the wrong picture of the Orient in America," Wentwood accused.

"No worse than some of our own intelligence," another commented.

"Well, this has been the blackest three months in the history of the Allies," Haizlett, the Australian, announced, and Alex was inclined to agree. "It has to get better. Can't get any worse."

The sound of a plane blurred the voices, and then a tremendous explosion rocked the island. Alex, falling to the floor, saw great flames through the open door. His own PBY had been hit, and its remnants began to float in the lagoon, like an oriental funeral pyre, as the dock also caught fire.

"Gentlemen, with your permission, our conference will be delayed while we seek more adequate cover."

The American captain turned to his fellow officer. "In other words," he translated, "run like hell."

All around, the shore batteries opened up, and the men raced for the sandbagged trenches. Alex stuffed his handkerchief into his mouth to avoid concussion from the heavy guns.

When the battle was over, the twelve men finished their conference, with recommendations for the high command. Certain that the secluded port would be attacked again at dawn, the twelve, under cover of the moonless night, left Port T.

Alex accepted a ride to Townsville, with the American captain, Wentwood. His diplomatic days were in limbo for a time. Now, he would become involved in a game every bit as dangerous. Only this time, the enemy would not know his name.

On May 1, 1942, while the two U.S. task forces moved into the Coral Sea, the Japanese were heading for Tulagi, a small island in the Solomons.

The Solomon Islands lay in an elongated chain that stretched from Bougainville all the way to San Cristobal in the south, as if some giant had haphazardly strewn emerald stones to make a necklace for the sea. A narrow corridor, designated "the Slot," divided the two parts of the chain.

On the northeast lay the islands of Choiseul, Santa Isabel, and Malaita, and to the southwest, Vella Lavella, New Georgia, and Guadalcanal. Only the Sealark Channel separated the eastern coast of Guadalcanal from Tulagi, seat of the Solomons Protectorate.

On that afternoon, fifty-one-year-old Giles Canupp, the manager of a copra plantation, sat on the verandah of his island home and looked across the channel toward Tulagi. Great clouds of smoke spiraling into the sky made much more of a display than the wisps of smoke from the two volcanoes on Bougainville to the north.

From Rabaul, on New Britain, the Japanese were expanding their foothold into the Solomons. Tulagi, victim of recent Japanese air attacks, was now being readied for abandonment by the few men left on the island. Most of her inhabitants had already fled, and now, as the great warehouse stores of goods were being destroyed by fire, Giles, twenty miles across the channel, had a ringside seat.

For fourteen years, the copra plantation had been his home. And for the past two years, he had served as a coastwatcher relaying messages by the mammoth teleradio set up in a radio shack attached to his house.

Timi You, one of his Melanesian servants, walked onto the verandah. "Master Giles, KEO is calling you."

Immediately Giles got up and rushed to the teleradio. Putting on his headphones, he responded, "This is CRE. Come in, KEO." At first, there was only static. Then as Giles repeated his call letters, he heard Ken Otwell to the north.

"Two Japanese convoys headed your way. Seaplane carrier, with corvette, coming down the Slot toward Tulagi. Twelve transports, two heavy cruisers, one aircraft carrier following to the east."

With a quiet expertise, he relayed the message through the network. And within half an hour, it was received in Townsville by Eric Graham of the Coast Watchers headquarters.

Alex Ramsay, sitting in the office with Eric Graham, listened to the ensuing conversations. He had been receiving a crash course in the use of the Playfair code. And when the rush was finally over, when the task forces in the Coral Sea had been alerted, Eric turned his attention to the man in his office.

"That was your chap, Giles Canupp," Eric informed him. "The one you're going to replace on Guadalcanal. All hell's breaking loose, as you heard. Are you still willing to go into that Jap nest? You can back out if you want."

"No. I'm already committed."

"Well, then, let's finish up. Your plane leaves at sixteen hundred."

An hour later, Alex was on another PBY flying low over the Coral Sea toward Guadalcanal.

"Jesus, just don't let any Jap planes be concerned with one little PBY," Marston, the pilot, muttered religiously to Alex's chagrin.

Sitting in one of the blisters, Alex watched for the enemy. But he was flying so close to the water that it was difficult to see anything except the whitecaps below. Alex had a feeling that a Zero could come out of the clouds and be sitting right on top of them without their seeing or knowing.

But as time elapsed, there was no sign of any ship or plane—neither the eastern prong of the Japanese convoy heading for Papua New Guinea, nor the U.S. Task Force 17, heading for the rendezvous point where it would link up with Task Force 11, built around the carrier *Lexington.*

Once more, the pilot's nervousness transmitted itself to Alex. "We're taking a powerful chance going into the lagoon blind. If the Japs see us, they could blast us out of the water."

"We've had good luck so far," Alex acknowledged. He

did not mention the disaster at Port T.

"Yeah. Maybe it'll stay with us." Marston, to make sure, reached out before he brought the plane down, and touched his rabbit's foot dangling from the instrument panel. Alex couldn't blame him.

The plane touched water and the pilot cut his motor to allow the plane to glide to a stop. Trying hard not to appear in a hurry to discharge his passenger. Marston said, "You're sure someone's coming out to meet you?"

"Yes. Timi You, Canupp's native boy. He will have heard the plane come in. He should be here in a few minutes in his outrigger canoe."

The pilot resigned himself to the wait. Five minutes passed, and then ten. Finally, Marston spoke. "They say there're still some headhunters on the islands around here. One planter disappeared three years ago, and nine months later, someone recognized his shrunken head hanging over some chief's door. You got your pistol with you, Mr. Ramsay?"

"Yes. But I doubt that I'll need it against the natives. I understand that most are friendly."

At that moment, a canoe came in sight. But as Alex and Marston watched, the canoe headed out to sea instead. Five minutes later, a second canoe emerged, manned by three natives. The canoe followed the same path as the first for a time, and then quickly swung back toward the floating plane. Alex took his seabag and climbed onto the wing of the PBY.

"Masta Ramsay?"

"Yes?"

"I am Timi You," one of the natives said. "Masta Giles wait for you."

"Good. I was beginning to think you weren't coming."

Sheltered from land view, Alex climbed into the outrigger canoe and Timi You motioned Alex under the palm fronds in the stern of the boat. "We fish for hour. Then come back."

Unprotesting, Alex lay under the palms while Timi You hurried to catch up with the other canoe. Unable to see around him, Alex heard the PBY take off. And from the direction of Tulagi, explosions permeated the air. A few minutes later, the chug of a boat caused Timi You to speak again. "Be still, Masta. Patrol boat coming."

The Melanesian pulled up his net of fish just as the patrol boat slowed. A brief exchange ensued, with questions concerning an unidentified plane. Timi You acknowledged seeing one. Then, he gestured toward Tulagi. And the Japanese, satisfied, picked up speed and disappeared around the northern tip of the island.

With the smell of fish in the boat beside him, Alex remained still while the outrigger returned to shore. The boat hit the beach; the natives jumped out and began to drag it into a thicket of palms. The patrol boat had gone for the day.

"Everything's okay. You get out now." Timi You's voice was little more than a whisper, but Alex, after waiting for over an hour to hear the words, wasted no time once the signal had been given. He climbed out and stood up. His left foot was asleep. To get the circulation going again, he flexed the muscle in the calf of his leg.

Within moments, there was no sign that a boat had been brought ashore or hidden under palm fronds. Alex, following Timi You, crept silently through the jungle toward the plantation high above the lagoon.

On the verandah, Giles Canupp had watched the entire operation.When he saw the new man was safe, he put up his binoculars and searched for a cool beer. The copra plantation had served its purpose, but now it was too close to the lagoon to be safe for anyone. Ramsay would be better off two miles farther up in the hills, at another plantation.

Everything was arranged. He'd seen to that—the radio set up, the house well stocked. And if the Japanese should invade the island and Ramsay be forced to abandon the house, there were enough goods stored to last a year in the cave at the other plantation.

Giles looked down at his bandaged hand. He felt no pain. But, of course, that was one of the symptoms of the disease. Leprosy. Only Sister Birghitta, the native nun, knew—and Wani, his servant. Giles was reconciled to it now. But Eric had not wanted him to go to Savo.

"It's suicide, Giles. You'll never get out alive."

"But think how much good I can do, spotting the convoys as they come down the Slot."

Giles had made up his mind. He would go out in style rather than linger with his rotting flesh. After the natives helped him dismantle the giant teleradio and get it to the isolated island of Savo, he would send them back—all except Wani, who had vowed never to leave him, regardless of what happened.

Giles finished his beer. He left the verandah and, walking through each room of the plantation house, he walked through the fourteen years of memories. Soon, when he put a torch to the house, they, too, would be gone.

Chapter 11

THROUGH THE JUNGLED INTERIOR OF THE ISLAND OF Guadalcanal, Alex Ramsay followed Timi You. As he looked backward, like a traveler marking a trail, he saw no sign, no evidence that indicated where the three men had walked.

After the canoe had been hidden beyond the beach, the other natives vanished, leaving Alex with Timi You and Obadiah, who now carried his seabag.

For a while, they traveled along the winding riverbank, where Timi You gave Alex the first lesson of the island. "Not wish to swim in river," he advised.

Alex had no need to ask why, for a large crocodile suddenly left the sunny bank and plunged into the water.

Along the river, thatched huts, built on stilts, were surrounded by small vegetable plots. Primitive decorations hanging on the poles and woven into textures of the thatched awnings, showed that the people had been shark worshipers before the missionaries came.

With the Japanese landing on the northern portion of the island, most of the Europeans had been removed, except for a few French nuns who'd taken refuge in the caves. Only one white Dutch priest and six black nuns, native to the Solomons, remained in the mission village inland, with its church and small hospital. But Alex did not see it. Timi You, anxious to bring the man to Giles Canupp as he'd been told, avoided the mission village altogether.

Hot and thirsty, with pesky mosquitoes swarming all a-round him, Alex slapped at his neck. "Is the plantation much farther?" he inquired.

"Few more kilometers," Timi You assured him.

Soon, a cricket pitch came into view—an incongruous sight in the midst of a jungle. Alex smiled, for it was a standard colonial mark upon the land—a game exported by the British, even as they imported native rubber, copra, or tea for England.

Then, the copra plantation, itself, appeared. Set on a rise far above the lagoon, the plantation house with its enormous verandah combined the flavor of the tropical islands and the comforts of the British.

The portly Giles Canupp, with a shock of white hair partially hiding his forehead, walked down the steps of the verandah to meet Alex.

"Welcome to Shangri-La," he said, his penetrating eyes assessing the man before him. "I'm Giles Canupp."

"Alex Ramsay," he replied, and held out his hand in greeting.

Giles, in a breach of etiquette, ignored the extended hand. Instead, he waved the two natives inside. And motioning for Alex to join him on the verandah, he called for Wani to bring his visitor a cool lager to drink.

"You won't be staying here long," Giles announced as he eased himself into the wicker chair and motioned for Alex to take the other one. "As soon as you finish your beer, Timi You will take you to your place, two miles farther up the mountain. Eric told you about it, I assume."

"Yes."

"I'm leaving the island at dawn," Giles said. "As soon as you get to Bohorok, I'll buzz you on the teleradio, to make sure you have the hang of it. After that, we'll begin dismantling and packing. The next time we talk, I'll be on Savo. Do you have any questions now?"

"I'm interested in the cave. How will I find it?"

"I've already told Timi You to show you first thing in the morning. There'll be no activity for a while in the Slot, and if there is, one of the other coastwatchers will be on duty north of here. You need to know the location of the cave as soon as possible.

"When the Japs come—and they will—there'll be no time to pack. But you needn't worry. I gathered almost all the abandoned supplies in the company's store—staples, canned goods, benzine to operate the radio—and plenty of quinine and Atabrine. You'll have to have plenty of antimalarial drugs. And as to water, you'll have to catch it in a rain barrel. Most of the water on the island is disease-laden— except for the spring on this property, and a cascading waterfall high in the mountains. But it rains every afternoon, so it shouldn't be a problem. If you need to, you can sit out the entire damned war if you get stuck on the island."

But Alex did not intend to spend the rest of the war on Guadalcanal. He would do his bit until his new orders from intelligence came in.

"What about the others on the island? Can they be relied upon in an emergency?"

"Trust Timi You, of course," Giles advised. "Beyond him, you can trust Father Waal, the priest, and Sister Birghitta. But the fewer people who know your business, the better. If the Japanese take over, the others can be bribed too easily."

Timi You appeared again. Alex put down the empty beer mug and stood. He did not offer his hand again to Giles.

"Well, so long, old chap," Giles said. "And good luck. I'll ring you up tonight."

"Good-bye, Canupp. And thank you for your help."

Giles watched until the two disappeared. He would miss Timi You, but he'd made him promise to stay with the new man, Ramsay. Where Giles was going, he had no need for a houseful of servants. He and Wani would manage.

As dusk came to the viridian green isle, with its lagoon turning to lavender and aubergine and its trade winds rippling the coconut palm fronds on the beach, Alex approached the second plantation situated nearly three thousand feet higher than the first.

Called Bohorok, for the trade winds, it was almost a replica of Canupp's — with one exception. The verandah was enclosed with screen mesh wiring, a welcome relief from the winged night life that inoculated unsuspecting victims with malarial parasites. The disease, if left untreated, could cause devastating chills and fever, and even death.

The temperature had dropped twenty degrees from the heat of the day. And the billowing breeze began to dry Alex's shirt that had stuck to his back for the past four hours.

Once Alex arrived, he searched for the teleradio already set up in the house. It was not hard to find, for it occupied the entire wall facing the front of the house. Alex did not envy Giles the job of dismantling and moving his own radio to Savo. It would take a dozen or more men to carry the parts — transmitter, speaker, receiver — all weighing between seventy and a hundred pounds each, with additional weight of storage batteries and the engine and benzine to charge the batteries. With an average range of five hundred miles, the teleradio could operate either by telegraph key or voice.

The Playfair code was simple and did not require mastery of a complex cipher system. Alex was slightly disappointed at its simplicity, for he had been brought up in Indian ways, by a tutor who taught him to use his faculties much like the child, Kim, whom Rudyard Kipling had created.

Alex had been taught to use his powers of observation, to estimate at a glance the number of jewels in a box, or the number of elephants on the plain. With sleight of hand, he could transfer small objects from one place to another without being observed, as he had transferred the ruby to Chuang in the Red Dragon Restaurant. He had also been taught to remain still for hours, in full control, without a muscle twitching.

Yet, with all his expertise, one woman, Sunny Fitzpatrick, had caused him to lose control of his emotions.

With a feeling of utter self-disgust, he had returned late that night to the wattle bushes in the Sydney park, where he'd flung her apricot-colored sandals. By the next day, she'd already left the hotel before he could return them with his apology.

Alex walked from the radio room and found his bedroom, where Timi You was chasing a winged inhabitant from the armoire prior to hanging up his clothes—the few suits of cotton khaki, and his ancestral kilt, so out of place in the jungle.

A large bed stood in the middle of the room, with a mosquito tent, or bar, hanging from the ceiling to protect the sleeper from the mosquitoes that might penetrate the mesh screens.

On the table lay a Flit gun to deal with the intruders. Even that reminded Alex of Sunny and the hospital ship. He had seen her use a similar gun filled with melted paraffin to spray on the wounded, to protect their agonizing burns and seal in the moisture that oozed from their wounds.

He wandered through the rest of the house, taking note of the furnishings, the family mementoes and pictures left behind by the owner. It was as if he expected to come back any day. In the kitchen, Alex found a refrigerator that ran on benzine, like the radio. Personally, he could do without iced drinks, if he had to, but the fridge would be useful to store the perishables, fruits and vegetables.

More concerned though with the locations of all the doors and windows, Alex checked them, in case he would have to leave the plantation house in a hurry. Mentally filing the house plans in his mind, he went back to the radio to await Canupp's call.

"GC, calling MDAR. Come in, MDAR."

"MDAR here. Awaiting your message."

Giles Canupp switched to the Playfair code, using the telegraph key. The man gave the sign-off for his station watch. It was the last message Giles would deliver from the copra plantation. Just as he had changed initials to call Alex, he had chosen another name, Black Pawn, to use when he broadcast from Savo. That way, the Japanese would not know that he had moved.

Using the telegraph key, Alex sent a message of his own. "Luck." Then, he switched over to hear the final strains of "God Save the King." Giles was leaving in style.

While Timi You served Alex his dinner that night, Giles , in the other plantation, dismantled the teleradio. Through the night, the native bearers carried its parts in the opposite direction from which Alex had come. Hidden in the fleet of outrigger canoes, the transmitter, receiver, speaker, and batteries waited to be transported at dawn to the other island, closer to the Slot.

By morning, a Japanese flying boat, a Kawanisi, flew over the burning plantation house. The fire provided the necessary diversion while Giles and the natives left Guadalcanal.

Down below, in the mission village, Sister Birghitta looked up at the smoke from the burning plantation house. It was fitting that the man had set fire to all his belongings. It would not do for an unsuspecting squatter to live in a house where leprosy had dwelled.

Chapter 12

HOLDING THE MAP IN HIS HANDS, ALEX RAMSAY TRUDG--ed behind Timi You, who was cutting their way through the dense, matted jungle beyond the copra plantation.

That morning, shortly before dawn, Alex had seen the fire coming from Giles Canupp's plantation house. It was surprising, for he had evidently set it himself. That meant that Giles never intended to return to Guadalcanal, or at least, not to the house he had called home for over fourteen years.

It took a certain type of man to do that—destroy everything around him before leaving a place. The British were no good at it, even when ordered. And it was one of the reasons the Japanese enjoyed British modernization in Malaya.

Careful where he stepped, Alex continued to follow the trail made by Timi You. At times, he stopped to look back, to get his bearings, as if memorizing the turns, the configuration of landscape, measured in angles from the lagoon, the reef, and the stretches of beach visible below. By tomorrow, there would be no trail, no path to indicate where he and the native had walked today.

A parrot protested the invasion of his domain, while a bush rat, the size of a rabbit, scurried through the undergrowth. A lizard, the color of the tree bark, narrowly missed having his tail cut off by Timi You's *kukri* knife as he hacked his way through the tangled vines rooted to the same bark.

Alex's pistol rested in its holster on his belt. But unless it was a dire emergency, he knew better than to use it. He wanted no weapon fire to draw attention to himself on an island that contained not only Japanese on the northern tip, but villages of natives, none too civilized, in the interior.

Timi You stopped and held up his hand for Alex to do the same. They waited and listened. From the jungle, a grunting sound came—a wild boar rooting about for food. Through the trees, Alex caught a glimpse of the boar as it lifted its head and seemed to look in his direction. It was an ugly, dangerous beast, with curved tusks able to rip a man apart in seconds.

Alex's own grandfather had been killed by a boar, and his father had become obsessed with destroying every wild pig on his ancestral lands. Alex was twelve years old that year when his grandfather had died—old enough to go hunting with the men, yet young enough for his mother to worry about him.

His mother. He had not thought of her in a long time, for they had never been that close except for a brief period in his life, almost too early to remember—long before his grandfather had died, when they were still in India.

Although he had trouble recalling his mother's face, Alex remembered well the sounds and smells of that particular summer, as if it were yesterday.

With a few servants traveling with them, he and his mother had gone into the mountains to seek relief from the heat of Delhi, and to escape the stench of the jungle and the holy river swollen from the monsoon rains. Perhaps that was what had stirred his familial memory, even before he saw the boar.

Like one returning to the past, Alex had been aware of the odor of the jungle, gradually dissipating as they climbed to a higher elevation where the air was pure as the spring water hidden in the rock crevices above.

When the boar moved on, Alex relaxed his grip on the pistol handle. Timi You began to hack the vines again, and Alex's attention returned to the map.

The landscape was a series of hills and valleys, stretches of matted jungle suddenly ending in a clearing, a plot of land that had once been a vegetable garden for some village now deserted by its natives. Before they crossed a clearing, Timi You cut leafy twigs, placed them around his head, and Alex did the same, disguising his bush helmet and making a cloak of vines for his shoulders, in case the Kawanisi should fly overhead.

He'd seen an entire Japanese battleship disguised like a small island, complete with palm trees, anchored off the coast of Java. It had remained there, undetected from the air, while Alex floated by on his raft and saw the men moving about on deck.

Now, with his own disguise, Alex, like a moving bush, raced over vulnerable open space, stopping at times and then proceeding a short distance until he and Timi You were again undercover.

The higher up along the range Alex went, the more he felt a sense of remoteness. For two hundred years the island had been bypassed by civilization. Despite their initial discovery, no trade routes had linked these islands to the outside world. Only now did they assume an importance, as the Japanese undertook to cut off Allied access to Australia and New Zealand.

At intervals, the two men rested and then continued, hurrying toward the cave before the afternoon rains began.

In the period of time since they'd left Bohorok, Timi You had spoken less than a dozen words. Now, with a sense of accomplishment, he stopped, turned to Alex, and said, "The cave is there, Masta."

Concealed so skillfully, the opening was not apparent to Alex. Low clouds sat on the tips of mountains overhead, while below was a magnificent view of the lagoon, the channel, and the surrounding islands. A tall tree blind, appearing for all the world like a natural extension of the tangled jungle, hung over the precipice, a marvelous aerie to the watcher lodged within. The surrounding jungle, looking the same in any direction, refused to give up its secret to the naked eye, even when Alex was standing before it.

Appreciating the craftiness that had gone into its design, Alex smiled. "Fantastic," he whispered, motioning to Timi You to reveal the opening to him.

The native took seven or eight steps, leaned over and loosened a gate made of roped vines. Natural debris, fallen from the forest onto the vines, made pockets that held plants and ferns similar to the surrounding floor of the jungle. The cavernous hole was black, and from its entrance, there was no indication that it held a treasure cache of goods.

"I light lamp for you, Masta," Timi You offered. He took a long stick and, using it as a prod, he found the lantern hidden beyond the entrance. Careful not to touch the lantern with his hands, he brought it out into the open. A number of insects scurried onto the ground, and the Melanesian, satisfied that most had vanished, lifted the globe and lit the wick.

Behind him, Alex pulled the gate closed and followed the path of light through the cave. Surprised at the expanse, he walked through the first chamber, empty to everything except a few crawling creatures. But once they had turned into the second chamber, all that changed.

Cases of food—tins labeled as meat, vegetables, fruits—lined the walls; dried staples—rice and flour in waterproof bags—added to the enormous cache, with cases of whiskey, and first-aid supplies, including quinine and Atabrine, marked with a red cross, piled high on the opposite wall. Farther down the chamber sat drums of benzine, more than thirty in number, with ammunition and a wooden box marked RIFLES. And beyond them, a few cots and bedding supplies.

"How long have the supplies been stored in here?"

"Six, seven months."

"Who else knows about this cave?"

Timi You hesitated. "Wani."

"No one else?"

"Obadiah, maybe."

Alex had seen enough. He needed to get back to Bohorok. The marquess of Dalhousie struck a match and, holding it to the corner of the map, he began to burn it.

"What you do—burn map for?" Timi You inquired, his face aghast at Alex's action.

"I no longer need it," Alex answered. At Timi You's incredulous expression, Alex challenged him "Shall I lead you back to Bohorok from here?"

"You never find—with map gone." Timi You looked toward the charred remnants that Alex was crushing into the dirt floor with his boot.

"If I don't, I'll prepare dinner tonight for both of us."

Timi You suddenly grinned. The two left the chamber. At the entrance to the cave, the native snuffed out the light and hid the lantern behind a rock just inside. Then, as Alex watched, he closed the opening. Careful to put the leafy gate back the way it had been, he smoothed the jungle floor to erase any footprints before the cave.

"You need," Timi You urged, and took his fiercely sharp knife from the waist of his khaki shorts.

Alex accepted it. He stood for a moment and gazed over the terrain. Then he proceeded down the ridge, with a dubious Timi You trailing him.

If Alex had put any markers along the way to serve as a guide back, they were soon obliterated when the afternoon rains began. Thunder called from one mountain peak to another and lightning flashed into the sea.

Watching the sudden, startled flutter of leaves in the wind, Alex was reminded of the Indian prayer flags of his adopted land, and the Hindu belief that the wind could whisper their messages in the ears of the gods above.

Rarely did Alex have to use the *kukri* knife to chop his

way through the jungle. He seemed to possess a sixth sense as to how they had come. And Timi You watched while Alex stopped from time to time to get his bearings and then press forward.

But when the first hour had passed and the second begun, Timi You became smug. Alex had turned in the wrong direction. Certain now that the man would have to cook dinner that night—if he was an honorable man who kept his word—Timi You watched for Masta Ramsay to get hopelessly lost before he said anything.

Alex took the *kukri* and began to hack his way through virgin territory. Timi You's chest expanded. Soon now, the man would ask for his help.

Alex finally stopped and turned toward the native, but the words Timi You expected to hear were not uttered. Instead, Alex said, "I think we should be able to pick up the trail now—below the open range that was so dangerous."

A surprised Timi You, native to the island, began to recognize the trail again. The white man had found a better way down. Reconciled to preparing dinner that night, Timi You continued to follow behind Alex. Yet, he was not disappointed, as he had been in the cave when Alex had burned the map.

His respect for Masta Ramsay began to grow. He and Masta would make a good team. His sense of pride that had been given a beating when Giles Canupp selected Wani to go with him to Savo was resurrected. And by the time they reached Bohorok and the man returned his knife, Timi You's allegiance to Alex Ramsay was firm.

By morning, the storm had abated and the sunbirds were once more flying about the plantation house. Alex walked out to the verandah and gazed down at the lagoon and the palms lining the beach. Already in his place in a palm tree at the edge of the plantation grounds, Obadiah lowered his basket on a rope for Timi You to fill with food and drink for the day. Then he hoisted it, to disappear into the umbrellaed tree house strung with wires that served as an antenna for the giant radio inside Bohorok.

Alex settled down in a chair on the verandah to enjoy his pipe. But before he could get it lit, he heard the conch shell signal from Obadiah. He rushed inside for his binoculars, retrieved them, and looked toward the Slot. But no ships came into view. That could mean only one other thing—a visitor on foot.

A wary Alex approached the palm tree. "Who is it, Obadiah?"

"Good man. Priest from village. Father Waal."

Alex was still wary as he watched the man wend his way toward the house. With his pistol in hand, he remained hidden until the priest came into the clearing.

Father Waal was an incongruous sight. His priestly cassock lapped against his knees, while his long thin legs stepped from puddle to puddle like some black heron uncertain of the water's depth. Thin and gaunt, with a permanent tobacco gold glow from the sun, he exuded a supreme confidence as he walked.

When the man came close enough for Alex to discern his individual features, his wariness diminished. Despite the haphazard arrangement of eyes, nose, and mouth, the man's countenance was angelic.

"Hallo," the priest called, when he saw Alex on his way to meet him. "I'm Father Waal from the mission village below."

"And I am Alex Ramsay."

"I know. Giles told me you were coming."

"Will you come in?" Alex motioned for the priest to go before him onto the verandah. But before ascending the steps, Father Waal stopped to remove his muddy boots and lower his cassock. The he walked barefooted up the steps and onto the verandah.

As if caught in some biblical reenactment, Alex called for Timi You to bring a basin of water and a towel. And also, as if it were the most natural thing in the world, Father Waal allowed the native to perform the ritual of washing his feet.

When that was done, the priest reached into a pocket of his robe and pulled out a pair of black slippers.

Once the amenities had been dealt with and Father Waal was offered something cool to drink, the priest turned to Alex to reveal his purpose in walking all the way from the village to Bohorok.

"I thought you might be worried about Giles, so I came to tell you he got off all right. But later than he planned. One of the mission boys arrived just before I left. Giles's native bearers ran into a boat delivering a load of comfort women to the Japanese soldiers on the northern end of the island. They had to hide for several hours until it was reasonably safe to cross."

His casual mention of the women the Japanese government recruited to give aid to its soldiers far from home was followed by a chuckle.

"Don't be shocked for my sake, Mr. Ramsay. Living in these islands for the past fifteen years, I have seen every human condition—love, hate, greed, lust, birth, death. There is not much left to shock me."

Alex nodded. "Did you come by the burned plantation?"

"Yes. It was completely gutted. But Giles had one of the other boys monitor it so the fire would not get out of hand and spread. But it didn't matter, actually. The rain saw to that."

Finally, Father Waal rose to leave. "You're fortunate to have Timi You. He's a prince of a fellow. Obadiah, too. And All-Same-Barrel will be a good watcher, if he doesn't eat too many betel nuts. Well, so long, Ramsay. If I can help you at any time..."

Alex replied, "I thought you priests were determined to be neutral in this war."

"My bishop has given me permission to defend my flock from the wolf." His hand patted a bulge in his right pocket.

At the steps, Alex waited for Father Waal to remove his slippers, lace the heavy boots, and hitch up his cassock to protect the hem from the mud.

"We must have dinner together soon," Alex offered, walking to the edge of the clearing with the man.

"I look forward to it," the priest responded. "God be with you."

Watching the priest until he disappeared past the clearing, Alex felt comforted that he had a formidable ally on the island. As an afterthought, Alex began to wonder if Father Waal also knew the way to the cave sanctuary above Bohorok.

Chapter 13

DRESSED IN HER WHITE UNIFORM AND HER UN-
inflated Mae West, Sunny Fitzpatrick stood at the railing of
the *Good Hope*. With Kirk Singleton beside her, she gazed
toward the late afternoon horizon. Nothing but the trade
wind rippled the waters, turning up the white-capped
waves of the sea. To Sunny, it was ironic that one of the most
beautiful bodies of water in the world was now braced for
death and destruction.

Early that morning, they had heard the planes take off
from the carrier to intercept the Japanese convoy. And as
they waited for the planes to return, Sunny commented, "I
hope they all make it back to the carrier."

"That's a little too much to hope for, Fitzpatrick." The
man had reverted to her last name, as was his custom. And
then in a fit of restlessness, he said, "I swear this waiting is
nerve-wracking. I'd rather be in the middle of the fighting
than standing around, waiting."

Sunny smiled. "Now you know how the women at home
feel."

Kirk laughed. "And so one Amanda Fitzpatrick decided
she was not the waiting kind, and joined this man's navy."

"You're absolutely right."

A slight sputtering sound stopped their conversation.
Kirk took his binoculars to search for the noise. "I think he's

one of ours."

Sunny, with no need of binoculars, saw the dark funnel of smoke coming from the tail of the plane. "He's in trouble," she said, and immediately thought of her brother Jack.

"Yes. He'll never land on the carrier deck. Too dangerous. He'll probably try to ditch in the sea."

Kirk removed his binoculars and handed them to Sunny. "If the pilot's lucky, he'll be your first customer."

The battle of the Coral Sea began, and with it a devastating comedy of errors that plagued both sides. The Japanese believed two vessels, a U.S. oil tanker and a cruiser, were the vanguard of the U.S task force. They sought them out and sank both. Meanwhile, the actual task force passed by unmolested.

On the Allied side, the sighting of the small carrier *Shoho* by a scout plane diverted the Americans from the two main Japanese carriers. And in the dark, with poor visibility, Japanese pilots, mistaking the *Yorktown* for one of its own, attempted to land on deck, like homing pigeons, but beaten off by U.S. gunners.

At the same time, the *Lexington* was mistaken for the enemy by Allied bombers, who did their utmost to sink her before the error was discovered.

For two days, the enemy task forces drew within a hundred miles without a single salvo fired at each other. Only the carrier pilots engaged in battle.

Shortly before dawn on May 8, as Tulagi was invaded by the Japanese, Commander Matt Willoughby listened to the planes being launched from the two aircraft carriers, *Lexington* and *Yorktown.*

The *Lexington* was the more ponderous and plodding of the ships, and it was that carrier that the *Viscount* had been ordered to protect.

Moving south in the night, the U.S. task force had left the cover of rain squalls and clouds. As morning came to the Coral Sea, the ships lay exposed in brilliant sunlight, while the Japanese remained blanketed in layers of clouds to the north.

Aware of the lack of cloud cover, Matt stood on the bridge of the *Viscount* with his executive officer, Pearson. "I have a feeling we're going to see some action today," Matt confided.

"That will suit the gunners fine. They're just itching to blast a few Zeros out of the sky—or torpedo one of the Jap carriers."

With the elementary radar on the *Lexington* signaling aircraft approaching from sixty-eight miles away, the convoy was put on alert. Five fighters were dispatched to intercept the aircraft since the radar could not distinguish friend from foe. Twenty miles away, the fighters found the enemy—an ugly assortment of torpedo planes, dive bombers, and fighters, all with one purpose. To sink the *Lexington.*

Now, the destroyers moved into battle formation to await the enemy planes. On the *Viscount,* Matt's warning was engraved on each gunner's mind: "They'll come in two groups, more than likely, and drop their torpedoes on both bows at the same time. If the *Lexington* tries to parallel one group of torpedoes, the other group will hit her broadside. It's up to us to keep that from happening."

When it finally came, the hum of planes in the sky was no surprise. "That's my baby," one of the gunners shouted, earmarking the first plane to blast out of the sky.

With geysers as high as the ships themselves, the Coral Sea responded to the dropped torpedoes. Everywhere there were planes, flak, noise, and fiery crashes into the sea. Several large fish, blasted from the waters, landed on the *Viscount's* deck, though no one much noticed. The men were far too busy defending the huge, lumbersome carrier from air attack. Down below, men, shirtless in the heat, fed shells to the gunners above.

Directing the battle from the bridge, Matt watched each new wave of bombers. "My God, that's one of ours," he said to Pearson, standing beside him. The gunners made no distinction. Anything in the air above them was fair game, even to the American plane that had somehow become mixed in with the enemy. It was the only time in the battle that Matt wished for his gunners to miss their target.

Despite the protective stance of the cruisers and destroyers surrounding her, the *Lexington* took a hit on her port gun gallery, wiping out its crew and setting fire to the ship. Two other torpedoes hit port side and sent large wakes over the sea. But none was totally annihilating. The *Lexington* still sat in the water, seaworthy despite the fires.

The battle raged; each cruiser, each destroyer determined to ward off a deadly blow to the great aircraft carrier. The sky was filled with fireworks, with pungent odors of flak, black and white shell bursts that slowly disintegrated and drifted to meet the slow-moving clouds on the far horizon, while fresh bursts of flak supplanted the old.

At first, Matt was not aware of the sudden silence that encompassed the scene of the naval battle. His ears still rang from the gunners' bombardment. But as he looked up, he saw that the sky was now empty of planes. The Japanese fighters and dive bombers had gone.

Matt looked to the north, but there was no sign of a second attack. By all calculations, the Japanese had retired for the day. Nine minutes in all—nine minutes of sound and fury—that felt like eternity, and then the battle was over. He turned his eyes to the south and, in the distance, he saw black smoke rising from the carrier, *Yorktown.* But there were no explosions, and so he assumed the damage was not crippling.

He was proud of his men. "All hands, now hear this," Matt began, his voice reaching the innermost recesses of the destroyer. "The Japanese attack has been beaten off, and our carriers are still seaworthy. Congratulations to you all."

A great shout arose from the *Viscount*, even from those attending to their wounds and burns. Completely exhausted, the gunners dropped amid great graveyards of empty shells that littered the deck, and went to sleep.

But their sleep was rudely snatched from them. A huge explosion rocked the carrier *Lexington,* and the gunners on deck witnessed a series of fires breaking out amidship. As a new battle raged—this time within the carrier—the crew of the *Viscount* could only stand by. Despite the firefighting belowdecks, the returning flight squadron, coming from their bout with the enemy task force, landed safely on the top carrier deck. But then, the situation became grave. By late afternoon, the carrier's power shut down. There were now no water pumps in service to contain the spreading fires.

At the call for help, Matt brought the *Viscount* alongside to deliver the requested fire hoses. But the pumps on the destroyer hadn't been designed to deal with a fire the magnitude of the one that now threatened the life of the giant carrier.

Finally, the admiral gave orders to abandon ship. The *Lexington* could not be saved. All vital signs had vanished.

The surrounding destroyers and cruisers lowered their boats and prepared to receive the crew from the *Lexington*—the wounded first, brought alongside in wire cages, while the able-bodied shinnied down the knotted ropes into the sea, to await rescue later. Others, uncertain of their prowess in the water and ability to stay afloat, raided the planes on the carrier deck, pitched their yellow rafts into the sea, and jumped after them.

As one explosion after another rocked the carrier, the race began—to remove all hands. The fire spread to the planes on deck, and with the explosion of their gasoline tanks, all remaining survivors jumped into the sea.

Then the ammunition for the carrier's heavy guns exploded. Twenty thousand pounds of ignited torpedoes sent steel plate and missiles into the air. A great ground swell encompassed the sea. The sky lit up with flames a hundred feet tall. And the remainder of the task force waited for the ship to break up and sink. But she continued to burn, lighting up the night sky with a powerful force, outlining her still-proud form.

For three hours the task force had been immobile, gathering the survivors and watching the pride of the fleet in her death throes. Now, it was past time to move on. The waters were infested with Japanese submarines, and the *Lexington* served as a beacon for a hundred miles or more to any sub that wished to attack. At 19:15 the admiral of the fleet gave orders to regroup and sail south—all except one destroyer, one commander.

Matt Willoughby, designated to preside over the *Lexington* demise, received orders to remain behind and send her to a watery grave with his own torpedoes.

If the *Lexington* had to be sunk, it was far better for it to be done with dignity and honor. Still, it was heartrending to preside over the death of the carrier.

As Matt stared at the burning ship, he became a twelve-year-old again, with all the accompanying rage he had felt when his horse, Orion, had splintered his leg and had to be destroyed. He would never forget that day and the argument with his father over the horse's destruction. But tears had not deterred his father.

"Orion is in agony, son. Can't you see it? There's nothing else to do but put him out of his misery. Go back to the house, Matt."

His father's voice had been harsh, like the admiral's. But now Matt was a man, ordered to stay behind to preside over death.

One last time, the *Viscount* circled the *Lexington* to make sure there were no survivors still in the water. They had no need for a searchlight. The burning ship gave ample light.

Floating eastward from the ship's bow, a large piece of debris, resembling the wing of a plane, caught Matt's attention. He watched it for a moment, then another part of the ship's wreckage demanded attention. For some unexplained reason, his eyes returned to the plane debris.

"Mr. Pearson, take a look at the wreckage off port bow,"

he said. "Does that look like someone in the water?"

Guided by Matt's pointing, the executive officer adjusted his binoculars. "Could be," he admitted. "But I don't see any movement, sir. Probably dead."

"Nevertheless," Matt countered, "order a rescue boat, Mr. Pearson."

The rescue team, alerted, lowered a boat and cautiously sped through the fiery waters to the floating debris, while from the bridge of the destroyer, Matt watched. Pleased, he saw the members of the rescue team pull a man into the boat. He appeared to be alive.

Matt immediately left the bridge to go on deck and await the return of the last survivor. A few minutes more and the man would have gone under with the *Lexington.*

As the man was hoisted onto the deck, Matt saw that he was covered in black oil, camouflaging his body and the remnants of his uniform except for the winged insignia on his shirt and his rank.

"You cut it a little close, didn't you, Ensign?" Matt inquired.

The ensign appeared to be in shock and he was slow to respond to Matt's question. Finally, he managed to say, "Thank you, Commander, for rescuing me."

Matt nodded. Motioning for the medical corpsman to take the pilot to sick bay, Matt left the deck and returned to the bridge.

Now, the *Viscount* eased away from the starboard side of the *Lexington.* "Give orders for the torpedoes, Mr. Pearson."

Four torpedoes were released, coursing through the waters to find their target. Within seconds, new explosions shook the *Lexington,* causing a great updraft, with hissing and screaming as fire and water, natural enemies, met in one last battle.

Standing by to give a final salute to the carrier he had sworn to protect, Matt Willoughby, the commander of the *Viscount,* watched her go down. She sank slowly, majestically, as the waves washed over her and committed her spirit to the sea.

When the fires were out, when the ghost of the *Lexington* was no longer visible, the destroyer fired all engines and rushed to catch up with the rest of the fleet.

Chapter 14

AT GENERAL MACARTHUR'S HEADQUARTERS IN MEL-
bourne, Irish Fitzpatrick glanced at his watch. He had lost
track of time. Now, he realized he should have let Kenna
know, over an hour ago, that he was working late. But at
least, she would understand.

Thankful that Kenna was not like some of the other
generals' wives, he smiled as he thought of her. They had
been married almost twenty-three years—time enough for
his passion to have dulled. But that was not the case.
Sometimes he thought he loved her even more now, more
than when they first married—if that were possible.
Suddenly impatient to get back to the apartment, Irish
snapped off the overhead light, locked his office, and
prepared to leave the building.

"General Fitzpatrick, sir." The voice in the hallway
caused him to turn.

"Yes, Corporal?"

"The news has come over the wires. The *Lexington* has
been sunk."

At the message, Irish, the general, became a father,
alarmed over the welfare of his son. Yet, his military bearing
did not betray him. Forcing his voice to remain calm, he
inquired, "And the men on board? Were they rescued?"

"Some of them, sir. Others, I believe, went down with the

ship. The first communiqué was slightly confusing."

"How soon will you have a complete list of survivors?"

"Probably not for the next several days. The admiral is all right, though."

"What about the air squadron?"

"I haven't heard anything about them, except they landed on deck while the *Lexington* was burning." The corporal watched the general's mouth. It was set in a hard, straight line.

"Did you know anyone personally, sir, in the air squadron?"

"My son, Jack. Ensign Jack Fitzpatrick."

"I didn't realize…I'm sorry, sir. If you'd like to come into the radio room, there'll be other reports coming through the night."

"Thank you, Corporal. Yes. I'd like to stay and listen in."

Irish followed the corporal down the hall and prepared for a long night.

"Would you like a cup of coffee, General?" one of the men inquired.

Irish nodded. But the coffee grew cold as he listened to the updated news. The ship had been sunk by an American destroyer, after there was no hope of her survival. If that were the case, then the ship would have been evacuated beforehand and survivors picked up by a friendly ship. Knowing that, Irish felt better.

"Most of the survivors will be coming into Darwin on the hospital ship, General," the radioman relayed to Irish.

With that news, Irish stood up. "Thank you, Corporal," he said, and walked out of the radio room. He would learn no more that night. Slowly he walked past the guard at the door, returned his salute, and headed for the apartment three blocks away. Now, he knew that Kenna would be alarmed since it was well into morning. And with good reason. There was no way he could hide the news. She would have to be told.

Asleep in the chair, Kenna heard the key turning in the

lock. On the table in the alcove of the apartment, Irish's plate and wine glass remained empty, a silent accusation against the man who had not come home for dinner. But Kenna, knowing by instinct that something was being planned for "MacArthur's Navy" had resigned herself to his absence. How much more difficult it would have been for her to have remained in the States, when the rest of her family were all in the Pacific.

"Irish?"

"Are you still awake, Kenna?"

"I fell asleep in the chair. I was waiting for you to come home for dinner."

"I know. I'm sorry." He walked toward his wife and tenderly brushed the strand of hair that had fallen out of place as she slept. And then he took her in his arms, and held her.

Struggling to shake off the drowsiness that encompassed her, Kenna backed out of his embrace.

"What's wrong, Irish?" she demanded, her gray eyes suddenly fearful.

"Kenna, there's still hope," he assured her. "But the *Lexington* went down tonight in the Coral Sea."

Once again she was in his arms, and he comforted her as her tears began to flow. "The survivors were picked up. They'll return to Darwin on the hospital ship in several days. We won't know for certain until then whether Jack…"

Kenna brushed her tears away. "Jack's alive. I know he is."

"But we'll have to be prepared for the worst, Kenna."

"No." She began to walk away from her husband.

"Where are you going?"

"To pack. I'm meeting the ship in Darwin."

Irish looked at her, saw the tilt of her head that showed her determination, and knew there was no stopping her. He remembered that day at Fort McPherson, long ago, during another war, when she'd climbed over the fence to the fort and straightway into his heart. She had been determined then to go overseas as an army nurse because of her missing brother. There had been no stopping her, then, as well.

Irish sighed. "You won't be able to get air transporation," he warned.

"Then I'll go by train."

The next day, Kenna left Melbourne for the overland trip north—a difficult, time-consuming journey through the interior of the continent. Kenna put that out of her mind. She was lucky to have gotten a ticket on the train at such short notice.

"Bluey here will help you with your luggage, ma'am. He's a dinkum bloke."

Kenna smiled as she recalled the stationmaster's words. It was only later, after becoming settled in the train, that she began to wonder at the translation. Just as the Australians seemed amused at her own accent, she also found it difficult to understand them. She'd given up asking them to repeat what they'd said, for she could understand no better the second time.

A large woman in a flowered hat sat across from Kenna and fanned herself. She appeared so calm in contrast to Kenna, who still felt the effects of her mad dash to board the train. For a half hour, neither one spoke. Finally, Kenna decided to break the silence.

"Are you traveling far?" Kenna inquired.

"To Alice Springs," the woman answered. "My daughter lives there. And you?"

"To Darwin."

Again there was silence, except for the clack of the train wheels. Then the other woman said, "You're an American, aren't you?"

"Yes."

"Have you been in Australia long?"

"Less than a month. My husband's with the American army."

"My own husband is dead," the woman confided, "but

I have two sons who are Diggers."

"I beg your pardon. Diggers?"

"Soldiers," she replied. And then she asked, "Do you have sons?"

Kenna's voice was almost a whisper. "Yes. One. I also have a daughter."

"My daughter's husband was killed in Crete."

"I'm sorry."

The sadness in Kenna's face communicated itself to the other woman. Seeing the tears, she realized the American had sorrows of her own. Rather than witness her distress, the Australian watched the passing landscape as the train left all remnants of civilization behind.

A few minutes later, Kenna had regained her composure and she, too, began to look at the changing landscape. Suddenly, a raucous sound outside the open window startled her. "Gracious, what was that?" she inquired aloud.

The woman opposite her laughed. "You've never heard a kookaburra bird before?"

Kenna shook her head. "No. And I'd just as soon not hear it again."

"It does make a rather intimidating noise," the woman admitted. "But we're all so used to the sound that it doesn't bother us anymore."

The exotic landscape took Kenna's mind off her reason for traveling. At one point, she saw a wallaby in the distance, with her baby, or joey, barely visible in her pouch. And in one of the eucalypt trees, Kenna was almost certain that she saw a koala bear. The farther north she traveled, the more aware Kenna became of the vastness of the land, settled indirectly because of America's independence from England.

Once the undesirables and the debtors could no longer be shipped across the Atlantic, Australia became the land for banishment. But like the colony of Georgia, few convict ships docked along the coast of Victoria. And so Melbourne, like Savannah, was a proud coastal city, just as pompous in in its culture.

When Kenna finally reached Alice Springs, the former shantytown surrounded by red clay hills, she found the atmosphere very different. Gone was the cosmopolitan ambience of Melbourne, and in its place was a Wild West town, filled with hardened cowboys and with aborigines comparable to the Indians of North America.

A sense of estrangement overwhelmed her as she watched the people gather their packages and prepare to leave the train. Kenna looked toward the platform and saw the throng of people milling about.

"I didn't realize Alice Springs would be so lively," she said.

"Only once a year. Just for the Bangtail Muster. You see the abo over there?"

"The dark-skinned man?"

"Yes. He'll be winning a prize, more than likely. They're all excellent horsemen. My little Stanley won't stand a chance, but I promised I would come anyway, to watch him ride. Poor little fatherless tyke. Well, good-bye and good luck on the rest of your journey up the track."

"Good luck to you, also."

From the window, Kenna watched the woman in the flowered hat embrace a smaller replica of herself, waiting on the platform. A boy who looked no older than thirteen proudly took her packages. Then they disappeared from Kenna's line of vision.

"Mrs. Fitzpatrick?'

"Yes."

A young American officer—a lieutenant— stood before her. "I'm Lt. Smathers, ma'am. Your husband, General Fitzpatrick, has arranged air transportation for you the rest of the way to Darwin. I have a jeep waiting to take you to the airport immediately."

"Those are the most beautiful words I've heard in two days, Lieutenant," a tired Kenna responded. While the lieutenant reached for her luggage, she closed the book she'd been holding and stood up.

* * *

Alisdair Shannon leaned against the fuselage of the small civilian plane and watched the cloud of dust in the distance. He was in his fifties, his dark hair graying at the temples, his skin a leathered bronze. The color of his eyes was hidden behind the squint against the sun as he removed his dark glasses to polish the lenses with his bandanna. Tall and lithe, he exuded an animal magnetism, a strength akin to the land itself, free and untamed.

"There's the pilot now, Mrs. Fitzpatrick," the lieutenant said, coming to a stop at the airstrip. "Looks like he's ready to leave."

"Then we arrived just in time, didn't we?"

Alisdair watched his passenger emerge from the jeep. Solemnly he took note of the woman who in no way resembled the stereotype of a general's wife. He had not looked forward to this unwanted passenger, but he had been roped in, just like one of his steers at roundup time. But he would make sure to reclaim the favor from his friend Martin the next time he went to Canberra.

"Mrs. Fitzpatrick, may I present Alisdair Shannon."

"How do you do, Mr. Shannon." Kenna held out her hand and smiled.

At the touch of her hand in his, Alisdair frowned. Standing before him was the most beautiful woman he'd ever seen — petite, with eyes the color of the sea in winter, shimmering gray — an ageless beauty for whom the years seemed to have taken little toll.

He dropped his hand quickly. "If you're ready, Mrs. Fitzpatrick, we'll be leaving now."

"Of course."

"Smathers, just put her luggage on the strip. I'll stow it behind the seat in a minute."

Kenna turned to the lieutenant. "Thank you for rescuing me from the train, Lieutenant."

"It was my pleasure, Mrs. Fitzpatrick."

Alisdair Shannon brought a flight jacket from the plane and handed it to Kenna as she climbed aboard. "Here, you'd better put this on. We'll be flying higher than usual and you might get cold."

Lt. Smathers waited in the jeep and watched Alisdair start the propeller, climb into the pilot's seat, and start down the long, dusty runway. Shielding the dust and grit from his eyes, he heard the plane become airborne. Looking upward at the vanishing plane, John Smathers questioned the general's sanity. He knew if he had a wife who looked like that, he would never let her out of his sight, especially to travel alone with one of the richest cattle barons in Australia.

In the air, Alisdair Shannon made no effort to converse. The less he knew of the woman beside him, the better off he would be. But Kenna's curiosity and interest in the land below forced grudging answers from him. Gradually, without realizing it, the man began to relax, and the shield he'd placed between them when he first met her started to disintegrate.

"What animals are those?" Kenna asked, seeing several wolflike animals below.

"Dingoes—wild dogs," he responded. "They kill sheep and newborn calves. Every station owner has to guard against dingoes."

"They must be like the wild coyotes we have in the West," Kenna replied. "And you have wild horses, too, I understand."

Alisdair nodded. "And a few camels also—an experiment years ago in the desert. Now, the animals are used only for races several times a year. Quite a ridiculous sight."

The smoke from a bush fire swirled over the land, obliterating the scenery. Alisdair climbed higher in altitude, circled, and reached for his transmitter. Kenna listened to the pilot attempting to contact a sheep station in the fire's path. He remained in a holding pattern until he was successful. Then, he began to fly north again.

"Edwards will alert the transportation people," Alisdair explained. "If you'd remained on the ground, you'd have been in for a long delay."

"Then I'm eternally grateful to you, Mr. Shannon, for the plane ride."

From her words, Alisdair had a feeling that the woman's trip might not be a frivolous one, as he'd first assumed. "Your trip to Darwin is that important to you?"

For an instant, Kenna hesitated. Then she explained, "My son was on the *Lexington*, Mr. Shannon. The survivors will be coming in on the hospital ship sometime tomorrow."

"Then you'll be at the dock in plenty of time to welcome him."

"Yes. If he's still alive." Kenna's voice was almost lost in the wind.

"But you received word that he was picked up?"

"No."

Her words opened up an old wound, for Alisdair was no stranger to the anguish of not knowing whether a son were dead or alive.

Jaded for years of avoiding entrapment by eligible young women determined to marry his fortune, Alisdair Shannon had the rotten luck of being stirred on that afternoon by a woman completely unaware of him.

He glanced at the sad, proud profile of Kenna Fitzpatrick. So brave, yet so vulnerable. He wanted to take her in his arms to comfort her. Instead, he asked, "Do you have a place to stay tonight in Darwin?"

"I thought I'd try a hotel…"

The man became thoughtful. She would never accept his hospitality. But if she didn't know the apartment was his… First, he'd call Cochoran to see if he might bunk in with him. Then, he would leave his own apartment for the woman seated beside him. Deciding that, he began to look for the airport outside Darwin, and to prepare for landing.

Chapter 15

DIRECTLY SOUTH OF THE DUTCH OIL FIELDS THAT HAD
been bombarded time and again by the Japanese, the city of
Darwin was surrounded by lagoons and swamp-lands,
where crocodiles and exotic birds vied for attention with the
monsoon rains.

Strategic as a port, Darwin was the only Australian city
so far to have felt the bombs of the Japanese — an event so
traumatic that Australian troops on their way to Rangoon
had been recalled by the prime minister for home defense,
thus bringing about the schism between the Aussie and the
British government.

Unlike Melbourne, where the change of weather could
come in a day, from hot to cold, Darwin remained the
same — extremely hot. Only the monsoon season determined
whether the city would be wrapped in a wet heat or dry. By
the time Kenna arrived in Darwin, the monsoon rains had
not yet begun.

Helping Kenna from the plane, Alisdair Shannon said, "I
have friends in Darwin, Mrs. Fitzpatrick. Let me make a few
telephone calls. I might be able to find a place for you to
stay."

"I've already been enough trouble for you, Mr. Shannon."

The man was insistent. He motioned for Kenna to wait
while he went inside the building to call the superintendent

of his apartment house. Cochoran, he could contact later.

"Gregory, I have a favor to ask of you," Alisdair began. "I want you to open up my apartment for a Mrs. Fitzpatrick. She'll be there within the half hour. But under no circumstances is she to know that it's my apartment. Do you understand?"

"Yes, Mr. Shannon. But what about your personal things?"

"That's where I'm relying on you. Get in there and remove the papers from my desk top. I'll pick them up later. And by the way, she'll insist on paying you, I'm sure. Find out the going rate for an average hotel room and charge her accordingly."

"Yes, Mr. Shannon. Is there anything else?"

"Not at the moment." Alisdair hung up and went back outside the hangar. He returned to Kenna with a smile. "You now have a place to stay for the night. It's not far from the harbor. Belongs to a friend of mine who's out of town. I just talked with the super. He'll let you in."

"But won't the owner mind—having a total stranger using his apartment? It's not that I'm ungrateful to you, but…"

"Don't worry about the owner. He's always happy to make a little extra money." Alisdair adjusted his dark glasses. "Now, let's find some ground transportation into the city."

By late afternoon, Kenna was settled in the apartment. It was clearly a man's abode, all leather and wood, with no feminine influence apparent.

A startling aboriginal carving greeted Kenna in the entrance hall, and inside the living room, a Maori shield hung over the leather sofa. Overhead, a ceiling fan circulated the slight breeze that came in from the bay through the open balcony doors.

"I don't have to remind you, I'm sure, Mrs. Fitzpatrick," Gregory had said a few minutes earlier, "that the blackout draperies will have to be drawn before you put on any lights. The Japanese, you know."

"I understand."

"And if you want to use some of the tins of food or the plonk in the pantry, keep an account and we'll settle up when you check out."

"Thank you, Gregory," Kenna responded. She had not even thought about food.

For a while, Kenna stood on the balcony. The view of the botanical gardens and the bay was breathtaking.

Reluctantly turning back, Kenna walked inside to search for the bedroom where Gregory had taken her luggage. It, too, was a masculine retreat. The bed was wide and comfortable, with a tailored brown and white cotton spread woven in some animal skin design. And above the bed hung another ceiling fan, turning slowly.

Kenna opened her luggage, took out a white negligee, and found the bath, where she drew a cool tub of water to remove the dust of travel from her body. Her muscles were still tense from the strain of the past two days.

She longed to call Irish, just to hear his voice. But there was no reason to do so until she had news of their son. Tomorrow would be soon enough—once the ship had docked.

Later, feeling fresh and clean, with her hair newly washed, Kenna walked to the pantry, where there were tins of food and biscuits, and bottles of wine lay on their sides.

Plonk, indeed. She smiled as she thought of the word Gregory had used. The wine was of the finest label, not a cheap wine as indicated by the slang expression. The owner of the apartment evidently had more expensive tastes than Gregory imagined. And Kenna, alone for a night of uncertainty, opened a bottle and poured a glass to sip along with her supper of biscuits and squid.

With the draperies open to catch the last light, Kenna turned back the spread, climbed into bed, and picked up the novel she had brought with her.

It was then that Kenna noticed the oil painting on the wall opposite the bed. A magnificent white house, with a porch that reminded her of some Victorian mansion in the South, dominated the canvas. Yet the landscape, unlike the magnolia one she was accustomed to, was raw, desolate, giving a primitive feeling of danger and unrelenting savagery that at once drew her to the painting even as it repelled her. It was the same feeling, reborn from old ashes, she'd had with Irish Fitzpatrick that summer day so long ago at Fort McPherson.

Kenna shuddered and returned to her novel. But as the sun sank into the bay and dimmed the room, she gave up her reading. As if mesmerized, she watched the patterned trail of twilight play upon the painting until darkness fell. With the breeze of the bay bringing coolness to the room, Kenna fell into a troubled sleep.

The night passed, and the sun again invaded the room. The painting of the mansion, deliberately placed by the owner, no doubt, to be the last thing he saw before sleeping and the first he saw when he awoke, greeted her.

Kenna became fully awake and her thoughts left the painting. She hopped from the bed and rushed toward the bathroom. The hospital ship would be docking sometime that morning. And she wanted to make sure she was at the harbor in plenty of time.

Kenna didn't bother with breakfast. She pulled her light blue dress with jacket from the closet, where it hung beside a safari suit of tan khaki, zipped up the side of her dress, and brushed her hair in place. Like Sunny's, it curled on its own, a blessing in the Australian climate. With a dash of lipstick across her mouth and powder on her nose to remove the shine, Kenna left the apartment.

From the residential section of the bay area, Kenna rode a tram to the waterfront, a teeming commercial and business district, now overflowing with military supplies being shipped across the Pacific.

Mutton and beef, wheat and grain, wool from the prize Merino sheep, waited to be loaded on cargo and supply ships. There were people everywhere, military as well as civilian, swarming over the harbor area.

Kenna took her place with the others, walking up and down, stopping in a pub for a strawberry fizz and a sandwich to stave off the hunger that had come over her. Then she began to pace again, her nervous energy keeping her from finding a place to sit and watch as the others were doing.

Out on the horizon, a large, white hospital ship, with its green band surrounding the waterline and its red cross declaring its pedigree as a ship of mercy, became a small speck upon the water. Seeing it, Kenna's heart began to beat more rapidly. A small exclamation of anguish escaped her lips even as she watched the blue-green water off the great barrier reef.

"Oh, God, please let him be on the ship," Kenna prayed silently.

All at once, she was surrounded by a crush of people waiting for the same ship. Along the wharves, a row of ambulances sat, with medical corpsmen and nurses. The scene reminded Kenna of another war, when she had waited with Wells, the ambulance driver, at the railway station in Toul, France, for the hospital train to come in from the front. Now, a new war was being fought, on the water as well as land, with the navies of the world locked in mortal combat.

When the giant ship finally cast anchor, a great cheer went up. Some spectators along the wharf held flags as the launches left harbor to remove the casualties from the *Good Hope.* But Kenna, with no flag to wave, clutched her hands tighter, her knuckles turning white, while her nails dug into the palm of her hands until the pain caused her to loosen her closed fists.

The crowd closed in and Kenna's view was blocked. Frantically, she searched for another position, finding it on a tall wooden platform that gave her height.

"Lady, no one is allowed on that platform," a husky voice called to her.

"Please, I can't see over the crowd," she protested.

The man stepped forward, ready to argue with her until he caught a signal from his boss standing in the window of a building overlooking the wharf.

"All right," he said, changing his mind. "But be careful. I'd hate to fish you out of the harbor."

She smiled her gratitude at the stevedore, his muscled arms rippling with tattoos and sweat glistening on his bare chest.

From her vantage point, Kenna watched each launch come into harbor and unload. She searched each face as the survivors passed by her, some men on stretchers, others able to walk. The more serious had been removed from the ship first. Her son, Jack, was not among them.

For an hour, the unloading continued and a frantic Kenna remained on the platform near the water and watched. Wives and sweethearts, recognizing their own, gave thankful greetings, while others, with no one special, merely greeted them all. "Nice go, Yank. Good luck." The men smiled back, their gratitude for the welcome showing in their eyes.

Soon, they were all loaded into the ambulances and buses. "That's all the casualties, folks," a voice called out. "Please move back. The crew will be coming ashore now."

A griefstricken Kenna Fitzpatrick closed her eyes to press back the tears. Her trip had been for nothing. She dreaded calling Irish in Melbourne to tell him that Jack was still missing in action.

As she waited for Sunny to come ashore, she remembered her daughter's concern on the day she'd surprised her in Auckland. "Something's happened to Jack. You've come to tell me…" Like a foreshadowing, the words had come true.

The crowd on the wharf dispersed, with only a few people remaining. Kenna stepped down from the platform. The stevedore passed by without noticing her. And the man at the window above continued his watch, while Kenna stood alone on the wharf below.

Filled with passengers in white and khaki, the launch made its way once more from the anchored ship in the harbor, obscured from view off and on by the jutting peninsula. The craft cut its engine shortly before reaching the wharf.

Kenna, biting her lip, waited for the launch to unload. She could not see the passengers clearly through her blur of tears. They seemed to come all at once — nurses and doctors, medical corpsmen and ship's personnel, like one body moving along the wharf. And then a voice in front of her said, "I thought you might be here to meet the ship, Mother."

"Oh, Sunny. Your brother—"

"I know, Mother. It's been a tough three days for you. When I heard the *Lexington* had sunk, I wanted to call you. But there was no way to get in touch."

Directly behind Sunny stood a tall young man, dressed in white. His hands were wrapped in bandages, but the smile on his face was broad. "Well, aren't you going to say hello to me, too, Mom?"

Kenna quickly brushed away her tears. The young man, now in clear view, looked so much like Irish, with his dark hair, his shining topaz eyes, that her throat hurt. Kenna's voice faltered. "Jack? Oh, darling, you're alive. You're alive."

The tall son, towering over his mother, stepped forward and embraced her, with his bandaged hands held out awkwardly. "They let me come last, with Sunny," he explained.

"All right, Ensign. Let's go. The bus has waited long enough."

Kenna protested. "Jack…"

"I have to go now, Mom. But Sunny will tell you everything. And I'll write—" He gazed down at his bandaged hands. "I'll get someone to write you and Dad tonight." Jack Fitzpatrick turned to Sunny. " 'Bye, Sis. And thanks for the bandages."

With a slightly unsteady gait, Jack walked down the wharf to the waiting bus. The doctor beside him put out his hand to steady him.

"He's going to be all right, Mother," Sunny assured Kenna. "He has a slight concussion, so they'll keep him in the hospital for a while."

"What about his hands?"

"They'll heal well. I don't foresee any problem. He'll probably be back on active duty in a month."

"I traveled for three days," a rueful Kenna began.

"And you got to see him for less than two minutes," Sunny finished. "I know."

Kenna suddenly smiled and put her arm around her daughter. "But it was worth it, just to know he's alive. Come, darling. Let's find a telephone and call your father with the wonderful news."

Hesitating, Sunny looked toward the ship's officer standing patiently nearby. And Kenna, noticing her hesitation, immediately said, "Have I spoiled your plans, popping up like this?"

"No, Mother. But Singleton is taking me out to dinner tonight, if you don't mind. Just let me speak with him a moment. Then we can go somewhere and I'll fill you in on Jack."

The next hour was an emotional one, with the call to Irish and the conversation with her daughter. Sitting in a garden restaurant overlooking the bay, Kenna sipped a lemonade while she listened to Sunny relating the events of the battle and the sinking of the *Lexington.*

"…And it was Matt who rescued Jack. I'll always be grateful to him for that. He found him floating in the water, shortly before the ship went down. Jack was the last survivor to be picked up."

When there were no more questions to be asked, when Kenna was satisfied that she had heard everything Sunny could tell her, she glanced at her watch.

"How long are you staying in Darwin, Mother?"

"Since Jack has been flown out, I think I'll try to leave by this afternoon. Now, don't worry about me. You go ahead and catch up with your friends. Oh, Sunny, in all the rush, I forgot to bring your apricot sandals."

"My sandals? You have them?"

"Yes. Evidently you lost them. Your friend, the marquess of Dalhousie, was kind enough to give them to me before your father and I left Sydney."

"The marquess of Dalhousie is no friend of mine," Sunny bristled.

"Well, at least you could be grateful to him. He went out of his way to return them."

Sunny swallowed and forced herself to remain silent. How could she tell her mother that Alex Ramsay had also gone out of his way to take them from her and throw them into the wattle bush beyond the park bench.

"I really have no use for them. I haven't worn the apricot silk dress since the party at the governor-general's."

"But it's a beautiful dress. You'll find another place to wear it, I'm sure. And you'll be glad to have the matching shoes."

Kenna paid the bill, and at the entrance to the gardens, she parted company with her daughter. "The next letter you write to us, Sunny," a lighthearted Kenna chided, "please don't give the censor so much work to do."

"A slice of Swiss cheese, huh?"

Kenna nodded. "Or a holy writ."

"Very funny, Mother." Sunny leaned forward and gave her mother a kiss on her cheek. "Have a safe trip back to Melbourne. And tell Dad how much I enjoyed the chat on the phone."

When Sunny was out of sight, Kenna began to walk toward the apartment. She was not sure how soon she would be able to leave Darwin. Perhaps Gregory would be able to help her.

Once she reached the apartment complex, Kenna found Gregory at the desk in the foyer. "Please make up my bill," she informed him. "I'd like to leave Darwin this afternoon, if possible. Do you think you might see if there's a train going south within the next few hours?"

"I'll find out, Mrs. Fitzpatrick, and let you know. It might be morning, though, before something is available."

"Thank you, Gregory." Kenna left the foyer and walked to the apartment. It was still cool, despite the extreme heat outside. She removed the short jacket of her blue dress and went into the bath to wash her face. Then she settled down to wait for news from Gregory.

Twenty minutes later, there was a tap at her door. Kenna rose from the chair. "Yes?" she called out before opening the door.

"It's Gregory, mum. Can you be ready to leave in an hour?"

Kenna opened the door. "Yes, of course."

"Then I'll come and get your luggage when you're ready. A man will be in the foyer at three o'clock to take you to the station."

"How kind of you, Gregory. Thank you. Now, if you will check in the pantry to see how much I owe you...I opened a bottle of wine last night and had a tin of squid with biscuits. No breakfast this morning."

"I'll take your word for it, Mrs. Fitzpatrick. And you can pay your bill when you come downstairs. I'll have it ready then."

Once Gregory was gone, Kenna hurried into the bathroom, slipped out of her clothes and into a tub of cool water. A little later, she felt fresh again—and happy. She pulled the lavender dress from the closet and packed her other clothes. A white wisp of a shawl—a fine blend of silk and wool—lay on the chair for her return journey. There was no telling what the weather would be like once she left Darwin.

She placed her luggage outside the door, locked the apartment, and went downstairs to pay her bill.

Gregory noticed the miraculous difference in one day's time that had changed the sad, beautiful woman into one whose face was filled with a special radiance. Yet even in her radiance, there was an air of vulnerability that made a man want to be generous—even one as hard as Alisdair Shannon.

When the hour was up, a taxi stopped in front of the apartment house. "There's your ride, Mrs. Fitzpatrick," Gregory announced. He picked up her luggage and followed her to the pavement.

Standing before the taxi was the man, Alisdair Shannon. Kenna hesitated when she recognized him. "I had not realized I would be seeing you again, Mr. Shannon."

The bronzed, gray-templed man smiled. "How else would you get to the airport?"

"The airport? But I'm going back to Melbourne by train."

"And what would you do when you came to the end of the track?"

"Do you mean there's no through connection?"

"Not at the moment. Perhaps in another ten years." He motioned for Kenna to get in, as Gregory placed her luggage in the front seat of the taxi. "See you, Gregory," he said, climbing into the taxi beside her. He signaled the driver, and the taxi drove away from the plush apartment house by the bay.

Chapter 16

IN THE AIR HIGH ABOVE THE NORTHERN TERRITORY, THE plane piloted by Alisdair Shannon held a contented Kenna Fitzpatrick.

The reddish cast of the land reminded Kenna of north Georgia red clay hills. But unlike the Georgia hills, the land was dry and the grass became the color of ripe wheat bending to the wind.

Kenna wore the same flight jacket over the lavender dress, and used her white silk and wool shawl as a lap robe against the coolness of the afternoon sky.

"You're happy now, aren't you?" the pilot inquired. And before she had a chance to answer, he confirmed his own observation. "There's a vast difference in you, now that you know your son is safe."

Kenna smiled at him. "I suppose it will always be that way—a parent worrying over her children, especially in time of war. Do you have children, Mr. Shannon?"

He barely hesitated. "No. I'm not so fortunate as you."

"A wife?"

"My wife died a long time ago."

"I'm sorry."

"But I'm not entirely alone, so there's no need for you to feel sorry for me."

His eyes were hidden behind the glasses. Of course. That

type of man would never want for companionship. And Kenna, realizing it, knew she should not have allowed her curiosity to override her politeness. But he did not seem offended. He merely changed the subject, calling attention to the expanse of land below, as they soared over the landscape.

"The man who owns the sheep station below crossed the imported Merinos with some of his native sheep, and now he has the best of both breeds — a hardy, healthy animal with excellent wool."

"How large is his station?"

"About three hundred miles."

"That's a tremendous size, isn't it, even for Australia?"

"Not when you realize how few sheep can actually live on an acre of grass out here."

Kenna laughed. "You see how little I know about sheep. Now, if you talked about horses, I'd be able to converse more intelligently."

"You enjoy riding?"

"Yes. And that's what I miss most out here, I suppose. My husband and I rode with a hunt club at home. Of course, I always felt sorry for the fox," she added quickly.

Now it was Alisdair's turn to laugh. "We Aussies are not that civilized. We hunt, too, but we don't feel a bit sorry for the animals."

"You fox hunt here, as well?"

"No. We hunt dingoes, the wild dogs I mentioned earlier. Periodically, we band together to get rid of them when they become a nuisance to the stock."

Suddenly, Alisdair inquired, "When is your husband expecting you back in Melbourne?"

"Not until Saturday. He'll be quite surprised to see me tonight, thanks to you, Mr. Shannon."

An easy, comfortable silence now enveloped the two. Kenna continued to watch the land below, noticing a gradual change in the topography of the land, in the trees, and in the appearance of cattle.

"I hope you don't mind," Alisdair said. "I need to make one stop before we proceed to Melbourne."

"Not at all. It will give me a chance to stretch. I'm not always a good traveler on long journeys," Kenna confessed.

In the distance, an airstrip paralled a fence, and a long, straight road broke off from a more winding one. When the pilot passed over a clump of trees, he began to make his approach toward the runway. But instead of landing, he pulled up, circled over a large white house, and then came in from the opposite direction.

Kenna, aware of the boxes adjacent to her own luggage, decided the pilot had an important delivery to make at this ranch that evidently spread for miles.

Alisdair brought the plane down, stirring up the red dust and causing a few cattle in the far pasture to scatter. By the time Kenna was helped from the plane to the ground, she saw a utility truck headed in the direction of the airstrip.

"That's Leahy coming to meet us," Alisdair said, taking the flight jacket from Kenna. "He's the manager for Koraburra Station."

Kenna hesitated. "I hope the owner won't mind your bringing an uninvited guest with you."

"Don't worry. The owner is seldom at home. That's why he has Leahy living on the property."

The truck stopped within a few feet of the plane. The man, Leahy, jumped out to greet Alisdair. "I'm glad to see you, Mr. Shannon," he began, walking toward the two.

"Kenna, this is John Leahy. John, my guest, Mrs. Fitzpatrick."

An amused Kenna acknowledged the introduction. A subtle change had come over the pilot once he'd landed, even to calling her by her first name, as if intimating to the manager of the station that she was more than a mere passenger to him.

"There're two boxes in the back, with Mrs. Fitzpatrick's luggage."

"I'll get them right away, Mr. Shannon."

Once John Leahy loaded the back of the truck and climbed aboard, Alisdair started the motor and left the airstrip.

Beyond the range, the sun began to disappear. There would be little daylight left for their trip, and Kenna, glad to make a stop, nevertheless hoped they wouldn't stay too long. She didn't like flying at night, especially over territory as rugged as this part of Australia.

Halfway to the house, Alisdair met an aborigine driving several milk cows toward the barn. He slowed and waved as the truck edged by on the narrow, winding road. Then the road branched off, showing a straight vista bordered by clumps of eucalypt trees.

For the first time since flying over Koraburra Station, Kenna's vision of the magnificent house was unobstructed. White, with a steep-pitched roof, a wrap-around porch, and architectural trim that seemed sturdy, yet delicate, the Victorian mansion looked vaguely familiar. Then, Kenna remembered the painting in the apartment.

Kenna turned to Alisdair. "It's the same house, isn't it?" she accused. "The one in the painting at the apartment in Darwin."

"So you recognized it."

"Yes. And I feel as if I'm an interloper."

"The owner doesn't mind, I assure you."

"And how do you know?" Kenna asked, her voice slightly exasperated. "Are you on such good terms with the man?"

"At times. But if you wish to thank him, yourself, you can do so later—at tea."

"I thought you said he was seldom home."

"That's true. But he'll be back in time for tea."

Only slightly mollified, Kenna allowed Alisdair to help her out of the truck as the housekeeper opened the door of the mansion.

"That's Molly O'Leary, the housekeeper," Alisdair announced.

The white-haired woman, dressed in a blue cotton print dress with a large white apron over it, smiled as she saw the two. "Mr. Shannon, how good it is to see you."

"Kenna, this is Mrs. O'Leary. Like your Chicago O'Learys." He smiled in the housekeeper's direction. "Molly, take Mrs. Fitzpatrick to a downstairs bedroom so she can freshen up from her long trip."

"Right away, Mr. Shannon."

They went inside the house, while Alisdair remained outside. Beautiful English antiques were combined with the same aboriginal art that had graced the apartment in Darwin.

"I hope I won't be too much trouble," Kenna announced, "descending on you so unexpectedly."

"We're always ready for visitors," Mrs. O'leary responded, "although they don't come so often, with the gasoline shortage, you know. Will you be staying long?"

"Oh, no. I have to get back to Melbourne tonight."

The woman raised her eyebrows in surprise, but said nothing until they arrived at the door of the bedroom down the long hall.

"The bath is on the other side of the bedroom," she said. "And just as soon as Mr. Leahy unloads the truck, I'll have Corky bring in your luggage."

"But I—"

"You wish anything now, Mrs. Fitzpatrick?"

A flustered Kenna decided she need not explain to the housekeeper. "No, nothing else, Mrs. O'Leary. Thank you."

"Tea will be served at six."

Mrs. O'Leary closed the bedroom door. Later as Kenna gazed in the mirror of the bathroom, she saw how travel-worn and tired she looked. It would be nice to change before tea, before meeting the owner of this vast station. All at once, Kenna realized she had not even bothered to learn his name.

When Kenna returned from the bathroom, she saw that her luggage had been placed inside the room and the white coverlet turned back from the bed. She quickly made up her mind. Taking the pale pink silk dress from the bag, she hung it up in the closet and walked back to the bath, where she turned on the faucets to the tub. Once she had freshened up, she might even have time for a short nap before getting dressed.

A little before six, Kenna, who had not actually gone to sleep, rose from the comfortable bed. She brushed her teeth and began to apply a little makeup, using more than she normally did. It was vain of her, she knew, changing from her travel dress to a flimsier one for tea when she would have to change again before leaving. But as the wife of a high-ranking general, she was used to dressing for the occasion wherever she was.

Taking her white shawl with her, Kenna walked onto the porch of the house, where she studied the flower garden forged out of alien land into a beautifully manicured plot, with its stone walkway passing through beds of roses and other flowers of blue and deep rose.

She left the porch and followed the formal walk past the house, and there at the side, set apart from the main house, was a white gazebo with an ornate white wooden bench. Here, the greenery tracing the fence was wilder, less formal, no longer clipped into shape but flowing over the fence with tendrils of color that spilled over onto the stones.

Forgetting her flimsy dress, she sat down on the bench and drank in the view. A sense of happiness overwhelmed her. Used to the uncertainties of war, she wanted to remember only that moment of beauty, as the hills turned purple and the shadows spread slowly over the garden. Too soon, this moment of peace would be gone. But for now, she felt sheltered, happy that her son was alive.

Alisdair Shannon stood silently in the garden, and for a time, he watched the woman while his heart protested. It wasn't fair that she was married to someone else. Yet, he knew that he had done what he had to do—bring her to Koraburra, even though he knew he would live to regret it.

With the two glasses in his hands, he moved on to the

gazebo. "I thought you might be out here," he said, holding out a glass for her to take.

"Oh, hello, Mr. Shannon. I was just enjoying the beautiful view."

"A toast," Alisdair said. "To the most beautiful woman who has ever been to Koraburra."

Kenna smiled. "You're too kind, Mr. Shannon. And I expect the owner has his own opinion. By the way, where is the owner?"

"That's what I wanted to clear up, before we go in to tea. I have a confession to make."

"Yes?"

"I'm the owner, Kenna."

Chapter 17

KENNA LOOKED AT THE MAN WHO HAD JUST ACKNOW-ledged his deceit. The ruggedness and grandeur of the land that now surrounded him was reflected in his face, in the easy stance of his lean, tanned body.

"And I suppose the apartment in Darwin is yours, also?"

"Yes. I didn't intend being secretive, especially at first. Please remember that. But later, as the trip wore on, I realized you were in no state to search for a room on your own once we reached Darwin."

Suddenly, Kenna laughed.

"And what do you find so amusing?"

"Poor Gregory, trying to settle up the bill. I suppose that's when I should have become suspicious, Mr. Shannon."

"My friends call me Shan," he interrupted.

She ignored his comment.

"And what did Gregory do to make you suspicious?" he prompted.

"He called your beautiful wine 'plonk,' for one thing and charged me accordingly."

Now it was Alisdair's turn to laugh. "Well, now that I know you recognize fine spirits, drink up." He held his glass in tribute, and Kenna, with good grace, lifted her glass and took a sip.

"What is it?" she asked, not recognizing the taste.

"A sundowner," he replied.

"I thought a sundowner was a tramp who arrived at a station too late in the day to do any work for his food."

Shan smiled. "That, too. But it's also a drink as old as the colonies, themselves." Indicating the space beside her on the bench, he asked, "Do you mind?"

"Be my guest," she answered, and took another sip of the sundowner.

With Shan seated on the bench beside her, Kenna held the crystal glass in her hand and gazed toward the setting sun. "Do you have any other surprises for me, Mr…..Shan?"

"No. We'll leave for Melbourne directly after we eat. Shall we go in?"

Kenna stood and, with his hand at her elbow, she walked down the steps of the gazebo and onto the stone path leading through the garden to the porch.

In the formal parlor, where they had gone to wait for tea, an oil painting of a mother and son hung over the mantelpiece. "Your family?" Kenna inquired.

"Yes. My late wife and son. She died years ago. My son, in North Africa."

"I'm sorry." Now, Kenna was no longer angry at Alisdair Shannon. She remembered his hesitation when she'd asked about children. And she began to understand his generosity to her.

As a father who'd lost a son and gone through the terrible grief, he was trying to make it easier for her. Her hurt had become his also. But he was right in one respect. If she had known he was giving up his apartment for her, she would have refused, regardless of the reason behind it.

"I believe our tea is ready," Shan said, seeing Tapoa, the aborigine, standing at the door.

Kenna would never get used to a meal called "tea." For her, it was an afternoon event, with more conversation than food. Now it was the opposite. Suddenly self-conscious, Kenna fell silent.

"Are you…"

"Did you..."

They began at the same time. "I'm sorry. What did you start to say?" Shan insisted.

"It wasn't important, really, I—"

"Shan! Where are you, Shan?" a voice called from the hallway.

Recognizing the voice, Shan stood up. "Excuse me, Kenna. That's one of my neighbors. There must be something wrong."

"Oh, there you are, darling. I was hoping you'd be back today."

The young woman swept into the dining room and, unaware of anyone else in the room, she rushed toward Shan and kissed him.

The man cleared his throat. "I have a guest, Cece," he admonished. "Kenna, may I present the daughter of my good neighbor, Cece Bennigan. Cece, this is my guest, Mrs. Fitzpatrick."

"How do you do, Miss Bennigan."

"Mrs. Fitzpatrick," Cece answered in a rather hostile voice. She was tall, dark haired, willowy. To Kenna she seemed more child than woman.

"Sit down, Cece," Shan urged. "I'll have Tapoa bring you a plate."

"Thank you, no. I have one other stop to make. If I'd realized you were entertaining tonight..."

"Mr. Shannon was kind enough to give me a ride from Darwin," Kenna explained, anxious for her not to get the wrong impression. "My son was wounded, and he came in on the hospital ship."

Cece relaxed at Kenna's explanation. She no longer felt threatened by the beautiful woman sitting at Shan's table.

Kenna, realizing it, regained her poise. No longer self-conscious as she had been a few minutes earlier, Kenna listened as Cece told her reason for coming.

"Dad's beside himself, Shan. His prize bull has been killed by dingoes. He's getting up a party of men to hunt them down, first thing in the morning. Can you come to help?"

Shan hesitated. He looked toward Kenna. "Mrs. Fitzpatrick needs to be back in Melbourne by tonight. I doubt I could get back here in time..."

Having discounted the other woman as any threat, Cece said, "Maybe she wouldn't mind waiting until after the hunt tomorrow. And then I could ride with you to Melbourne. I have some shopping to do. And we could return to Koraburra together."

"Kenna, is it imperative for you to be back tonight?"

Kenna looked from Cece to Shan. He was well aware that Irish would not be expecting her so soon. "I can wait until tomorrow, Shan, if you feel you should join the hunt."

"I have an obligation to help the Bennigans," he replied. "Then, too, others of us could lose our own prize cattle if the dogs aren't dealt with."

"Then that's settled," Cece said. "I'll tell Dad you'll come. Seven o'clock."

Cec got up to go, and Shan stood to walk with her to the door. "Excuse me for a moment, Kenna."

"Certainly. Good-bye, Cece," Kenna said, and she was left alone in the dining room.

Cece's attempt to whisper to Shan was not succesful. Her voice carried into the dining room. "For a moment, Shan, darling, I was actually jealous — until I realized you wouldn't be interested in a woman her age, however beautiful she is."

"She's closer to my age than you are. Have you thought of that, Cece?"

"But men are different. You always said that. And I agree."

"You should have married Dair before he volunteered, Cece," he commented sadly.

"He would have gone anyway, Shan. You know that. Besides, I was already in love with his father."

Kenna deliberately blocked out any further conversation between the two. She had not wanted to listen in, any more than she wanted to spend the night at Koraburra. But now, it was too late for both.

Shan returned to the dining room. And in an easy camaraderie, they finished their meal. Conversation was no longer stilted. In a strange way, Cece's interruption had eased their sudden awkwardness.

"Would you like to sit on the porch for a few minutes?" he asked.

"Yes. That would be quite pleasant. But if you have something else to do, please don't feel that you have to entertain me."

"No. Nighttime on a busy station is for relaxation. My son, Dair, and I used to play chess after supper. I don't suppose you play chess, Kenna?" he asked wistfully.

"As a matter of fact, I do."

Shan's blue eyes lit up in delight. "Forget the invitation to sit on the porch. I'll see you in the parlor in five minutes."

By the time Kenna, after returning to her bedroom for a moment, walked into the living room, Shan had set up the board. "White or black? I'll give you your choice."

"White," Kenna answered and sat down at the table opposite Shan.

The only sound came from the grandfather clock in the hall as it steadily chimed the hour and half hour. Occasionally, a sigh from Kenna's lips heralded the losing of a pawn or knight. But she played to win and Shan liked that.

Finally, the clock struck ten, and Kenna stifled a yawn. "Checkmate," Shan said. He stood up. "One turn around the garden for exercise and then I'll allow you to nip off to bed."

"That's a bargain."

As they walked along the stones where the air was perfumed with roses, Shan suddenly asked, "Are you in love with your husband, Kenna?"

"Of course. What made you ask such a question?"

"I don't know. I don't usually ask such a personal question. I suppose I *should* apologize."

"Unless you allow me the same impertinent one."

"Fire away."

"Are you in love with Cece Bennigan?"

He laughed. "Some days she tells me I am. On other days, I'm not so sure."

He became serious. "Tomorrow, while I'm away, I hope you won't be too bored. If you'd like to ride, Corky will saddle a horse for you. But you must stay within sight of the house. It's too easy to get lost out on the range, especially for someone unfamiliar with the land."

"Thank you, but I doubt I'll take you up on that offer. A lazy morning, doing absolutely nothing, appeals to me."

Shan's serious expression changed to one of amusement. "If that's the case, you can even have breakfast in bed," he teased. "Just let Mrs. O'Leary know."

They walked back to the porch and into the house. "Good night, Kenna."

"Good night, Shan. I hope your hunt tomorrow is successful."

Later, Kenna climbed into bed. In a clump of trees not far from the main gate, a dingo's yellow eyes gleamed in the dark. A howl suddenly penetrated the darkness and brought a shiver to Kenna. She wrapped the blanket around her shoulders and continued to read until she could no longer hold open her eyes. She reached out to snap off the light and soon drifted into a sound sleep. Off and on during the night, the strange howl continued, but Kenna, tired from the long day, did not hear the wild animal once she had gone to sleep.

Chapter 18

KENNA RETURNED TO MELBOURNE, AND SUNNY LEFT Darwin on the *Good Hope.*

Now, the war in the Pacific took on a new intensity. The battle of the Coral Sea, considered a strategic victory for the Japanese, ironically worked to the Allies' advantage and set the stage for the victory at Midway.

On Guadalcanal, Alex Ramsay spent his days watching the Slot for enemy ships and gradually set up his network of scouts, with the help of Father Waal, to monitor the comings and goings of the Japanese at the northern end of the island, where the comfort women had settled in for a long stay.

Almost immediately, Alex became an important link in the Coastal Command, as he relayed messages from Giles to the other islands and provided information of his own.

May passed into June, and with the month came new dangers. Picking up radio signals between Alex and Giles, the Japanese began sending landing parties to try to locate the radios set up in the hills of the surrounding islands. But at each landing so far on Guadalcanal, the natives had warned Alex. He merely holed up and maintained silence until the enemy departed.

How he chafed at this hiding from the Japanese. He wanted to engage them in battle instead. But he had been specifically warned by Eric. "Your job is *not* to fight—I repeat — *not* to fight — or do anything to endanger your work as a coastwatcher. You are doing a far more important job, reporting the movement of ships and convoys."

On that morning in June, as Alex recalled the conversation with Eric, he sat and listened in to the teleradio. It had been five days since he'd last heard from Giles, and he was getting worried about him. Finally deciding there would be no message from Giles that morning, he stood up and stretched. He began to walk to the kitchen when he heard the conch shell signal from Timi You, on watch duty in the treehouse platform.

Alex rushed to the porch and, standing on the steps, he put his binoculars to his eyes. Black, billowing smoke arose as an oil tanker, with two destroyer escorts, chugged past Tulagi and headed south into the Coral Sea. The presence of a tanker was always an important discovery, for it indicated an armada of ships somewhere, waiting for refueling.

There had been no signal from any coastwatcher closer to Bougainville. Valuable time had already been lost. The only thing left to do now was broadcast on the x-frequency, and hope some ship within the vicinity would hear and respond, without waiting for the message to reach the Coastwatchers headquarters in Townsville, and then be relayed back again.

"MDAR to X. I repeat, MDAR to X. Three ships passing Tulagi at ten hundred hours. Headed south. One oil tanker. Two destroyers."

Alex used the telegraph key since it could broadcast a hundred or so miles farther than the human voice. He repeated the message three times and then signed off.

Hovering off the coast of San Cristobal near Kirakira, the destroyer *Viscount*, waiting to be reassigned for another major sea battle, had just completed its training of new gunners and other personnel in a mock battle with the destroyer, *Collier*.

In the *Viscount's* radio room, Signal Corpsman Holliman, with nothing better to do, played with the dials in hopes of picking up some good music. As he turned the dial to the x-frequency, he heard Alex's message. After decoding it, he promptly alerted his commander.

"Did the coastwatcher give the exact bearings of the ships?" Matt asked.

"Heading south, sir, directly between Tulagi and Berande Point."

Matt looked at the map. "Change course, Mr. Pearson," Matt ordered, giving him the exact position of latitude and longitude. "Let's get a piece of that oil tanker."

"Aye, aye, sir." Peason smiled as he began the maneuver.

Spinning the destroyer around like a coin on a tabletop, Pearson changed course and headed out to intercept the tanker. Directly behind the *Viscount*, the *Collier* followed suit. Now, their new gunners and torpedo men were going to get a taste of actual battle.

On the island of Savo to the north, Giles Canupp remained hidden in a small indentation barely large enough for his massive frame. Over it, a rotten palm tree lay crosswise, its palm fronds and growth of vines obscuring his presence. Approximately fifteen feet away, in a small, bombed-out crater, his man, Wani, also hid and waited.

For five days they had been chased over the island by the Japanese officer, Kyoto, and his platoon of soldiers searching for the elusive Black Pawn and his teleradio.

Now, Kyoto was closing in and Giles sensed it. He and Wani had nowhere else to run. Their water was gone. Also their food. And Giles, with aching chills and fever, knew he was coming down with another bout of malaria.

When he heard the excited voices getting closer, like the bark of dogs cornering a fox, Giles, hidden in the earth den, tried to keep his body from shaking. He longed for a cool drink of water for his parched tongue, but it was useless. Kyoto had stationed guards at the spring, and even at the river. Now seeing Kyoto in full view, Giles had a premonition that he had chosen his own grave.

The officer bore no resemblance to the propaganda posters of short, buck-toothed men in thick horn-rimmed glasses. Kyoto was tall, with the proud bearing of a warrior. Cold and impassive, he gave directions to his men to fan out and explore every inch of ground.

Giles held his breath as a soldier took his bayonet and began to thrust through the debris at the edge of the crater. Suddenly, voices erupted into excitement; soldiers surrounded the crater.

Unable to see anything but the soldiers' backs, Giles became heartsick. And he waited for the inevitable — the sight of Wani being pulled out of the crater by the soldiers.

The black man, dressed in a lap-lap, with one of Giles' blue shirts on his back and a pair of brogans on his feet, was hurled out of the crater, even as he clung to the dirt sides of the hole. A cry of triumph came from one of the soldiers. It was answered by the others, while Wani, crouching on the open ground, waited for the prick of the nearest bayonet.

"Black Pawn. Where is Black Pawn?" Kyoto demanded in pidgin English.

Wani remained silent. Again, Kyoto demanded an answer. Wani said nothing.

With an order in Japanese, Kyoto pointed to a nearby tree and walked away with several soldiers. The few left behind tied Wani to the trunk of the tree. Giles hoped they would leave the native and join the others in their search for Black Pawn. Instead, he saw one of the soldiers begin to rip the blue shirt from Wani's body with the tip of his bayonet. At the same time, he baited Wani to answer his question.

It became a sport, with each unanswered question left as a mark somewhere on Wani's body. The other Japanese soldiers laughed and found more comfortable seats to watch the ensuing trial.

Directly above Giles, one of the soldiers sat down on the rotten palm, causing debris to fall into Giles' eyes. But Giles did not move.

For an hour, the soldier continued his sport with Wani, while Giles gritted his teeth. Now naked, the native, who had tattooed his body with white in a tribal ritual when he'd first become a man, was now tattooed in blood.

Finally tiring, the Japanese soldier gave up his place to another. With a gleeful banzai cry, the second soldier ran toward Wani with a full thrust of the bayonet. Laughing, the others lined up to take turns using Wani for target practice.

Giles could stand it no longer. He upended the tree where the soldier sat. The Japanese fell into the dirt as Giles emerged with pistols firing.

In that short time, with surprise on his side, Giles brought three soldiers down. He barely felt the sting in his own flesh as the enemy recovered from their surprise.

For the first time in the hour, Giles heard Wani speak. "Masta, kill me. Please."

With the pistol aimed at Wani's heart, Giles fired. He saw the man's head slump to his chest. He then turned the pistol on himself as the soldiers rushed him with their drawn bayonets.

He fell to the ground. And with his last breath, Giles Canupp gasped, "Steak and eggs," the code of a coastwatcher closing down his station for good.

Two days later, the *Viscount* lay at the bottom of the sea—and Matt Willoughby, with a broken leg and assorted cuts, lay in a berth on the hospital ship *Good Hope.*

Sunny had spent as much of her off time as she could with him, trying to cheer up the unhappy commander.

"But you sank the tanker, Matt," she defended as they spoke that evening. "You can't dismiss that."

"I lost my ship, Sunny. Even worse than that, Pearson is dead. And over half the crew—Holliman, Michinikowsky, Swinton, and old Earl Mason."

Refusing to be comforted, Matt turned his face to the bulkhead. He wanted no sympathy from Sunny. He wanted to feel the grief wash over him; he wanted to mourn the death of each of his men.

Finally, Sunny left him. She remembered the day when

she'd blamed herself when one of her patients had died. It was small comfort at the time to know he would have died anyway, regardless of what she had done to try to save him, just as it was small comfort to Matt that the submarine, trailing the tanker, was the culprit that had sunk the ship. Sunny knew it would take Matt a long time to stop blaming himself.

At the end of the passageway, Benita bumped into Sunny, returning to quarters. "How is Commander Willoughby tonight?"

"Medically, he's all right, Benita. But you know how it is when you blame yourself for something the enemy did."

"I've seen it time and again—men unable to separate themselves from their jobs—whether it's a boat or a business. Their egos become so wrapped up with what they're doing, that if something happens to the job, part of them dies, too."

"But what's the answer. Benita? How can Matt be made to see that he's valuable for himself?"

"He can't. The only thing that will erase this depression is for him to be assigned to another destroyer, as soon as possible."

"Which is at least six months away." Sunny left Benita and continued to her quarters.

With the war accelerating in the Pacific and casualties on the islands mounting, a second hospital ship had been assigned to the lollipop run. The two ships occasionally passed each other in their biweekly runs, as one filled and hurried back to port with the wounded while the other began a fresh trip. Because of it, the *Good Hope* was almost empty.

Beyond the few injured survivors from the *Viscount,* there were only about a dozen or so other patients on the wards—a sailor transferred from the admiral's flagship because of an attack of appendicitis, a marine with severe jungle rot, one young soldier injured by his own grenade, and a downed flyer picked up by a sub in one of the island lagoons.

After performing the emergency appendectomy, the surgeons had been left with nothing to do. And the dentists with their empty dental chairs, had devised a checkup for the entire ship's personnel, in the hopes they could find a cavity or two to fill, or a good reason for a root canal.

When Sunny reached nurses' quarters, she found Wendy in bed, nursing a swollen jaw.

"So the dentist finally found a cavity," Sunny commiserated.

"It barely showed up on the x-ray, " Wendy complained. "And as for the shot he gave, it was absolutely horrendous. I won't be able to find my upper lip for two days. But just wait. Sometime when *he* needs a shot, I'm going to volunteer. Then I'll find the dullest needle in the sterilizer — preferably one with a hook on the end — and pay him back."

Sunny laughed. "Revenge is a potent emotion, isn't it?"

She watched Wendy trying to smile. But her mouth, dull with the effects of the novocaine, refused to cooperate.

"How's Matt?"

"Depressed. He discounts the fact that he sank the oil tanker and one of the destroyers. All he can think of is his men. And he acts as if he's sorry he didn't go down with the ship, even though he was the last one off."

"Sometimes I get scared, Sunny," Wendy confessed, "when I think of this hospital ship going down. As often as we've practiced evacuating the patients to the boats, I know it won't be that smooth if it actually happens."

"What I worry about is the men with heavy casts on their bodies. They don't stand a chance." Sunny shuddered. "Why did you bring up such a gruesome subject? Talk about something more pleasant — ghosts, cholera, or even leprosy."

"How about love? I think I'm in love, Sunny."

"And who is it this time — Van Johnson?"

"No. Hank Brogdon. I think I'm in love with the shrimp."

"Then why do you act so miserable when you say it?"

"Because if I marry him, I won't ever be able to wear sling heels. And you know how much I adore dressy shoes, like your pretty apricot sandals."

"Maybe Brogdon hasn't finished growing, Wendy. Have you thought of that?"

Wendy attempted another smile. "What a lovely idea. He *is* awfully young."

"Well, I'm off to the showers," Sunny commented, leaving Wendy to daydream about Brogdon's height.

Sunny had just turned on the showerhead and reached for her shampoo, when the bulkhead reverberated with an awful explosion. The lights flickered, and she reached out to steady herself. With sirens piercing throughout the hospital ship, Sunny grabbed her uniform and put on her Mae West lying beside it.

Before she finished getting into her shoes, a second explosion rocked the *Good Hope*. She ran from the shower and started belowdecks to the wards. Then, the lights went out and Sunny felt herself hurtling through space as the deck collapsed and the ship emitted a grinding, screeching noise, like an animal in its death throes.

Chapter 19

WITH HANDS REACHING OUT FUTILELY TO GRASP ANY-
thing to stop her rapid fall, Sunny fell through a hole in the
deck and landed hard on a top bunk mattress in the surgical
ward below. A flashlight beam caught her in its light and
followed her rude descent through the overhead as the ship
heeled.

Momentarily stunned, Sunny bounced off the bunk to
the ward deck, where she sat until she could regain her
breath. She did not notice that the second explosion had
blown off one of her shoes.

Three men, also stunned from the torpedo hit that had
lifted the ship out of the water, held to the sides of their
bunks—Arrio, the appendectomy case, Rehoboth, the
temporarily blind pilot, with bandages over his eyes; and
Grainger, with his feet encased in surgical stockings.

"What's happening," the blind pilot demanded. "Has the
ship been hit? Are we going to abandon ship?"

The fear in his voice was akin to her own, but the task
ahead took precedence over her fear. Forcing herself to
respond in a calm voice, Sunny replied," Yes, we've been hit.
But we probably won't have to abandon ship. Just to be on
the safe side, though, we're going to report to the lifeboat
station on deck."

Her calm, take-charge voice amid the disaster seemed to soothe the men. By rote, she repeated the instructions drilled into the nurses for evacuation of the wards. "Now, let's get in single file, hands on shoulders. Arrio, may I have your flashlight?"

Shining the light through the darkness of the ward, Sunny saw that the door was not blocked. "I'll lead the way," she continued. "Arrio, you're next, then Rehoboth, and you, Grainger, last."

While she took blind Rehoboth's hands and placed them on Arrio's shoulders, Grainger was busy grabbing a few personal items to stuff into his pillowcase.

"All right. Let's move out."

Avoiding the beams that had fallen through and narrowly missed her patients, Sunny led the three past the wreckage and into the passageway. In the eerie glow of the flashlight, smoke began to curl and billow overhead.

Grainger coughed and Sunny stopped the procession. Flashing the light up and down, Sunny debated with herself. What if she were leading them straight into the path of the fire? As she stood still and listened, a sound of water rushing in with a steady whoosh came from behind her. Then, she felt the water begin to slosh against her feet. Sunny decided she had little choice but to press forward. If they remained below, they could easily be drowned.

Sunny could hear voices in the dark—shouts above her and a dragging sound, like a firehose, that disappeared in the maelstrom of crackling flames and a new explosion that forced the nurse and her patients to their knees. All around them, bells rang, and through the darkness that made the escape more hazardous, the voice of the captain repeated over and over, "Abandon ship. This is no exercise. Abandon ship."

"We're sinking. I can feel the ship list," Rehoboth said.

Then, another light appeared in the passageway. "Come this way," a voice urged the four. "Fire is blocking exit five."

They quickly climbed to their feet, held on to each other,

and joined another line. Recognizing Benita in the second group, Sunny demanded, "Have you seen Matt, or anybody else from the officers' medical ward?"

"No. Heinman said they got a direct hit. They're trapped below."

Sunny groaned, but continued to help her patients. By the time they reached the top deck, the bridge was surrounded by smoke. The mast began to disintegrate, sending down fiery missiles to land among the men and women preparing the boats and rafts.

"Has anybody got a knife? I can't get the rope loose," a male voice shouted.

There was no need for a flashlight. The deck was like a huge bonfire, lighting up the frightened faces and giving them a surrealistic quality, no longer human, but alien in shape and color.

When some of the Carley rafts had been cut free, the men threw them into the water. Some jumped, while others climbed down the paravane ropes hanging over the side and swam to the rafts.

"Those Shinto bastards," a voice sobbed, and Sunny was only vaguely aware that it was Heinman speaking as he stood and helped the others over the side.

With the three from the surgical ward delivered safely to the lifesaving station, Sunny no longer heeded the rules. She left them and began to run toward the aft deck, that had taken the brunt of the torpedo. She would have to find Matt, for she could not leave the ship without him.

"Where're you going, Sunny?" a voice demanded.

"To look for the other patients," she shouted back.

"You don't have time. The ship's going to blow at any minute."

She paid no attention to the voice, but continued running in the other direction. The deck was hot, and the foot that was not protected felt the blistering heat. Sunny hopped and limped along, until she found another shoe, devoid of its owner, and stooped to put it on, not caring that it was another right shoe instead of left. She clambered down a ladder, her hands slipping on something wet. The flashlight casing hit her cheekbone with a powerful wallop. When she felt solid deck beneath her, she wiped her hands dry on her uniform. And only then, in the dim light provided by the flashlight, did she realize it was blood.

A hiss, like escaping steam, grew louder, and Sunny, groping along the passageway, jerked her hand back from the heat that permeated the bulkhead. Droplets of sweat ran down her face, and a suffocating feeling enveloped her as she realized there was little oxygen in the passageway for her to breathe.

With twisted metal and open, gaping holes where walls had stood, Sunny was hard put to remember the physical layout of the hospital ship. As if in a labyrinth, Sunny ran one way and then another. But when she was over the space where she thought ward 3 had been, she called out," Matt, can you hear me? Where are you, Matt?"

Black smoke surrounded her and Sunny began to crawl on all fours to make use of the little remaining oxygen close to the deck.

"Sunny? Is that you, Sunny?"

"Matt? I can't see you. Keep talking so I can find you."

"Sunny, don't come down," he warned. "You can't help me now. Go back on deck."

"No, Matt. You know I won't leave you. Especially after you saved Jack."

"You don't owe me anything for that. Please, Sunny. Save yourself. It's too late to get me out."

The ship shifted and Sunny fell to the edge of an abyss. And in the hole below, Matt Willoughby, with the heavy cast upon his leg, was trapped with no way out.

Hank Brogdon, directly behind Sunny, had also started for the medical ward with his portable gas-powered saw. The doctors had laughed at his invention, made after the Japanese Zero attacked the *Good Hope*. But he realized that if the ship sank, a man in a heavy body cast would go straight to Davy Jones' locker, like a Mafia victim with a concrete block tied to his body.

He followed the sound of the voices, his makeshift miner's hat with light leaving his hands free to grope along the same passageway where Sunny had come.

"Fitzpatrick," he yelled. "It's Brogdon. I'm coming to help. Hold on."

By the time Brogdon reached the two, Sunny was already in the hole with Matt. A heavy beam lay across the cast of his leg, pinning him under the wreckage. And when Sunny saw it, she became pessimistic. There was no way a human could lift the beam to free Matt. It would require special equipment.

But then, Brogdon was at her side. And with the buzz of the high-powered saw, he began the delicate operation of removing the cast from Matt's leg. Sunny held her flashlight, but Brogdon didn't need it. The light from his tin hat was sufficient.

In an emergency, no one is ever able to gauge the time in minutes or hours—and Sunny least of all in that dark abyss, with the sound of the saw adding to the screaming, shifting noises, the creaks and groans of the ship settling deeper and deeper into the water.

Finally, with the bunk removed from on top of him, Matt Willoughby was pulled free. The cast, cut in two, remained under the heavy beam, like an empty cocoon.

"I just hope they don't get me for practicing surgery without a license," Brogdon commented.

"I'll be the first to defend you," Matt vowed.

After stacking several bunks on end, the three climbed from the hole. For Matt, it was an excruciating trip, but the pain didn't stop him. They crawled through the labyrinth, and Brogdon, with a sixth sense, brought them topside as the ship began to disintegrate.

"She's breaking up. Jump," Brogdon urged.

Sunny looked over the railing. Heads bobbed in the water, while survivors clung to the rafts and boats. With the explosion somewhere behind her, Sunny didn't take time to climb down the roped side of the *Good Hope*. Holding her nose, she jumped. Down she plunged into the sea, and before she surfaced, she thought her lungs would burst.

Like the sweet smell of death that permeated the fighting beaches, Sunny would never forget the taste of fuel oil floating upon the water's surface. Gulping the air, she swallowed a mouthful. But it came up immediately, gagging her and imprinting on her mind forever the sickening, thick consistency.

"Over here, Sunny," Madeleine called out. "Can you swim to the raft?"

She didn't dare open her mouth again, even to answer. She was tired, and the slow strokes brought her only a short distance toward the raft that kept drifting farther away. But she had not come this far to drown in a sea of thick, black oil. In a supreme effort, she kicked her feet and forced one arm over the other until she felt strong arms beneath her, lifting her up onto the raft.

She lay there, exhausted, her eyes still closed. Then, she felt a cloth wiping her face free of the layer of oil.

In the deep of the night, candled by one great flame in the sea, the boats, the rafts drifted away from the sinking hospital ship. The *Good Hope* sat in the water longer than anyone expected.

When they were nearly three miles away, the ship went down. And when the final explosion came, with boiler plate and missiles shooting into the sky like fireworks on the Fourth of July, the raft, holding Sunny and a few other survivors, flipped over, dumping the occupants into the sea. But a few minutes later, they climbed again into the righted raft.

Spread over a wide range of sea, the rafts and boats drifted apart during the night—carried by the current toward the Japanese-infested islands of the six-hundred-mile chain of the Solomons.

Chapter 20

AMID THE SERENITY AND QUIET OF DAWN, SUNNY FITZ-patrick awoke. She stared at the mackerel sky with its soft, high clouds, and at the vast expanse of sea, coming alive in neptune colors of emerald and foam.

There was no sign of any other raft beyond the two that had been lashed together during the night. The only thing visible in the distance was the faint outline of a land mass — a tropical island that seemed to beckon with the breeze.

Curled up beside Sunny, her friend Madeleine slept peacefully, as if the previous night of horror had never occurred. A slight snore came from Heinman, stretched on his back and taking up part of the space that should have belonged to Rehoboth. The only other occupant of the raft was tall, lanky Sleepy Joe Tyler, the ship's anesthetist.

Sunny turned on her side and brushed her sticky hair from her eyes to get a better view of the raft trailing behind them. On the second raft were Brogdon and Matt, Wendy and Benita. At first, she couldn't tell who the fifth one was until he reached into a pillowcase and hurriedly popped something into his mouth. She recognized the slightly overweight Grainger, who had stuffed chocolate bars into his pillowcase before they left the surgical ward. Unaware that anyone was watching him, he quickly put the rest of the candy into the pillowcase and hid it under his Mae West.

Sunny sat up and yawned.

"Good morning, Fitzpatrick," a male voice croaked in her ear.

"Good morning, Heinman." She whispered so she wouldn't disturb Madeleine. "And it *is* a good morning, isn't it?"

"You bet it is. Last night, I thought I wouldn't ever get to see another one."

Rehoboth, roused from his sleep by Heinman's moving, sat up. The bandages on his eyes were still miraculously clean. "Can anybody see land?" he asked.

"Yes," Sunny replied. "Only, I can't tell how far away it is. Ten miles, maybe."

"More like fifty to a hundred," Sleepy Joe corrected.

"Commander Willoughby should know," Heinman said. And then he called out, "Commander, are you awake?"

Sunny looked at the survivors on Matt's raft and was shocked at their motley appearance. Each was covered in fuel oil, with assorted cuts and bruises to the skin. Sunny looked down at her own uniform, torn and dirty, and realized she must look the same.

"Yes, I'm awake. What is it?"

"How far do you think that island is?" Heinman asked, pointing toward the speck in the distance.

For a moment, Matt was silent. "At least a hundred miles or more," he finally replied.

"No. It can't be. It's got to be closer than that."

"Distances on the water are deceiving," Matt replied.

His estimate put a pall over the group of survivors, who had almost nothing in the way of food or water. Most of the provisions had gone under when the rafts capsized.

Realizing their greatest need was to survive until they reached land, or were spotted from the air, they took stock of what they had with them. Grainger remained silent, but Sunny mentally added his small cache of goods along with the rest.

Those with tin hats turned them upside down to catch

the rain, if they should be so fortunate. And Brogdon, unraveling part of a rope, made a fishing line and attached a sharpened metal hook from his life preserver. As he dropped it into the sea, the rest set up a watch for coconuts that sometimes floated out to sea from the island lagoons.

"Have you taken a look at your shoes, Fitzpatrick?" Heinman asked. Before she could answer, he said, "They don't match. Or else you've got two right feet."

"I'm lucky to have two shoes, so don't make fun of them."

"Madeleine acts as if she's been anesthetized," Sleepy Joe commented. "Do you think we should wake her up to make sure she's all right?"

At this suggestion, Sunny looked down at her friend. "Madleine. Wake up, Madeleine."

She didn't stir. Sunny, reaching out to give her a gentle shake, felt the coldness of her hand. Quickly, she placed her fingers on Madeleine's throat to feel for a pulse. And when there was none, she gave an anguished cry. She continued trying to elicit any small sign of life, but was unsuccessful.

"What's wrong with her, Fitzpatrick?"

She had seen death often enough—soldiers wounded on battlefields—soldiers gradually dying from their wounds. She had become reconciled to the fact, however difficult. But nurses weren't supposed to die, especially nurses like sweet, kind Madeleine.

Heinman's question went unanswered. Sunny gathered Madeleine's lifeless body into her arms and began to rock her back and forth like a baby. Tears streamed down Sunny's cheeks and with heartbreaking sadness, she spoke her friend's name over and over. "Madeleine. Madeleine." Her lips moved, but no sound came from her throat.

Heinman reached out toward the young woman in Sunny's arms. Seeing the area of blood behind her left ear, he lifted the matted hair. Barely visible was the slender piece of metal, the projectile that had taken Madeleine's life some-time during the night. "The Shinto bastards," Heinman said, repeating the words he'd spoken on the deck of the *Good Hope*.

On the second raft, Benita and Wendy seemed to sense that something was drastically wrong. "What's the matter?" Wendy called out.

"Tindol is dead," Heinman announced.

"No. Not Madeleine." The two women on the second raft clung to each other. "It can't be true." But they saw Sunny in her grief, and they, too, began to weep.

A harsh voice reprimanded them. "Save your tears. She's just the first."

For an hour, Sunny held Madeleine and refused to give her up, refused to think of what they would have to do. But Sleepy Joe said gently, "You'll have to let her go, Sunny. For the good of the rest of us."

No one had ever been buried at sea from the hospital ship, for it contained a refrigerated morgue. But they were not on the hospital ship. They were on the steaming, open sea, with no certainty of ever reaching land.

"Commander, you know the service, don't you?" Brogdon inquired.

"Yes."

"Then let's get on with it."

With the blazing hot sun upon their heads, Matt began the service for the dead. His voice rose above the gathering wind and his final words became a prayer for those still alive on the rafts.

Madeleine Tindol was committed to the deep and quietly grieved by the three who had shared her life on the *Good Hope*. The men swallowed hard to keep back their tears.

By the middle of the afternoon, a squall came up and tossed the rafts about like flotsam. While part of the crew bailed out the seawater, others, with tin hats, captured the rain to be used later for drinking.

Each took advantage of the sudden rain—Sunny lifted her head and let the water trickle down her parched throat, while others did the same.

Once the squall subsided and the sun came out to stay, it was clear that the intense heat was their most formidable enemy. Sunny had protested the heartless removal of Madeleine's dress and shoes, but Sleepy Joe was more practical. He and Heinman rigged up the white cotton uniform over the raft like an umbrella to stave off the fierce rays that had already begun their devastating work on tender skin. And in the other raft, the men took off their shirts to do the same.

As twilight came upon the water, Rehoboth said, "I'm hungry."

"Me, too," Heinman agreed.

"What's on the menu for tonight, Fitzpatrick?" a sardonic Sleepy Joe asked.

Hank Brogdon's fishing line had not lured any fish. And Sunny wasn't sure she could eat raw fish, anyway. But they were all hungry, nevertheless.

"Maybe Grainger will share his chocolate bars with us," Sunny announced.

"Hey, Grainger," Heinman called. "When are you going to bring out the food?"

"What food?"

Sunny's face tightened. "The chocolate bars in the pillowcase, under your Mae West."

A guilty expression spread over Grainger's face. "I thought we'd be hungrier by tomorrow. I planned on saving it till then."

"We'll worry about tomorrow when it comes. Bring out the chocolate now, Grainger," Matt ordered.

In the heat, the chocolate had stuck to the foil, but it made little difference. It was divided equally among the nine, and those fortunate to have a small piece of tin foil licked it clean, once the chocolate was gone.

Then a tin hat was passed around for each to take a drink of water. The law of survival became a strict task-master. No one was allowed to have more than another.

Grainger had learned his lesson quickly. His pillowcase, with the few remaining items of food, had been confiscated by Brogdon, appointed by Matt as the mess officer for all.

The daily ablutions were taken care of quietly and efficiently by slipping over the side of the raft and into the water. But by the second day, dehydration had set in and the trips over the side became less frequent.

The nine became indolent as they conserved their strength in the heat. They moved little and talked less, with the exception of Rehoboth, whose need for conversation was greater because of his blindness.

It was now their third day on the water. While the others slept the afternoon away, Sunny kept watch. They had no food; they had drunk the last of the water. And the sun bore down relentlessly on the Coral Sea.

Shielding her eyes from the blinding rays, Sunny squinted over the monotonous miles of water. In the far distance, a tiny, moving speck appeared. She watched it getting gradually larger, until there was no mistake. It was a ship, coming in their direction.

"Wake up, everybody," Sunny called out. "There's a ship coming toward us. Look."

In her excitement, she tried to stand, but with the shift of the raft, she quickly sat down again. "Did you hear me? I said there's a ship coming."

"Where? Is it one of ours? Can you tell?" The questions all came at once as the other eight awoke.

Wendy began waving and shouting. "Yoo-hoo. Can you see us? We're over here."

Benita, in her quiet voice, said, "Thank heavens. I don't think we could have lasted another day out here."

Matt's voice dashed all hopes. "Be quiet, everybody. And sit down."

"Why should we do that, Commander?" Heinman challenged, caught up in the excitement.

"Because it's a Japanese cruiser," he informed them. "Pray to God she moves on without seeing us."

He ordered the reflective white umbrella sails to be taken down. He would rather see them all dead in the sea than captured by the enemy—especially the three nurses. He remembered what happened to the Dutch nurses when the Japanese had invaded the East Indies.

"Now, lie down and don't make a sound."

Aware of their own breathing, the nine lay still and listened. But suddenly, Brogdon's foot jerked upward.

"God, I think I've caught a fish," he announced in a groan, as the rope, wrapped around his ankle, tightened. "What a helluva time for that to happen." He grabbed at the rope to keep from being pulled over the side.

"Grainger, help him," Matt whispered. "We can't afford to lose the fish."

With Benita and Wendy holding on to Brogdon, Grainger tugged at the line. In the distance, they could hear the laughing voices of the sailors on the Japanese cruiser as she came closer.

The fish jumped out of the water with a splash. A magnificent specimen, it was large enough to feed nine people if they could hold onto it. And if they could get past the cruiser without being seen. The actions of the fish trying to get loose cut their chances considerably. Yet, if Brogdon allowed the fish to go free, it would mean losing the line, too. And he couldn't afford to do that.

The fish tired. For a few minutes, the tautness of the rope relaxed. Then, with renewed energy, the fish made a bid for freedom, heading straight into the path of the Japanese cruiser. "Hell, Commander, what do I do now?" Brogdon groaned.

Matt was ready to give the order to release the fish when it suddenly changed course, pulling the rafts in the opposite direction.

The cruiser passed uncomfortably close, but continued its speed. And when it was finally out of sight, Sleepy Joe exchanged places with Benita in the other raft and helped to bring in the fish.

That evening, with their stomachs full, the survivors lay quietly and looked up at the stars.

"I never thought I would eat sashimi," Sunny remarked, "and live to say I actually enjoyed it."

"What's sashshimi?" Rehoboth inquired.

"The Japanese name for raw fish."

"Please, you don't have to remind me," Heinman teased. "I pretended it was steak while I was eating it."

"Hey, Brogdon, why do you think you were luckier today than yesterday, or the day before?" Sleepy Joe asked.

"I tied a piece of red cloth on the hook this morning. Guess he was just a sucker for red."

In the night, the rafts became caught in the current, pushing them toward the reef that formed a barrier to the island lagoon. No longer spinning haphazardly at the whim of the wind, the two flimsy crafts continued steadily toward the southern tip of Guadalcanal.

By morning, as the tide washed in to the palm-studded shore, it brought the nine survivors from the *Good Hope* closer to the island that had appeared like a mirage for the past four days.

To celebrate the presence of land so near, Sunny removed her ill-fitting shoes and replaced them with Madeleine's. She knew her friend would not mind.

While she gazed at the incredibly beautiful island, now within reach, Sunny vowed that she would make a memorial to her friend. It would be Madeleine's Beach, with an appropriate marker for the nurse who had given her life in the service of her country.

Chapter 21

ONCE THE RAFTS HAD CROSSED THE BREAKERS INTO THE sheltered lagoon itself, they were safe from the tide that might have carried them out to sea again.

All nine began to paddle in concert like the natives they'd seen in their outrigger canoes. But they had no oars, and so they used their hands instead. Even Rehoboth was able to help, with Heinman guiding him.

"I hope the natives are friendly," Wendy whispered to Benita on the second raft.

"Yes, I hope so, too." She did not voice aloud her fear that even now they might run into the enemy. Yet, the same fear brought a silence to the group as they continued to paddle, and to watch the approaching beach.

At first, there seemed to be no sign of life on the beach. But then Sleepy Joe caught sight of a native darting into a pile of palm fronds.

"I think we're being watched," he commented to Heinman.

"Well, if we are, I hope it's by a friendly native. I'd hate to have my head decorating some native hut," Heinman said, "after coming all this way."

Matt and Brogdon were also aware of the movements on the beach, a bush moving slightly to the right, a palm tree swaying under a sudden weight, causing a coconut to fall to the sand.

"You think we should call out to them?" Melvin Grainger asked.

Matt and Brogdon were in agreement. "No," Matt replied. "Just keep paddling and act as if you don't know they're watching us."

Undiverted by the movements on the beach, Rehoboth listened to the slight drone behind them. "I think I hear a plane," he said. "Can anybody see it?"

For a moment, the four on the lead raft stopped paddling to listen. Heinman broke into a grin as the sound grew louder. "It's got to be a rescue plane, looking for us. Oh, hallelujah! We'll be back to civilization in no time."

His enthusiasm was contagious, until the plane flew low over the lagoon. Painted on its fuselage was the symbol of the rising sun. It was not a rescue plane after all, but a patrol plane belonging to the enemy.

"It's going to dive on us," Matt warned. "Paddle for all you're worth."

Desperately, they paddled and prayed to get to shore without being strafed. The natives were forgotten. The enemy plane presented a much more ominous danger.

The curious natives watched from their hiding places while the plane came in low to strafe the rafts. Until that moment, they had feared the rafts. Now, they knew they did not belong to the Japanese whom they hated. Kelia, the chieftain, waited until the plane had disappeared. Then, he gave a signal for his men to uncover the canoes and row out into the lagoon for any survivors of the sinking rafts.

The men and women of the *Good Hope* bobbed in the lagoon in their life preservers. Heinman, holding on to Rehoboth, felt the sting of salt on his arm.

"Did you get hit, Rehoboth?" Heinman asked.

"I don't think so."

Heinman knew from his answer that the blood in the water was his.

Farther away, Sunny hardly recognized Sleepy Joe Tyler,

the tall, slender man whom the patients had loved. He now resembled a limp rag doll floating upon the water.

She looked back to see what had happened to the second raft. She saw Brogdon holding on to Wendy's life preserver and carrying her along with him. Matt was swimming alongside Benita, and Grainger, slightly behind them all, kept looking out to sea.

"Shark," he yelled, seeing something move through the water.

His cry brought new panic to the group trying to reach shore. The blood in the water was a certain attraction. But Grainger was wrong. There were no sharks in the vicinity.

When they saw the canoes coming out to meet them, their hope of rescue was renewed. Brogdon removed his life preserver, for he was a strong swimmer, but Grainger, unable to do anything but dog paddle, bobbed about in the water without gaining distance.

Soon, black hands reached down to drag Sunny out of the lagoon. She fell into the canoe and, with a smile of gratitude on her sunburned lips, she looked up into the fiercest face she had ever seen in her life.

The native's skin, black and glistening, was ridged where he had been mutilated in tribal ritual; his white teeth, filed into sharp points, declared his cannibalistic heritage and gave a menacing countenance. But Sunny had finally reached that dangerous period when the struggle for survival seemed too overwhelming to continue. Quiet resignation took its place. She was too exhausted to care.

She sat in the canoe and, viewing the scene like a dispassionate observer might, she saw the others in the lagoon taken up into boats—Matt and Benita in the same boat, with Grainger holding on to the second canoe while he looked behind him for fins of the nonexistent shark.

"Don't give up now, Sunny," Matt urged, reaching out to touch her hand. The touch comforted her, as his presence on the other raft had comforted her the last four days. Yet, it was strange that, during that time, she had not asked to trade places with Benita so she could be closer to him.

The canoes, with their occupants, reached shore. Those who could walk unaided stumbled onto the sand and collapsed in the shelter of the palms.

A possessive Brogdon allowed no one else to touch Wendy, whose hand was bleeding despite the tourniquet he had fashioned from his shirt. Heinman also shook off any help as he guided Rehoboth with his good arm. But Matt, with his broken leg, and Grainger, with his surgical stockings still intact, were unable to walk without assistance from the natives.

Sunny, forgetting her fear, looked up into the fierce face staring down at her. "Thank you," she said, "for saving my life."

The native smiled back at her, and in words incomprehensible to any of the survivors, he spoke to one of his men. Then, from a hiding place under the palm fronds, he brought out a wicked-looking machete.

"Oh, God, he's going to kill us," Wendy moaned.

Too weak to do anything but watch, Sunny waited for the fatal blow. But the blow came to a coconut, its top lopped off with a precise chop. The native offered the coconut first to Sunny.

Her unsteady hands reached out for it. Quickly, she took a long sip of coconut milk and passed it to the next in line. Soon, each survivor had his own coconut—the Papuan milkshake that Heinman had once disparaged, but now praised as his thirst was quenched.

The leader of the group spoke again, pointed to the interior of the island, and left with his men.

"Are they going to leave us here on the beach?" Wendy asked, puzzled at their sudden departure.

"They're probably going for help," Brogdon decided.

"Well, I can't walk another step for a long time," Sunny said, resting her head against the trunk of a palm tree while she applied pressure to Heinman's wound to control the bleeding.

At the same time, Benita attended to Wendy, loosening the tourniquet at intervals before reapplying it. No one mentioned Sleepy Joe Tyler, whose body still floated in the lagoon. But once Brogdon saw that Wendy was being looked after, he quietly left the group, waded into the water, and swam to recover the anesthetist's body.

When Brogdon had brought him ashore and placed him farther down the beach, no one mentioned his name. How hardened they had all become since Madeleine's death. It was almost as if, by denying his former existence, his death had not occurred.

As the sun began to lower over the lagoon, Matt said, "If the natives don't come back soon, we'll have to move out. We can't stay on the beach. It's too dangerous."

"But you can't walk, Matt," Sunny reminded him.

"Grainger has trouble, too," Heinman added. "Because of his jungle rot."

"Maybe I'd better start looking for something to use as splints for your leg, Commander." Brogdon motioned for Sunny to help him search. Out of the eight survivors, there were only three without injury—Sunny, Brogdon, and Benita. And with Benita watching over Wendy, the exhausted, sunburned Sunny was the only one left to help.

A half hour later, Matt, with his leg wrapped in wooden splints and tied by vines, stood up with the help of two strong poles. "We'd better move out," he said, as the last vestiges of light lingered upon the lagoon.

They had taken only a few steps when the natives returned, this time accompanied by a priest and two native nuns, as dark as Kelia.

"I'm Father Waal," the priest said, introducing himself. "Chief Kelia tells me he rescued you from the lagoon."

As the senior officer, Matt became the official spokeman for the group. "Yes. I'm Commander Willoughby of the United States Navy. And these are the survivors of the hospital ship, *Good Hope*. Carefully, Matt introduced each one, with proper rank and identification.

Brogdon reached out and shook hands with the priest. "We're awfully glad to see you, Father. We had no idea any missionaries were still on these islands."

"There are a few of us left," the priest replied. "Although most have been evacuated, or executed by the Japanese." Then he introduced the two nuns: "My right hand and my left—Sister Birghitta and Sister Agnes."

Standing behind them was a group of native bearers with stretchers for the wounded. Within minutes, Matt, Wendy, Heinman, Rehoboth, and Grainger had been hoisted into the air on strong shoulders, two natives for each stretcher. And Sunny, with Brogdon and Benita protesting that they could still walk, followed behind with the two nuns and the priest.

"I'm glad I happened to be visiting Chief Kelia's village today," Father Waal began, looking toward Brogdon, with whom he was walking.

"Not half so glad as we are, Father," Brogdon responded.

Sunny stumbled on a root, but Sister Birghitta reached out to keep her from falling. "You are a nurse, also?" Sister Birghitta asked.

"Yes. The three of us," Sunny answered, pointing to the other two women. A curious Sunny finally asked the question she'd been longing to ask ever since she found out the two black nuns were nurses. "How is it that you remained on the island with Father Waal?"

The black nun looked toward the priest. "It was difficult to persuade him. He wanted us to go with the others. Yet, these are our people. They need our help. For Father Waal, it is not so simple. His white skin makes it dangerous for him here. He should have left before the Japanese landed."

"You mean they're already on this island?"

"Yes. One group on the northern end; one group on the southwest tip. And it's only a matter of time before they take over the entire island."

A subdued Sunny saved her strength for the trek through the jungle. When they reached the native village in the interior, the eight who had been together night and day since the ship went down were separated, with the men in one hut and the three nurses in another with Sister Birghitta and Sister Agnes.

Once they'd been fed and Sister Birghitta had dressed Wendy's wound, they were left alone while she went to help Sister Agnes attend to the other survivors.

With Benita already asleep on a pallet, Wendy turned to Sunny. "I'm scared," she whispered. "Did you notice how fierce the natives all look? I'm afraid to shut my eyes for fear they'll murder us in our sleep."

"Sister Birghitta said we'll move out first thing in the morning. Father Waal came to settle a dispute, since there's no civil authority left on the island now. We'll be all right if we stay with him."

"What kind of a dispute?"

"Kelia's son killed a Japanese soldier last week. He was raiding his pig trap. The chief wanted to make sure Father Waal would not punish him for it."

"Well, will he?"

"Not according to the Sister. Only he's not sure the tribe can tell the difference between the Japanese and any other man with light skin. So he wants to get us away from here before there's further trouble."

"I think you brought trouble with you, Sunny. I saw the way the chief was looking at you tonight, after we came back from the bathing pool."

"The sun has baked your brain, Wendy. The way we both look now, neither one of us would bring even *half* a wild pig in the native marriage market. And we've lost so much weight, they wouldn't want to eat us, either."

"Oh, Sunny. That's what I love about you. No matter what we've been through, you can always make me feel better."

It was just as well that Sunny had no inkling of the argument going on at that moment between Father Waal and Kelia.

Sister Birghitta, and the other nun, Sister Agnes, returned to the leaf hut to find Sunny awake. She was still worried
about their departure the next morning, knowing it would
be tough for Matt with his broken leg—and for Grainger,
too.

"Are we still leaving tomorrow morning?" Sunny
inquired.

Sister Birghitta hesitated. "Yes. Father Waal has planned
our departure at dawn."

Reassured, an exhausted Sunny went to sleep. But long
before dawn, Sister Birghitta, standing over the blonde
nurse, awoke her.

"Quickly," she urged. "You are to put on Sister Agnes's
robe."

Confused at being awakened so soon, Sunny sat up. "I
don't understand."

"Ssh! Don't make a sound."

"What is it? The sun hasn't even come up."

"Father Waal's instructions. You and I are to leave at
once. The others will catch up with us later."

Sensing immediate danger, Sunny acquiesced. She put
on the black habit belonging to Sister Agnes and followed
Sister Birghitta. Hiding her face, she walked within a few
feet of the native stationed by Kelia to watch over the leaf
hut during the night.

Chapter 22

SUNNY HURRIED ALONG THE FOOTPATH WITH SISTER Birghitta, as if the devil himself were after them. What had she done to be ostracized from the others? To flee from the village before dawn, with the mosquitoes buzzing about her head and a nun's black habit disguising her uniform?

When she had tried to question the sister, the woman had not answered, choosing instead to walk even more quickly, while stopping only occasionally to listen to the sounds behind her.

"Please, Sister, tell me what I've done," Sunny begged, once they were beyond hearing distance of the village.

"You have caught Kelia's eye," she responded. And in a disapproving voice, she added, "You never should have washed the dark grease from your hair."

Sunny remembered the day the *Good Hope* had stopped at Pago Pago and Kirk Singleton had been forced to come to her rescue because of the native pulling her hair. "If the chief wants a few strands, why didn't he ask me? I wouldn't have minded cutting some of it to give him."

"My dear Miss Fitzpatrick, you don't understand. He wanted your entire head. It would have brought him a fortune."

A sick feeling swept over Sunny. So Heinman's remark about headhunters was not so far-fetched after all. Now that she understood the urgency, Sunny picked up speed, and when it was time to stop and take a rest, it was Sister Birghitta who suggested it.

The sun came up and still they traveled. Sunny began to limp, for Madeleine's shoes were too big for her and rubbed up and down on her heels. When the sister chose another resting place, Sunny selected some soft leaves to line the heels of her shoes where the blisters had begun to form.

"No, not those," Sister Birghitta cautioned. "They're poison. Here, these are safe," she said, reaching onto another shrub to replace the leaves Sunny had chosen.

Once the leaves were in place, the sister stood up and motioned for Sunny to follow. "We don't have much farther to go before we can stop and wait for the others."

"You think the rest will be all right? Kelia will let them go?"

"Yes. He will be too busy looking for you to bother with the others."

Twenty minutes later, the two came to a stop. Sister Birghitta parted the branches of a bush and before her was a natural hiding place, a bower large enough for two and surrounded on all sides by vegetation. "This is where we wait," the nun announced, and indicated that Sunny was to climb in first.

Seated beside each other, with the long, black habits covering their legs which were drawn up to their chins, they listened for sounds along the path.

But the sounds they heard came from the opposite direction. The nun put her hand on Sunny's shoulder, to caution her to remain quiet. Warily, Sunny listened to the voices, to the same inflection she'd heard from the Japanese cruiser as it sailed by their rafts. Then she saw them—twelve Japanese soldiers. Sunny drew in her breath and clasped her hands to keep them from trembling.

The soldiers stopped within a few feet of the hiding place, shifted a chest upon their shoulders, and then disappeared in the direction of the water. A few minutes later, Sunny heard the sound of a launch leaving the lagoon.

An irate Sister Birghitta recognized Father Waal's chest. The previous week, scouts had alerted the priest that the Japanese were beginning to raid the villages, killing their chickens and pigs and carrying off anything that took their fancy. But this was the first time they had bothered the mission village.

Sister Birghitta glanced at the nurse beside her. She knew the Americans would not be safe in the village for long. The Japanese would come again. Father Waal would have to find another place to hide them until they could be rescued from the island.

Ten minutes after the launch had departed, Father Waal and the others reached the bower where Sunny was hidden. The two women, watching a gecko lizard sunning himself only a few feet away, remained as still as the lizard until the priest actually appeared on the pathway.

"Sister," he called out softly. "Are you there?"

"Yes, Father," she replied and rose from the leafy bower, with Sunny following.

Sister Agnes, walking with Benita and Wendy, looked like any other islander, with her brightly flowered muumuu in place of her nun's habit.

"How glad we are to see you, Sunny," Wendy said, reaching out to hug her.

"We thought something terrible had happened to you," Benita added, "when you weren't in the hut this morning."

"Evidently something terrible would have happened if Sister Birghitta hadn't spirited me away."

The three nurses set off together, apart from the natives. Matt and Grainger were on individual conveyances similar to an Indian travois, a platform fastened to poles that dragged on the ground behind the men who could walk— Brogdon, Rehoboth, Father Waal, and Heinman.

Alerted to the raiding party by Sister Birghitta, Father Waal increased his pace, hurrying them along without stopping to rest. He cautioned them to be quiet, as well.

Keeping up the steady walk, they finally reached the edge of the mission village.

From a distance, the village looked undisturbed. But as they approached the compound, Father Waal stopped. Spread in the pathway at the entrance was a dead parrot, with its neck obviously broken and its beautiful tail feathers strewn on the ground beside it.

Father Waal removed the harness from around his chest. A great sadness came over his face as he walked to the bird and gently lifted it from the ground. "Poor Kira. I should never have left you alone."

He placed the bird on a palm frond and walked back to the travois to take up the harness. But Matt, with the help of the poles Brogdon had found for him the previous day, stood up. "I can walk the rest of the way, Father," Matt said. "Attend to your pet."

The mission village was deserted when they entered. With Father Waal burying the bird, Sisters Birghitta and Agnes led them to the priest's quarters, where they sat and rested on the small verandah.

"Did you actually see the Japanese, Sunny?" Brogdon asked.

"Yes. There were twelve of them. They passed within a few feet of our hiding place, and then disappeared toward the beach. Later, I heard the motor of a launch,"

"Probably going back across the channel to Tulagi," Matt said.

"We're lucky, then, that we didn't meet them on the trail," Wendy said. "That would have been disastrous."

"Yes. They sound so barbaric. Just look what they did to Father Waal's bird." Benita's voice was sympathetic.

Joining them on the verandah, Father Waal corrected her. "It wasn't the Japanese who killed poor Kira."

"Then who did?"

"One of Kelia's men."

At his answer, a sudden wave of fear swept over Sunny, causing her to shudder despite the afternoon heat. "And the reason?" she asked, afraid to hear the answer, yet certain of what he was going to say.

A worried Father Waal looked at the young woman still wearing the nun's habit. Her pale moonbeam hair was hidden, but not the brilliant topaz eyes. He had no wish to alarm her, yet her life was in imminent danger, "To show Kelia's displeasure that I kept a certain prize from him."

"Sunny," Wendy affirmed, "I saw the way the chief was looking at you. And I knew he wanted you for his woman."

Neither Sister Birghitta nor Father Waal corrected her. And Sunny remained silent, too.

Later that afternoon, Father Waal decided that he must take the young nurse high in the hills to the copra plantation. He knew Kelia's men would be back, and the small group could not protect her. The mission village was too vulnerable.

Brogdon, also feeling they were in a vulnerable place, but more because of the Japanese than the natives, finished the meal the sisters had prepared.

"I think we'll have to find another place to go until we're rescued," he said to the group seated at the large table. "We can't stay here forever. It puts Father Waal and the sisters in too much danger."

Sister Agnes, dressed again in her nun's habit, broke her usual silence. "I remember when Giles Canupp, the coastwatcher in the hills, rescued a downed flyer not long ago. He sent a message out on his radio and a few days later, a submarine appeared in the lagoon to pick up the man."

That was clearly the best news that Brogdon had heard. Trying to keep the excitement out of his voice, he asked, "Where do I find this Canupp fellow?"

"He left Guadalcanal almost a month ago," Sister Agnes answered.

"But there's another coastwatcher farther up in the hills," Sister Birghitta said. "I've never seen him, but Father Waal has."

"Then he'll have a radio, too," Brogdon said. He and Matt

looked at each other. They still had a chance to get off the island alive.

That afternoon, as Sunny slept soundly in the *fale*, despite the heavy downpour of rain, Father Waal was in conference with Matt Willoughby and Hank Brogdon, the two ranking naval officers.

"I'll leave my pistol with you, Mr. Brogdon, while I take the young woman to the copra plantation," Father Waal explained.

"And do you think she will be safe there, for the time being?" Matt asked. Silently, he swore at his broken leg that left him almost immobile and unable to defend Sunny, who had risked her life earlier to save him.

"Yes. It's the only thing to do, because of Kelia. After the coastwatcher sends the message, she can stay there until word comes that you will be rescued. Then, she can join you at the appointed hour."

"The rest of us can't stay here at the mission for long, though," Brogdon began.

"That's true. I've decided we'll move inland as soon as I get back. There's a village not too far from here, where the natives are still friendly."

"But are they civilized?" a doubting Matt asked.

"More so than Kelia, who's fast falling back into his old ways. But you must remember, this is a different world, where at least forty dialects are spoken and one tribe's culture is alien to another. I daresay there're natives in the interior, far over the ridge, who've never seen another tribe, much less a white man."

"The Japanese will change that," Brogdon said. "They seem to be invading every island along the Slot."

"What they've seen of the Japanese, the natives don't like. That's why Kelia didn't butcher all of you in the lagoon."

Awakened again from a sound sleep, Sunny sat up and tied her shoes. Then she stood and held her arms up for the nun's habit to go over her head again.

There was no time to say good-bye to Matt or any of the others, except Wendy and Benita, before Father Waal swept her surreptitiously out of the village. He chose a back route that led them through the rough buildings that housed the remaining animals, and on into the jungle beyond. If anyone were watching the gates, he would not see them passing through.

Shortly after they were gone, a small black man suddenly appeared in the middle of the compound.

Seeing the native, Wendy became afraid. "Is that one of Kelia's men?" she asked Sister Birghitta, standing beside her.

"No. That's Patingo, coming for his wife's medicine. I'd better go to the dispensary to meet him."

A relieved Wendy sat down on the mat. "Benita, I wish I were back on the hospital ship, don't you?"

She nodded. "Maybe they'll send a rescue plane for us within the next few days."

"Wouldn't that be wonderful?"

"How's your hand, Wendy?"

"Sore. I wish I had some sulfa powder to sprinkle on it. Heinman could use some, too. I noticed his arm is already swollen."

"And Grainger's feet are infected again."

"I hate to say it, but I didn't like him much on the raft. Now that we're on the island, he doesn't seem quite so obnoxious."

"Well, your Mr. Brogdon more than made up for Grainger's shortcomings."

"You remember in Pago Pago, when you told me character isn't measured in *inches*?"

"I remember."

"Well, it is. And Brogdon's ten feet tall, as far as I'm concerned." She stopped for a moment and then continued. "But you know what surprised me most?"

"What?"

"That Matt and Sunny weren't really that close. On the raft, I mean."

"It's a little difficult to live out your fantasies with a four-day growth of beard and your stomach growling from hunger. Perhaps it's better that they saw each other at their worst."

"Yes. I guess it's hard to stay on a pedestal all the time. And Sunny *did* look different with greasy black hair, didn't she?"

"Now, let's not get too catty, Wendy," Benita cautioned. "As I remember, you didn't look so glamorous, yourself."

"Oh, Benita, why are we talking like this—not even making sense. I'm scared, Benita. Scared the Japanese will come. Scared we won't ever get off this island."

"Hush! We've come this far. We've just got to believe that things will turn out all right. If Sunny gets a radio message through tonight, then help will soon be on the way."

"I'll have to remember that. Especially tonight, with Sunny gone. I miss her already."

On the trail that climbed steadily to the higher elevation, Sunny followed the tall, gaunt priest. The two were both dressed in black. And once again, to avoid dirtying the hem of his cassock, Father Waal hitched it above the tops of his brogans. And Sunny did likewise to the habit. On her arm she carried the basket the two sisters had given her with Madeleine's tattered uniform, rescued from the lagoon.

She had not put a marker on the beach in Madeleine's memory. Too much had happened at once—the strafing by the patrol plane and their struggle to get ashore. And she hoped that the natives had given Sleepy Joe a proper burial.

In the quiet of the late afternoon, as the evening shadows began to gather, Sunny thought of her mother. She would be frantic with worry; she and her father would have heard about the hospital ship by now. But if the coastwatcher could send out a message, it wouldn't be long before they knew she had survived.

Gradually the jungle came alive with sounds of animals rustling through the dried leaves, and brightly plummaged birds sounding off alarms from tree to tree as the intruders passed through their aerie. Spectacular with color, the surroundings were both beautiful and dangerous.

They came to the edge of the destroyed plantation where Giles Canupp had lived. Vines encircled the ruins, coaxing them to join the jungle, to deny that the spot had ever been cultivated and manicured in the style of a colonial settler. As the two passed by the ruins, a wild creature left its newly found home and scurried across their path.

"What's that?" Sunny asked in a whisper as she stepped back.

"Merely a bush rat," Father Waal replied. And with his haphazard features taking on an amused expression, he added, "It's more afraid of you than you are with him. So he won't bother you."

At that moment, Sunny thought of Kirk Singleton, and wished he were with her to see it. He had always bragged about his Texas grasshoppers and other animals that were always larger than anyone else's; his stories always taller tales than anyone else's.

For one brief moment, she lifted her eyes to the darkening sky. "Please, God, let Singleton still be alive," she prayed.

"Did you say something, Miss Fitzpatrick?" the priest inquired, glancing over his shoulder.

"No, Father. I was only thinking out loud."

He nodded and returned to his brisk pace.

In the thickening twilight, with the sounds and smells magnified around him, Alex Ramsay sat on the screened verandah and smoked his pipe. He now had another native scout, along with Timi You and Obadiah, as part of the trusted team that watched the channel and monitored his section of the island.

They had made a charmed circle around the approach to Bohorok, the plantation house, as the more cautious and ferocious natives did with their village compounds—layers of dried, hollow bamboo sticks that went off as loudly as firecrackers when stepped upon by a man. Animals could come and go without setting off the trap, unless it was an extremely large animal, such as a wild boar. Only one place had been left free—a silent escape if Alex should have to leave the house in a hurry.

A few hours before, the native with the pidgin-English name of All-Same-Barrel had returned with news of a raft being strafed by a Japanese plane farther down the coast. Only one dead man was found on the beach, and the remnants of coconut shells strewn on the sand. If there had been survivors, they had vanished. But that was not surprising. Landing parties of Japanese were becoming more common every day.

A loud noise erupted—a bamboo stick. Immediately, Alex dashed into the house to retrieve extra shells for his pistol. He hid along one side of the house, while the natives took up their positions, decided on earlier—Obadiah with his wicked *kukri* knife; All-Same-barrel with his double-barreled shotgun, a relic given to him by Giles Canupp, and Timi You with a pistol and a long, slender knife stuck into his lap-lap.

Knowing that it was dangerous to come onto the grounds of Bohorok in the dark, the priest said, "Wait here, Miss Fitzpatrick. I'll go ahead."

The landscape gave no hint that a house was anywhere near. The jungle had encroached gradually on Bohorok, and Alex had done nothing to clear it away, for the foliage provided the camouflage for his teleradio station.

Sunny swallowed. "Father, I hate the dark," she confessed. "Please don't be gone long."

Walking closer, Father Waal began to whistle very softly, Sunny, behind him, recognized the first line of "Onward Christian Soldiers." Almost immediately, the second line was returned.

Timi You, hidden to the left of Alex, also heard the signal and recognized the priest. He relaxed his hand on his pistol and slipped from the hiding place, to circle behind the call. He wanted to make sure the priest had not been followed.

He came in the darkness, his tattooed face, his dark, glistening body bare except for the lap-lap. Seeing another figure, he crept soundlessly to get a better glimpse, and in his hand he held the long, thin dagger.

Uneasy at being left alone, even for a few minutes, Sunny watched the darkness and listened for the least sound. She turned her head and saw the native staring at her.

Certain that he was one of Kelia's men, Sunny's only thought was to escape capture. With the native blocking her path in the direction Father Waal had gone, Sunny raced downward through the jungle. Within minutes the jungle had swallowed her, but she kept running through the dark, without stopping to rest.

Chapter 23

AS HE RECOGNIZED FATHER WAAL EMERGING INTO THE clearing, Alex Ramsay put his pistol back in its holster and left his hiding place to meet the priest.

"Good evening, Father. I'm surprised to see you about this late."

"I've come on urgent business, Mr. Ramsay."

"Then let's go onto the verandah."

The priest shook his head and remained in the clearing. "I have brought someone with me—to seek sanctuary with you until she can leave the island. That is, if you will take her in."

Alex hesitated. Bohorok's strength lay in its being hidden, with few people knowing of its existence. Alex felt the situation must be grave for the priest to risk making a long trip at night.

"A woman?" Alex inquired, making certain that he had heard correctly.

"Yes. A very brave one, whose life is in mortal danger at this very moment."

Thinking he meant one of the French nuns who'd refused to leave the island, Alex replied, "Then of course I can't refuse, can I? Where is she?"

"Waiting beyond the clearing. I'll go and get her."

"All right. Take Obadiah with you," he advised.

The native, still on guard, appeared at Alex's words, and followed Father Waal as he retraced his steps.

With his hands slapping at a mosquito, Alex hurried back onto the verandah to await the priest's return. But it was Timi You who returned, instead.

"Masta," he said, with a worried expression. "Nun run away in jungle."

"What do you mean, Timi You?"

"I look for Japanese soldiers. Make sure they not follow Father. I see nun. She see Timi You. Run away."

"Don't worry, Timi You. It wasn't your fault. Father Waal will find her."

Timi You shook his head. "No time soon."

The native was right. For an hour, Alex remained on the verandah, but no one else returned—neither Obadiah, nor the priest. Alex began to get worried. If the sister were in such danger, why did the priest leave her alone to begin with? Why had he not risked bringing her into the clearing with him?

Alex stood up to go inside. The moon, rising higher in the sky, brought light to the edge of the clearing, and in its shadows, a figure appeared, carefully picking her way toward the house.

In one great rush, Sunny sped across the open ground, past the flowering vines, and bounded up the steps to the verandah. She saw the man standing up and ran toward him. In a hoarse whisper, she begged, "Please help me. Kelia's man is after me."

"It's all right, Sister. You're safe here," he assured her. He reached out to touch her shoulder, to calm her. "You mustn't be afraid."

She continued to tremble as her breath came in uneven gasps.

He led her inside and struck a match to light the lamp. And in the wick's sudden flare, he saw the brilliant topaz eyes staring at him. His hand, in an awkward motion, hit the lamp and almost overturned it.

Unbelieving, they stared at each other. "Amanda?"

"Alex?"

"What are you doing here, on Guadalcanal?" he demanded.

"The *Good Hope* was torpedoed. But you—I thought you'd gone back to England."

He motioned for her to sit at the table. "Would you like something to drink?"

She shook her head. "I can't stay. I have to find Father Waal." She turned as if to go, but Alex reached out to stop her.

"Sit down," he ordered. "You're in no condition to go traipsing about in the jungle at this time of night."

"But Father Waal—"

"...Will return here with one of my native boys when they can't find you. Timi You," he called. "Bring two glasses and a bottle of whiskey."

Once Sunny sat at the table, she knew she would be unable to get up for a long time. The muscles in her legs trembled, and she became aware of a great weakness now that her adrenaline no longer prompted her to run for her life. Yet, when Timi You appeared with the whiskey, Sunny tried to stand, for the native who'd put her to flight was coming toward her.

"This is my trusted scout, Timi You," Alex said. "I believe you saw him earlier tonight?"

Seeing the apologetic look on the man's face, Sunny realized she had made a mistake. He was not one of Kelia's men, after all. "I thought he was someone else," she managed to say.

"He didn't mean to scare you, Amanda. He was every whit as surprised to see you as you were to see him. But he needed to make sure that no one had followed the priest up the trail."

"Timi You sorry," he said, placing the two glasses and the bottle on the table. "Not want to scare Sister."

When Alex and Sunny were alone again, Alex said,

"Now tell me what happened. And why are you in such danger?"

Taking a sip of the whiskey, Sunny felt her throat catch fire. But the whiskey served its intended purpose, and soon she had relaxed enough to begin her story.

"I'm almost embarrassed to tell you. It seems the native chieftain, Kelia, who rescued us in the lagoon, admires my hair."

Alex's eyebrow went up in a questioning gesture.

"…So much so, that he wants my head."

"My God! How bloody barbaric."

"Not only that, but dangerous for my neck. That's why Father Waal spirited me away from him. But he knows we went to the mission village. Father Waal hoped that you would hide me until a ship or sub came to pick us up. But now, of course, I can't stay here…"

"Why do you say that?"

"I didn't realize that *you* are the coastwatcher."

"You would prefer the shelter of a total stranger?"

"Yes."

"And may I ask why?"

"We're not friends, Alex Ramsay. I'm sure you would resent my being around, even for a few days."

"Allow me to decide that, Amanda Fitzpatrick."

Ignoring his last comment, she asked, "How soon can you send out a message for rescue?"

"First thing in the morning. You should be off the island in several days."

Father Waal returned to Bohorok, with Obadiah. When he saw Sunny seated at the table with Alex Ramsay, he said, "Thank heavens you're safe." He did not question her disappearance.

"Timi You, another glass for Father Waal."

The priest joined them. "Miss Fitzpatrick has told you of their hope for rescue?"

"Yes. I've already promised to send a message on the teleradio."

"I had word three days ago, Mr. Ramsay, that the Japanese executed the nuns at Rabaul. I want no such thing to happen here. So when the rescue boat comes, I would like to send Sisters Birghitta and Agnes with them. And a Chinese family too—a mother and her two children—if there's room."

"That can be arranged."

Father Waal quickly downed the rest of his drink and stood. "Just send Obadiah to me when you have word of the rescue boat," he asked. "I'll have everyone gathered together."

"It's too late, Father, for you to travel tonight. Stay here, and you can take back the message with you in the morning."

He hesitated briefly. Then he smiled. "A good idea. Thank you." And he sat down again at the table.

Sunny, opposite him, felt relief. She did not want him to walk in the jungle at night. Neither did she want to stay alone with Alex at Bohorok. But by morning, certain that rescue was on the way, she would take her chances with Kelia and return to the village with the priest.

That night, the higher altitude was much more comfortable than the humidity of the village below. Surrounded by a mosquito net, companion to the one in the next bedroom where Alex slept, Sunny fell into bed and was soon asleep. She had stayed up late; for neither she nor Father Waal had eaten. After the meal, she listed the names of the survivors for the message to be sent out.

Alex Ramsay had done it all before—for two flyers whose plane had been shot down. Sleepily, she'd listened to the discussion on the best place for the boat to come, the signal to guide the boat to the proper stretch of beach. And in her dreams that night, she saw her mother, Kenna, waiting anxiously for word of her daughter.

In the morning, Sunny was awakened by the sound of a conch shell in the distance. She sat up quickly, her pulse beating fast, as the habits of the past days warned her that she had slept too soundly — like the evening on the raft when she had fallen over the side and awakened in tepid, black water.

She knew the conch shell was a signal of some sort — a warning. Sunny threw back the mosquito netting and, slipping on the black habit, she rushed into the hallway, where she bumped into Alex.

"What's that?" she demanded.

"I'm just going to see," he answered, brushing past her to the verandah and the hidden lookout post in the tall palm tree.

Standing beneath the overlook, Alex called out, "What do you see, Obadiah" The channel revealed no ships passing by.

"Japanese patrol boat in lagoon."

"Do you see many men?"

"Heap plenty — thirty, forty."

Alex was not surprised. An hour previously, he'd sent the message over the teleradio. Now, the Japanese knew something was astir. For the rest of the day, he would maintain radio silence so his position would not be discovered.

In a few minutes, Alex had sentries stationed along the path to Bohorok. If the Japanese got that far up, he wanted to make sure he had ample warning to escape into the bush.

Sunny stood on the verandah and watched Alex return to the house.

"What did your sentry see?" Sunny asked.

"A Japanese patrol boat has landed on the beach below. They'll be searching the island for the radio."

"I'm sorry if we've put you in danger."

He dismissed her apology. "Every time we broadcast, there's a possibility we'll be discovered."

"Where is Father Waal?"

"He left early this morning to get back to the mission."

"But I was planning on going with him."

A scowl marred Alex's brow. "Have you looked at

yourself in a mirror lately? Heaven knows you're in a better condition than I was when the destroyer picked me up. But you're still in no condition to run all over this island." His voice grew harsh with a final blow to her ego. "No wonder Kelia only wanted your blonde hair. The rest of you is entirely too skinny and scratched up for any man to desire you."

She looked at the man whose beard, a sandy red shade, covered his chin, the way it had when she'd first seen him. All of those difficult days of caring for him on the hospital ship flooded her memory.

With her eyes sparkling in anger, she drew her small frame up in a haughty manner, tilted her chin, and in exact mimicry of the marquess of Dalhousie, said, "I am not one of your freaks in a side show, my lord, to be stared at..."

His hearty laugh filled the verandah. And then he caught himself. In a much quieter voice, he said, "Touché, Miss Fitzpatrick. Now go on into the kitchen and fix yourself a cup of tea."

She hesitated. "Who owns this house, Alex?"

"The copra plantation company. But I'm sure they never expect to see it again."

"Then, you think it's all right if I use some of the things in the bedroom?"

"Such as...?"

"Well, there're some cosmetics—and a comb. And I found a cotton dress."

"Use anything you want," he answered, "except the radio."

The next time Sunny saw Alex was in the evening, slightly before twilight. The Japanese patrol boat had come and gone without discovering their whereabouts. And Alex, deeming it safe, turned on the teleradio to pick up messages and news from the outside world.

Sunny stood in the doorway and listened to the sounds of static that came from a BBC broadcast. Another station, coming in loud and clear, overshadowed the first— the familiar voice of Tokyo Rose, with her excellent American accent, broadcasting to the homesick soldiers and sailors in the Pacific. It was a familiar agenda, using real names, current pop songs, and bits of news from home, designed to lower the morale of the fighting men.

Sunny left the doorway to walk onto the verandah, when the next news caused her to stop. "This is a special message to the unlucky eight from the *Good Hope* who managed to reach Guadalcanal. If you're listening out there, Amanda, Wendy, Benita, Hank, Matt, Corry, Josh, and Melvin, you might as well surrender tomorrow when Lieutenant Ishimoto returns to find you. No ship is coming to rescue you. They have forgotten you, and you'll die in the jungle if you don't surrender. And while you're thinking about that, I'll play Matt's favorite song: 'As Time Goes By.'

"On Guam yesterday—"

Alex turned off the radio and stood up. "You heard?"

"Yes. It's frightening, isn't it, that she even knows our names?"

"She's good at that. But she's not always right. So don't let what she said tonight bother you unduly." He did not mention his suspicion that the Japanese had broken the code.

Despite her worried face, Sunny looked like a different person. The long rest had relieved the haunted look around her eyes. Dressed in the yellow cotton dress, with straw sandals, and the pale pink lipstick giving added color to her face, she no longer looked like some waif. Even her sunburned nose was faintly disguised by powder.

Late that afternoon, Sunny had decided to make herself useful. She realized she had upset the routine of the plantation house; had invaded the coastwatcher's privacy and created more work for them all—which kept Timi You out of the kitchen and guarding the path to Bohorok, instead.

For that reason, Sunny prepared the evening meal—an American one, slightly different from the native meal she and Father Waal had been given the evening before.

"I've fixed us a before-dinner drink, Alex. Where would you like it?

"On the verandah?"

"Yes. I'll bring it out."

A few minutes later, a clean-shaven Alex sat in the bamboo chair and stared out in the direction of Tulagi. But visibility was bad, due to the threatening storm. It was still quiet, but in the distance, streaks of lightning zigzagged across the sky that was now colored in gray-hued tones of purple. The banana trees around the plantation house began to bend, while the tall palm tree that served as a lookout rustled its fronds in signal to the rising breeze.

Alex stood briefly when Sunny returned to the verandah. She placed the tray on the bamboo table between the two chairs, and then sat in the one opposite Alex.

"Your drink, my lord," she offered with a smile.

"Thank you, my lady." He took the tall glass offered him and smiled also.

They sipped their drinks in silence and watched the darkening landscape, the large white clouds gathered and driven by the wind like some fleet convoy skimming through the sky.

When they had finished their drinks, Sunny took the tray. "Dinner will be ready in a few minutes. I'll call you when it's on the table."

Alex nodded. Neither one had felt like talking. They had gone through the motions of civility. Yet, Alex sensed a sadness in the young nurse. Despite his encouragement, Tokyo Rose had done her damage. Amanda Fitzpatrick was too intelligent not to realize that she might never see the outside world again.

Chapter 24

THAT EVENING, WITH THE RAIN WHIPPING ONTO THE verandah, Sunny and Alex sat at the table in the large dining area and ate their dinner by candlelight.

Around them were the mementoes of another family, long gone—the pictures in tarnished brass frames; the embroidery, half finished, in a basket by an easy chair, as if the woman of the house had merely put it down to check on her native servants, or perhaps a crying child.

Alex, watching Sunny from across the table, felt the ghosts in the house as he ate his evening meal.

"You don't have to tell me, Amanda. I can taste the difference. I know Timi You had nothing to do with dinner tonight."

"Oh, but he did. He killed the chicken for me. I could never have done that." Then she tilted her head, as if to challenge her own last statement. "But then, perhaps I could. I never thought I could eat raw fish, but that's the only thing that kept us alive on the raft." She smiled. "A need to survive can make you do almost anything, can't it?"

He nodded. "The instinct for survival is a great equalizer, Amanda. Thousands of years of civilization can be wiped out in an instant. And we become no better than the most barbaric tribe."

"How did you survive on the open sea, Alex?" she asked.

"As you well know, it was touch and go. But I suppose I owe my life to the bird that flew right into my face. Its meat lasted for three days. Like Timi You," he added, "I had no hesitation in killing it."

They returned to the food on their plates, and became silent once more. There was a kindred feeling between them—no longer antagonism, or a wish to lash out. They had suffered through the same life-threatening experience, and now, each was making an obeisance to a more civilized way of life.

The soft glow of the candlelight erased the scratches on Sunny's face. In the simple yellow cotton dress, she was extremely feminine looking. Her hair, newly washed, curled of its own accord, giving her a chic look that belied the earlier, unruly appearance. Now, she resembled more the young woman at the governor-general's dinner in Sydney.

That was the first time he'd seen her out of uniform— that evening when he'd arranged for her to be his dinner partner. He had barely escaped escorting the big-bosomed widow of an M.P., and a titled woman in her own right, to the dining room—a breach of protocol on his part.

"Are you ready for dessert?" Sunny asked, breaking into his quiet thoughts.

"You mean there's more?"

"Of course. My specialty. You're lucky you have banana trees growing all around you."

"I don't much care for—"

"Now, don't be a spoilsport, my lord. Especially after I've gone to the trouble of transporting a recipe over ten thousand miles from home."

"A Georgia specialty?"

"No. From New Orleans. But it's still Southern—Creole. Bananas Foster," she announced.

Now came the reason for the candles at the table. She had reserved the kerosene lantern for another purpose. Alex, fascinated, watched while she blended the butter and brown sugar into the saucepan over the fire, then stirred in the bananas and poured the rum over the concoction. She set fire to the rum, and a blaze flared up quickly. With deft hands, she spooned up the flaming mixture onto the dessert plates and topped it with whipped cream made that afternoon from a tin of condensed milk.

She waited expectantly for him to sample the creation.

He took a second bite in silence. Finally, becoming impatient, she said, "Well?"

"My compliments to the chef, Amanda. I've never tasted anything so delectable."

A pleased Sunny beamed at the compliment. Then, her face took on a sadness. In a soft voice she said, "Do you think you could call me Sunny? Tokyo Rose knows where Amanda is. But just for tonight, I'd like to think she has no idea that Sunny Fitzpatrick exists."

"If you promise not to call me 'my lord' again."

"Of course, my…Alex."

When the meal was over, Sunny took the plates to the kitchen. By the time she returned to the living room, Alex had put a supply of old records on the gramophone.

"You still owe me a dance, Sunny," he said, and held out his arms.

Vulnerable to the mood that had pervaded the entire evening, Sunny responded. It was a slow, love song, and somehow Alex's arms around her brought comfort. For a short time, she could pretend that the world was a safe place. There was no war going on around her; no Tokyo Express traveling through the Slot to destroy the Allied navies; no Tokyo Rose broadcasting homesickness and despair to thousands of soldiers far from home.

She felt his lips brush her forehead, and she became aware of him as a man, gentleness and strength at the same time, while her body curved into his, their movements becoming one, no longer responding to the beat of the music, but to their own inner rhythm of desire.

His lips became more insistent, exploring her face, the curve of her neck, a tantalizing, teasing feeling that drove her to distraction.

His mouth possessed hers in the same manner that had brought her such distress in Sydney. But this time, she didn't fight him. Soft, pliant, she remained in his arms, the dance steps forgotten, while desire reached an unendurable, magnificent aching that demanded consummation.

The raucous scratch of the needle on the gramaphone brought Sunny back to reality. She opened her eyes and became aware of her surroundings. What was she doing in Alex's arms while Matt waited for her in the mission village below? She began to push away from Alex.

"Please. No more," she begged. "We shouldn't…"

"Sunny," he whispered, his voice hoarse.

"No, Alex. Please let me go."

The mood was broken. He saw the fright in her eyes and reluctantly let her go. As she left the room and sought the safety of her bedroom, Alex walked out of the house and stood on the steps. He didn't care that the rain drenched him.

At that moment, Alex regretted the circumstances that had brought Sunny Fitzpatrick into his life again. Bohorok would never be the same once she'd gone. But the sooner she left, the better off he would be, putting his mind back on his mission. He was a fool to allow the atmosphere of the stormy night to entice him into dancing with her. He reached up to feel his chin, where his beard had been until that afternoon. He'd been a fool to shave because of her. Standing on the steps in the rain, Alex talked himself out of love.

Shortly before dawn, the message came. Relayed from the control station on Malaita, the cipher contained instructions for the pickup of the eight survivors, with the other refugees. Now came the problem of getting the message to Father Waal; for if Tokyo Rose were right, they could expect another visit that day from Ishimoto.

The safest way of alerting Father Waal was to send Obadiah or All-Same-Barrel to the village. The Japanese were used to seeing the natives come and go. Obadiah had even crossed the channel to Tulagi to get firsthand news at the Japanese post. So far the Japanese camp on the northern tip of the island had not presented an undue problem to Alex. How long that would remain true, he didn't know. Probably until some native betrayed their position and led the Japanese over the rugged terrain.

Even in the short time he'd been on Guadalcanal, Alex had become aware of the change in some of the natives. They were not nearly so friendly to the Allies, since the Japanese now occupied the other islands.

After Alex sent Obadiah on the errand to the village, he heard the conch shell sound coming from the lookout. Climbing to the platform himself, Alex saw that the landing party was not merely a patrol party. Down below, he saw the landing crafts, heavy equipment being unloaded, and swarms of workers coming ashore. And a disconcerted Alex realized that an encampment and perhaps an airfield were in the works. The Japanese were on the beach to stay.

Obadiah, the Fijian, who had been baptized when he was thirteen by a Methodist missionary, still retained many of the ways of his native people. Naturally friendly, he'd left his own island and wandered along the vast chain of the Solomons—working for the white settlers when he needed money, or when he'd decided he'd traveled enough for a while.

With Wani, his best friend, he had remained on Guadalcanal to work for Giles Canupp. Now, Wani was dead. Obadiah had taken his outrigger canoe to Savo; to look for him when the old Masta had stopped broadcasting. He had found them both and buried them before returning to Guadalcanal by way of Tulagi, where he avenged their deaths. It was a foolish thing, killing the Japanese sentries, for Ishimoto had almost caught him. Only pretending not to understand had he gotten past the officer and rowed on to Guadalcanal.

He didn't like the Japanese, for they never paid the natives for their work. A little rice was about all they received for their labor. He was sorry the Japanese had more weapons and more men, for they were taking over all the islands. Soon, Masta Alex would have to move on, or risk being caught, too.

Following the path of the meandering river, Obadiah passed by the deserted houses on stilts. A crocodile, sunning himself on the riverbank, splashed into the water to catch his breakfast, while two parrots, with a warning cry, took flight to another tree.

Obadiah stopped and listened. In the distance he could hear Japanese voices and loud groaning of saws interspersed with a steady hammering against wood. Quickly climbing into a tree to get a better view, he looked down on the beach. Japanese soldiers swarmed all along the lagoon, carrying logs and lumber as they built a large landing dock out into the water — the same type of dock as Tulagi's across the channel. And they had already conscripted native labor to help them.

Obadiah climbed down and began to hurry toward the mission village. A new wariness gripped him and he became more careful. He had not worn his gun belt, for it would have been a dead giveaway if the Japanese should see him. The only weapon he carried was the knife.

He met no one on the trail. By the time he reached the mission village, the jungle appeared deceptively peaceful and quiet. No birds sang in the trees; no voices greeted him as he stood before the open gate. The village appeared to be just as deserted as the houses along the riverbank.

He knew better than to walk into the village by the gate. Darting from tree to tree, he made his way to the far corner of the mission. Sensing danger in the air, Obadiah knew that Father Waal had fled. He left the mission behind and began the trek toward the next village, the one inhabited by Sister Birghitta's people.

At the edge of the next village, the old chief sat before his leaf hut and chewed on his betel nuts. The brown stain dribbled down his chin until he took his hand and wiped it away. He barely noticed Obadiah approaching him.

"I look for Sister Birghitta," Obadiah said to the old man. "Is she in village?"

He shook his head without looking up. "All gone. Boys all gone. Japanese come for work boys. Women hide."

"And Father Waal?"

The old man didn't respond. "Boys all gone," he repeated, shaking his head. A toothless old woman, dressed in a muumuu, walked toward her husband with a basket of breadfruit. Obadiah was unable to get a response from her, either. How could he give the message to Father Waal if he couldn't find him?

Obadiah walked to a nearby palm. He shook the tree and a large coconut fell to the ground. He sat down near the old chief and his woman. With his sharp knife, he made an incision in the coconut. Once he'd satisfied his thirst, Obadiah got up and left the village.

Now, he retraced his steps toward the beach. He had to be careful when he infiltrated the work crew the Japanese had conscripted. But he needed to find out where the sister had gone. And that seemed to be his only hope of finding out—from one of the village boys.

Obadiah, blacker than most of the men on the work crew, waited until the Japanese guard had turned his head. Then, he took his place beside a young man about his own size.

In the same rhythm, he lifted the other end of the long log and helped him carry it toward one of the carpenters.

"Where is Sister Birghitta?" Obadiah whispered.

"You! Stop your talking and work," a guard yelled at him.

Ishimoto, standing by a palm, looked up at the commotion. Obadiah hung his head, but too late. The Japanese officer had spotted him.

Quickly, the young man dropped his end of the log. "In

the sand crab cave," he whispered as he bent to retrieve it.

By then, Ishimoto was standing directly over them. His face, proud and cold, glanced from one to the other.

"You have been to Tulagi," the officer said, frowning at Obadiah as if trying to remember the circumstances.

The first time at Tulagi, Obadiah had pretended not to understand the pidgin English when challenged by Ishimoto. A decided change came over the native now. He smiled and nodded. "Brought great fish," he said. "Last week. Swap for rice."

At his friendliness, Ishimoto began to relax. Momentarily accepting Obadiah's explanation, he motioned for him to continue working. The two picked up the log again and carried it toward the water. Obadiah took on an awkward gait, and Ishimoto, watching him, decided that he was probably harmless. So many of the natives looked alike. Yet, there was something about this man that still worried him.

For the rest of the morning, Ishimoto's eyes returned to Obadiah, who waited for the appropriate moment to vanish. It was while he was standing in line with the others for his handful of rice at lunchtime that Ishimoto remembered the puzzling circumstances surrounding the killing of his two sentries.

At the edge of the work area, Obadiah found a log to sit on. He looked up to see Ishimoto and a menacing looking foot soldier coming toward him. He put down his meal and, careful not to appear hurried, he deliberately made an impolite bodily noise as he strolled toward the cover of bushes.

Ishimoto and the soldier stopped. They waited for Obadiah to reappear. But the native vanished from the work camp. Fleet of foot, he raced through the jungle and headed for the cave where Sister Birghitta and the others were hiding.

Chapter 25

HANK BROGDON, DELIRIOUS WITH FEVER, LAY ON THE floor of the cave. He was oblivious to the sand crab sidling its way toward his bare arm.

Seated beside him, Josh Heinman took a stick and, with his good arm, knocked the crab against the cave wall opposite him. "These damn crabs," he barked. "They're enough to drive a man crazy."

"A woman, too," Wendy responded. "Don't leave us out."

The seven survivors, waiting for the two nuns with Father Waal from a food-foraging trip, were despondent at their current situation. Forced to hide from the Japanese, they had been taken to a cave assiduously avoided by any sane human being. Yet, it was for that reason that they were relatively safe from human harm. But that did not extend to the vermin of the island.

Benita, the only able-bodied one since Brogdon had come down with malaria, bent over to place a cool, wet cloth across the officer's brow. They had no quinine, no Atabrine left. And if they weren't rescued within the next few days, it might be too late for the entire group.

With danger all around, they had set up a twenty-four hour watch just inside the entrance to the cave.

Now, Matt Willoughby, finishing his morning watch, relinquished his place to Grainger. "Be careful with the pistol, Grainger. We don't have any bullets to spare," he reminded the man, as he turned the pistol over to him.

Using his makeshift crutches, Matt dragged himself away from the entrance and slowly progressed toward the others deeper within the cave. When he reached Brogdon and Benita, he paused.

"How is he, Benita?"

"Running a high fever," she answered, with no attempt to disguise the seriousness of his condition.

"Maybe Father Waal will bring back some quinine," Matt wished out loud. Then, he continued past the two until he reached the large mat where Rehoboth was already asleep. Holding on to a crutch, Matt lowered himself and stretched out to go to sleep.

At the entrance to the cave, a nervous Grainger, holding the group's only weapon in his hand, watched for Father Waal and the two sisters to return.

Melvin Grainger had never been brave. Even in childhood he'd stayed at home, rather than play in the park with the others. An urchin had given him a bloody nose when he was six, and it had been such a trauma to him that he had not ventured out again for a long time. But as he grew up, even his older brother had picked on him regularly.

Then he was drafted and sent overseas to fight. At one time, he'd been so scared that he almost shot himself in the foot, just to get out of the fighting. But he decided it would hurt too much. He chose, instead, to stop taking his Atabrine tablets, in hopes he would come down with malaria or dengue fever. That hadn't happened, either. He was so busy trying to devise a way to get out of the swampy jungle, he'd forgotten orders to change into dry socks. With his boots wet for days at the time, he'd developed jungle rot. And that had been his passport to the hospital ship and safety. Only, the ship had been sunk. And he was not safe.

He was as afraid of the natives as he was of the Japanese—especially Kelia's men who had stalked them from the time Sunny Fitzpatrick had disappeared. And he was deathly afraid that his own shrunken head would wind up in Kelia's leaf hut, too. Grainger, thinking of the double danger, gripped the pistol handle even tighter.

Obadiah had almost reached the entrance to the sand crab cave when he stopped. He began to whistle softly the signal for Father Waal—the first line of "Onward Christian Soldiers." But the second line never came. Instead, a shot rang out. Surprised, Obadiah clutched his side and fell.

With the sound of the shot, Matt awoke. He grabbed his makeshift crutches and dragged himself toward the entrance to the cave.

"What's wrong, Grainger?" Matt demanded.

"A native peering from the bush. I think I got him."

"Damn you, Grainger. Put the pistol down. I thought I told you to be extremely careful."

"But he might have been…"

"Perfectly harmless," Matt finished. "And you've alerted the entire island to our whereabouts."

Matt looked out of the cave. He saw no one. And yet, he heard a faint whistle, weak, but no mistaking what it was—a hymn taught by the missionaries. Matt, standing in the full sun, softly whistled the same tune. He listened, and when he heard the response, he went out to look for the native.

Obadiah lay beside a rotted log. By the time Matt found him, he was bleeding badly. "I'm sorry," Matt whispered as he looked down at Obadiah.

"Father Waal," Obadiah gasped. "Message from Masta."

"I'll take it to him."

"Ship come at mouth of river—midnight. Two days from now. Put white flag on beach for him to see."

An angry Matt Willoughby could hardly contain himself. Grainger had not only shot an innocent native, but a valuable one, with a message for their rescue. He hobbled back inside the cave where Grainger was watching. "Get a mat to bring this man inside the cave. He's bleeding to death."

Within a few minutes, the two nurses, with Heinman and Rehoboth, had carried Obadiah inside with them. While Benita worked hard to stop his bleeding, Wendy returned to the outside of the cave, where she began to clean up the telltale signs of blood that had dropped from the mat.

She spread fresh palm leaves over the dirt and, taking some of the wild sweet potato cuttings, she hurriedly planted them in the more worn spaces. With the help of the afternoon rain, their hiding place could still be secure, despite Grainger's mistake.

Father Waal, gathering breadfruit and bananas, heard the shot from the general direction of the cave. He immediately signaled for the sisters to take the baskets, while he picked up the large jug of spring water resting on the level rock.

The three hurried down the path from the ruins of Giles Canupp's burned-out plantation.

"Do you think the Japanese have found them, Father?" a worried Sister Agnes inquired.

"No, I don't think so. There was only one shot. But I pray that nothing is seriously wrong."

"A snake, perhaps?" Sister Birghitta suggested.

"Perhaps," the priest responded, gathering speed as he trudged downhill. A group of small rocks dislodged from the path, and Father Waal stumbled, splashing some of the water as he reached out to steady himself.

The priest regretted taking the seven survivors to such an inhospitable place as the cave, but they were all lucky to have escaped being found in the village when the Japanese came. With God's help, they would soon be off the island, along with the Chinese mother and her two children, still hiding with the other women from the village.

Father Waal had planned to return to Bohorok as soon as it was dark. If there were a message waiting, Alex wouldn't know where to deliver it.

By the time the priest and the two nuns reached the opening to the cave, Matt had taken charge of the pistol and was again keeping watch.

"I'm afraid I have bad news for you, Father," Matt informed him.

"What is it?"

"One of the natives—Obadiah—was accidentally shot."

High in the hills, above the cave, the day grew dim. Like a repeat of the previous evening, the soft white cumulus clouds began to gather on the rising wind.

Alex Ramsay was worried. Obadiah had not returned. And he had a strange feeling that something was wrong. Had Obadiah gotten through to deliver the vital message to Father Waal and the members of the *Good Hope*?

For the entire day, the sentries—Timi You and All-Same-Barrel—had watched the activity on the beach below. Now, only a skeleton crew was left at the site. The others had returned across the channel to Tulagi. Relieved that the Japs had not come to stay—at least for a while yet—Alex felt that Sunny and the others still stood a good chance of getting off the island safely. That is, if Obadiah had been able to deliver the message.

After taking one final look at the lagoon, Alex walked back inside the plantation house and went to the teleradio. As much as he hated to say it, he got more telling news from Tokyo Rose than from the Allied broadcasts. He glanced at his watch and turned on the radio as thousands of Allies all over the South Pacific did the same.

Setting the table for dinner, Sunny heard the familiar voice and hurried into the radio room to listen. All day she had avoided Alex because of the previous evening. But now, she was in control of her emotions. Two more nights and she would be with Matt and the others.

Sunny sat down in the chair beside Alex. Busy listening, he barely acknowledged her presence.

Tokyo Rose began her broadcast in the usual way, with her soft, seductive voice commiserating with the homesick soldiers. More songs than news, the program continued at a leisurely pace. And Sunny stood up to return to the kitchen and check on dinner. She had gotten to the door when she heard her own name.

"I have a special condolence for Lieutenant Amanda Fitzpatrick, wherever she is tonight...."

Sunny whirled from the doorway and rushed back to the radio set.

"The High Command has informed me, Amanda, that your father, Brigadier General John Ireland Fitzpatrick, was shot down over the Coral Sea three days ago. What a pity, Amanda, that he never knew you survived the sinking of your ship. Now he's dead because of you. And so, in your sorrow, Amanda Fitzpatrick, I dedicate this next song..."

"Sunny."

"No. It can't be true."

Alex switched off the radio. But Sunny ran from the room before he could stop her. Forgotten were the meal on the stove—everything but the terrible news she'd just heard. Her fault. Her fault. Out onto the verandah and down the steps into the darkness Sunny ran, with her hands over her ears as if to erase the tragic news that raced through her brain. "Oh, Dad. Dad, I'm sorry. I didn't mean to hurt you."

She collapsed by a palm tree at the edge of the plantation grounds, sobs wracking her body.

Alex found her and gathered her in his arms to comfort her. "It might not be true, Sunny. She might be making it up."

"No, he would have been searching for me. I know it. And I caused his death. I'll never forgive myself."

An angry Alex Ramsay spoke harshly. "Stop it, Sunny. Your father was a soldier. If he's dead—and I said *if*—then it was done by the Japanese, not you."

She refused to be consoled. Oblivious to the swarm of mosquitoes, she lay with her head against the trunk of the palm, until Alex, swearing at the biting insects, picked up Sunny and carried her back into the house.

Aware only of her grief, Sunny did not protest Alex's

arms. She didn't notice the charred, burned odor coming from the kitchen. It was left up to Alex to take the scorched pot from the fire, and then return to the sofa where he'd placed her. Trying to get through to a weeping Sunny, Alex repeated. "He was a soldier, Sunny. With a soldier's duty — to face death every day. You're not responsible…."

"No, Alex. He was safe. It was only because of me that he died. I can't ever face my mother — to see *her* grief. And Jack won't forgive me either. I failed them, Alex. I failed them. It's all my fault."

The rains began, with a sudden downpour upon the roof. And the sky, darkening, burst forth in a clatter of thunder, with flashes lighting up the heavens like some fierce battle between Titans — frightening, startling in its dramatic intensity.

The wind slammed the doors to the verandah shut, and the candles on the table flickered and then were snuffed out, leaving Sunny bereft, with darkness all around her.

Alex reached out and held her close, to comfort her. Yet, no words served to stop the anguished groan that came from her lips. Alex, unable to stand the sound any longer, covered her mouth with his, mingling his breath with hers, to breathe new life into the woman he loved.

His need became hers, and in her sorrow, Sunny clung to him and did not resist the passion that grew in deep measure with her anguish, an aching that intensified and was made into such exquisite, sweet sorrow.

In concert with the wildness of the wind, Alex Ramsay, marquess of Dalhousie, claimed what had been his from the beginning of time. Before God, he took the woman in his arms as his, like an ancestor chieftain of his ancient clan. He needed no words beyond his own, spoken in Gaelic, to make her his wife.

In the darkness, he lifted Sunny from the sofa and carried her to his bed. With the lightning invading the room, Alex made love to the woman who had haunted him for so long. Sorrow and passion ignited into an unquenchable fire, building an altar of flames in which they were both consumed. The raging storm outside was of little consequence.

Later, Sunny lay quietly in Alex's arms. She should have felt guilty at her own behavior, for she had done nothing to stop Alex. She removed her arm from around his neck and rolled onto her side. Alex whispered in her ear, "Are you sorry, Sunny?"

Sunny's reply was languid, distant, as if another person were speaking. "I should be," she acknowledged. "But strangely, I'm not."

"It wouldn't make any difference. You and I both know it was going to happen between us, sooner or later."

"Yes," she admitted. "I think I knew it the second day on the hospital ship. That's why I fought so hard against you. Strange, isn't it, that it took the loss of a loved one to make me realize why I was always so antagonistic to you?"

"Sunny, after the war—"

She put her hand over his mouth to stop the words. "No recriminations—and no promises, Alex. That's the way I want it to be."

"But I feel a responsibility for you now."

She propped herself up on her elbow and gazed into his strong, sharp-angled face. Forcing herself not to touch him, she said, "Your responsibility is your job here. Mine is to care for the wounded. Beyond that, we have no responsibility—especially to each other."

When his eyes protested, Sunny lay down again and, without looking at him, said, "Don't make too much of this night, Alex Ramsay. It could just as easily have been Matt as you."

"I don't believe you. You were never in love with Matt Willoughby."

"Who mentioned the word 'love'?" Sunny inquired. "You didn't hear me say it tonight, did you?" Before he could answer, she continued, "Grow up, Alex Ramsay. A woman has the same needs as a man. And she certainly doesn't have to be in love to go to bed with him."

Alex sat up on the side of the bed. He didn't trust himself to speak, but Sunny felt his anger. She reached out for the discarded yellow dress and fled toward her bedroom.

She lay awake until morning, careful to keep her crying from being heard in the next room.

In the morning, Alex left Bohorok. The noise of the hammers and saws resumed on the beach and grew to a frenzied sound that penetrated the island. Alex stopped along a ledge and, using his binoculars, he watched Father Waal carefully picking his way to the ruins of Canupp's place. On his shoulder, he carried a water jug, and Alex assumed rightly that he was heading for the pure spring hidden behind the bougainvillea vines that entwined the giant banyan tree.

Looking for Obadiah was a priority for Alex, for he knew he wanted no words with Sunny that morning. She had made it clear that the evening spent with him had been a mere dalliance, to be taken lightly by them both. Now, he was glad that he had spoken in Gaelic—that she was not aware of the extent of his emotions—to call her his wife at the moment of consummation.

But in the past few hours, he had realized she was right. In little less than two days she would be off the island, and then as a coastwatcher, temporarily assigned to the Australian navy, he could get his mind back on the reason for his being on Guadalcanal in the first place. And it certainly wasn't to serve as lover and protector for a shipwrecked nurse.

With care, Alex negotiated the remainder of the path until he was hidden beyond the spring. From his vantage point, he could see the priest looking vaguely from left to right, yet having no idea that he was being watched.

Just when Alex was ready to call out to Father Waal, his eyes saw a slight movement of branches that had nothing to do with the wind. A native, moving to the other side of a tree, also watched the priest. Carefully removing the pistol from its holster, Alex remained hidden while the black-robed man bent over to dip water from the spring.

The native made no effort to become known to Father Waal. Like Alex, he remained hidden. The tattoos on the man's body proclaimed a more militant tribe, fiercer looking than either Obadiah or Timi You. Baffled, Alex wondered why he was keeping tabs on the priest.

Then, Alex remembered the reason Sunny was hiding at Bohorok. Yes, that must be it. Through Father Waal, the native hoped to find the woman whom his chief coveted.

Like a chameleon blending into the landscape, Alex didn't stir. Finally, Father Waal picked up the water jug, slung it over his shoulder, and retraced his steps. Watching him, Alex knew he would have to warn the priest not to come to Bohorok before the survivors left the island. Nothing must go wrong. For his own peace of mind, Alex knew he had to get Sunny off the island as soon as possible.

Down the trail Father Waal went, with the native a short distance behind him. And with the same amount of space between them, Alex Ramsay tracked the native.

Chapter 26

IN THE COMFORTABLE TWO-BEDROOM APARTMENT IN Melbourne, Kenna Fitzpatrick sat in an easy chair and gazed out the window to the street below. She had been in the same position for an hour, the cup of cold tea untouched at her side.

Her life had turned into a nightmare. First, Sunny. And now, her husband, Irish. Sunny was still alive. But not Irish. The sea had claimed him, with only the wreckage of the plane where he'd gone down. At that moment, her only consolation was knowing that one wreck had not been responsible for the other; that Irish's mission had nothing to do with the sinking of the *Good Hope*, or the search for survivors.

On the table, the official notification lay—the same dreaded telegram—the same color paper—that she'd received in two separate wars. One for her brother, the other for her husband.

She had not accepted her brother's death in France. Something had made her keep up hope that he was alive. But now, over twenty years later, there was no such spark that even faintly lived in her heart. Irish was dead. She felt it, a burden that weighted her down, like some monstrous rock. And to add insult to injury were the words spoken in kindness an hour earlier by the young officer bringing the official telegram, corroborating the earlier report.

"You won't have to vacate the apartment immediately, Mrs. Fitzpatrick. General Milton, who's to take your husband's place, won't get here before the end of next week."

Then he added, "When you feel like talking, just call me. I'll send some men over to help you with your packing. And I'll arrange your transportation back to the States."

There were few personal effects in the furnished apartment for Kenna to pack. Most of the furniture she'd had in Pearl was in storage. Only the few pictures, Irish's uniforms, and her own clothes remained. Giving up the apartment would not be that heartrending, except for its being the last place shared with Irish. But leaving Australia while Sunny was still to be rescued would be impossible.

The faint knock on the door went unchallenged. Kenna remained seated, until the persistent sound finally prompted her to do something about it. How she longed for Mattie, the large black woman at home.

For two days there had been a steady stream of visitors offering their condolences. Most of the high-ranking officers had already made their official calls and left. But if Mattie had been with her, or even the island girl, Kahani, the visitors could have left their calling cards on the silver tray, rather than come face-to-face with the grieving widow.

Kenna rose from the chair and unlocked the door.

"May I come in?"

Standing before her was Alisdair Shannon, the man she hadn't seen since her trip to Darwin.

"Yes, of course," she said woodenly, and stepped back for him to enter. She walked ahead of him and indicated the chair before the fireplace where an anemic-looking flame struggled to bring heat to the room. "Will you have a cup of tea?" she inquired. "I was just going to heat up the water."

He glanced over at the full cup beside the twin chair. "You sit down," he urged. "And I'll fix us both a cup."

"But you don't know—"

"Sit down, Kenna," he repeated. "I can find what I need." He removed his sheepskin jacket and laid it across the chair. Then, he took her cup to the kitchen with him while Kenna did as she was told, taking her place once more in the chair that faced the window.

In a short time, he returned, with not only the cups of tea but a tray of sandwiches.

"Kenna, I'm sorry. I didn't know until this morning."

"How did you find out?"

"I had an appointment with Martin in Canberra. He's the one who told me. So I flew on to Melbourne when I'd finished my business there."

"Thank you, Shan, for coming."

He held the plate of sandwiches before her. She shook her head, but her refusal didn't seem to matter. He continued holding out the plate. Knowing how stubborn the man was, she finally took one and laid it on her plate. "Eat, Kenna," he commanded, still not satisfied. And so Kenna, who'd eaten nothing all day, took a bite.

Alisdair Shannon, with a special aura about him, filled the room with his presence, as Irish had done when he was alive. His hair, gray at the temples, was slightly ruffled from the wind. But his blue eyes, worldly and sober, held no hint of merriment as they had previously when he'd touched down on the runway to his cattle station.

He put his cup on the adjacent table. "What can I do to help you, Kenna?"

She stood up and walked to the window, to keep him from seeing her tears. "There's little for anyone to do, Shan. I'll be going back to the States soon."

"You won't be staying in Australia?"

"No. I have to give up this apartment by the end of next week."

"Mrs. O'Leary and I would welcome you to Koraburra— for you to stay as long as you wish."

"Thank you, but I no longer have military clearance. So I couldn't take you up on your offer, even if I wanted to."

Forcing a smile through her tears, she said, "It seems that generals' widows are merely in the way when there's a war on."

Shan came to the window where Kenna stood, with her cashmere sweater draped around her shoulders. He reached out and touched the woman whose beauty had grown with the years. Fine-boned, with high cheek bones and a sensuous mouth, she still caused heads to turn as she walked down the street, yet she didn't seem to notice.

For Shan, that innocence, despite her obvious sophistication in other matters, was a blessing. If Kenna Fitzpatrick had known the strong feelings she spawned in Alisdair Shannon at that moment, she would have been even more distressed, if that were possible.

"Telephone me, Kenna, if I can help you. I mean it," he said. He picked up his jacket and headed for the door, but then he stopped. "You won't go home before your daughter is rescued, will you?"

"How did you know she was missing?"

"I have my sources."

"Then I'm sure you won't say anything to jeopardize her chances for rescue."

"No, not at all. But you haven't answered my question."

"I'll do everything possible to stay until I see her again."

Nodding at her answer, he said, "Good-bye, Kenna. Keep your chin up."

She managed a slight smile. "Of course. And thank you, Shan, for coming."

The next day, Alisdair Shannon flew to Townsville, where he met with Eric and the rescue team that had the responsibility of removing the survivors of the *Good Hope* from Guadalcanal.

Months before, with an eye toward eventual invasion, U.S. intelligence officers had combed Australia for anyone familiar with the uncharted islands of the Solomons, since their only source of information came from German maps of 1916 vintage.

Shan had come to their attention, for he knew Guadalcanal well. He'd once panned for gold in the hills, and had spent his summers working on a copra plantation, until his father had grown old and needed him to take over Koraburra.

"See as much of the world as you can now, Son." He remembered his father's words as if he'd spoken him that instant. "For once you take over Koraburra, you will be tied down with its responsibility for the rest of your life — or until your own son can take over for you."

But Shan's son had been killed in North Africa. There was no one to come after him, unless he married a woman young enough to give him other children.

Two days later, as the clock in Kenna's apartment in Melbourne struck eleven in the evening, all wheels had been set in motion for the rescue of the American men and women hiding on Guadalcanal.

The American submarine *Porpoise*, with Alisdair Shannon on board, already lay hidden beyond the barrier reef in the half-crescent lagoon off the island. Father Waal, with Sisters Agnes and Birghitta, Pearl Li, the Chinese mother, and her two daughters, Jade and Isabella, traveled in slow procession with Matt, Brogdon, Grainger, Wendy, Benita, Rehoboth, and Heinman. Only Sunny was missing. But she was coming from another direction and planned to meet them near the mouth of the river shortly before midnight.

Silently leading the group in the moonlight, Father Waal was thankful that Alex Ramsay had warned him away from the sand crab cave, especially with one of Kelia's men tracking him. He was not so certain, though, that the hiding place had remained a secret. For that morning, a blood-stained leaf lay in plain view when he went out from the entrance. The blood was not Obadiah's, for the rain had washed away any trace of it. No, the leaf had been placed in front of the cave, deliberately, like the poor dead parrot, Kira, in front of the gates of the mission, as a warning. But it was too late to worry about that now.

Only a small work detail had been left by the Japanese to guard the nearly finished dock. And for that, Father Waal was also thankful. Within a day or two, there would be a permanent camp of Japanese on the beach, and the opportunity for evacuation would be lost.

In the distance, Matt heard the unmistakable sound of "Washing Machine Charlie," one of the Japanese planes, with its whirring, uneven motor designed to damage the nerves of anyone in its path. He had heard it regularly ever since they'd been on the island. In the cave, they were safe from its flares, dropped to light up the jungle in hopes of catching the enemy in its glare. He stopped for a moment and listened—hoping the plane would keep going to the other side of the island without picking up their crippled procession in its glare.

Brogdon was still out of his head, and Benita, getting him ready for the trip earlier, had no alternative but to gag him with a strip of cloth from his shirt, to keep him quiet.

On the submarine *Porpoise,* Captain Greg Guest was uneasy at the sound of the plane. His vessel lay exposed off the lagoon, vulnerable to the plane and to the Japanese patrol boats regularly plying the waters. Using his periscope, he watched for the white flag to appear on the beach; for he would not send the team in their boats until he knew the people were already waiting. The rescue team had little time to spare before the enemy patrol boats would come again, and he didn't want to expose his men unnecessarily. It would be hazardous enough even without hitches in the schedule.

At precisely five minutes to midnight, Father Waal came alone to the beach, tied Heinman's shirt to a pole and wedged it upright in the sand. Then he left the beach and hurried to the mouth of the winding, meandering river. By the time he reached the group, the young nurse from Bohorok should be at the rendezvous point, as well. He did not expect the French nun, even though he'd sent word to her. She had refused to leave twice before, but at least his conscience was clear in alerting her of the rescue.

The lookout on the *Porpoise* saw the flag and alerted his captain shortly before he spotted it through his periscope. Immediately, the captain gave orders to lower the rubber boats.

Alisdair Shannon, dressed completely in black like the others, took his place in the lead boat. Surrounded by lush, tropical growth, he guided them past the coral reef, their oars dipping into the water with rhythmic precision. In the distance, Shan again heard the sound of a plane and saw a bright flare lighting up the countryside. It was away from the beach and at a higher elevation, much closer to the ridge where he'd once panned for gold. In the mountainous terrain, the glow resembled a volcano's sudden eruption.

Now came the dangerous part for the boats getting past the breakers without having the flimsy vessels turn over. Like a surfer choosing the right wave to ride, Alisdair waited. Then, at his signal, the men rowed with all their strength until the wave forced them forward, toward the beach and calmer water.

The next boat was not so successful. Caught in the pounding force, the vessel overturned, dumping its occupants into the sea. As the men struggled to regain the boat and its oars, the third boat passed by, and also the fourth, leaving the second one to take its place at the end of the procession.

And in the procession on land, the women, all disguised in nun's habits, with their faces blackened, resembled silent crows on their way to roost. They stopped in groups of twos and threes, scattered along the riverbank wherever a tree, a bush gave them shelter. A child coughed, and Pearl Li, the Chinese mother, quickly muffled the sound with her hand.

Earlier, Sunny Fitzpatrick had said her good-byes to the cool, withdrawn Alex Ramsay. With Timi You to guide her, she had left Bohorok for an uneventful trip to join the others at the mouth of the river.

Father Waal, seeing the black-robed figures coming from the other direction, smiled with relief. Now they were all accounted for. Like clockwork, the boats navigated the river and appeared at the rendezvous point where Father Waal waited. He stood up from his hiding place, waved to the men, who brought their vessels close in to the banks.

Using sign language, Father Waal directed the loading — Brogdon first, with Benita and Wendy; then the children with their mother. As soon as one boat was full, it was pushed off and another took its place near the bank. Father Waal kept account of the number loaded in each boat — the injured interspersed with the healthy. At last, there remained only three on the bank — Sisters Birghitta and Agnes, and the priest.

"Father, please come with us," Sister Birghitta whispered. "There is nothing left for you here."

Father Waal shook his head, and twice made the sign of the cross. With sadness, he walked into the water and helped to push the last boat from the sandbar. For a long time he stood and watched, until they were all out of sight. The crocodiles had not bothered them, a small blessing in the night.

A few seconds later, the island came alive. The plane returned and dropped another flare dangerously close to the priest. He fled into the jungle even as the boats headed for the submarine in the lagoon.

By now, the small contingent of Japanese soldiers left on the island to guard the finished dock sensed that something was underway. As the boats passed from the river and edged out into the crescent lagoon, the soldiers ran onto the dock and turned on the searchlight.

"Hurry it up, Angus," Alisdair admonished. "We've been spotted."

At that moment, the Japanese began to fire at the water and the silently moving vessels were caught in the glare.

The next few minutes turned into a nightmarish race. Unable to submerge until the rescue squad returned, the submarine lay dead in the water. Then, from the channel, a Japanese destroyer, with her heavy guns, moved in to sink the *Porpoise,* while Washing Machine Charlie strafed the deck and narrowly missed the conning tower. Now, the captain had no choice.

"Fire all engines," Captain Guest ordered. "We submerge in two minutes."

"Can you see any sign of them, Harry?" a voice called out.

"No. Wait a minute. Yeah, I see something moving. That's them."

"Come on, you guys. Haul like hell," the gunner urged as he crouched on deck and waited for the plane to make a second pass at the sub.

With an earsplitting noise, the gunner aimed his shells at the plane flying low over the water. And while he and his buddy were busy defending the sub from attack above, other sailors made a human chain, lifting the survivors from each boat, rushing them along the deck, and then pushing them down the hatch with no thought for propriety.

The large guns from the destroyer began to roar, and a whoosh passed a hundred yards off port bow of the *Porpoise.* By the time the last group fell onto the deck, water was already ankle deep.

Finally the last man on deck, the gunner's mate, dived for the hatch. He battened it down a split second before the submarine submerged.

A short distance from Bohorok, the plane crashed against the mountain range.

With the enemy destroyer blocking their way, it was too late to reach the channel and the open sea. The captain of the *Porpoise* ordered all engines off, and in silence and darkness, the submarine sank to the bottom of the lagoon while her occupants listened for the torpedoes and depth charges searching out her hiding place. They made no effort to converse with each other. Now they were in even more danger than they'd been on land.

For two hours they remained on the bottom of the lagoon, with the submarine shaking from the near misses of each depth charge and torpedo. Finally, with a sudden rain squall, the captain decided it was time to move out into the open sea. Skirting close to the coral reef, the *Porpoise* traced the southern tip of the island. Finally, out of range of the Japanese destroyer, closer to Tulagi, life on the submarine returned to normal.

The lights came on again; everyone cheered. And Alisdair Shannon, with his wet black shirt and pants clinging to his lithe frame, saw the people he'd rescued—for the first time.

"Which one of you is Amanda Fitzpatrick?" he inquired. "I have a message from your mother."

Wendy waited for Sunny to answer. "Sunny, where are you?"

There was no reply.

"Come on, Sunny. Speak up," Benita demanded, looking at the blackened face of the woman sitting in the shadows.

"You are speaking with me, madame?" the French voice inquired.

In the far corner of the hold, Matt lifted his head. He struggled to stand on his good leg. "Where is she? Has anybody seen her?"

"No. I thought..."

"Who are you?" Wendy demanded, standing in front of the woman the same size as her friend.

"Why, I am Soeur Marie. Is anything wrong?"

"She isn't here," Wendy wailed. "We left her. Somebody tell the captain to turn around. We've got to go back for her."

Mistaking Wendy for one of the nuns, the executive officer said, "That's impossible, Sister. All the boats were lost. We didn't have time to deflate them and get them aboard. If somebody didn't make it to the beach, they'll just have to wait for another rescue operation."

"Shan, did you see anybody else on the beach?" one of the men on the rescue team asked.

"Only the priest. And he gave us the signal to leave."

A heartsick Alisdair Shannon looked from one face to the other. The only reason he'd agreed to come on such a dangerous mission was because of Kenna. How was he going to explain to her that it was her own daughter, Sunny, that he'd left behind on Guadalcanal?

Chapter 27

TWO HOURS AFTER THE RESCUE ON THE BEACH, A BRUISED
and bleeding Timi You raced toward Bohorok. His breath
came in gasps; his head ached abominably where he had
been struck by one of Kelia's men.

He had failed Masta and his woman. And for him, that
ache was worse than any pain in his head.

No stranger to pain, himself, Alex Ramsay stood on the
steps of Bohorok and gazed toward the lagoon. Mercifully,
the lights were out; all was quiet again. But he felt no peace.

Amanda Fitzpatrick had disrupted his life, disrupted his
beliefs, and was now disrupting his sleep. He kept telling
himself that he was better off without her; that he'd been
glad to see her go.

She had succeeded in alienating him after their
lovemaking, as if she had deliberately set out to do so. He
would have accepted her tears, her recriminations—
anything but her flippant words that any man would have
been welcome in her bed that night.

He knew he should put her out of his mind, to forget her
completely. And perhaps he could, once Timi You returned
with news that she was safe.

One last time, Alex made a night patrol of the
plantation's borders. Above him, on the ridge, the flames of
the crashed plane had been doused by the rain squall. But he

needn't worry about the enemy pilot. The explosion had taken care of him.

Alex walked back to the verandah and glanced at his watch. It was now 3:00 A.M.—past time for Timi You to be returning. Finally, in a fit of restlessness, Alex walked into the kitchen and pulled a can of beer from the refrigerator. Then, he went back to the screened verandah and settled himself in a bamboo chair. He looked at the empty chair beside him, and was again reminded of Sunny. Swearing under his breath, he stood up and, with the beer in his hand, he walked into the bedroom, brushed the mosquito netting aside and, fully clothed, stretched out on the bed.

No peace came to him, even in his own bed. For he remembered the softness of the woman beside him, the taste of her lips—and the ache began again, with love unfulfilled.

In disgust, he sat up, brushed his hair from his eyes, and began to pace up and down, until his own steps were answered by steps onto the verandah, and the slight creak of the door as it opened.

"Timi You, are you there?" Alex turned on the lantern light and saw the native before him—dried blood on his head and agonizing sorrow in his eyes.

"What's wrong? Didn't she get to the river safely?"

"Masta…" Timi You stopped and began again, his voice quivering with weakness and fatigue. "Masta, Kelia took woman."

With Timi You's words, Alex knew he'd been right to worry that night. Sunny had not gotten off the island after all, as he'd feared. And he knew what he must do.

"You know the way to Kelia's village, Timi You?"

"Yes, Masta. I lead you there." Timi You turned toward the door.

"Sit down, Timi You," Alex ordered. "You can't start out anywhere until you rest. And we can't just barge into the village. We'll have to devise a plan to get her back."

Alex brought a shot of whiskey for Timi You to drink. A few minutes later, he returned with the first-aid chest and cleaned the native's head wound. While he bandaged him, Alex asked questions—the size of the village, whether Kelia had guns. Anything that might be of use.

But it was Timi You who came up with a master plan—one so ridiculous that Alex dismissed it until he realized that Timi You was a better judge of the barbaric Kelia than he.

"Kelia, him chief of tribe, with tribe robe. You bigger chief of tribe with finer clothes. Not matter how many men. Challenge only chief to chief."

"You mean I should go alone and challenge Kelia in hand-to-hand combat?"

"You all same fellow twice to Kelia. Him small fellow. Him not want to fight."

"But I'm not a native chieftain like Kelia. There's no use pretending, Timi You."

"You big chief. I know. I hang tribal clothes in closet," he insisted.

The scout got up from the chair and took the lantern into Alex's bedroom. Immediately, he brought out Alex's Scottish tartan, his kilt, the sporran made of the head and skin of a badger, with all the accoutrements of the clan Ramsay, including the deadly looking dirk and the crest badge of the unicorn surrounded by strap and buckle. Here were the hereditary colors that Alex had worn to dinner at the governor-general's, and had brought to Guadalcanal with him because it was the only reminder of his Scottish heritage in an alien land.

"You put on. Then, we go. Before sunrise."

Alex stared at Timi You and then at his tartan. Without a word, he began to remove his khaki shirt.

Alex Ramsay had gained back all the weight he'd lost on the raft and during the time he was ill. Well over six feet tall, with broad shoulders, muscular calves and thighs, he was an imposing figure. Once he'd finished dressing in the red tartan, he presented himself to Timi You for final inspection.

There was a disappointment in the native's face. "You not have cockatoo feathers," he said, pointing to the glengarry Alex held in his hand. "Kelia have cockatoo feather headdress."

Not aware that feathers were much more valuable to the natives of the Solomons than any amount of money, an impatient Alex said, "Well, I don't have time to go out and shoot a parrot. We need to leave now if we're going to get to the village by daylight."

"Wait. Timi You fix."

He left the house, went to the leaf hut where he spent his nights, and dug up a long, slim parcel wrapped in banana leaves. And once he'd returned to the plantation house, he unfolded the riches set aside for his old age—feathers in magnificent colors, their plumage in shades of white, blue, yellow, orange and green, gathered over the years, as had Papageno, the birdman, stealing a single feather from an unsuspecting bird before it could take flight from the tree where he'd lain in wait for hours.

Once satisfied with Alex's appearance, Timi You was ready to lead him to Kelia's village.

In that short period of time before dawn, when the grayness of the night began to move out like a visible entity, a fetid, decaying odor arose from the jungle floor, took form in plumes of steam, and traveled with the grayness toward the horizon.

Through this blurry mist, the two men traveled until they came to a pathway bordered by poles. And on the poles, the shrunken heads, hidden by Kelia for Father Waal's visit earlier, were again in prominence as a warning against intruders.

Hurrying down the pathway, Alex saw the faint outline of the huts taking shape through the mist, and one lone sentry asleep at his post before the leaf hut in the middle of the village.

Alex put on his headdress. With the magnificent feathers pointing upward from his glengarry, he looked at least seven feet tall. He waited for the sun to break through the trees. And during that time, he went over in his mind the ferocious war cry of his clan, that brought terror to anyone who heard it.

He had been well rehearsed by Timi You. As he roared, Alex was to remain where he was, not entering through the village gate itself, but placing a foot on the stone before it, as if it were the Stone of Destiny—challenging who would be chieftain, and who would be tanist of the clan.

The sun broke through the trees in a blinding light behind Alex. And he chose that moment for the war cry to come from his throat—awesome and ferocious in the stillness of the early morning.

"Kelia," he shouted. And he waited for the village to come awake.

Timi You had chosen well. The effect on Kelia of seeing a giant in the first blinding rays of the sun was not disappointing.

With anxious eyes watching him from the openings of the huts, Kelia, dressed in his ceremonial robe and cockatoo feather headdress, slowly walked toward Alex.

Kelia was a small man, wiry and strong—no shorter, no taller than most of the men in his tribe. But his face, deliberately crisscrossed with cuts into which various dyes had been poured before healing, matched the hardness of his eyes.

Timi You became the translator. "White Chief has come to challenge Kelia to fight."

"And what has Kelia done to anger White Chief?"

"Kelia has stolen his woman. Will Kelia fight for her?"

The native chief hesitated. He consulted the man who stood beside him and served as his second. "What weapon will White Chief use in his fight?" Kelia finally inquired.

Alex pulled the dirk from its sheath. Its gleaming blue steel caught the sun, and Kelia moved back a step. Again, he consulted his second.

"Kelia trade three village women for White Chief's woman," he bargained.

Timi You translated it for Alex and then gave back Alex's

answer. "No. White Chief fight for his own woman."

Alex kept his foot on the stone. Kelia, a few yards inside the compound, remained where he was. With talk going rapidly back and forth between him and his second, Kelia, looking sour, finally capitulated.

"Woman only woman. Not worth fighting."

With a signal, Kelia motioned for his prisoner to be brought to him.

No longer dressed in the black habit, Sunny Fitzpatrick wore a flowered muumuu. On her feet were sandals woven of straw. Plaited bamboo bound her wrists as she was led out of a nearby hut by a short, plaited rope.

Her lips trembled when she saw Alex and Timi You. But Sunny's voice was silent. Her captor led her to Kelia, who took the rope. In a display of disgust, he threw it on the ground.

"Take woman," he said, and turned his back to Alex.

Timi You motioned for Sunny to step outside the gate. He bent down, picked up the rope, and placed it in Alex's hand.

"Don't say anything yet, Sunny," Alex urged her. "Walk slowly behind me until we're out of sight."

In regal steps, Alex walked along the pathway guarded by shrunken heads. Sunny, with the rope still tied about her wrists, followed. But once the pathway ended and they emerged into the jungle again, Alex took his dirk, sliced the rope from Sunny's wrists, removed his glengarry to Timi You's care, and motioned for them all to start running. For now, all three were fair game, not only for Kelia's warriors, but for the Japanese, too.

Chapter 28

WITH A GREAT CLANG AND CLATTER, THE JAPANESE landing barges lowered their ramps to discharge the trucks and earthmoving equipment onto the beaches of Guadalcanal. Within minutes, soldiers began setting up their tents.

Alex, hurrying toward Bohorok with Sunny and Timi You, stared down at the lagoon from the ruins of Giles Canupp's house. This was what he had dreaded—not the occasional landing party, searching for the teleradio, but a permanent encampment. The earthmoving equipment also presaged a landing field for planes, to strike anywhere in the Coral Sea, New Guinea, Australia, or New Zealand. Seeing the enemy swarm the beaches, Alex realized his days at Bohorok were numbered.

He looked at Sunny, dipping up a handful of water from the spring to drink, and then taking another one to splash on her face. He swore at Kelia for preventing her from leaving the island with the others.

"Have you rested enough?" Alex asked, impatient to get back to the plantation. He, too, perspired from the heat, even though he had removed as much of the wool tartan as he dared.

"I'm ready," she replied, denying the tiredness that had plagued her every step since they'd left the village.

Choosing not to walk along the route that was slightly worn—a telltale sign to any patrol—Alex and Timi You hacked their way through rougher jungle.

Earlier, Alex, realizing that his red tartan was entirely too eye-catching, had disguised himself with foliage—the same as he and Timi You had done when traveling in the open toward the cave on the ridge. As they slowly progressed toward Bohorok, Alex began to go over in his mind the terrain between Bohorok and the high ridge. If the Japanese were on the island to stay, their foraging parties would spread out in ever-widening circles. He only hoped that the nurse walking behind him could get off the island before they had to resort to the cave.

Alex looked at Timi You, with his head still wrapped in a bandage. He thought of the wounded Obadiah, in the care of the priest. Only All-Same-Barrel was healthy. But he was the one Alex was not completely sure of, even though he'd left him to act as sentry while he and Timi You had gone to Kelia's village to rescue Sunny.

High over the ridge, not far from where Alex had seen the crash earlier that morning, the young Japanese pilot, Yamuto, regained consciousness. He lay in the sun, with his head throbbing and his arm under him. He vaguely remembered being thrown out of the plane at the moment of impact. Surprised to feel pain, he realized he mustn't be dead, after all.

Slowly, he moved his body—his legs first, then one arm. When he tried to move the other, he felt the pain again. He couldn't get his right arm to obey him, and he knew from that, it was broken. Off-balance, he struggled to sit up. A wave of nausea swept over him and he felt disgust that one of the warriors of the emperor should be so weak. He lay down again, this time guarding his right arm, while his eyes looked toward the sky and traced the pattern of clouds skimming along toward the mountains.

A few minutes later, Yamuto sat up again. Still dizzy, he was not overcome with nausea. But he made no effort to stand. Instead, he examined the terrain around him—the jungle foliage scorched from the fire, and the wreckage itself a mere hundred yards from him. After a while, he stumbled to his feet. A short distance from where he stood lay the cave, with the coastwatcher's hidden cache of supplies.

He took a step and then stopped to rest. Then, another step, until he finally reached the wreckage of the plane. The singed scarf he'd worn was draped over a nearby bush. Seeing it, he took it up, to be used as a sling for his broken arm, while behind him, the cave entrance waited to give up its secret.

With the Japanese clearing the land for an airstrip nearer the beach and Yamuto searching his plane ruins on the ridge for something to eat, Alex returned to Bohorok. Without resting, he went immediately to the radio room to broadcast news of the Japanese landing and to inquire about another vessel for Sunny's rescue from the island.

A few minutes later, a disappointed Alex walked into the living room of the plantation house. Sunny was sound asleep on the sofa. He didn't wake her. Instead, he walked past her, into his own bedroom, where he removed the Highland tartan, placed it back in the closet and, after a bath, dressed in the more comfortable cotton khaki shirt and pants.

Three hours earlier, the U.S. submarine *Porpoise* had surfaced in the harbor near the military installation at Townsville. Ambulances were waiting to whisk the survivors to the hospital under a cover of censorship. No reporters greeted the group. Briefed by the executive officer of the submarine, the survivors had been given instructions to talk with no one except their immediate families. And the only information to be given, even to their next of kin, was that they were safe. Nothing else.

Wendy and Benita, acting as official spokesmen for the group from the *Good Hope*, cornered Alisdair Shannon, the mystery man, to beg that he do something about Sunny.

"I don't know why she didn't reach the beach," Wendy

whispered. "But I know she's still on the island. And somebody just *has* to go back for her."

"I'll see what I can do," Shan replied. "But you realize I have no power to promise anything. I'm merely a private citizen."

The two nurses nodded. But Wendy felt a little better, for there was something about this man that gave her hope. She still didn't know his name. No one on the submarine had volunteered it.

"Is there any way I can get in touch with you later?" Wendy asked. "I mean—if you find out something."

"I'm sorry. You see, for all of you who were picked up, I don't exist. I was never on this expedition."

As Wendy climbed into the ambulance, she caught one last glimpse of Shan, dressed in black, walking rapidly from the dock. She had not even seen him clearly, for, unlike the others, he had neglected to remove the charcoal that disguised his face.

Eric never got a full night's sleep anymore. That night, he'd even gotten less than usual, waiting for Shan and the *Porpoise* to return from their mission. He'd dozed on the cot set up in the corner of the telecommunications room. He hadn't removed his clothes in two days. The stubble on his chin attested to matters more important than shaving.

Two of his coastwatchers had not reported in. And he was afraid they'd been overrun by the Japanese. Combined with the dangerous rescue attempt at Guadalcanal, the shrinking of his network gave him an uneasy feeling, forcing him toward another ulcer attack.

"Eric, are you awake?" Shan's familiar voice caused him to sit up quickly. He was alert in an instant.

"Thank God you're back. Everything go all right? You got them off the island?"

"It was touch and go for a while. We had to dodge a Jap destroyer for several hours. And Washing Machine Charlie did a little damage to the gun emplacement. We got everyone off the island, Eric, with the exception of one nurse. And she's the reason I've come to see you."

"What happened to her?"

"We don't know. She was the one at Bohorok. Amanda Fitzpatrick, the general's daughter. She evidently never made it to the beach. Do you think you could rouse Ramsay and find out what happened to her?"

Eric groaned. "I'll have to, or else there'll be hell to pay from the general."

Shan did not inform Eric of Irish Fitzpatrick's death. He watched while Eric went to the vast network to call the coastwatcher on Guadalcanal. And he waited for the sound of the keys to respond. For a half hour, Eric tried to make contact through Malaita, but Guadalcanal was silent. Finally, Eric turned back to Shan.

"No one can get him. He's probably asleep. Why don't you go and wash up, and I'll have the kettle on for something to drink. I'll try again in an hour."

An hour later, there was still no response. "There's no need for both of us to stay. Why don't you go on to my apartment to get some sleep? I'll come later, when I've heard something."

Shan knew that he would only be in the way if he stayed around. He left the telecommunications center and went on to Eric's apartment, where he took a bath but did not go to sleep. Instead, he borrowed one of Eric's books and tried to read while he waited.

Later that afternoon, he heard the apartment door open. Shan got up from the chair and went to meet Eric. "Did you contact him?"

"Yes."

"Well, what happened to her?"

"She's all right, and safe for the moment, back at Bohorok."

"I'm ready to leave anytime you set up another rescue operation. Just give the word, Eric."

"You're not going, Shan."

"You can't send someone else. It's extremely dangerous ,

at best. Nobody knows the territory like I do."

"You don't understand, Shan. It's too dangerous for *anyone* to go. The Japs landed a huge force on the island this morning. They're building an airfield. The girl will have to stay until the U.S. Marines invade Guadalcanal."

A sick feeling came over Shan. "And how far off is this planned invasion? Three — four — five months?"

"I'm not at liberty to say."

"Damn!" Shan said, and pounded his fist in the palm of his hand.

"I don't know why you're so concerned about one nurse. It's a shame she didn't get to the sub. But she's lucky even to be alive, right now."

"What do you mean? What happened?"

"Seems Ramsay had to rescue her from one of the local headhunters."

"Oh, my God. What are you going to tell her family?"

"Nothing. After you left, I found out the general was killed recently. At least we won't have any grief from him. The War Department thinks it might be better to keep her listed officially as missing, since there's no guarantee she'll ever get off the island alive. Shan, where are you going?"

"I've got to get back to Melbourne — and then to Koraburra — to see about that shipment of beef."

A determined Alisdair Shannon, with his blue eyes the color of angry flint, left a puzzled Eric and, taking a tram, he rode toward the airport where his plane waited.

At Bohorok, Alex Ramsay walked past the sleeping Sunny. There was no need to wake her. She would learn the bad news soon enough. The navy could not send another rescue vessel anytime soon. So she was stuck on Guadalcanal. Whether she liked it or not, Alex was the only man she was apt to see for the next month or more — that is, if they were both lucky enough to stay alive.

The house was still quiet when Sunny gradually awoke. But outside, the late afternoon rains began — the steady drip onto the roof, the plopping sound of water on the leaves of the banana plants. No lantern had been lit. No candle waited on the table. With a gust of wind, the steady drops of rain developed into a squall, and Sunny sat up.

In the encroaching darkness, she tried to remember what she had been dreaming, what she'd promised herself not to forget, even as she struggled to open her eyes. But it was useless. The dream, the promise, disappeared. She was left with only a sadness surrounding her. And then, she suddenly remembered why. The submarine had left without her. And the Japanese had come on the island to stay.

Always priding herself on being completely self-reliant, even when she was a small child, Sunny was now faced with one hard, cold fact she couldn't deny. If it had not been for Alex coming to challenge Kelia, she would probably be dead. For one of the few times in her life, she was forced to eat her own words. No other man would have done so well. Only Alex Ramsay, marquess of Dalhousie, could have pulled off such a trick — in that ridiculous outfit.

Thinking of Alex standing before Kelia's gate and demanding her freedom, Sunny giggled aloud.

"And what do you find so amusing?" a voice inquired from the shadows across the room.

"Oh, Alex, I didn't mean to laugh. But do you have any idea how ridiculous you looked this morning? Especially with those cockatoo feathers practically reaching to the treetops?"

Alex stood and walked over to light the lantern. "I presume you won't repeat that in front of Timi You. It was his idea and I don't think it would be cricket to hurt his feelings."

"I'm sorry."

In the glow of the lantern light, Sunny saw Alex's face. His eyes were squinted, and he was trying hard not to laugh, himself.

"And what do *you* find so funny, Alex?"

His own laugh erupted, full voiced, despite his attempt to stifle it. "All those times my cousin Malcolm and I stood on the moothill and practiced that ferocious war cry. We barely managed to scare the pigeons, much less a human being. But it worked with Kelia."

"And for that, I'm grateful. I really am, Alex." Sunny's face became earnest. She walked toward the man and gazed up at him with her large topaz eyes still velvet soft from sleep. "You can't imagine how terrified I was."

Alex reached out and gently brushed a wayward strand of the silvery blonde hair that had gotten her into trouble. "Yes, I think I have an idea," he responded, his voice strangely sympathetic.

She moved back a step. His hand dropped to his side. Sunny's eyes became noncommittal as she rapidly changed the subject. "Did you receive a message about when I'll get off the island?"

Alex moved from the lantern light, where Sunny could not see his face. "There won't be another rescue attempt until after the Allied invasion of the island."

"I don't believe it."

"It's true. Right now, Sunny, it looks as if you're stuck on this bloody island with me for at least another month or more."

"I can't. I can't stay on this island with you. It's impossible."

It had been hard enough to disguise her feelings after their night together. The prospect of an entire month with him was disastrous. Even his hand on her face a moment before had made her want to hurl herself into his arms.

Seeing how miserable she looked, Alex became distant and cold. "You have no choice, even as I have no choice. But rest assured, Sunny Fitzpatrick, the moment any transportation is made available, I'll be happy to see you off."

Chapter 29

IN MELBOURNE A DESOLATE KENNA FITZPATRICK CLOSED her last suitcase. Irish's uniforms had already been shipped back to the States, to the house they'd shared all their married life with the exception of the two years in Egypt, when Irish had been a consultant for King Fuad on the cotton textile mills — that dark period in her life when her brother, Neal, had died in Atlanta.

Kenna was no stranger to sorrow, for when she was a child, her own mother and father had gone down with the *Titanic*. Perhaps that was why she had been so fierce in her devotion to the rest of her family — for Neal, when he was shot down over Verdun and listed as missing, just as Sunny had been listed at sea. If Kenna had refused to accept Neal's death without some proof, how much more did she now refuse to give up hope that her own daughter was still alive.

That morning, she had been notified that Sunny was not in the group rescued from the island. That was all. No explanation as to what happened to her; no information or names of others who had been more fortunate. And now, because Irish was dead, the military door to any further information had been slammed in her face.

She gazed around at the apartment that seemed sterile without the family pictures, the small mementoes that made an alien environment into a more palatable place. She was supposed to be out by the next day, although MacArthur had decided to move his headquarters to Brisbane. But how could she leave Melbourne, or Australia, itself, while Sunny was still missing?

The young major had already arranged transportation for her on the ship that was leaving the Sydney harbor to San Francisco. Her rail ticket from Melbourne to Sydney was in her purse.

Kenna wondered if she would need a special visa if she stayed in Australia, An apartment or even a room to live in was imperative. She wouldn't mind what it looked like, just as long as she could wait for news about Sunny.

Quickly, Kenna walked to the waste basket and retrieved the newspaper. She sat in the easy chair, switched on the lamp, and turned to the want ads. But there were no apartments, no rooms to rent in Melbourne. The paper was full of ads placed by people who were looking, just as she was. She brushed her hair back, and a small smudge from the newsprint remained on her temple.

A knock at the door went unnoticed. But it became insistent, and Kenna, putting down the want ads, rose from her chair to answer the knock.

"May I come in?"

Like a reenactment of another day, Kenna stepped back to allow Alisdair Shannon to enter. "What are you doing here?" she asked.

Shan hesitated. He had debated with himself as to how much to tell her. Seeing the suitcases in the hallway, he said, "Are you leaving?"

"Yes. No. Oh, Shan, I'm supposed to leave for Sydney tomorrow, but I can't go home yet. Sunny wasn't rescued. She's still missing."

"I'm sorry. More than I can tell you, Kenna."

"She was on an island. I don't even know which one. And there was a rescue last night. But Sunny wasn't with them. What could have happened to her, Shan? Did the Japanese take her? Did she become ill with malaria or some other dreaded disease? I'm beside myself with worry."

Shan's mind was busy. Kenna's distress touched him deeply—her anxiety over her son, her husband's death, and now the tragedy of her daughter. Just how much did a country demand in wartime from a woman? Everything that she possessed?

Shan suddenly made up his mind. The military lid had been placed on the rescue operation in large part because of his own role in it. And although he would never do anything to jeopardize a military action, it was over now. And Kenna had a right to know about her daughter. She would rest easier realizing that, as long as Alex Ramsay was alive, Sunny was relatively safe.

"Your daughter is still alive, Kenna." He waited a moment before going on. "That's the reason for my coming today—to tell you."

"How do you know? How…"

"I can't give you my source. I can only assure you that she's still alive."

"You know where she is? What happened to her, Shan? Tell me."

Shan went to stand before the empty fireplace. "She's on the same island as Alex Ramsay. Somewhere in the Coral Sea."

"I don't understand. Are Sunny and Alex together?"

"Yes."

She quickly brushed aside that information. "I suppose it doesn't really matter. The important question is: When will another rescue operation be set up?"

"That's just it, Kenna. She's stuck on the island until the marines invade it."

The light went out of Kenna's eyes again. "And how long will that be?"

"Nobody knows for sure."

Kenna walked to where Shan was standing. "It's either Guadalcanal or New Guinea, isn't it?"

He didn't deny it.

"And it might be six months or more before the Allies are ready to take either island."

Again, he offered no denial. "I debated about whether to tell you at all."

"I'm glad you did. But you realize it's impossible for me to leave Australia now."

"So, what are you going to do,?

"I was looking through the ads when you knocked. If I can find another place to stay in Melbourne, I *must* stay until she's rescued…."

"There's nothing available in Melbourne."

"I know. I just discovered that." Kenna moved to the window and stared at the street below.

Behind her, Shan's voice casually remarked, "I think I have the solution."

The stunningly beautiful woman turned and waited for him to continue. With the room's shadows touching the lovely bone structure of her face, she looked little older than her own daughter.

"You could come with me to Koraburra." His face revealed nothing as he watched the surprise register in her winter gray eyes.

"But I couldn't—"

"Mrs. O'Leary and I would welcome you, Kenna. There's plenty of room. And you can stay for as long as it takes for your daughter to be rescued."

Alisdair Shannon began to walk toward the door. "I'll be back in the morning. That should give you enough time to think about it. If you decided to accept my hospitality, we'll fly to Koraburra by noon. If not, I'll take you to the train station for your return home."

An hour later, Kenna sat by the fire. It had become cold, and she was burning the last of the peat. She stared into the meager fire like some seer, to divine an answer from the flames. "Oh, Irish, what should I do?" she said aloud.

She didn't want to leave Australia, especially now. Shan had offered a temporary solution to that problem, just as he had seen to the apartment in Darwin earlier. Perhaps he might allow her to use that same apartment again, instead of going to Koraburra. Even as she thought it, Kenna knew that Darwin was too far away and too dangerous, with the Japanese stepping up their bombing of the city. The better plan was for her to go to Koraburra.

Kenna withdrew her hand from the fire's warmth. What was she thinking, even to consider it—with all the gossip that might follow, however innocent she was?

The best thing for her to do was to seek permission from the authorities to stay in Australia and then look for a place on her own. But she didn't have any time. By tomorrow, she would have to give up the apartment she was in.

Kenna began to think about her daughter. If Sunny had to be surrounded by the Japanese, Kenna was glad that Alex Ramsay was with her. She prayed for them both.

That night, Kenna watched the tiny patterns of light on the ceiling as the moon's rays slipped through the old-fashioned lace under drapery at the bedroom window. She had not bothered to close the heavier draperies. Complete darkness had been too threatening.

Toward morning, she made up her mind. As much as she wanted to stay, she realized she could do nothing to help Sunny. It was a selfish thing—to inconvenience other people because of her own desires. Perhaps it was for the best that she go home.

When Shan returned to the apartment, Kenna was ready. She opened the door and pointed to the luggage that was to go with her.

"Have you made up your mind?"

"Yes."

"Well, then, which is it to be—Koraburra, or the train station?"

"The train station."

He did not argue with her. He merely nodded and picked up the luggage to take down to the waiting taxi.

Kenna remained in the apartment, taking one last look to

make certain she'd left nothing of value behind. She put on her coat—beige, with a matching scarf—and then picked up the smart little hat, a smaller replica of the Australian hat, with one side pinned up by a jaunty little feather.

After placing the spare key from her purse on the table, she cut off the last light and was at the door by the time Shan returned.

They walked down the steps onto the pavement, where Kenna climbed into the taxi. "To the train station," Shan informed the driver once he'd taken his seat beside her.

"You have your ticket?"

"Yes. It's in my purse." Kenna unconsciously rubbed the leather design of her glove as they passed through the morning traffic of trams, bicycles, military vehicles, and a few private cars and taxis.

It didn't take long to reach the station. The taxi, with its charcoal burner on top, pulled up in front, stopped, and the driver got out to open the door. Kenna reached into her purse for money, but Shan stopped her. "Don't bother," he said. "The taxi will wait for me. I'll pay him later."

"You're leaving Melbourne right away?"

"Yes. It's past time to get back to Koraburra."

"You don't have to walk all the way with me, Shan. I can get a porter to help with my two bags...."

"I don't mind," he replied and continued to walk beside her.

The voice announcing her train came over the loudspeaker. They hurried through the gate and onto the platform, where puffs of dark smoke with particles of soot slowly drifted to earth.

Kenna stopped and held out her hand. "Thank you, Alisdair Shannon. I won't ever forget your kindness."

Shan drew her hand to his lips. Their eyes met. Kenna felt the soft brush of a kiss on the back of her hand where the cutout design of the glove left her skin bare. People milled around them while he continued to hold her hand and gaze into her eyes.

"Are these your bags, lady?" The porter's voice broke the spell.

"Yes. Please put them on the train for me," Kenna replied. And in a quiet, serious voice, she said, "Good-bye, Shan."

"Good-bye, Kenna. God go with you."

He helped her onto the step of the passenger car. Then he began to walk from the platform toward the gate.

All at once, above the noise of the crowd, Kenna called his name. "Shan."

He stopped, turned around. Then, seeing her step down from the train and start toward him, he rapidly retraced the distance to meet her.

In a breathless voice she said, "I've changed my mind. I want to go to Koraburra."

No surprise registered on his face. He merely said, "We'll need to get your luggage off the train."

While she waited on the platform, Shan reclaimed her baggage. As the train pulled out of the station, both Alisdair Shannon and Kenna Fitzpatrick walked past the gate and returned to the taxi on the street.

Chapter 30

WHILE KENNA FLEW TO KORABURRA WITH ALISDAIR Shannon, her daughter, Sunny, sat at the breakfast table with Alex at Bohorok. The two quietly ate their morning meal, with few words in conversation.

Now, it was even more hazardous on the island, and the measures for safety that Alex had taken in the past would have to be increased.

"I know you don't want to be on Guadalcanal anymore than I want you to be," Alex began. "But that doesn't change the fact that you are. The Japanese may overrun us any moment, so you're not going to be treated as a visitor, Sunny. You'll have to do your share of work."

Her topaz eyes were hostile as she returned his gaze. "I fixed the breakfast, if you didn't happen to notice. And there have been a few other meals, too."

"I'm not talking about work in the kitchen, even though food is important. I mean you will have to take your turn in the lookout and the radio room. Obadiah is a liability, even to Father Waal, until he gets well. That leaves only Timi You and All-Same-Barrel to patrol and warn us of approaching danger."

Instead of becoming angry, Sunny nodded. "Just tell me what to do, Alex."

That morning, Sunny was again dressed in the yellow

cotton, with straw sandals on her feet. She had recovered quickly from her sleepless night in Kelia's village. Seeing her that morning, with the freshness of youth, with her smooth skin completely healed from the scratches and effects of the sun, Alex recognized the resiliency so taken for granted by the young. He'd never asked her age. Even now, it didn't really matter, although he could guess that she was not much older than twenty-one or twenty-two. At thirty-six, he felt old enough to be her father. No. That wasn't quite true. The feelings she forced from him were not fatherly at all.

"What do you want me to do?" Sunny asked again, prompting a response from him.

He frowned. "The first thing you need to do is find some trousers to wear. You can't shinny up a palm tree in that dress."

"That won't be a problem. The lady of the manor left some of her shirts and pants in one of the drawers of the chest in her bedroom."

Alex smiled in spite of himself. "For your first lesson in observation, look at the family pictures on the table. Tell me what you see, and then we'll discuss the owner of the trousers."

Sunny rose from the table. She picked up the picture and examined it. A man, a woman, and a boy dressed in khaki like the man, stared up at her from the ornate frame.

"I see a man, a woman, a little boy about twelve years old. The woman has on the dress I'm wearing now. The man and the little boy are dressed almost alike—in khaki. And there're posed against the steps of Bohorok."

"So who might be the owner of the trousers in the chest?"

"They could belong to anyone of the three," a stubborn Sunny replied. "Just because the woman in the picture has a dress on, doesn't mean she can't own shirts and pants, too."

"You saw them in the drawer?"

"Yes."

"Did the trousers have a fly in the front or a placket on the side?"

"I didn't unfold them, Alex. Since they were in the chest, I assumed—"

"In this business, you do not assume anything. Go and look, and then come back and tell me." Sunny put the picture in its place and walked to the bedroom. She pulled open a drawer, took out a pair of khaki pants small enough for either the woman or the boy—but when she saw the front fly she realized they belonged to the boy.

She walked back into the room where Alex was taking a last sip of tea. "Did you discover the owner?" he asked.

"Yes. They belong to the boy."

"How many shirts and how many pants are in the drawer?"

Exasperated, Sunny replied, "You didn't ask me to count them."

"But you opened the chest. From that, you should be able to answer any question I might ask you concerning its contents."

Ignoring her angry look, he continued to scold. "Once you climb up to the observation platform in the tree, you will have to observe a multitude of things at the same time. If there's one aircraft carrier in a Japanese convoy, you mustn't miss it, even though it's surrounded by cruisers and destroyers. And recognizing the enemy flag is of little use if you can't tell the number of ships, the kinds, and the direction in which they're headed."

"Lord, you're a hard taskmaster already. Will I have my head lopped off if I happen to miss a few?"

"Not by *me*." Alex's words had a sinister implication. Sunny thought of the encampment below, and the double danger they were in. Getting up from the table, Alex said, "Don't bother with the dishes. There's a booklet by the teleradio with the shapes and descriptions of all the Japanese vessels you're apt to see. I suggest you start learning them as quickly as possible."

"After I change into trousers, if they fit me. You remember, you gave me that prior order, Masta."

Alex ignored the name the natives called him. "So I did," he said and, unable to stifle a laugh, he added, "I believe there's hope for you after all, Sunny Fitzpatrick."

Armed with binoculars and Alex's booklet of ships, Sunny, dressed in the boyish khaki pants and shirt, sat on the platform of the palm tree and looked out beyond the lagoon to the channel.

Even as high in altitude as she was, she could hear the sound of the earthmoving equipment below. Droning steadily, the equipment swallowed great chunks of uneven land, uprooted trees, and then spit them out to the side, where men, Lilliputian-sized, burned them to clear the land for the airfield.

The afternoon sun, glittering across the channel, caused her eyes to water and made it difficult for her to see. Then something moving—dark gray in color—interrupted the unceasing glitter of the sun on the water. Sunny wiped her perspiring face on her shirt sleeve and returned the binoculars to her eyes.

Consulting the booklet, she sought verification of the shape. It was a cargo ship, carrying supplies. Alone, with no escort, the ship didn't seem to be in any particular hurry.

Like Timi You and the others before her, Sunny picked up a conch shell and blew into it. The sound brought Alex toward the clump of trees at the edge of the plantation grounds that overlooked the ledge.

"What is it?" he asked. "What do you see?"

"One cargo supply ship—Japanese," she answered. "With no escort."

From his position below, Alex watched the ship pass by. It was not of sufficient importance to risk using the teleradio in the daytime.

"All right," he said. "You can come off duty now. All-Same-Barrel will take over in a few minutes."

Sunny wasted little time in leaving the platform. Her water was gone, and the mosquitoes had plagued her all afternoon. Crawling down the tree, she sought the footholds, the loops nailed along the trunk. She negotiated the final few feet with an agile spring to the ground, landing on the soft earth near Alex. She quickly got up and brushed herself off before Alex had a chance to help her.

"You don't seem to be a stranger to climbing a tree," he commented.

"I don't seem to be a stranger to the mosquitoes, either," she replied, rubbing a spot on her neck. "Do you happen to have any Atabrine? I'd hate to be any further trouble to you than I already am."

"You don't feel feverish, do you?" he asked, his voice changing to one of concern.

"No. Just hot and thirsty."

"Come with me. I'll get the medication."

"Sister Birghitta said the other coastwatcher developed leprosy."

"Giles Canupp?"

"Yes—the one killed by the Japanese on Savo. Did you know him?"

"I met him once, when I first came to Guadalcanal."

With Sunny's information, everything began to fit in place—Giles's refusal to shake hands when they met; his burning down his plantation house when he left. Now, Alex understood why the man had chosen such a suicide mission. He'd had no future, except as an outcast.

In an instant, Alex recalled the full image of the man— the bandage on his hand. Alex had chastised Sunny for not being observant enough. Now he realized he was at fault, too.

And he should have thought to offer Sunny the Atabrine tablets before she had to ask.

Alex signaled for All-Same-Barrel to take Sunny's place in the lookout. Even smaller than Timi You, All-Same-Barrel had resorted to his native attire rather than the khakis and shoes worn most of the time by Timi You. Barefooted, with only the lap-lap to cover his body, he could more easily slip through the jungle without being suspected by the Japanese. That morning, he had gotten past them to visit Obadiah, left by Father Waal at a friendly village some distance from the one the Japanese had raided for workers.

Walking beside Sunny, Alex stopped. "Go on in the house. I'll be there soon," he said. He changed directions and quickened his pace to catch up with All-Same-Barrel before he climbed the tree.

"All-Same-Barrel?"

"Yes, Masta?"

"Where did you go this morning?"

"To see Obadiah, Masta."

"How is he?"

"Him come back to Bohorok. Soon."

"Did you see Father Waal also?"

The native shook his head. "Obadiah say Father hide from Ishimoto. Him not like priests."

Satisfied at the reason given for the native's disappearance, Alex said, "When you get hungry, lower your basket. Timi You will bring you some food."

"Yes, Masta."

Alex stood below and watched All-Same-Barrel scale the tree with his bare feet. Then, he hurried inside to find the Atabrine tablets for Sunny.

But once he reached the house, the teleradio demanded his attention. Alex rushed into the radio room to receive the message from another coastwatcher.

Brad Gillespie, at the northern end of the island approximately fifty miles away, was making his final broadcast. "BG to MDAR," the calm voice intoned.

"Go ahead, BG. I read you."

"We are closing down and moving inland. Japanese marching up the hill. Will broadcast from another position in a few days, if possible."

The connection was suddenly broken. A sober Alex Ramsay released the transmitter. Any message, any encouragement he might have given was too late. A sense of loss spread over him, for there was no guarantee that Gillespie would get out alive. And with his radio shut down, there remained only one other coastwatcher broadcasting from the western part of the island, separated from Alex by the range of mountains and facing away from the Slot.

Now, Alex was the last watcher between Bougainville and Malaita, and even his situation was becoming more hazardous each day. Finally taking up the transmitter, Alex relayed Gillespie's message.

By the time Alex located the Atabrine tablets, over a half hour had elapsed since Sunny had gone off duty. Not seeing her in the living quarters, Alex knocked at the closed door to her bedroom.

"Sunny, are you in there?" When he got no answer, he called again. "Sunny?"

In his hand, he held a glass of water and the bottle of Atabrine. He waited and, when there was still no answer, he pushed the door open and looked inside.

Veiled by the mosquito netting over the bed, Sunny was sound asleep. Alex looked at the malaria tablets and back toward the bed. He decided to wake Sunny to give her the medication.

He placed the glass and tablets on the bedside table and pushed back the netting. "Sunny?"

He reached out to rouse her, and touched soft, silken skin, tanned with a faint golden glow. She had removed the khaki shirt and trousers, and now wore only a bra and panties. She was so beautiful, so vulnerable, that his throat began to ache.

"Sunny," he called again softly. "I have your medication. Do you think you can wake up enough to swallow the tablets?"

She stirred and a slight noise came from her lips. Taking the sound for an assent, Alex retrieved one of the tablets, placed it on the table beside the water glass, and then lifted Sunny in his arms. Alex held the water glass to her lips long enough for her to swallow the bitter tablet. Feeling her soft breast against his chest triggered another memory—on the hospital ship, when *she* had been the one offering *him* something to drink.

All his anger against her vanished. He held her tenderly in his arms, her body unprotesting in sleep. A possessiveness raced through Alex's brain—a need to keep her safe from harm. Yet, every passing hour put her in greater danger.

After brushing his lips gently against her mouth, Alex released her, drew the mosquito netting and, walking out of the room, he pushed the door shut behind him.

That night, All-Same-Barrel watched as the meager lights were turned off in the plantation house. He couldn't understand it. Timi You had told him how Masta Alex had gone to Kelia's village to claim his woman. But the woman slept in her own room, while Masta slept in his. There was something wrong. And whatever it was had made Masta irritable. Going over the strangeness in his mind, All-Same-Barrel decided he would have to do something to make the woman return to Masta's bed. And he began to make his plans accordingly.

In the dead of night, when only the rustling of the jungle spoke of wild animals about, All-Same-Barrel set a trap. It wasn't long before he'd caught a bush rat foraging for food. Once the animal had quieted down, All-Same-Barrel returned to the plantation house with the bamboo trap in his hand.

Outside Sunny's window, he waited. Carefully, he lifted the thatched shutter over the window and, opening the trap's door, he dumped the animal onto the bedroom floor.

Because of her nap that afternoon, Sunny slept lightly. In the darkness, the gnawing noise from the animal awoke her. Now it sounded as if it were in her bedroom, But, no. The shutters were tight; the doors closed. And the walls had no holes in them. It was impossible for an animal to wander into her room.

What if it weren't an animal at all, but a person—a Japanese soldier or one of Kelia's men? Frightened, she called out, "Who's there?"

The room became silent.

"I said, who's there," she asked, a little louder this time.

From the dark corner of the room, an alien shape and glowing eyes appeared to be watching her. Sunny didn't dare get out of bed. Instead, she called out for Alex. "There's something in my room, Alex. Can you please bring your lantern? Alex, can you hear me? It's Sunny. I need you."

She heard a stirring from the adjacent bedroom. A light turned on, and a door opened.

"What's wrong, Sunny?"

From behind the netting, she replied, "I think there's something in my room."

Threatened at the approach of Alex with the light, the bush rat began to run about the room. The only escape was the open door between the two bedrooms.

"It's going into your room," Sunny warned.

Alex moved quickly with the lantern and shut the connecting door, leaving Sunny alone in the darkness. Warily, she listened to the noise emanating from the other side of the door. Alex did not use his pistol. Evidently he'd chosen some other method to deal with the intruder. Then, all was quiet, except for Alex's footsteps through the house. A door opened, closed, and then the footsteps returned.

Alex pushed open her bedroom door slightly and held up the lantern. "Everything's under control," he assured her.

"Did you kill it?"

"Probably not. But I stunned the animal enough to get it outside without biting me."

"It was bush rat, wasn't it?"

"Yes. Tomorrow, I'll have to find out how it got in."

"Thank you, Alex. I'm sorry I had to wake you."

"Don't think anything about it. This is all a part of living in the jungle. You'll be all right, now?" he inquired.

"Yes, thank you."

Unable to conceal his amusement, Alex suggested, "Then

why don't you lie down again?"

Until that moment, Sunny was not aware that she was standing on the bed.

Outside the plantation house, a disappointed All-Same-Barrel watched the lantern go out. He saw only one shadow. The woman was still in the other bedroom, and Masta was alone. His plan had not worked. He decided he would have to think of another way to bring the two together.

Chapter 31

THE NEXT AFTERNOON, AS A CAPRICIOUS ALL-SAME-Barrel made new plans, Father Waal began to sort out his possessions. He planned to take one wicker case—that was all he could carry. Of primary importance were the sacrament vessels—the outward symbols of confirmation, baptism, matrimony, penance, and the Eucharist.

A momentary sadness touched his heart. For twenty years he'd been on the island, taking care of the natives' souls while the sisters of mercy took care of their health. That afternoon, he especially missed Sister Birghitta and Sister Agnes, for they had been with him the longest. He had converted them, overseen their growing faith, and sent them off for nurses' training. And when they had chosen to return, to work with him, he had felt satisfaction at their dedication.

He looked over at the pallet where Obadiah was resting. He had been brought to the cave a few hours earlier by two natives who had been warned ahead of time that Ishimoto was planning a raid on their village because he suspected their friendliness to the priest and Obadiah, who had vanished from the work camp. But the priest and Obadiah could not survive in the cave for long. That hiding place, too, would soon be discovered. They would have to move on, by nighttime, take to the hills and seek sanctuary, first at Bohorok, and then beyond.

After adding a change of clothes, the priest shut his wicker case. He felt in the pocket of his cassock for the gun. He had wondered if he would ever have the courage to use it, for he considered all life sacred. But the knowledge of what had happened to the nuns on Bougainville had hardened his heart against the Japanese.

Noticing that Obadiah had awakened, Father Waal said, "As soon as it grows dark, my son, we will start toward Bohorok. Do you feel strong enough to walk?"

"Yes, Father," he replied. The native had already confessed his killing of the sentries at Tulagi. Father Waal had given him no further penance. Philosophical, Obadiah had accepted his own injury as the penance God had imposed on him because he had killed the sentries in anger and not self-defense.

In the early evening, as the priest and Obadiah, with a long stick to aid him, began their journey toward Bohorok, the residents of the plantation compound had problems of their own.

Timi You and All-Same-Barrel were not speaking because of some useless quarrel. Sunny had burned her hand on the stove, and Alex, searching the house for some way in which the bush rat could have entered, had come to the conclusion that someone had deliberately placed the animal in Sunny's room, for the shutter at her window had been tampered with.

After dinner, Alex and Sunny sat in the living room and, in the dim light provided by twin lanterns, attempted to read. Occasionally, Alex glanced up at the restless Sunny. She seemed to have little interest in her novel. Finally, she closed the book.

"Well, I think I'll be off to bed," she said. She stifled a yawn as she spoke.

"I'd like you to do something for me, Sunny."

A tired Sunny had taken her turn in the lookout; she had prepared the evening meal, washed the dishes, and cleaned the house. "I hope it won't take long. I'm tired from the long day," she complained.

"I want you to sleep in my room tonight."

A furious Sunny, growing angrier by the minute, launched an attack against Alex. "Absolutely not, Alex Ramsay. I'll never share your bed again. If you think—"

"Calm down, Sunny. I never asked you to *share* the bed. I merely want you to swap bedrooms tonight, in case the bush rat gets in again."

"Oh. Well, why didn't you say so in the first place?"

"You didn't give me a chance, in your eagerness to be offended."

"I'll have to get my gown."

"No hurry. I'll just sit here and finish my pipe."

"Don't you think you'd better claim your pajamas before I turn in?"

"In case you've forgotten, I don't wear pajamas."

With a wide-eyed innocence, she ignored his comment. She picked up her lantern. "Good night, Alex."

"Sleep well, Sunny."

She disappeared into her own bedroom, and a few minutes later, Alex heard the water running in the archaic bathroom at the back of the kitchen. With teeth brushed and face freshly scrubbed, Sunny walked into Alex's bedroom. She held the lantern high to examine fresh bed linen, to make sure no island inhabitants were hiding between the sheets. Satisfied, she climbed into bed, snuffed out the lantern light, and drew the netting around her.

Sunny stared at the ceiling and listened to the soft music coming from the gramaphone in the living room. Alex had turned it low, but the song reminded her of one particular night, when she had felt Alex's arms around her, when they had danced. She remembered the comfort of his arms in an even more intimate moment, in the very bed where she now lay—alone.

It was strange that, in this bedroom, she was more aware of his presence than she'd been while sitting beside him in the living room. She waited for the music to stop, then for his footsteps. Finally she heard them in the hall. They paused for a second outside his own bedroom door, then moved on. She heard the springs creak from his weight as he lay down on her bed. And Sunny wondered if the same thoughts were going through his mind.

In the silence, Sunny gradually relaxed. The rigors of the day were forgotten. Her eyelids closed, and she floated into a reverie—not totally asleep, not completely awake. Her foot twitched as her muscles lost their tenseness—like the family pup, McCracken, relaxing before the fire at home and drifting off to dream a puppy's pleasant dreams.

Outside the window of Sunny's bedroom, where Alex now slept, All-Same-Barrel adjusted the shell-and-feather headpiece. His body was streaked in dyes of white and blue, in the same design used by Kelia's tribe. The previous night, his plan had backfired, for the woman was not sufficiently afraid of the bush rat. But there was no mistaking her fear of Kelia. Once he'd frightened her, she would not want to sleep without Masta at her side to protect her.

Reaching his hand inside, he unlatched the window shutter and silently climbed through the window. In the full moon of the night, he began to weave and writhe in a grotesque dance, moving slowly toward the netting. At the first sign of a scream, he planned to jump through the window and disappear.

His bare feet, making little noise as he walked across the flooring, began to take on a rhythmic pattern upon the wood as he brought his heel down with every dance step. The anklets rattled suddenly when he jumped into the air.

All-Same-Barrel frowned. There was no stirring from the bed covered by the gauze netting. A little bolder, the native approached the bed and made a groaning sound. He lifted his arms and swayed back and forth from side to side, so that the large shell on his forehead and the others hanging about his neck made a clacking sound with each snap and tilt of his head.

All-Same-Barrel could not see the woman, for the sheet

covered her entire body. And she was still surrounded by the mosquito netting.

In an instant, almost quicker than his eye could follow, a muscular arm reached out and captured him in a vise-like grip. All-Same-Barrel yelped in surprise and pain. He struggled to escape, but the more he struggled, the harsher the pain.

Alex Ramsay's deep voice said, "I should string you up in the nearest tree, All-Same-Barrel, for what you've done tonight."

"Please, Masta," the native begged. "I meant no harm."

"No? Then why did you break into this bedroom?"

"I wanted to scare woman...." He yelped as Alex tightened his grip . "It was all for you, Masta. Please let me go."

"Explain yourself first, All-Same-Barrel."

"White woman not come to your bed. You unhappy. She unhappy. All-Same-Barrel fix." He smiled to show his goodwill, but Alex did not return his smile.

"I almost shot you when you slipped through the window," Alex confessed. "It's a good thing I recognized you, despite your grotesque appearance."

"Thank you, Masta."

Alex loosened his hold on All-Same-Barrel. "You put the bush rat in here last night, as well, didn't you?"

"Yes, Masta."

"I want to warn you, All-Same-Barrel. If you *ever* pull such a stunt again, I promise I will shoot you. Is that understood?"

A contrite All-Same-Barrel swallowed. "Yes, Masta."

"All right, then. Go out the same way you came in. And wash off that paint immediately, before Timi You sees you. Otherwise, your life won't be worth a rupee, or a molted cockatoo feather."

All-Same-Barrel fled toward the window. He climbed out quickly. "Latch the shutter behind you, All-Same-Barrel."

Alex Ramsay walked back to the bed, covered up his

naked body with the sheet, and went on to sleep, while Sunny, in his bed in the other room, continued her dreams, undisturbed.

Down below, Father Waal and Obadiah stopped to rest at the spring near the old plantation site that Giles Canupp had once occupied. They drank the cool, pure water, hidden by the overgrowth of vines. Feeling a sense of urgency, they did not linger, for they still had several miles to go.

With the help of the strong stick, Obadiah managed the steep trail. The wound in his side was healing well, but he had lost a lot of blood and was still weak. He craved green leafy vegetables rather than the breadfruit cakes that were a staple of his diet. And Father Waal fed him plenty of canned red meat rather than the usual fish caught in the river.

The priest kept glancing back to make sure the man was following. When he came to a safe spot, Father Waal signaled Obadiah to stop and rest.

By midnight, with the moon high in the sky, the two weary travelers stood at the edge of Bohorok. They knew better than to walk in unannounced. Finding a comfortable place sheltered by green branches, they made a pallet for themselves and lay down to sleep the rest of the night until the sun came up.

By breakfast time, Bohorok claimed six inhabitants—the three native sentries, Timi You, Obadiah, and All-Same Barrel; one priest, one shipwrecked nurse, and one coastwatcher—a minute band to deal with the three dozen soldiers, led at that moment by Ishimoto, who had located the signal of the teleradio high in the hills.

"Father, it's good to see you again," Sunny said, eager to hear the news of the other members of the ship. "Did the rescue go off as planned?"

"It was a narrow escape," the priest admitted. "And, of course, I was extremely disheartened when I realized you were still on the island. And I'm afraid, Alex, your feat in Kelia's village has been reported to the Japanese."

Alex was philosophical about it. "A man can hardly

walk through the jungle in a bright red Scottish tartan and kilt and not attract attention."

A frantic blowing of the conch shell disturbed the gathering at the table. "Excuse me," Alex said, quickly putting down his fork.

A worried Sunny watched him rush out of the house and head for the lookout tree, where Timi You was on duty. Her attention was divided between what was going on outside and Father Waal at the breakfast table. "Will you have another muffin, Father?" she inquired, holding out the small basket with the warm muffins wrapped in a large white napkin.

"Yes, thank you," he said, taking another to put on his plate. He smiled. "If I seem overindulgent, my child, it's because I have been a victim of my own cooking lately."

The two, making casual conversation, watched the door to the verandah. Like a man possessed, Alex rushed back into the house. "Grab your things, Sunny. We're leaving Bohorok in five minutes."

"What's wrong, Alex?"

"The Japanese have discovered us. They're well past Canupp's place and heading this way."

"But where will we go?"

"Up to the ridge," Alex said, already halfway to the radio room.

While Sunny headed to her bedroom to grab her comb and brush, the Atabrine, and a change of khakis, Father Waal took the basket still half-filled with warm muffins and placed in his wicker case.

Alex sat at the teleradio and began to broadcast the distress signal. He used the key, for it broadcast several hundred miles farther. "MDAR, shutting down. Japanese on way." Then he closed with the same signal that other coastwatchers in the Solomons used when shutting down their stations: "Steak and eggs."

A shattering sound came from the radio room. The set, too large to carry, was too important to be left intact for the

Japanese to capture and to use.

As the morning sun touched the banana trees and drank the dew from the patches of tall grass next to the platform that overlooked the azure lagoon, six people began the dangerous trek toward the ridge high in the clouds.

"Wait. Timi You forget something."

"You don't have time to go back, Timi You. The Japs will be here in a few minutes."

To the consternation of Alex and the group, the native turned and ran back to his leaf hut. Quickly, Timi You dug up the parcel wrapped in banana leaves — the cockatoo feathers, the wealth for his old age. He could not leave those behind. They were much too valuable and, to him, as important as his life. He strapped the parcel to his back. As the first Japanese soldier emerged in view at the plantation's edge, Timi You ran out of his leaf hut to join the others.

The soldier called out; a sudden spattering of machine gun bullets followed Timi You's path as he disappeared, unharmed, into the jungle.

Then, the yard filled with soldiers, calling out to each other and rushing to surround the house. A short distance away, Timi You caught up with Alex and Sunny.

They ran, attempting to put as much distance between them and the enemy as possible. Sunny dropped a khaki shirt, but she didn't stop to pick it up. Father Waal glanced at Obadiah. All-Same-Barrel was beside him, to help in case he should stumble. With his wicked-looking *kukri* knife, Timi You began to hack through the tangled vines.

Alex, visualizing the map he had destroyed, prayed at that moment that his memory would not leave him. He was thankful he'd destroyed the map, for it would have meant disaster if it had fallen into the hands of the Japanese. Now, if they could get to the ridge, they would be safe for a while. But Alex knew they were in for a rough time.

With the Japanese taking over Guadalcanal, as they had the other islands along the Solomons, there was no assurance that the Allies would arrive in time to make any difference to any of those escaping from Bohorok that morning.

Chapter 32

KENNA CHALMERS FITZPATRICK AWOKE AT KORABURRA, the magnificent cattle and sheep station owned by Alisdair Shannon.

It had been a week since she'd left Melbourne. Kenna had sent her change of address to her son Jack. Lest he misunderstood, she had told him little about her host.

For four days now, Shan had been away. Only she and Mrs. O'Leary had been together, with two aborigines coming in daily to help in the house and kitchen. And, of course, the overseer took care of the efficient running of the station, with the help of his stockmen.

At night, Kenna slept in the same bedroom she had used on her first visit. And during the day, she rode the horse, Barringo, when she felt the need for exercise. Other than that, her life was quiet, spent in reading or playing the piano which was slightly out of tune, or working in the sadly neglected rock garden.

No one had come to visit and Kenna was relieved. The constant round of social activities as a general's wife, with prescribed protocol determined by a husband's rank—from the row in which the captains' wives could sit to the spots on which the colonels' wives could stand at formal teas—had been relegated to the past. Kenna was content now in an unstructured life, where she was free to choose what she wanted to do and when she wanted to do it.

Dressed in her robe, Kenna carried her breakfast tray back to the kitchen. "Thank you, Mrs. O'Leary, for an excellent breakfast," she said, setting the tray on the table.

"You didn't have to bring the tray back, Mrs. Fitzpatrick. Oona could have gotten it from your room later."

Kenna smiled. "I needed the exercise after such a generous breakfast."

"Will you be going for your morning ride?"

"Yes. As soon as I put on my jodhpurs."

"Then I'll send word to Corky to bring the horse around front."

"Thank you. I shouldn't be long."

Twenty minutes later, Kenna trotted down the winding lane with clumps of eucalypt trees interspersed in an irregular pattern. Off to the side, in the distance, was the landing strip for Shan's plane.

"Come on, Barringo, boy. Let's go for a gallop."

Down past the trees Kenna flew, and across the field with red hills in the background. Unafraid of getting lost, she headed toward the river, where she had ridden the previous day. The river and the small lake were unspectacular because of the recent lack of rain. Yet, there was a beautiful area with trees growing over the riverbank — a small oasis of peace where small animals came to drink. It was a secluded spot where she could sit and sort out all the events and subsequent emotions that had plagued her for the past few weeks.

So totally different from anything she had shared with Irish, Kenna felt the healing balm of the raw, powerful land. She had always been tied to the land, growing up as she had in the South, where heritage was measured in acres and bloodlines. Fleetingly, she thought of Shan, and wondered about his own heritage—whether his ancestors had come over on a convict ship from England years ago. Kenna smiled. How little that mattered in the long run. It was the man, himself, who was important.

Kenna heard the sound of the plane. She looked up toward the sky and recognized the Cessna preparing to land. So Alisdair Shannon had finished his business and come home to Koraburra.

She remained by the riverbank. There was no need to rush back to the house. Barringo was content to graze in the grass by the bank, and she was even more content to stay where she was. She lay down on the soft earth, stared up at the sky, and unconsciously chewed on a thin blade of grass that more resembled wheat because of its color and texture.

The picture of Irish and Sunny the last time they were together in Sydney invaded her thoughts. Tears came to her eyes, and Kenna did nothing to stop their flow, for she was alone, in her own sanctuary, where she came each day, away from Mrs. O'Leary and the others—where she could deal with her grief in the only way she knew how.

She was glad she was able to cry, for she'd been so numb. Now, she knew her tears were the first small step in the long process of accepting that death and danger had come to her life, without adequate warning.

Unashamed of her tears, Kenna allowed them to flow until none were left. Feeling enormously drained, she lay still for a long time, with her hands clasped under her head and her face shaded from the sun by the low-hanging branch of the tree.

"I thought you might be here," a man's voice challenged.

Kenna immediately sat up. "Shan?"

He moved closer, walking with his own horse, and tied the reins to another limb not far from Barringo. One horse neighed, and the other answered.

Not looking at him, Kenna said, "I heard the plane."

"Yes. I got home almost an hour ago. You've been all right these past few days—while I was away?" He came and crouched close to where she was sitting. He saw her face, still tearstained, but made no mention of it.

"Yes. But I'm afraid I've been quite lazy while you were gone."

"Mrs. O'Leary said you've been working in the rock garden."

"Oh, that." She made a little moue. "I hope you don't mind my tackling the project, even if I haven't made much headway."

"If you're interested in continuing, I'll get one of the boys to help you."

"Yes, I'd like that."

Shan walked to the riverbank, dipped his handkerchief into the water, and brought it back to Kenna. "Here, wash your face before we start back. I'd hate for Mrs. O'Leary to think I've been cruel to you."

"Is it that noticeable?"

"I'm afraid so."

She took the offered handkerchief, wiped her face, and mopped at her neck before returning it. "Thank you, Shan."

He made no acknowledgment. Instead, he said, "Let's ride for a while together. Then, we need to get back to the house. As soon as we've eaten lunch, we'll leave for the Bennigans'. They're having a party tonight at Barrah."

"Oh, no. You go on. I'll stay at Koraburra."

"It's too late for you to back out. I've already accepted for you." He sounded so much like Irish in the earlier days of their marriage that she didn't dare argue for fear the tears would begin again.

Shan rode beside Kenna, as he had that day not so long ago—when he first realized why he'd stopped off at Koraburra with Kenna Fitzpatrick. He'd been attracted to her all along, but it was after the dingo hunt, when he'd ridden to find her, that he understood what had happened to him.

It was at the river that he'd discovered her that day, before they flew back to Melbourne. Then later, he felt almost guilty that her husband had died—David, coveting Uriah's wife, and then sending him into battle to be killed.

Shan was not responsible for General Fitzpatrick's death. But he had coveted his wife, nevertheless. And he had taken advantage of her dilemma, for Shan was certain that once she left the continent, he would never see her again.

Now, he would have to be patient and kind. And allow her to get over her grief before he could even dare hope she would grow to love him. And she would need his love more than ever. Eric had told him of Ramsay's last call, just as the Japanese were surrounding Bohorok. The future for her daughter, Sunny, was not bright.

"I'll race you to the trees," he suddenly called out. Kenna took up his challenge and allowed Barringo his head. Neck and neck they raced, with Shan holding his horse, Bowral, back slightly toward the end, until Kenna was ahead.

She held up at the clump of trees, and when Shan reached her, she said, "I don't want you to *give* me the race. One day, I'll beat you fair and square. Just wait and see."

Shan smiled. The color was back in her face, and there was no trace of tears that had wrenched his heart.

They trotted at a leisurely pace for a few minutes, then slowed to a walk while the horses cooled off from their gallop. By the time they reached the white house with its Victorian-gabled roof, Corky was there to take the mounts to the stable.

"By the way, Kenna," Shan said as they walked onto the porch. "Pack a bag. We're staying overnight at Barrah."

Once again, Kenna climbed into the Cessna. Her bag was already stashed behind the seat, but she was still reluctant to leave. "What if someone should try to reach me about Sunny?" Kenna pleaded, unable to conceal a worried look.

"I've already left instructions for Mrs. O'Leary. Any message is to be relayed immediately to Barrah."

Every argument for remaining behind had been countered. With no further excuses at her disposal, Kenna buckled the seat belt and watched Shan prepare for takeoff.

Soon, they were airborne. Shan circled the white house once, straightened up his wings, and then proceeded in a westerly direction, toward the sun and Barrah.

When they touched down at the other landing strip, four planes, similar to Shan's, were lined up. A utility truck drew up and Kenna recognized Cece Bennigan, who smiled and waved as the Cessna taxied by before coming to a full stop.

The moment Shan climbed out, Cece was there. "Shan," she said, hurling herself into his arms. "I'm so glad you finally got here."

"I see the others beat me," he said, playfully tweaking her nose instead of kissing her expectant, upturned face.

"Yes. I'd hoped that you would be first. Shall we go?"

"As soon as I help my passenger out."

Kenna looked at Shan and then toward Cece, who seemed surprised that Kenna was along. At Cece's questioning look, Shan quickly said, "I suppose your father mentioned that I was bringing another guest?"

"He mentioned it," a grudging Cece responded.

"Well, aren't you going to welcome us both?"

"Of course. How do you do, Mrs. Fitzpatrick?"

"Very well, thank you. And you?"

"All right, considering how busy we are this season." She turned to Shan. "Just put your luggage in the rear of the truck. I'm afraid we'll be a little crowded. Mrs. Fitzpatrick, would you mind riding in the back?"

An amused Kenna, used to the best seats in the house as a general's wife, did not have time to reply.

"Really, Cece," Shan admonished. "Where are your manners? Mrs. Fitzpatrick will ride up front with you, and I'll ride in the back."

"I'm sorry. I tend to forget that people lose their agility as they get older. Even Dad can't move as fast as he once did."

Shan laughed. "That properly puts us in our place, doesn't it, Kenna?"

"I didn't mean *you*, Shan. You'll always be young."

"Your father is only five years older than I am."

"My father has been old ever since I can remember. You and he have nothing in common except the cattle stations. And maybe one other item—you're both without wives."

Cece laughed. "One by choice, and the other—not."

Kenna watched the road and didn't enter into the banter between the two friends. Although she longed to ask what had happened to Cece's mother, she knew better than to do so.

"In case Shan hasn't told you, my darling mother ran out on Dad and me five years ago. She went back to Canada because she couldn't take the isolation from society any longer."

"I'm sorry, Cece."

"Oh, you don't have to be sorry for either one of us. We've done quite well without her."

The truck pulled into a circular driveway, where a gray limestone house with curved portico stood. Even more splendid than the house in which Shan lived, it rose out of the middle of nowhere, with red ocher hills and range as a backdrop, while a fountain beyond the driveway stood empty.

As if she could read Kenna's mind, Cece said, "I wanted to start up the fountain again, just for the party, but Dad said the sheep needed the water more. We haven't had much rain lately."

When the truck came to a stop, the tall, slender, dark-haired Cece swung easily to the ground, while Shan, after jumping from the back of the truck, walked around to help the petite Kenna from the vehicle that was much too high off the ground for her to maneuver easily.

"Juno, take the bags inside," Cece commanded the waiting servant.

"And you can put up the truck. We won't be needing it again today."

Curious to meet Shan's mysterious American houseguest, Todd Bennigan rose from his chair when he heard the truck arrive.

With snow white hair and a slight bend to his shoulders, he looked much older than Shan. Because of the war and the tremendous need for wool and meat, he had parlayed his smaller acreage into a better-paying station than ever.

Still, the house took too much money to run, and he recognized that Shan had been smarter than he. Todd would have been happier with a simpler house, too. But his wife, Megan, had persuaded him to renovate, adding a wing they didn't need at all, plus the fountain that wasted water in a land that had no water to waste.

"Shan, how are you?" Todd boomed, holding out his hand to grip Shan's.

"Couldn't be better," Shan replied with a friendly squeeze.

"Mrs. Fitzpatrick, this is my father, Todd Bennigan," Cece began. And to her father she said, "Mrs. Fitzpatrick's husband is an American general."

Shan frowned and quickly corrected the introduction. "Mrs. Fitzpatrick—Kenna—is actually a widow, Cece."

Kenna held out her hand toward Todd Bennigan. "How do you do, Mr. Bennigan."

Todd took one look at the beautiful woman before him, and he smiled at what he saw. The evening was going to be much more interesting than he had anticipated.

"So glad you could come, Mrs. Fitzpatrick. But may I call you Kenna?" he asked. "I'm afraid there's no formality in my house."

"I don't mind at all, Mr. Bennigan."

"Todd. Call me Todd. Well, Cece, take our lovely guest to her room. We can't have her standing in the hallway, when everyone will be eager to meet her." He turned again to Kenna. "Take your time to freshen up. Come on downstairs whenever you like."

"Thank you, Mr....Todd."

As Kenna followed Cece up the stairs, a wary Alisdair Shannon looked at his friend. Todd Bennigan had lost the slight droop to his shoulders. Suddenly, the fifty-six -year-old man was standing straight, with a decided gleam in his eyes.

A feeling of consternation invaded Shan as he realized

that Todd was still watching the woman he'd brought from Koraburra.

Chapter 33

WHEN KENNA RETURNED DOWNSTAIRS, SHE WAS DRESS-
ed in a sophisticated black silk suit that the dressmaker in
Hawaii had made for her. And draped over her arm was the
gossamer-soft wool shawl, oyster in color, to match the
shade of her blouse. Although Kenna was not tall, her
slender legs, her curved swan neck gave her the appearance
of being so.

She followed the sound of voices and clinking of glasses
to an open door. And at its entrance, she paused for just a
moment, her soft gray eyes vulnerable, as she searched for
someone she knew.

Two men stood immediately and began to walk toward
her—Shan and Todd. But it was Todd who reached her first,
took her arm in a possessive way, and drew her into the
room.

"This beautiful lady is Kenna Fitzpatrick, an American.
Now, I'm going to introduce each one of you, but I'll give
you fair warning. She is *my* special guest tonight, and I don't
want any man in this room to forget it."

Everyone laughed except Shan. Suddenly, Cece
appeared at Shan's side. "Darling, can you get me another
drink, please?"

Four couples—three about the age of the host, and a
much younger one—made up the group. With Cece and

Shan paired together, it was only natural for Todd to pay attention to the only woman who was alone.

"How long will you be staying in Australia, Mrs. Fitzpatrick?" one of the older women asked when introduced.

Kenna hesitated. "Perhaps for another month or so."

"And then you'll return to the United States?"

"Yes. Those are my plans."

Shan, on the other side of the room, was not pleased with what he overheard. Once the introductions were over, Todd reluctantly gave up Kenna to the group of women and joined the men congregating before the fire.

They were the same men who had gone with Todd on the dingo hunt when he'd sought their help—Adam Duckett, Trane Mallory, Marvin Hunsinger, and the much younger Trilby James, who had inherited the ranch on the other side of the Bennigans. And, of course, Alisdair Shannon from Koraburra.

"There they go again, talking business. Marvin promised he would be sociable tonight," his wife complained.

"Why should tonight be any different from the rest?" Etta Mallory inquired. She turned to Kenna. "This always happens, you know. The sheep and the steers manage to divide us."

The wives commiserated with each other as they sipped their drinks. "But they work so hard," said the gray-haired Ruth Duckett. "And with such little help. Both our boys are in service. Adam had to come out of retirement to take over again. Do you have children, Mrs. Fitzpatrick?"

"Yes. A son and a daughter—both in the navy—one a pilot, the other a nurse."

"How commendable. But then, I suppose the boys in the States have no choice, do they? In Australia, there is no draft. All are volunteers."

"Trilby wanted to volunteer, too," Rita James offered. "But the government refused to take him since he was in a vital industry—raising wool for uniforms and beef to feed the armies."

"Your husband, Mrs. Fitzpatrick? Didn't I hear from Cece that he's a general?"

"My husband was killed recently, Mrs. Mallory."

"I'm so sorry." She quickly changed the subject as Kenna struggled not to allow her eyes to mist.

Cece Bennigan, dressed in a stylish red hostess dress, returned from the kitchen. "Dinner's on, everybody," she announced. "So grab your partner, and let's go into the dining room."

She immediately headed toward Shan to claim him as husbands and wives put down their drink glasses and met each other halfway.

Offering his arm to Kenna, a smiling Todd asked, "May I?"

She left her shawl on the sofa by the window and walked into the dining room with the owner of Barrah.

In spite of herself, Kenna was entertained by the wit and talkativeness of the group. And she could find nothing wrong with Todd's gallantry. He made her feel quite special—sitting to her left and watching to see if she needed anything.

Once dinner was over, they filed into the new wing of the house where a screen had been set up to preview a film—a documentary made at Barrah and the other ranches. This was the surprise that Todd had kept from them, and the reason for the gathering. He had gotten a copy from the Public Information Service.

"I hope, Kenna, you won't be bored with the film," Todd began. "It's not often that your neighbors turn into movie stars."

Ruth Duckett leaned over and whispered to Kenna, "The government filmed this several months ago, to show that the people at home—the ranchers and the farmers—are doing their bit, too."

"Are you in it?" Kenna asked Ruth.

"I think so. Unless I wound up on what you call 'the

cutting room floor.' "

Sitting between Todd and Ruth, Kenna was kept properly informed as to which ranch or station belonged to whom. But the two need not have bothered. The owners laughed and chortled in delighted horror as they recognized themselves, caught in the camera's eye.

The group was closely knit, their friendship going back over the years and forged by several generations into a strong bond against their common enemies—fire, flood, disease, and wild animals that threatened their folds, herds, and livelihood.

Finally, Kenna recognized Shan's white, Victorian house that slowly came into view, with the camera panning the clumps of eucalypt trees and the rugged red hills in the distance. She listened to the narrator explain the extent of Shan's holdings—the largest station in Australia, with large export capabilities. She watched Shan, lean, tanned, a man equally at home on the land or in the city. The documentary faded as he climbed into his Cessna and took off over the vast land dotted with cattle and sheep being fattened for the Allied armies in Europe, Africa, and the Pacific.

When the lights came on, the group applauded. Ruth, leaning across Kenna, whispered to Todd, "I had forgotten just how wealthy Shan is. When Cece marries him and Barrah and Koraburra are merged, their children are going to have quite a legacy."

"Don't bury me yet, Ruth," Todd teased. "Who knows? If I find the right woman, I might marry again. And Cece might not be the only heir to inherit Barrah."

A surprised Ruth, always used to saying what she thought, commented, "Aren't you and Megan still married?"

"It's been five years since she left—long enough for me to know she's never coming back. It's past time to bury that marriage—for both of us." Todd turned to Kenna, "Would you like another drink? Or would you prefer a walk around the garden?"

"If you don't mind, Todd, it's been a long day. I think I'll just say good-night and go on to bed."

A disappointed Todd inquired, "Do you ride, Kenna?"

"Yes."

"Then let's meet for breakfast. I'd love to show you Barrah in the morning sunlight. Nine o'clock?"

"That would be lovely, Todd. Thank you."

Kenna said her good-nights to everyone except Shan. He was occupied with Cece, and she did not want to disturb him as she left the group. She walked out of the viewing room, now fully lit, retraced her steps into the hallway, and found the curving stairs to the upper floor and her bedroom.

Upstairs, Kenna removed the jacket of her black silk suit and hung it in the closet. When she looked for her shawl, she realized she had left it in the living room before dinner.

She opened her door to the hallway. A light was still on, but the house was silent. Deciding she'd rather retrieve the shawl then than wait until morning, Kenna left her bedroom and walked downstairs.

The embers in the fireplace in the living room provided a faint glow, making it unnecessary for Kenna to turn on the light. The dim outline of the twin sofas in the corner beckoned her. She was almost to the sofa when she heard a faint giggle from the other corner, where a matching chair and ottoman rested.

"I'm afraid we've been caught, Shan," Cece's amused voice rang out.

Kenna stopped at the sound of the voice. "I'm sorry. I didn't mean to intrude. I came downstairs for my shawl...."

"Kenna..." Shan's voice sounded strange, as if he resented the intrusion.

"It's all right," she assured him. "I won't be but a moment." Hastily she grabbed up the oyster white shawl and fled the room. "Good night," she called behind her, and rushed toward the staircase.

Kenna had trouble going to sleep that night, even though she was exhausted. But it was nothing new. She had not slept well for some time. Finally, in the wee hours, she drifted into a sound sleep.

She was still asleep when the maid knocked at the door the next morning. "Mister Todd is downstairs, waiting for you, Mrs. Fitzpatrick."

"Thank you, Milly. What time is it?"

"Eight-thirty, ma'am."

Hurriedly, Kenna got up. She had a half hour to bathe and put on her jodhpurs. While in the tub, she recalled the embarrassing situation downstairs the evening before. At least riding with Todd for the morning would give Shan time to say good-bye to Cece before they left for Koraburra.

Kenna was directed to the second, less formal dining room. Todd was there to greet her.

"Good morning, Kenna. I see you're already dressed for our ride."

"Good morning, Todd. I thought it would save time," she commented.

She looked at the man before her—at the snappy plaid cravat, his khaki shirt and darker brown jodhpurs and freshly polished riding boots. His face looked slightly craggy in the early morning light.

"Well, help yourself to the buffet," he said, urging her to take a plate.

There were only two places at the small table, and when Kenna was seated, she said, "Aren't the others coming down to eat?"

"Oh, I usually spoil the women by having their breakfasts sent up," he hedged.

"And the men?"

"Stayed up late last night. They'll come down when they're good and ready."

No one else came. Todd and Kenna had the small dining room to themselves. And when they had finished, Kenna followed Todd to the stables, where she selected her own horse— a mare with white markings on her nose.

They rode out the gates, past the circular driveway and toward the native trees scattered over the land. The land looked rugged and barren, less fertile than Koraburra. But Kenna, used to the lushness of the American South, decided she was no authority in a land that had such scant rainfall.

They had ridden for almost an hour, away from the house and toward the river that was a mere trickle. A willow tree at what must have been the riverbank defined the river's size in better seasons.

Todd and Kenna stopped at the willow to rest the horses. As Todd helped her dismount, he remarked, "You certainly do sit a horse well, Kenna."

"Thank you, Todd. Horses have always been an important part of my life."

The man took the reins of both horses and tied them to a tree. When he returned to where Kenna was standing, his jaw was resolute. "Last night, you said you would be in Australia for another month or so. Will you be at Koraburra the entire time?"

"I'm not sure. My plans are uncertain at the moment."

"I find you quite a fascinating woman, Kenna. And I'd like to come and call on you, if you don't mind."

Her gray eyes looked up at the man waiting for an answer. She was determined to say nothing that would hurt him, especially since he had been so hospitable to her.

"I'm afraid I won't be good company for anyone for quite a while, Todd. My grief is entirely too new. But if I were going to receive anyone, you'd be the first I would welcome."

A disappointed Todd Bennigan accepted her explanation. But it didn't keep him from making plans of his own—the first, to contact Megan in Canada with an ultimatum. Come home, or he would file for divorce. And he already knew that she would never return to Australia.

Todd and Kenna started back to the house. It was almost noon and Kenna was beginning to get hungry again. The crisp, fresh air and the long ride had combined to make the little she'd eaten for breakfast only a distant memory.

They traveled down the graveled lane and onto the

circular driveway near the still-silent fountain. The jeep waited at the front of the house, and sitting inside it were Shan and Trane Mallory.

"Good morning, you two," Todd called out in a friendly voice. "You should have been with us. I was showing Kenna over Barrah."

"Yes, it was a lovely ride," Kenna affirmed.

Before Todd could dismount and help Kenna, Shan was already at her side. His face showed his irritation. "I've been waiting for you for the past thirty minutes, so we could leave."

"I didn't realize you would be in a hurry this morning. I'll run in to change and pack. It won't take long."

"I'm afraid you won't be able to do either one." He pointed toward the luggage already in the truck. "Milly packed for you. I'll give you five minutes. Then we'll be on our way."

Todd gave the two horses to one of the stable boys and joined Kenna and Shan. Overhearing the last of the conversation, Todd protested. "But you never leave, Shan, until after lunch is served. The spread will be on in a few minutes."

"I'm sorry, Todd. I have to get back to Koraburra immediately. Something's come up."

Kenna's face turned white, for she feared news of Sunny had been forwarded to Barrah. "Is it Sunny?" she demanded, the fear showing in her voice.

"No, I've heard nothing. This is something else entirely."

Unnerved, Kenna said, "I won't be long." She hurried into the house to wash up, while Todd remained outside with Shan and Trane.

"She's really something, Shannon," Todd confided. "Thank you for bringing her. My life may never be the same after meeting her."

He grinned but Shan did not return his smile. Realizing something had upset his friend, Todd said, "You and Cece haven't had a quarrel, have you?"

"You'll have to ask Cece," a noncommital Shan replied. Kenna walked down the steps and toward Todd Benni-gan. She held out her hand in friendship. "Thank you, Todd, for inviting me to Barrah."

"You'll have to come again soon. And if Shan won't bring you, just get on the wireless and call me. I'll fly over for you."

Shan rushed her to the truck, helped her up, and climbed into the driver's seat, with Trane Mallory sitting in the rear. The graveled rocks spun from the wheels as Shan took off.

"I know you're in a hurry, old man," Trane commented. "But for the sake of my ailing back, can you slow down a little?"

"Sorry," Shan replied, easing up slightly on the accelerator as he drove toward the airstrip where his Cessna waited.

Chapter 34

ON THE ISLAND OF GUADALCANAL, THE SOUND OF A search plane skimming over the jungle brought Alex Ramsay to a halt. The group desperately needed to rest—especially Obadiah and Father Waal, who had already put a nitroglycerin tablet under his tongue to relieve the angina pain in his arm.

The soldiers had evidently given up trying to follow them, for the jungle was now quiet except for the Washing Machine Charlie overhead. At Alex's signal, a grateful Sunny dropped to her knees and cradled herself on a bed of leaves. Her rapid breathing gradually slowed to near normal, while around her, the rest of the group also found a resting place.

Alex's hand was now a mass of blisters because of the constant hacking against the lianas—vines tying tree to tree and shrub to shrub, with massive runners that denied easy access through the jungle. Even Timi You, more used to the teeming foliage, had removed the bandage of gauze from his head and wrapped it around his right hand.

"How much farther do we have to go?" Sunny whispered.

"Several hours more. And then we'll be at the cave."

"Do you think we'll be safe there?"

"It's the safest place on the island," Alex assured her.

"And there's food stored there, too?"

"Yes. Enough to last for six months or more."

"Is anyone hungry?" Father Waal asked.

The three natives on the other side of the priest lifted their heads and waited for someone to answer.

"Would it make any difference, Father?" Sunny inquired.

"It might." He smiled. "This is as good a time as any to bring out the muffins you made this morning, my child." He turned to All-Same-Barrel, who had carried his wicker case for the last few miles. "Open up my case, All-Same-Barrel," he asked, "and bring the basket of muffins to me, please."

Surprised, Sunny watched as the native brought out the rest of the muffins she'd baked that morning for breakfast. There were six of them left—enough for everyone to have a muffin. But instead of doling them out whole, Father Waal broke three of them in half.

He held out the basket, first to Sunny. "We may have to feed the multitude again with the crumbs," Father Waal said, "so let's take only a half muffin for now."

"They don't look like loaves and fishes, Father," Sunny said with a laugh. "More like manna from heaven, don't you think?"

He smiled as he went through the ritual of blessing each piece of bread and offering it to the next in line. The six sat and ate quietly, taking small pinches of the half muffins and popping them into their mouths, as if to record the taste forever. While they were eating, the priest returned the last three muffins to his wicker case for later on.

"I wish we had some water to drink," Sunny said in a wistful voice, for a crumb had gotten stuck in her throat.

"Another hour of walking, and we'll reach a waterfall," Alex assured her. He glanced toward Timi You and the native nodded. The humidity and heat of the island had an enervating effect on all of them. They desperately needed water. There had been no time to stop earlier, even to pick up a coconut. At a much higher level now, they were beyond the line of coconut palms, and the waterfall was the only disease-free source of water anywhere near.

But to reach it, they would have to take the route that Timi You had traveled the first time he directed Alex to the ridge and the caves. That meant going through the more dangerous open terrain with no trees to hide their progress. Even though the enemy plane was still scouting, Alex decided that they would have to take the risk.

"All right, let's travel on," Alex said, standing.

Reluctantly, Sunny pushed herself up from the ground. Soon they began the second part of the journey. The path was steeper, with rocky ledges that crumbled without warning.

Father Waal lost his footing and slid halfway down a hill before grabbing onto a bush. He hung suspended, with one foot searching for a firm toehold, while above, the others watched helplessly. But the priest managed to regain his footing and reach Alex's outstretched hand.

Sunny's few belongings had long ago been placed in Father Waal's wicker case. Alex wanted no items dropped along the way for the Japanese to trace their escape route. Then, too, Alex knew Sunny would need her hands free to scale the rough terrain.

The hour passed slowly. No one talked, for all were conserving their energy, all concentrating on the water not far away. Just ahead of them, Sunny saw the open space that divided the jungle from the deserted village and relatively level land.

"Water," she said. "I think I can even smell it."

"Let's hope not," Alex countered, still able to smile despite his thirst. "That would mean it's polluted with some dead animal carcass."

Sunny returned his smile. "You forget, I was on the raft long enough for small things like that not to bother me." She started toward the field, but Alex stopped her.

"Wait, Sunny. You'll have to camouflage yourself before you leave the shelter of the trees."

Alex and Timi You chopped some leafy twigs while the

others gathered ferns and vines. Within a few minutes, even the wicker case had become a moving bush.

They started out in pairs—slowly at first—a quick dash and then a stop—movement and then tableau, in case enemy eyes were watching the terrain. Timi You and All-Same-Barrel, with Father Waal's case, went first, followed by Obadiah and the priest.

At last, Sunny and Alex left the cover of overhanging branches. In a zigzag pattern, they skirted the edge of the jungle and then darted into the open, falling to their knees and remaining still, like a bush suddenly planted in the field. At the point of no return, they heard the noise of the plane. As the plane came into view overhead, Father Waal stumbled again and lost part of the green camouflage from his black cassock.

"Run, Father," Timi You shouted, dropping his half of the wicker case. All-Same-Barel did the same, and fled across the open vista as the plane came in low to strafe the field. But Father Wal remained still, his black figure a few feet from his wicker case.

Farther back, Alex and Sunny, well-camouflaged, also lay still while the three natives ran, unhampered by the case. Tracer bullets, machine gun fire ripped up the footprints made by the three only a split second previously. The plane moved out of range, then circled and came in again, even lower, so that Sunny could almost make out the features of the pilot's face.

"What do we do now, Alex?" Sunny asked, wanting to get up and run, yet knowing it might be the worst option.

"Stay where you are. Don't move an eyelid," Alex cautioned. He did not follow his own advice. With a sudden spurt of energy, he ran toward Father Waal, scooped him up in his arms, and carried him to a ditch, where he fell.

Directly behind Alex, in the spot where Father Waal had stumbled, tracer bullets plowed the earth. A few seconds more and the priest would have been dead.

The plane soared upward and Alex shouted, "Run now,

Sunny — toward Timi You."

She needed no further encouragement. Sprinting as fast as she could, Sunny took off, passing the ditch where Alex and Father Waal lay. Then Alex got up, hoisted the priest in his arms, and made it to shelter just as the plane returned.

With the field sufficiently torn up and with no one in sight, Washing Machine Charlie left the open range and disappeared in the high clouds toward the channel and Tulagi.

"Hope he crashes," Sunny muttered between gasps for breath.

Timi You and All-Same-Barrel, realizing the plane had gone for the moment, went back into the open field and brought what was left of Father Waal's wicker case.

"I apologize for being so clumsy," the priest said. "It made matters worse. The pilot might not have seen you, if it hadn't been for me."

Seeing the apoplectic red of Father Waal's face, Sunny asked, "How long have you had trouble with your heart, Father?"

"What do you mean?"

Sunny was not to be put off. "Remember, Father," she warned. "I'm a nurse."

"So you are, my child. I should have remembered. Only one other suspected my secret — Sister Birghitta."

"And that's why she didn't want to leave you. But you haven't answered my question. How long?"

"Almost three years," the priest finally admitted.

"All this running can't be good for your heart," Sunny said. She turned to Alex. "He shouldn't walk anymore today. Do you think we can devise some type of conveyance for him?"

"I'll carry him on my back," Alex replied.

"No," the priest insisted. "Leave me here with one of the native boys who knows the way to the cave. Once I've had adequate rest, we can follow later."

Alex shook his head. "We'll remain together."

"But I insist—"

"Father, for once you're out of your jurisdiction. You take care of heavenly matters, and I'll take care of the earthly ones," Alex chided.

As if the matter had been settled, Alex changed the subject. "I'd forgotten just how fast you can run, Amanda Fitzpatrick."

In spite of her tiredness, Sunny laughed aloud. She remembered Alex's disapproval on the hospital ship the evening her nurses' team had won the Golden Bedpan Award.

"She won a prize for it," Alex said, turning again to the priest.

"And what prize was that, Miss Fitzpatrick?"

If she had been close enough to Alex, she would have kicked him for bringing up the subject. Quickly, she said, "First prize in a relay race between two nurses' teams on the hospital ship's deck."

"She was the team captain...."

Sunny glared at Alex and her topaz eyes dared him to go on. It had been harmless fun that night—to take away the tensions on the ship. And the bedpans had been filled with nothing more than rainwater.

"It looks as if your wicker case is a casualty of war, Father," Sunny said, anxious to direct his attention to something else.

While Timi You and All-Same-Barrel brought the case for Father Waal to inspect, Sunny walked over to Obadiah. "How are you feeling, Obadiah?"

"I be okay."

"Good. You haven't felt any pain?"

"Not bad," he replied. She realized that the native was every bit as stubborn as the priest.

They moved out, slower this time, for Father Waal was being carried by Alex. "Sprained ankle," Alex muttered toward Timi You. The excuse was accepted with no suspicion.

No one talked after that. The cool water supply ahead was on all their minds. Especially for Sunny and Alex. Each was remembering those days on the open sea, without water, without food.

Sunny wished she'd eaten more breakfast that morning. Half a muffin was hardly enough to assuage her hunger for the rest of the day. Yet, the hunger pangs were less to Sunny than the terrible thirst that had already caused her tongue to swell.

She heard the water before she saw it. The small stream ran down the eroded rock, tumbling over a precipice and into a pool below.

Not caring about anything beyond the water, she began to run again. She brushed past the few vines that separated her from the idyllic spot in the heart of the jungle. As she knelt at the water's edge, she startled a lizard into flight. Not aware of the others around her, Sunny held out her hands to catch the cascading water. And when she had drunk to her heart's content, she finally looked up. Staring at her from above the ledge were four hostile looking natives.

"Alex," she whispered to the man near her. Her hand signaled for him to look upward.

"I know, Sunny. Pretend you don't see them."

Timi You slowly moved back from the waterfall. His right hand rested on the *kukri*, while Alex, making the motions of drinking, kept his hand on his pistol.

The four natives disappeared and Sunny again whispered to Alex, "Do you think they'll tell the Japanese where we are?"

"They're probably more worried at what *we're* going to do. But once we leave, they'll know we mean them no harm."

They rested by the pool, with Timi You keeping watch near the faint footpath. Fifteen minutes later, they moved out again, with the priest insisting on walking for a time to give Alex some reprieve from his burden. The man's face was no longer red, and the pain in his arm and shoulder had subsided.

At an elevation where the cumulus clouds seemed almost within reach, they began another climb upward. A rumble of thunder announced a coming rain squall, while down below, the Japanese soldiers finally returned to Bohorok. An entire range now separated the group from the copra plantation.

Alex looked at Father Waal to see how he was faring. He walked slowly, but with a sure step, and aid from a long pole he used to dig into the earth every few feet.

Conserving energy as best they could, they walked and slapped at insects buzzing around their heads. Earlier, when Sunny still had enough energy to talk, she'd been forced into silence. Now, she was silent through choice.

The only words spoken aloud came from Alex. "We'll stop here to rest again." And occasionally, when Sunny lagged, he gave an encouraging, "We'll be there soon."

Then, Alex spoke the wonderful, long-awaited words, "We're here."

Sunny looked around her. The heavily forested ledge seemed no different from the others. She saw no entrance to a cave—merely a dense growth of vines and shrubs already wet with the rain that had begun earlier. The wreckage of the Japanese plane, half-hidden by the green growth that encircled the burned-out fuselage, lay a hundred yards away.

"Where is it?" Sunny inquired, pushing her wet hair from her face.

"Timi You, would you like to show them?"

The native scout walked ten to twelve paces, pulled back the living gate of greenery to reveal the dark opening of the cave.

"I don't believe it," Sunny said in amazement. "I could have walked past it a dozen times without even knowing it was there."

"Caves dot the entire island," Father Waal said. "You have no idea how many people are hiding from the Japanese at this very moment."

The brigade, with blisters on their hands and feet, waited for Timi You to light the lantern hidden inside and to chase out the island creatures that had sought refuge in the cave. A small gecko rushed by Sunny and leaped onto a tree, where it remained motionless except for its throat fluttering in and out with fright.

Sunny got no farther than the first chamber before she dropped to the cave floor. She closed her eyes in exhaustion, while outside, the rain quickened to a downpour. Large drops pelted the leaves. The subsequent rush of rain flooded the ridge and cascaded over the ledge, causing a mudslide immediately below, where the wounded Japanese pilot had crawled into the wreckage of the plane to wait out the fury of the island storm.

Chapter 35

AT KORABURRA, THE WINTER SEASON HAD TURNED COLD and dry. The riverbank where Kenna rode each day was now a dirty brown, and her horse, Barringo, found little grass to enjoy as Kenna sat in her sanctuary, away from the house.

The overnight trip to Barrah had been a mistake for many reasons. If Kenna hadn't known better, she would have thought Shan jealous of the attention paid her by their host, Todd Bennigan. But that was ridiculous—just as Shan's attempt to apologize for his behavior with Cece was also ridiculous.

She had handled the situation badly. She realized now, too late, that if she had been a little more diplomatic, she could have warded off the breach between them.

But she had been miffed, herself, at Shan's high-handed decision to have the maid pack her suitcase, forcing her to remain in her dusty jodhpurs for the trip back to Koraburra. She would have understood if he had told her beforehand that he wanted to leave by noon. But he had neglected to do that.

The return trip was far different from the leisurely flight to Barrah. Shan flew swiftly, as if the devil were in the tail wind directly behind him. He'd made no attempt at small talk. It was after he landed and they were waiting for the utility truck to arrive at the airstrip that he had finally spoken to her.

"Kenna, I want to explain about last night—"

She cut him off. "It's none of my business, Shan. You're free to do what you wish. You don't have to give me the details."

A thunderous look came over his face. "I understand your reasoning, Kenna. This way, you won't be forced into telling me what happened between you and Todd."

"Exactly. But the trip made me realize I don't belong out here. Heaven knows I've tried to find an apartment in the city, but all my inquiries so far have been to no avail."

She ignored the stifled oath that came from his throat. Quietly, she said, "I believe the truck is here. Shall we get out since you're in such a hurry?"

Remembering their brief conversation four days previously, a restless Kenna stood up, brushed the seat of her jodhpurs, and began to walk along the riverbank. Barringo neighed, as if he resented being left behind, but Kenna paid no attention to him. She kept walking with her head down, her thoughts a maddening dervish. The strain of not knowing what had happened to her daughter was almost more than she could bear. And the set-to with Shan had not helped.

What should she do? Even if she remained in the Pacific, there was nothing she could do to help Sunny. Yet, the idea of leaving, of putting a distance of over six thousand miles between them, was heartrending.

She felt guilty using Shan to stay in Australia. And she'd felt guilty adding to Mrs. O'Leary's work. The white-haired woman had looked so tired lately that Kenna, not knowing when Shan would return, had given the woman the weekend off. She had left a few hours before, with her sister and her husband.

Barringo snorted and his action caused Kenna to look back. Skulking along the riverbank a hundred or so yards directly behind her was an unusually large and wild-looking dingo.

Kenna remained quite still, trying to decide what to do. She saw the frightened horse struggling to get the reins loose from the low-hanging limb of the willow tree. She looked at the ferocious wild dog blocking her path to the horse. But then, the dingo was joined by two others from the pack, their feral eyes watching her. Across the muddy trickle that passed for a river, another willow tree stood with its lower branches bending toward the bank. Not nearly so strong or large as the closer tree, it was still her best chance for safety.

With Barringo pawing the ground and trying to get free, the dingoes' attention turned to the horse. Kenna took that opportunity to run. She dashed across the water, fell in the mud; got up and ran again without looking back. As she began to climb the tree, the first branch broke under her weight. But she held to the next branch and swung upward while immediately below her, a dingo, that had chosen to follow her, growled.

"Barringo," Kenna shouted. "Come here, Barringo." She whistled for the horse.

While the horse struggled even more to get loose, a dingo closed in and delivered a vicious bite. In pain, the horse snapped the branch free from the tree. Again Kenna whistled. "Come here, boy."

The horse paid no attention to her. Barringo, dragging the small limb, raced away from the river before the dingoes could overtake him. Kenna watched while the horse hobbled out of sight with two of the dingoes trailing behind. Within a few minutes, one of the dingoes returned to join the other still on guard by the tree where Kenna sat.

Corky, the aborigine, was the only one who knew that she had gone for a ride. If the horse returned to the stable, would he realize what had happened and come looking for her? But no one, except possibly , Shan, knew of the place she used as a sanctuary. He had been gone for four days. There was no guarantee that he would return to Koraburra anytime soon. And she was not within cooing distance for anyone to hear her.

Kenna was more angry than frightened. She blamed no one but herself—and the dingoes that watched her, like animals waiting out their prey. How long could she stay propped in the tree? Already her body was beginning to grow tired in such an uncomfortable position. Her foot, still muddy, slipped and she grabbed hold of the upper branch anew. A slight cracking sound signaled that the limb was too weak to last under her weight for any length of time. She climbed higher.

The sun began to sink behind the red hills in the distance, and the temperature dipped steadily. Kenna's light riding jacket gave little protection against the wind that swept over the open plain and whistled down the long cut of the riverbank.

To give an even more sinister touch to the landscape, a kookaburra bird, flying to the adjacent tree, emitted the shriek that long ago had earned the sobriquet of "laughing jackass."

Finally, the land was no longer a mass of shadows. Pitch black, except for the yellow eyes that glowed in the dark, the evening passed slowly. Kenna made up her mind. Her riding crop was little protection. But by morning, if the dingoes had not left, she would arm herself with a branch from the tree and face the wild dogs. She had no other choice.

Kenna's eyes closed and her grip relaxed, like a driver going to sleep at the wheel of a car. Suddenly she came awake again and tightened her grasp.

As she looked out into the blackness, she saw a small light, dim at first, like a lantern hanging by the stable door or in one of the little houses that sheltered the aborigines working on Koraburra. Another appeared from a different direction, and still another, all progressing steadily over the land. And Kenna began to hope that someone was out looking for her.

She strained her ears for the "Cooee" call, used by trackers to locate someone lost in the wild. But no sound beyond the call of the wind reached her ears.

Then, barely perceptible, the sound rose above the wind—a shrill, high-pitched cooee. Just as a hopeful Kenna opened her mouth to answer, the kookaburra bird in the nearby tree responded with its shriek.

Frustrated, Kenna waited for the piercing laugh to diminish. Then, she answered. The dingoes moved from beneath the tree. The lights grew brighter, and Kenna, responding steadily to the man tracking her, called out until her voice grew hoarse with the strain.

Across the riverbank, the lantern stopped moving. "Kenna, where are you?"

"On the other side of the water. In the willow tree. Watch out, Shan. There're two dingoes nearby."

A shot rang out, but it was not toward the wild dogs. Rather, the shot went into the air, to alert the trackers that Kenna had been found. But the noise worked to drive the dogs away, as well. Their gleaming eyes no longer watched from the bank. By the time Shan had navigated the trickling stream, Kenna had dropped to the ground. Disturbed, the large bird emitted another loud shriek, causing Shan's mount to sidle in fright.

"Go away. Shoo," an annoyed Kenna chided the bird as she began to walk along the bank toward Shan and the light. "Am I glad to see you," she remarked, giving little indication of the harrowing experience she'd been through. "You have the most inhospitable creatures on your station, Alisdair Shannon."

"I warned you about that, Kenna, if you remember. But I'm sorry you had to find out in a more dramatic way."

The lantern was in her eyes, and Kenna held up her hand to shield them. "Well, no harm's done, thank heavens."

He leaned down and lifted her into the saddle with him. A blanket went over her and she shivered as his arms clasped her to him.

"Speak for yourself," he said in a low tone that vibrated

against her ear. "I'll never be the same again."

Content to rest her head against Shan's chest, a tired and hungry Kenna rode through the alien terrain until they reached the house, blazing with lights.

"Did Barringo get back to the house all right?"

"No, we found him a mile from the house. He has a rather nasty bite on his leg, but it will heal."

"I'm sorry he was hurt."

Shan was suddenly angry. "You have no idea, do you, what agony I've been through? And not because of Barringo. I thought the dingoes had attacked *you*, too, and that you were lying out there in the dark—hurt, or perhaps even dead. And here you act as if you've been out on a lark."

"How else should I behave? Would you rather have found me in tears and hysterics? Would that have satisfied your male ego sufficiently? Well, keep sniping at me, Alisdair Shannon, and your wish might come true."

"Oh, Kenna, let's not fight anymore. You're safe. That's what actually matters." He helped her down from the saddle. "Go on into the house and get Mrs. O'Leary to fix us a bite of supper while I take the horse to the stable and thank the boys for going out with me."

"Mrs. O'Leary has left for the weekend."

"I don't recall giving her that time off."

"Well, that's something else you can fuss about. *I* told her it was all right to spend the weekend with her sister's family since there was no need for her stay here on my account."

Kenna marched onto the verandah of the Victorian mansion without giving Shan a chance to answer. She heard the horse's hooves pounding against the graveled drive as he wheeled the horse from the steps. Alone, she sat in a chair and removed her muddy boots before walking inside.

By the time Shan returned from the stable, Kenna had taken a quick shower, put on a warm yellow dress with pale lavender trim, and gone into the kitchen to prepare food for the two to eat. And later, when it was ready, Shan walked into the kitchen.

"I've made a fire. We can eat before it, if you'd like."

"Yes, I'd like that. I still feel a little chilled."

Scrambled eggs, thin slices of beef, and John Dory fish with chunks of hot bread, jam, and butter occupied the less formal earthenware that Kenna had found in the kitchen. She brought the plates into the small family room off the kitchen, where they sat together on the blue wool plaid sofa with twin coffee tables made of Tasmanian mountain ash before it. Shane poured red wine into the matching earthenware goblets.

"To the gods for keeping you safe," Shan said in salute.

"To Koraburra and the man who owns it," Kenna replied, grateful that he had found her, despite her behavior that might have indicated otherwise.

Shan took a bite. "My compliments," he said, showing his approval at the meal. "Do you enjoy cooking?"

"Only when I'm extremely hungry."

Shan laughed. "I take it, then, that you've had a Mrs. O'Leary in your kitchen, also."

"Yes. But her name is Mattie. She's keeping the house in Macon in order, for our…my return."

"I see."

They fell silent, each taking a sip of wine and then picking up a fork to continue eating. Later, Kenna, staring into the fire said, "Houses have memories, don't they? I feel it in this house, too, Shan—happiness and sadness, joy and laughter—and children…"

"It's been a silent house lately," he admitted. "That's why I like to hear your voice." In confidence, he said, "This is the first time I've sat in this room since I received the telegram about Dair. After Miranda died, my son and I used to have our Sunday night suppers in here."

A sadness filled his voice and Kenna remained silent.

Suddenly, Shan reached over and took her hand in his. "Miranda has been dead for ten years." With a sense of urgency he continued, "Today, while I flew back from Townsville, I tried to remember what she looked like. But your face kept getting in the way, Kenna. I couldn't even remember the color of her eyes. I kept seeing those chameleon gray eyes of yours, changing with your moods, like a weather barometer.

"I wanted to hurry home, to apologize for my foul mood at Barrah. I was jealous of Todd's attention to you, especially after I had informed Cece the evening before that I was falling in love with you."

A distressed Kenna withdrew her hand and stood abruptly. "You shouldn't have done that, Shan. Cece made it clear that she plans to marry you. And this—"

Shan interrupted. "I don't want to marry a child bride who's the age of my own son. I want to marry a woman, Kenna—a beautiful, impetuous woman, capable of being the kind of wife I need and desire. The moment I saw you in the garden, when we'd stopped off from Darwin, I realized I wanted you. And I usually get what I want," he warned.

Kenna backed toward the fire. "It's too soon, Shan. My husband…"

He followed her. "I'm not asking you to marry me tomorrow, Kenna. I'm willing to wait while you deal with his memory in your own way." He gazed down into her serious, sober face. "But not too long, Kenna. You have to go on living. And it's easier to share your grief with someone who understands, rather than trying to manage alone. Especially with the news I have for you."

"What is it? Have you heard anything from Sunny?"

He hesitated. "Part of it will be in the newspapers tomorrow. So you might as well know. The Japanese have landed a large invasion force on Guadalcanal. Alex Ramsay broadcast an SOS from there a few days ago. The Japanese discovered his hideout."

"No, Shan." Kenna bit her lip and turned her head to stare into the dying embers of the fire.

"Eric told me there's a cave in the hills where they will probably be safe—at least for a while."

She faced the tall, lithe man, whose words held the only

hope for her daughter's safety. "I'm frightened for her, Shan."

"I know, darling." He put his arms around her to comfort her. She didn't protest.

Chapter 36

ON GUADALCANAL, THE AFTERNOON RAIN SQUALL
came in full force, and Timi You hid a barrel outside the
cave to catch the rainwater. Disease-laden, most of the rivers
and springs could not be relied upon for drinking water,
even that high up in elevation.

Inside the cave, Sunny looked down at her skin, irritated
from the poisonous sap of some of the trees they had passed
in the jungle. And she remembered Sister Birghitta's words
when they had left Kelia's village and hidden out until
Father Waal could catch up with them.

"Those leaves are poisonous. Here, these are harmless."
Sunny had put them in the shoes she'd worn—Madeleine's
shoes. Now using the healing sulfa powder Alex had given
her, she pressed along the ridges of the blisters that she'd
acquired again, much worse this time because of the more
difficult journey and the constant rubbing of the straw
sandals.

It was strange how rapidly one became used to dealing
with danger. Yesterday seemed a fantasy—the friends, the
hospital ship, the frivolous things that had occupied her
time on shore leave. Sunny had never worried before about
water to drink, or food to eat, or the possibility of being
captured by the enemy—whether by the Japanese or the
native chieftain, Kelia. And as for Matt Willoughby and the

others, how little she thought of them now. Reality was in the present—today, with Alex, Father Waal, and the three native scouts, all fighting to survive on a hostile island.

Even Bohorok was gone. Timi You had pointed out the fire an hour after their escape. The Japanese had destroyed it. Yet, Sunny was glad. She would not have been happy, knowing they were sitting on the screened verandah where she and Alex had watched the sun set, or sleeping on the bed she'd shared with Alex on the night she'd heard Tokyo Rose on the radio, with the sad news of her father.

"Are you recovered enough to select your bedroom now?" Alex asked, returning from the inner chambers of the cave.

"You mean I have a choice?"

"Yes—within reason, of course. It will have to be on this level and far enough away from the entrance so the lantern light won't show."

Sunny rose from the floor where she was sitting. "Lead on, Alex Ramsay."

They passed by the cache of supplies, the boxes and crates against the walls. Quickly, Sunny made out the labels denoting the food, benzene, rifles, and medication. "I had no idea," she commented, "that so much was stored away up here."

"Giles did it," Alex explained, "with the help of Timi You and Wani, the chap who went with him to Savo."

"Will you be able to broadcast from here?"

"We have the equipment. But we'll set it up at least a mile away from the cave."

"Surely the Japanese couldn't find you now that we've put an entire range between us?"

"Remember the scout plane that strafed us. I'm afraid the pilot will scour the entire island to find us."

Sunny saw the cots and she forgot everything else. "How lovely. I thought we would have to sleep on leaves."

"We're not quite that rustic."

Alex stopped. In three directions, the cave branched off.

"We won't use the middle tunnel. It leads to a pool below, and the dampness isn't healthy. You have your choice of either the left or the right corridor. Which will it be?"

Sunny hesitated. "Where will you and Father Waal sleep tonight?"

"In the same corridor as you. We'll put the scouts on the other side. But someone will be on duty all the time at the entrance."

Sunny chose a right turn from the main room, and no natural light reached them deep within the cave. "I don't really like the dark," she confessed.

"I didn't expect you would."

While Alex held the lantern high, Sunny walked behind him.

"Is there more than one exit to the cave?" she asked.

"Not that I've found so far."

The young nurse, dressed in khaki, shuddered. "I'd feel better if we had a back door in case someone came in the front."

"That would mean an extra guard," Alex pointed out. "And we don't have enough manpower for that."

Stopping at a place where the wall was indented, with an overhanging ledge, Sunny said, "I think I'll take this space, if it's all right with you."

Alex gave a nod. "I'll get All-Same-Barrel to bring your cot and set it up."

"I'm not sure I trust that fellow."

"And why do you say that?"

"I heard you two talking in my bedroom at Bohorok. He was the one who put the bush rat in there, wasn't he?"

Alex smiled. "You needn't worry about him anymore, I assure you."

Though not convinced, Sunny dropped the subject. "And where are the amenities—like a bathroom?"

"Outside the cave—anywhere you choose."

"Not in the middle of the night," Sunny protested.

An amused Alex suggested, "Then you can set up your own *chambre de toilette*, inside."

"On the hospital ship, we called it 'the head.' "

"Whatever you prefer to call it, you'll have sole responsibility of emptying it each day."

"Naturally. And now that that's settled, what about food? Am I expected to cook tonight? And what about the smoke from the fire? Do you think it will be seen this far up?"

"There's little danger in that. Any smoke will dissipate into the mist. Just to make certain, though, we can use the middle corridor for the kitchen. But not tonight. We'll open up a few cans and eat the food cold."

Conscious of their being completely alone for the first time that day, Sunny, denying the magnetic pull that drew her to Alex, continued to ask questions.

"Are there enough lanterns to go around?"

Alex stared into her worried topaz eyes and forced himself to answer. "We have only three. But I'll see that you get one of them."

"Thank you, Alex."

They continued to stare at each other while the silence built in intensity around them. Shadows from the lantern played upon the wall, forming a silhouette of a man and a woman leaning toward each other.

Suddenly, Alex set the lantern on the floor at their feet and took a step closer. In a voice filled with tenderness, he said, "Sunny, I'm sorry you had such a rough time today."

"It wasn't any worse for me than for the others," she replied, dismissing his apology even as she attempted to dismiss his tenderness.

"That's what I love about you," he confessed in a sad, bittersweet voice. "You won't ever cry uncle, will you?" He reached out to touch her cheek, a caressing motion that rapidly transformed itself to fire and passion.

She stepped back, but his eyes held hers, and in spite of her resolve, she began to move steadily toward him until she was in his arms.

His lips brushed against hers, a soft, tantalizing kiss that ripened into heated desire, his mouth claiming hers, not gently, but with all the longing that had gone unfulfilled. The dimension of time disappeared—the night in Sydney, the night at Bohorok—this very moment, all the same. He claimed her heart and soul with a kiss that seared and branded her with the knowledge that she would never be free from Alex Ramsay again.

He gently placed his hand under her chin and lifted her face until her eyes met his once more. "Why do we keep pretending, Sunny?" he whispered, "and denying our need for each other? That night at Bohorok, when I held you in my arms and loved you, I knew I wanted to spend eternity with you."

Sunny turned her head so that Alex could not see the tears that threatened. "But we don't have an eternity, do we, Alex? We both know we won't ever get off this God-forsaken island."

He didn't refute what she said. "Then whatever time has been allotted to us—a week, even a day—I want to love you, Sunny. I want to be a husband to you."

"I'm afraid Father Waal wouldn't approve."

"Didn't you see what he brought in his wicker case? He could marry us properly. Tonight, Sunny. If you'd say yes."

She looked at Alex and saw her own desire reflected in his eyes. At that moment, Matt Willoughby no longer existed. If she were going to die, she would much rather die as Alex Ramsay's wife than a lonely Sunny Fitzpatrick, denying even one night of ecstasy in Alex's arms.

"I can see the headlines now," she joked. "The bride wore khaki, while her attendants were dressed in cockatoo feathers."

Alex laughed. "Does that mean your answer is yes?"

"Why not?"

"Then All-Same-Barrel will be extremely happy tonight. He's wanted this all along."

"Yes, Masta."

"You little devil. Stop teasing me. Let's go and find the priest."

Retracing their steps through the cave to the first chamber, Alex and Sunny went arm in arm. Alex was unable to stand straight because of the low-hanging stalactites, formed centuries before by water dripping through the porous volcanic rock.

One hour later, with the lanterns surrounding the altar set up by Father Waal, Amanda "Sunny" Fitzpatrick and Alex Ramsay, marquess of Dalhousie, became man and wife.

In her hands, Sunny held a bouquet of hastily gathered greenery, with a small bunch of flowers known by the islanders as mountain coral because of its resemblance to the sea coral in the lagoon below. And witness to the ceremony were the three native scouts—Timi You, Obadiah, and All-Same-Barrel.

The cup from which the bridal pair drank had a small leak, courtesy of the plane that had strafed the open field where the wicker case had been dropped. But none of that mattered. With Father Waal's blessing, the two knelt, while Obadiah hummed the only hymn he'd learned from an early Methodist missionary: "Onward Christian Soldiers."

"Peace be with you, my children," Father Waal said as the service ended.

"Thank you, Father," Sunny acknowledged.

Alex leaned over to kiss his bride, while the three native scouts grinned in satisfaction, none more radiant than All-Same-Barrel, who took the credit for the fine state of affairs. Masta had finally claimed his woman, and he felt sure he had helped to bring them together.

With the wedding ceremony, plans for dinner changed. Timi You built a fire to heat up the canned food—Spam and potatoes—with fruit cocktail and canned datenut loaf for dessert, and hot tea laced with spirits. When it was ready, the six sat down together to share the wedding feast.

"Obadiah keep watch tonight," the scout offered.

"All-Same-Barrel fix sleeping quarters. Fine quarters," he boasted.

"And Timi You cook wedding supper," the third one said, pointing to the food they were consuming at that very moment.

"And I performed the wedding sacrament," Father Waal said with a smile, joining in the camaraderie.

"Thank you, each one," Alex said. "My wife and I appreciate what you have done for us tonight."

"Night not over yet," All-Same-Barrel said with a knowing grin.

"Please. Not another bush rat, All-Same-Barrel. I don't need that again."

A wary native looked at the young nurse and back to Alex, who laughed. A puzzled Father Waal waited for an explanation. But Sunny merely said, "A harmless joke, Father — not worth retelling."

With her words, All-Same-Barrel relaxed and took up the cup of tea, laced with more than his share of rum.

After the meal, the men and the lanterns disappeared, until only one light remained with Alex and Sunny. He drew her closer to him, now that they were finally alone. Alex took one piece of the datenut loaf, broke it in half, and fed Sunny with one piece, while she did the same for him. He took his cup, offered it to her first, and then drained the rest. "With all my worldly goods, I thee endow," he whispered, repeating the phrase spoken earlier.

His words affected her more than she wished to acknowledge. And Sunny responded in the same way she'd responded all her life when she was threatened by her own emotions. "Let me count them — a teleradio not yet put together, a cache of benzene, a barrel of rice…"

"…And my eternal love."

Her flippancy disappeared. She looked at him with a steady gaze. "It's going to take a little time, Alex."

"We have all night," he replied.

Alex stood up, took the lantern, and helped Sunny to her

feet. "Let's go and see how our fine friend, All-Same-Barrel , has prepared the bridal suite."

"Wait. I want to take my flowers." Sunny quickly gathered them up from the altar where she'd put them for safekeeping, and returned to his side.

Alex held out his arm. "Are you ready, my lady?"

She smiled and in a demure voice she said, "Yes, my lord."

The flickering lantern traced their path from the larger chamber into the labyrinth beyond. They took the right corridor until they came to the curved wall, the indentation that gave privacy to the sleeping quarters.

"Look," Sunny said, pointing to the massive garland of the same type flowers and greenery she held. Draped from the overhanging ledge, it served as a curtain to the cots. The perfume of the flowers was delicate, a barely perceptible scent upon the air that disguised the former musty odor. A bamboo rug had been placed upon the floor beside the two cots lashed together. Sheets, pillows, and a blanket completed the idyllic picture.

Sunny looked from the bower to her left hand and the ring of plaited grass. "All-Same-Barrel really is ingenious, isn't he, Alex?"

"One day, Sunny, I'll give you a proper ring."

She placed her hand on his lips. "No promises. Please. Just love me tonight, Alex. That's all I ask."

He needed no coaxing. In the curtained bower, deep inside the hidden cave, passion ignited with an intensity that matched the raging storm outside.

That night, high above the lagoon, the tropical rainstorm continued. The howling wind bent the trees to the ground and scattered the white coral blossoms over the ridge, while two lovers, with no promise of tomorrow, fell asleep in each other's arms.

Chapter 37

A WEEK LATER, ON THE ISLAND NINETY MILES LONG AND twenty-five miles wide, the six had settled into a domestic routine. An illusionary sense of security now enveloped them. The scout plane had not returned.

Down below, the Japanese seemed to be wholly occupied with building the landing field. The terrain separating Sunny and her group from the narrow strip of beach on the southern shore of the island, where the Japanese had a toehold, contained an almost impassable chain of mountains.

Alex and the three scouts built a leaf hut one mile from the cave, and set up the teleradio that had been stashed in the cave six months ago. Now, Alex was broadcasting again—but only at times of greatest urgency.

Because of Father Waal's heart, the priest was given nothing more strenuous to do than keep watch from the camouflaged platform beyond the cave. Monitoring his health, Sunny was satisfied at his good color and apparent recuperation after the climb to the ridge.

On that morning in August, a particularly happy Sunny left the cave she had labeled the *Guadalcanal-Carlton*. The news had come from Malaita. Because the Japanese landing strip was nearing completion, Guadalcanal was going to be invaded by the Allies earlier than originally planned. All the six on the ridge had to do was wait for the marines to take the island. And then they would be safe.

Each day, Sunny had gone a little farther to explore the land and gather wood for the cooking fire. On that morning, she took a different route, choosing instead to climb below, where an uprooted tree lay sprawled with its broken branches ripe for salvage. Sunny had learned early on to take a blanket to ease the burden of carrying the wood back to the cave.

As she stood looking down at the dead tree, she began to make out the wreckage of a plane, barely visible in the vines that had begun to grow over the fuselage. Curious, she edged her way past the tree and toward the plane.

There was a feeling of danger in the air, even though the wreck was not a recent one. But Sunny was not afraid. She had the pistol that Alex had given her to carry. It rested in the holster strapped to her waist, and it was fully loaded.

Careful of the undergrowth, Sunny persisted in her journey until she was on the same level as the charred hulk. The folding wing tip indicated it was a fighter from an aircraft carrier. And the faint round insignia of the sun on its fuselage left no doubt as to its nationality. The plane was the same type that had strafed their rafts when they passed beyond the coral reef and into the lagoon below. And Sunny, remembering Madeleine and Sleepy Joe Tyler, felt a certain satisfaction at its demise. No longer curious, she moved on, to begin gathering wood.

She was not prepared for the sudden movement of a booted foot jutting from the wreckage. Sunny stopped, pulled the pistol from its holster, and waited. There was no further movement—only a babbling of foreign sounds over and over. And although she couldn't understand the words, she recognized the pattern of a delirious patient. Still holding the pistol in front of her, Sunny crept closer to get a better view. The pilot was barely alive. His clothes were wet, soaked through, and beads of perspiration on his face indicated a high fever, the reason for his babbling.

Sunny looked at the man cradled in the wreckage, and then back at the pistol. She cocked it, aimed it at the enemy, but she could not bring herself to fire. He was ill. And she had seen his face. He was an individual, with individual features, completely different from the entire race she'd found so easy to hate since that day at Pearl Harbor.

Leaving the blanket, she quickly retraced her steps toward the cave to seek out Father Waal, the only other person within a mile's range. He could help her decide what to do, since she had failed so miserably in carrying out Alex's orders when he'd entrusted the gun to her.

Dressed in his black cassock, Father Waal sat and looked over the island jungle from his aerie high in a clump of trees. The channel had been empty all morning. No ships sailed in either direction, and it had been a quiet three hours, except for the occasional noise from below, where the locomotives the Japanese had brought in were busy rumbling along the Lunga Plain.

"Father," Sunny called from beneath the platform.

The priest jumped. For he had not heard anyone coming up behind him. Recognizing Sunny's voice, he answered, "Yes, what is it, my child?"

"I think you'd better come with me. I just found a Japanese pilot in the wreckage of a plane below us."

Quickly, the priest hoisted up his cassock and climbed down the tree. "Is he still alive?"

Sunny nodded. "But he looks as if he might die any minute. He's delirious with fever. What are we to do, Father?"

"Take me to him, and then we'll decide."

"I wish Alex were here."

"But he isn't. We'll have to deal with this ourselves."

"I don't think I can shoot him," Sunny warned. "Even if he *is* the enemy."

The priest didn't reply. He followed Sunny down the trail until the large tree came in sight. And just beyond it, Father Waal spied the wreckage. On the ground nearby lay the blanket that Sunny had dropped.

With the nurse beside him, the priest leaned over and peered into the charred hulk that served as a shelter for the wounded pilot. He listened to the rasping, uneven breath, the faint babbling of words. Then he straightened up and faced Sunny. "We have only one choice—and that is to take him back to the cave."

"I was afraid you'd say that."

With a knowing look passing over his haphazardly arranged features, the priest said, "We have both been trained to value human life, Sunny. That puts us in a vulnerable position. This man has done us no harm. But I think it wouldn't change matters even if he had."

"I know. When I first saw him, I thought of my brother Jack. If he crashed in enemy territory, it would break my heart to think no one would offer him water, to make him more comfortable at the end."

The two took the blanket, spread it evenly on the ground, and then pulled the delirious pilot from the wreckage. Not much older than a boy, the pilot was small, and the two rescuers had little trouble in rolling him onto the blanket. Then, they gathered the corners and dragged him up the hill, toward the entrance of the cave.

Sunny did not weigh the consequences of their deed. Later, when Alex returned to the cave, she would have to deal with it. But for now, she was more concerned with Father Waal's heart, to make sure he was not overexerting himself. She became a nurse again, monitoring two patients—the priest and the enemy pilot.

Once they got the Japanese pilot into the cave, Father Waal returned to his post. In the next few hours, it was almost as if Sunny were on the hospital ship again and fighting for a patient's life. Careful not to allot more liquid than he could handle, Sunny placed a small amount of water on the man's parched tongue. He swallowed, and Sunny gave him more, a little at the time. Then, using the two wooden splints, she taped his broken arm, and finally bathed his face, neck, and chest with cool rainwater. By late afternoon, she managed to get the Atabrine tablets down his throat.

As the sun dropped behind the mountain peaks and its final rays cast a golden glow over the jungle, alive with the evening songs of birds, Sunny began to listen for the sound of Alex and the others returning to the cave. Off and on, she glanced toward the man lying on a pallet not far from her.

Father Waal was the first to return to the cave. "How is out patient?" he asked, squatting to get a better look at the pilot.

"Still delirious," Sunny answered. "But his tongue is no longer swollen from thirst. I found a picture, Father, in his shirt. It must be his family." She walked over to the ledge and picked up the photo to show the priest.

* * *

Alex Ramsay was pleased as he left the leaf hut with Timi You. The coastwatcher on Malaita had given the secret signal. Guadalcanal was to be invaded by the Allies within twenty-four hours. When the bombardment from the ships began, prior to the marines' landing, it would be a dangerous time for anyone on the island. But the six were relatively safe in the cave. And that's where they would remain during the shelling. They could not afford to be caught on the hillside.

Anxious to return to the cave with the news, Alex began to walk more briskly. One week previously, he had believed he had no future. Now, with the coming of the Allies, all that had changed. His usefulness as a coastwatcher on Guadalcanal was ending, but the need for him in Burma and India was just beginning. His jaw hardened as he thought of the latest Japanese atrocities. At last he was going to get into the fight. Eric had relayed the message. Once he was off the island, he would join Chuang San Chu in Burma, as a British officer attached to the Chinese regiment. It was what he wanted, yet he had to be careful when telling Sunny.

Outside the cave, Timi You sat down and waited for Obadiah and All-Same-Barrel, while Alex hurried inside. Once he passed beyond the entrance, he followed the glow of the fire and the appetizing aroma of food cooking. He had a ravenous appetite, for Alex was a big man. The tin of fruit and hardtack, eaten in the middle of the day, had long since proved inadequate,

He had to hand it to Sunny. Even though she didn't like to cook, she had been diligent in her preparation of the two meals a day they all ate together. Seeing her leaning over the cooking pot, Alex rushed toward the fire. But he stopped short when he saw the prone outline of a man on a pallet not far from the fire.

The man moved, and a cautious Alex took the rifle from his shoulder. "Who is that?" he inquired, looking toward Sunny.

She released the soup handle and wiped her hands on the white cloth wrapped around her khaki trousers. "A downed pilot," an equally cautious Sunny replied.

Alex took the lantern, lit it and, standing over the man, scrutinized his features. Sunny waited for his next words.

"He's Japanese."

"Yes."

A thunderous frown moved over Alex's face, "I gave you the pistol, Sunny, so you could shoot any damn Jap who came within a mile of the cave."

"I know. But he's delirious, Alex. I couldn't do it. I kept thinking of Jack."

"Well, I hope your compassion extends to the six of us when he murders us in our sleep."

Blending into the dark shadows beyond the fire Father Waal sat. "I thought we might secure him at night, Alex."

The marquess turned toward the shadows. "So you're in this too, are you, Father? I seem to remember something a priest said not long ago about a shepherd protecting his flock from the wolf. Have you changed your mind?"

"No. But sometimes a shepherd can't bring himself to

shoot an injured cub when he seems to be of little danger to the flock."

Out of respect for the priest, Alex refrained from a retort. He took the lantern and headed to the entrance where Timi You sat. Within a few minutes, the native scout arranged a rope restraint so that the Japanese pilot would be unable to move freely, in case he came out of his delirium during the night.

The three native scouts eyed the pilot as they ate their dinner. A pall fell over the others, as well, and Alex, enthusiastic about the pending invasion, at first kept the news to himself while he concentrated on the bowl of soup laden with vegetables and chunks of beef.

Finally, he spoke. "No one is to leave the cave for the next twenty-four hours. Is that understood?"

"Why, Alex? " the priest inquired. "Do you expect the invasion forces to come?"

"Yes. Any moment. The secret message came from Malaita."

"What wonderful news," Sunny said, speaking for the first time since they'd sat down to eat. "This might even be our last meal together in the Guadalcanal-Carlton. I can't say that I'll miss it."

"Does this mean then that your mission as a coastwatcher is finished, Alex?" Father Waal inquired.

"Almost. I've just received news that I'm to go to Burma once this island is in Allied hands."

"And you, Sunny?" a concerned priest asked. "What will you do?"

"I'll ask for reassignment on another hospital ship, of course."

Alex looked at her as she spoke, but he made no comment. She had withdrawn from him, as if the ceremony by Father Waal had never taken place. Alex realized he was to blame. He should not have spoken so sharply to her. He watched as she left the fire to attend to the pilot. Ignoring his own order, Alex stood up abruptly and announced, "I think

I'll go to the lookout and see if any ships are coming into the channel."

With his rifle slung over his shoulder, Alex walked past the pallet to the cave entrance, where the gate of leaves and greenery had been fastened for the night. Carefully, he loosened it enough to slip past.

The night was black, with a mist covering the heavens. But as the clouds drifted, an occasional star shone through. Alex gazed past the channel toward Tulagi. He saw nothing, for it, too, was blacked out.

By the time he returned to the cave, Sunny had left the main chamber. Only Father Waal remained, keeping watch over the injured pilot.

"Father, I want you to witness a document," Alex said. "You and Obadiah."

The priest nodded and moved closer to the fire while Alex walked to the chest in the corner to retrieve pen, ink, and paper. By lantern light, Alex Ramsay, marquess of Dalhousie, wrote a last will and testament. And when he'd finished, his signature was witnessed by the priest and the only native who could write his name legibly.

Alex waited for the ink to dry. And when he was satisfied, he folded the document and placed it in the waterproof pouch with his marriage certificate. He did not return the pouch to the chest. Instead, he kept it in his hand, said good night, and began to walk toward the sleeping chamber.

He had no need of a light. Every step of the route had been memorized. But by the time Alex made the second turn down the labyrinth, a soft glow from Sunny's lantern guided him the rest of the way.

Acting as if the breach between them had never occurred, Alex sat down on the cot beside Sunny. "I want you to keep these documents on your person at all times, Sunny."

"What are they?" she asked, hesitating to accept the waterproof pouch with its long string.

"Our marriage certificate and my new will."

When she opened her mouth to protest, Alex paid no attention. "If something happens to me, these two documents should assure your being taken care of. You're to wear them around your neck from now on."

"But Alex, I don't need—"

Again, he cut her off. "We've been man and wife, Sunny. At this very moment, you might be carrying my son. Would you deny him his heritage because of your misplaced pride?"

"I'm not pregnant," she replied. "And if I were, it could just as easily be a daughter."

"True. Then you and she would be cared for by my private funds. But if I had no male heir, then the title and lands would revert to my cousin, Malcolm." He placed the stringed pouch around her neck.

"Do I have to wear it tonight?" she argued.

"If it's going to interfere with your sleep, then put it under your pillow. But promise to begin wearing it first thing in the morning."

"Alex, I'm sorry about the pilot. I even cocked the pistol this morning, but I couldn't bring myself to shoot him."

Alex smiled. "I understand, Sunny. Seeing him in the cave tonight took me by surprise, and I was too harsh with you. But actually, I would have been even more surprised if you had shot him. Forgive me?"

"Of course, Alex."

Knowing they would be separated soon, they clung to each other throughout the night. Shortly before dawn, they heard the aerial bombardment of Tulagi and Guadalcanal begin.

Chapter 38

FOR SOME TIME, THE JAPANESE STATIONED AT RABAUL IN the northern Solomons, had accepted their tour of duty as a veritable paradise. By day, their planes flew, unmolested, on sorties to New Guinea and the other islands. Their ships, the Tokyo Express, roved undeterred down the Slot and back. By late afternoon, most were home again and free to do what they wished — watch the movies that came regularly from Japan, trade goods with the natives, or visit the comfort women, mainly Korean, who had been shipped to Rabaul.

On the morning of August 7, 1942, the Japanese in the Solomons received the first indication that their claim to the tropical Eden in the Pacific was beginning to erode. The first major Allied offensive was underway. And sprinkled through the uncharted islands were the few coastwatchers that the Japanese had been unable to drive out.

Alex Ramsay, in the leaf hut above the Lunga Plain, monitored the battle below. He had not taken his own advice, but had chosen to remain on duty with the teleradio, to relay any messages.

The cruisers offshore bombarded the island, their shells setting fire to the fuel dumps and sending black smoke skyward. Hitting their targets, the shells ricocheted into the hills, with the telltale red of the tracers forming a shallow V, while below the clink of davits told of boats being lowered for landing on the beach.

Listening to the sounds of the battle, Alex felt sorry for the soldiers getting their first taste of Guadalcanal. The white sandy beaches lined with coconut palms were deceiving, for between them and the airstrip they were sworn to take were the foul-smelling swamps where crocodiles, spiders, leeches, and swarms of disease-laden mosquitoes waited for them—insidious enemies that could not be dealt with by bayonets or ammo.

And if they were fortunate enough to survive those obstacles and get to the Lunga Plain, another trial awaited them—the kunai grass, razor-sharp and tall as a man. The two-edged blades could draw blood from anyone coming in contact with them.

All that day, Alex stayed at his post, picking up and sending messages. But the Japanese had been taken by surprise. The construction workers, assigned to building the airstrip, and the sailors guarding it offered little resistance and fled to the hills as the U.S. Marines spread over the plain and took their objective.

Then, abruptly, the island became quiet—too quiet. It was not like the Japanese to give up something as important as the airstrip without a battle to the death. The construction workers' flight he could understand. They operated under no rules of *Bushido.*

Timi You, coming into the leaf hut, watched Alex close down the radio for the day. "Masta," the native spoke, "the Japanese come. Toward the ridge."

Alex swore when he heard the news. "From the airstrip?"

"Yes, Masta."

"They're probably headed for the caves, to hide out. How far away are they?"

"Two miles. No more."

"Well, we'll worry about them when they get here. You have someone on watch for the night?"

"Yes, Masta. Obadiah."

That night in the cave, Sunny didn't attempt to hide her

exuberance as she prepared a special dinner to celebrate the Allied landing. "They took the airfield, didn't they?" she said to Alex.

"Yes, they have it for the moment."

He saw the crestfallen look on Sunny's face. "What do you mean?"

He had not intended to take away her joy so soon. But Sunny needed to be prepared for the next phase. The battle for the lush tropical island was not over.

"The Japanese are not going to lose something as important as an airfield without putting up a tremendous fight," he explained. "The battle for Guadalcanal has just begun."

"Maybe this time the Japanese have overextended themselves," she countered. "Perhaps they'll turn to New Guinea instead."

"They need a land base to do that. Remember, Rabaul is too far away for the planes to make the airstrike."

"I won't worry about that tonight. The U.S. Marines are on the island, and I say, 'Hooray for the marines!' " She lifted her cup and saluted her own countrymen.

In spite of himself, Alex smiled. He, too, lifted his cup and joined in. Let Sunny have her brief celebration, he decided, for the next few days might bring little to celebrate.

"How is the patient?" Alex asked Father Waal, who was coming to join them at the table.

"Much better. He's alert now. I think he's no longer afraid we're going to kill him, even though we have him tied up most of the time."

"Most of the time?" a wary Alex repeated.

"He has to be untied occasionally, Alex. You know that."

"I suppose so. Just be careful, though, that he doesn't escape."

"One of the boys watches him closely. But he knows better than to run when a gun is aimed at his head."

Anxious to change the subject from the Japanese pilot, Sunny said, "May I fix you something to drink, Father? Don't pay any attention to Alex's long face. We're celebrating tonight."

"Yes, thank you, my dear."

The next morning, the island was still quiet. Alex, after warning Sunny of the Japanese workers making their way toward them, left the cave. As he walked past the Japanese pilot, their eyes met briefly. Alex made no effort to disguise his hostility toward the man. Outside the cave, he signaled for Obadiah to come off duty and for All-Same-Barrel to take his place. Then, he and Timi You headed for the teleradio a mile away.

It wasn't long before Alex intercepted the message that he'd been expecting. TRO, one of the few coastwatchers north, tapped out the news. "Twenty-five bombers headed your way." Immediately, Alex broadcast the news on the x-frequency, to warn all vessels in the harbor.

A short time later, Alex saw the two aircraft carriers head out for the open sea, where it would be difficult for the bombers to sink them. But he had not expected the troop ships to follow suit. In the midst of landing a second wave of marines, they fled the lagoon without even unloading the equipment that the first wave of troops, under Vandergrift, needed to hold the small stretch of jungle they'd taken the day before.

With the approach of the enemy bombers, Alex hurried back to the cave.

The Japanese bombers were thorough, bringing devastation to the island. On the plain, the Americans swore as the bombers struck, undeterred. And high on the ridge, the six fugitives did the same, with the possible exception of Father Waal.

Gathered in the lower chamber, where the black pool of water held fish with sightless eyes, and the crevices of the overhead ledges housed bats, Sunny listened to the bombardment above. She moved toward Alex when the walls reverberated in response to a nearby shell.

"I think I'd rather be outside," Sunny whispered. "This

place makes me shudder." She watched All-Same-Barrel fending off a bat that had detected the presence of a warm-blooded victim.

"The bombardment won't last much longer," Alex assured her. "The planes will run low on fuel and be forced to return to Rabaul."

Within the hour, the island was silent again. With Obadiah leading the way, the seven traipsed back toward the central part of the cave. Alex was last, to keep an eye on the Japanese pilot, entrusted to Timi You. Sunny carried one of the lanterns, and Father Waal walked directly behind her.

Once they reached the main chamber, an unbelieving Sunny saw the rays of the sun pouring into the cave from the large hole above. The chamber was in shambles, with tins of food strewn in every direction. The cot that had been used as a sofa was no longer recognizable as such. And the improvised dining table, made from wood crates, was a mass of splinters, with the small bowl of coral flowers resting on the debris like a funeral bouquet.

Taking over, Alex appointed Obadiah and All-Same-Barrel to help Sunny with the cleanup, while Father Waal guarded the Japanese pilot. Motioning for Timi You to follow him, Alex left the cave to assess the damage outside.

He surveyed the craters along the ridge and watched the fires of the fuel dumps on the plain. "It doesn't look good, does it?" Alex said.

"No, Masta. Much damage."

"I think I'll go to the leaf hut to check on the radio," Alex said suddenly. "You stay here and keep watch."

While Timi You climbed the platform, disguised by the few trees left, Alex walked along the trail to the leaf hut. Shortly before he reached the area, he stopped. A large hole occupied the ground where the leaf hut had stood that morning. With slow steps, he continued his journey and gazed down into the crater. No evidence of the radio remained, with the exception of a small piece of wire caught at the edge of the crater. Alex stooped to pick it up. The wire was still warm to the touch. Peering at it in his hand, Alex Ramsay, marquess of Dalhousie, realized that, with the destruction of the radio, his days as a coastwatcher had come to an end.

When he was halfway back to the cave, the rains began. And once he walked inside, he saw a torrent of water pouring into the cave from the large hole overhead.

"Get a barrel, Obadiah," Alex ordered. "At least we can use the water for bathing tonight."

"Speak for yourself, Alex," Sunny said from the corner. "Some of us have already had our baths."

He looked closer. Sunny's clothes were soaked. And her wet hair hung over her forehead as she attempted to light the wet wood for cooking.

"Don't bother with a fire, Sunny. We'll eat the food cold tonight."

He walked over to the tins of food that had been salvaged and began to make a selection, putting them into a backpack.

"What are you doing?" Sunny asked.

"Selecting the items to go with us. We'll have to move out first thing tomorrow morning. We can't stay on the ridge any longer."

"Where will we go?"

"South, over the mountains."

"I thought you said it was impossible to get to the beach that way."

"Difficult," he admitted. "But not impossible. It's the only way left."

"You don't think it will be safer just moving to another cave and waiting?"

"No. This ridge is going to get a massive beating within the next week or so, once the Allies get their act together. They're going to root out the Japanese in the caves all around us, and our being here is not going to matter one way or the other to the Allied bombers."

"Can't you radio out for help?"

"There is no radio anymore, Sunny. We're entirely on our own. With over a thousand Japanese within shouting distance," he added.

Alex looked up to see the interested face of the pilot. He frowned and whispered, "I wonder if that bastard understands English?"

"He's never spoken it," Sunny said. "In fact, he's spoken nothing at all since he came out of his delirium." She lowered her voice and inquired, "Are you going to leave him here tomorrow?"

"No. We'll take him with us. He's the only one who speaks Japanese. And no doubt we'll run into a few before we get to the south beach."

The seven moved out the next morning, each carrying his own supply of food and water. A new phase began, more hazardous, through territory that even the natives had never passed. They walked under the grueling sun and along the trails made into muddy bogs by the afternoon rains, until they dropped in exhaustion.

A weak Yamuto kept up with the others, for somehow he had a suspicion that if he did not, he would be left on the trail by Alex. Natives hid in the bush and watched them. Alex paid no attention, except to become more alert in case they attacked. But the natives of the interior were merely curious. They evidently felt safe from the baffling bombardments along the coast, or the occasional plane overhead, for which they had no name. The war had not yet touched the bush people, or made any difference in their lives.

For an entire week, the seven kept up the horrendous pace. Through sheer willpower, Sunny ignored the blisters, the heat of the day, and the howling winds on the peaks.

Close to nighttime, when they stopped to make camp, Sunny was always too exhausted to think of the next day and what it would bring. She only knew that, behind them, the fires continued to burn; the ridge was attacked time and again. But unknown to her and the others, Savo Sound had become a graveyard for more than a thousand U.S. sailors, caught unaware by Rear Admiral Mikawa sailing from Rabaul with his naval task force.

On the eighth day, they stood on a hill and looked down at the narrow strip of south beach. As Sunny's knees buckled and she dropped to the ground, she managed a smile through her tears. In spite of the odds, they had come over the chain of mountains and now looked down at the Coral Sea.

Once they had rested, Alex turned to Timi You. "We still have to scout out the beach and locate the Japanese camp. Are you up to going with me now?"

"You stay," Timi You said. "I go. Safer if yellow bastards see me."

Timi You was thinner, but little different from the way he had been except for the lap-lap he wore instead of his khaki shorts. Where he'd gotten it, Alex didn't ask. He only remembered the day Timi You had left camp to scout the surrounding territory, and returned in native dress.

Knowing he would be less conspicuous, Alex nodded. "All right. But don't take any unnecessary chances."

Later that evening, the small dark native returned. With him he brought a sack of coconuts from the palm trees below, and a few bags of food with Japanese labels. He grinned as he dumped them at Alex's feet.

No scolding words greeted him. The six, including Yamuto, dived for a coconut and waited in turn for All-Same-Barrel to hack off the tops. They drank greedily from the shells. Sunny rested her head against a banyan tree and recalled Heinman's disparaging remarks about the Papuan milkshake at Pago Pago. If she were fortunate enough to see him again, she would challenge his low opinion of the coconut.

Alex walked to the tree and sat down beside Sunny. "It won't be long now," he assured her. "Timi You has located an outrigger canoe. If our luck still holds, we'll be on our way to San Cristobal by morning."

There was so much that Sunny wanted to say to Alex that night. But she was too exhausted. "I love you, Alex," she said, and the other words didn't seem to matter.

Alex leaned over and, with a gentleness, brushed his lips against her tender skin. He answered her with Gaelic words—the same ones he'd spoken that first night at Bohorok, when Sunny had become his wife in a ceremony of his own.

Down below, the Japanese troops laughed and partied, drinking *sake* and enjoying their fish and rice. Their voices floated upward to where the six—Sunny, Alex, Father Waal, the three natives—and the Japanese pilot, Yamuto, listened and waited for the hour before dawn.

The voices grew fainter, stopped altogether, and Sunny, sheltered by the banyan tree, went to sleep in Alex's arms.

Toward morning, long before the sun began to make its journey along the lagoons, to bring emerald green color to the dark, tepid waters, Father Waal leaned over the sleeping coastwatcher. "Alex," he whispered, his hand on his shoulder giving the man a shake. "Wake up, Alex."

With a start, Alex sat up. "What is it?"

"Yamuto is gone."

"What?" He struggled to become awake.

"Yamuto has escaped. It's my fault. I untied him, to let him answer nature's call."

"How long ago?"

"About fifteen or twenty minutes."

Down below, a shot was fired. "I hope they shot him," Alex said. "It would serve him right." He leaned over, woke up Sunny, and urged Father Waal to do the same with the others. But the shot had already awakened the three natives.

"What is it, Alex?" a sleepy Sunny inquired. "Is it time to get up?"

"Yes. We'll have to rush for the beach. Yamuto has escaped, and he'll be bringing the bloodhounds with him." Alex turned to Timi You, who was already at his side. "You heard? Yamuto has escaped."

"Yes, Masta."

"We'll split up immediately. Take my wife, Timi You, to the canoe. All-Same-Barrel is to go with you. If the rest of us don't get there in five minutes behind you, you're to leave anyway."

"But, Masta..."

"That's an order. Do you understand?"

"Yes, Masta."

"All right. Start running,"

"Alex—"

He turned his back on her, joined Obadiah and Father Waal beyond the banyan tree, and proceeded along the hillside away from the beach.

"Come, Masta's woman," Timi You said, speaking to Sunny. And Sunny began to run with the two natives toward the beach.

When they had gone a short distance, they heard Japanese voices. Yamuto had evidently gotten through to the camp. Timi You stopped, held up his hand like a hunted animal who smells the scent of danger, and listened to the sound of Japanese soldiers running nearby.

On the hill farther back, a rifle shot sounded. Recognizing the Enfield rifle that had been hidden in the cave on the ridge, Sunny cried. "No, Alex." He would not have fired unless he intended drawing the soldiers away from the beach—and her.

At the sound of the shot, the Japanese soldiers stopped in their tracks, changed course, and left the beach.

"We go now," a sympathetic Timi You said. "Not much time."

Stumbling along behind the two natives, Sunny was heartbroken. Tears flowed down her cheeks as her hand reached toward the waterproof pouch Alex had made her wear from the time they'd first left the cave. "If something happens to me, these documents will assure your being taken care of."

The two natives uncovered the outrigger canoe, dragged

it to the lagoon, and waited. Hiding under the palm fronds in the bottom of the boat, Sunny listened and prayed. But the only sounds came from the Japanese soldiers and the gunfire in the hills. The sporadic noise of the Enfield rifle finally ceased against the constant, overpowering fire of Japanese guns. Then the air became silent, until a bloodcurdling *banzai* shout left no doubt as to the outcome of the brief battle.

Giving a push to the canoe, Timi You set it afloat. But instead of climbing into the boat with All-Same-Barrel, he watched until it was beyond the reef. Then, he started toward the hills. With his action, he disobeyed Alex Ramsay's orders for the first time.

The sun came up over the Coral Sea, and Sunny emerged from cover. As the outrigger canoe headed for San Cristobal, her tearstained face was turned toward Guadalcanal. She rued the day she had ever found the Japanese pilot, Yamuto, in the wreckage below the ridge.

Chapter 39

ON THE VERANDAH OF KORABURRA, SUNNY SAT ALONE
and looked out over the red hills at sunset. It had been
almost a month since the U.S. destroyer *Madison* had picked
her up halfway between Guadalcanal and San Cristobal.

In her hands, she held her new orders and the letter from
Kirk Singleton, the captain of the newly commissioned
hospital ship, *Consolation*. She had been pronounced fit for
duty. Her scars and blisters had healed, yet she knew she
would never be the same again. Alex had changed her
forever. But no one knew about their marriage—not even
her mother. She wanted no words of sympathy from
anyone. Her sorrow was too new to share.

The door to the house opened and Kenna emerged. "I
brought you a sweater," she said, holding out one of her
own cashmeres for Sunny. "It gets chilly on the verandah
this time of year."

"Thank you, Mother." Sunny accepted it and draped the
sweater around her shoulders as Kenna took the chair beside
her. "Koraburra is beautiful, isn't it?" Sunny commented,
watching the purple shadows spread over the raw, powerful
land.

"Yes. I'll miss it when I return to Georgia."

"When are you leaving?"

"As soon as you go back on duty."

Sunny changed the position of her chair so that she was face-to-face with her mother. "Are you sure it isn't *Shan* that you're going to miss?"

Kenna gave a start, and her hand went nervously to her hair. "What do you mean?"

"He loves you, Mother. I can tell. And somehow I have a feeling that you care a great deal for him."

Again, Kenna's hand fluttered, and she suddenly looked out at the red hills. "Your father has been dead such a short time."

"I know. But a person's need for love doesn't diminish, does it, when someone dies? I think Dad would be happy if he knew you weren't quite so alone. Shan looks like a tower of strength. And I like his eyes, too."

Kenna's hand reached out to touch her daughter's. "Don't make impossible plans for me, darling. He needs to marry someone like Cece Bennigan."

"You could stop that, you know."

"I'm not sure I want to," Kenna hedged. "Shan's only son was killed. He needs a woman young enough to give him other children."

"Sometimes a man has other needs beyond an heir."

Kenna looked sharply at Sunny. "And when did you become an expert on a man's needs?"

"On Guadalcanal."

"I was afraid of that. Alex Ramsay?"

"Yes. But we were married, Mother. Father Waal married us in the cave on the ridge. I even have the marriage certificate to prove it." Suddenly, Sunny was in her mother's arms. "Oh, Mother," she said. "I loved him so. But he's dead. What am I going to do for the rest of my life?"

Kenna said nothing, for no words could comfort her daughter. She kept her arms around her and wept with her.

"I didn't plan on telling anybody," Sunny confessed. "But I've never kept secrets from you."

"I'm glad you told me, Sunny. I knew something was

dreadfully wrong."

Kenna wiped her tears with her handkerchief. "We Fitzpatricks don't cry very well, Sunny. Hush now, so there'll be no trace by the time Shan returns. We're going to have guests for dinner—Cece and her father, Todd."

Sunny smiled and borrowed her mother's handkerchief, as if she were a small child again. "I'll go in and wash my face. And I think you'd better do the same."

By the time Todd Bennigan flew his Cessna from Barrah, with his daughter Cece as passenger, Kenna had reverted to her calm, gracious self. She had helped Mrs. O'Leary in the kitchen, as she'd gotten into the habit of doing, sharing the work so that Mrs. O'Leary would not be overburdened at the last minute.

Hearing the sound of the plane, Kenna realized that the Bennigans were arriving before Shan. With the truck waiting in the driveway, Kenna enlisted her daughter's help.

"Darling, can you run to the airstrip and pick up the Bennigans? I thought that Shan would be back before they arrived."

"I'll be happy to, Mother." Sunny dashed down the steps of the verandah to the waiting vehicle.

She arrived at the airstrip just in time. When the two guests emerged from the plane, Sunny waved and waited for them to walk the few steps to the truck.

"Hi. I'm Sunny Fitzpatrick, Kenna's daughter," she said. "And you must be the Bennigans."

"Yes. Todd is the name, and this is my daughter, Cece." With a grin, he added, "You're *almost* as beautiful as your mother."

Sunny laughed, warming to him immediately. "I take that as a great compliment, sir." And then she said, "You're more familiar with these vehicles than I am. Do the three of us squeeze in the front? Or does one ride the headlights?"

"I'll ride in the back," Todd suggested. "Then, you two girls can chat away up front."

"Where's Shan?" Cece inquired.

"He's late. He hasn't gotten back from Melbourne yet."

Almost as soon as they reached the house, the sound of another plane in the distance caught Cece's attention. "That must be Shan now. I'll drive back to the airstrip for him," she said, motioning for Sunny to get out with her father.

"My daughter's awfully bossy, Sunny," Todd said, taking the luggage from the back.

"And she probably drives on the left side of the road, too," Sunny added, her topaz eyes lighting up with amusement.

"Is there any other way?" Cece commented, not happy at the instant rapport between the two.

She hurled a few gravel pebbles from the tires as she sped out of the driveway. Sunny ignored the departing truck, for Corky, the aborigine, was waiting to take the luggage inside.

"Todd, how nice to see you again," Kenna said, coming to the door to greet them. "Didn't Cece come, too?"

"Yes. But she's driving back to the airstrip to pick up Shan." Before Kenna could comment further, Todd leaned over and kissed her cheek. "You have a beautiful daughter, my dear."

"We *both* have beautiful daughters, Todd," she corrected and smiled at Sunny.

At the airstrip, Cece pulled up and jumped out of the truck to run and meet Shan. As the propellers came to a stop and the door opened, Cece rushed to the Cessna.

The man deplaning was not Shan, but a stranger. Tall, with dark hair, he was dressed in a U.S. Navy pilot's uniform, with the insignia indicating the rank of lieutenant. Taken by surprise, Cece said, "Who are you?"

Inside the plane, Shan called out, "Cece, this is Kenna's son, Jack Fitzpatrick. I found him wandering around Melbourne."

"Good Lord, not another one," Cece said. "Koraburra is crawling with Fitzpatricks tonight."

Jack Fitzpatrick's laugh was loud and deep. His merriment showed that her words had no effect upon him, beyond amusement.

Cece glared at him, and then her attention turned to Shan. She leaned forward for the man to kiss her, and she tucked her arm in his as they walked toward the truck that she'd left running.

"May I drive, Shan?" Jack asked suddenly. Shan nodded, and before Cece realized what had happened, she was relegated to the back of the truck and ignored like a spoiled brat while Shan and Jack conversed all the way back to the house.

When Shan and Cece entered the living room, Kenna was seated with Todd and Sunny. She immediately stood to greet them both. Once the amenities had been dealt with and Shan had shaken hands with Todd, he again turned to Kenna.

"I brought someone back from Melbourne with me, Kenna. Could you please tell Mrs. O'Leary to set another place at the table?"

"Of course. But where is your guest?"

"He's waiting in the hallway."

"Don't you want to invite him into the living room with us?"

"I thought you might like to do that yourself. Kenna." Shan stood in the middle of the living room floor and watched Kenna disappear into the hallway.

"Hi, Mom," a casual voice called out.

Kenna stopped and looked toward the front entrance. "Jack? Is that you, Jack?"

He came out of the shadows. "Yes. Quite a surprise, isn't it? I bumped into Shan in Melbourne. And he invited me here for the night," he said as he walked toward her.

They stood and looked at each other, with Kenna remembering the time she'd met the hospital ship at Darwin. Her eyes went to his hands, and then she smiled and touched his shoulder. "You've gotten taller," she said, her pride in her son showing in her eyes.

"Is that all the motherly affection I get, after coming so far?" he asked with a grin. And then, without waiting for an answer, he picked her up off the floor in a great bear hug, swung her around, and planted a huge kiss on the top of her head before putting her down again.

Kenna was laughing and crying at the same time. "I'm so happy to see you, darling. But please give your mother a little more respect."

"I'll try to remember next time," he answered, not bothered at all by his mother's affectionate admonition. "Where's Sunny?"

"In the living room. The Bennigans are here, too—Todd and his daughter, Cece."

"Yes. I met the family brat earlier."

A grateful Kenna, realizing Shan had arranged the private greeting with her son, walked again into the living room with him. "My I present my son, Lieutenant John Ireland Fitzpatrick."

"Jack!"

"Hi, Sis." He leaned over and kissed Sunny. And with his arm around her, he walked over to Todd Bennigan and shook hands.

The dinner that night was elegant, and Kenna was happy. The conversation flowed well, with a special effort on Kenna's part. Shan, knowing how easy it would be for the three, far from home, to lapse into their own conversation, was amused at the deft way Kenna took charge, never allowing a reminiscence, however brief, to exclude the others at the table.

When dinner was over and they had returned to the living room, Cece, as if mapping out her exclusive territory, chose to perch on the arm of the chair in which Shan was sitting. Todd, slightly embarrassed, elected not to say anything to his daughter. But within a few minutes, Jack stood up and walked toward Cece.

He pulled her to her feet and said, "Come on, brat. Let's leave the older generation to themselves. I want to see the stables. Coming with us, Sunny?"

"Sure. I'm right behind you."

With his mouth open, Todd Bennigan watched Jack lead his wayward daughter out of the room without a murmur. "I don't believe it," he said. "She didn't even make a fuss. I'll have to invite that boy to Barrah as often as he can come."

Shan laughed. "There's a bit of the Pied Piper in all three Fitzpatricks."

"Yes. I've been a victim, myself," Todd replied.

"Wouldn't you two like to talk business while I help Mrs. O'Leary with the dishes?"

"You can't get off that easily, Kenna," Shan chided. "Stay with us and I promise we won't embarrass you again."

The hour slipped by quickly, and Kenna, hearing the laughing voices on the verandah, realized the three young people had returned from the stable. But they were in no hurry to come inside.

"I think I'll say good night," Todd remarked. "It's been a long day."

Gathering the empty glasses to take back to the kitchen, Kenna said, "Sleep well, Todd."

Shan, also getting up, said, "If I don't see you in the morning for breakfast, I'll call you later, Todd." He nodded to his friend and then followed Kenna into the kitchen.

"It's been a long time since all the bedrooms were in use," Shan commented, watching Kenna quickly wash the glasses and put them in the cupboard.

Kenna's eyes were soft as she turned to face Shan. "How can I thank you for all the things you've done for me these past few weeks—allowing Sunny to recuperate here, and then bringing Jack back with you tonight?"

"I can think of several ways," he remarked. "But now isn't the time to bring them up."

"Speaking of time," a flustered Kenna remarked, "when are you planning to leave tomorrow?"

"By seven o'clock. I promised Jack I would have him back by ten o'clock. That means Sunny will have to get up a little earlier than planned."

"That won't be a problem. She's been packed and ready for two days. I think she's anxious to get back on duty."

The two cut out the lights as they went along the hallway toward the front. The door opened from the verandah, with Cece, Jack, and Sunny coming inside.

"I'm glad you three decided to come in," Shan said. "Remember, we leave at seven o'clock."

"So Jack informed me," Sunny replied.

"Shan, will you have room for another passenger tomorrow?" Cece inquired.

The man hesitated. "I suppose so, if you don't have much luggage. But I can't promise when I'll be back. You may have to find another ride home."

"That's all right. I can wait for you."

"Well, good night, Mother," Sunny said. "Will I see you in the morning?"

"Yes. I'll have a cup of coffee with you." She turned to Cece. "Would you like breakfast before you leave?"

"No, thank you. Just a cup of tea will be fine."

"Jack?"

"A glass of milk. And a slab of bread with jam."

"Sounds as if you're running a cafeteria, Kenna," Shan said.

She smiled. "If I am, you haven't put in your order."

"Just coffee. I'll have breakfast in Melbourne."

"Looks like Dad and Mrs. Fitzpatrick will have a cozy breakfast together. And if I know Dad, he won't be in any hurry to leave."

Cece's remark caused Shan's jaw to tighten. "Kenna, I meant to tell you. Corky will be reshoeing the horses tomorrow. I'm afraid you won't be able to use the stables."

The lights went out, the voices stopped, and Koraburra settled down for the night. Kenna, alone in the bedroom adjacent to Shan's, stayed awake for a long time, and finally drifted off to sleep only a few hours before the alarm of her clock went off.

In that early morning, Kenna put on her robe and walked into the kitchen. And in less than an hour, she stood on the verandah and waved while the four climbed into the sedan, driven by Leahy, the overseer, who would take them to the Cessna.

She watched the blinking red and green lights of the plane disappear over the dark red hills. Then, feeling bereft, Kenna went back into the house and climbed into bed for another hour.

Chapter 40

THE HOSPITAL SHIP *CONSOLATION* RODE AT ANCHOR IN the Sydney harbor, beyond the magnificent bridge that the Aussies called the Coathanger. Sunny Fitzpatrick, dressed in her smart new navy blue uniform, requested permission to come aboard. Saluting the officer of the day, she presented her new orders. He gave a cursory glance to them, and then waved her on deck.

Unlike the *Good Hope*, the *Consolation* was not a luxury liner. She was one of the first ships since World War I to be commissioned by the U.S. Navy as a hospital ship. And her lines proclaimed this pedigrce.

Pristine white, with a clean green line along her hull, the red cross of mercy painted upon her deck, and a shiny newness of brass and wood, the *Consolation* sat proud in the water and waited for her maiden voyage along the Lollipop Run.

Sunny looked for familiar faces while she searched for nurses' quarters. The only faces she saw were friendly, but unfamiliar—like the ship. Finally, with the help of another nurse, she found her cabin—larger, more spacious than the cubbyhole she'd shared with Wendy, Benita, and Madeleine. Propped upon her dresser was a note—actually an order to report immediately to the captain's quarters. She smiled when she read it, for it was signed by Kirk Singleton.

She left her quarters and returned to the upper deck. A few minutes later, she knocked at the closed door.

"Come in."

Forcing herself to smile, Sunny pushed open the door.

"Surprise!" the voices greeted her. And a dumfounded Sunny saw not only Kirk Singleton, but Benita, Wendy, Hank Brogdon, and Josh Heinman rushing toward her.

They began to talk at once. "I don't believe it," Sunny said, wiping away her tears. "You mean we're all together on the *Consolation?*"

"Captain Singleton is directly responsible," Wendy admitted, putting the emphasis on his new rank.

"Yes. And we've been waiting for the past hour for you to get here," Benita added.

"We're glad to see you finally made it," Josh Heinman teased. "We thought we might send a submarine for you, but then thought better of it."

Sunny looked toward Hank Brogdon, standing beside Wendy. "I see you got over your malaria."

"Yes. They wanted to invalid me home. But I bribed the doctor to let me stay. You're looking good, Sunny."

"Drinks are on the house," Singleton interrupted. "But they have to be non-alcoholic. What would you like, Fitzpatrick?"

"How about a Papuan milkshake?" she answered.

"Oh, no." Heinman groaned. "You're back in civilization again."

The party continued for fifteen more minutes. Then, Captain Singleton declared the festivities over. He and his executive officer, Brogdon, had other duties to attend to.

The next morning, the *Consolation* left harbor and Sunny, with her old roommates, Wendy and Benita, and a new one, Moxie Logan, settled down to a new routine on a new ship.

* * *

At Koraburra, Kenna began to pack. Alisdair Shannon had completed his part of the contract—making it possible for Kenna to stay in Australia until her daughter was rescued. And the month of Sunny's recuperation had been good for them both. Koraburra had provided a calm, healing presence, despite their sorrows. But now, it was time for Kenna to leave, just as Sunny had left.

Mrs. O'Leary walked down the hallway and stopped at the open bedroom door. "I have your dinner in the oven, Mrs. Fitzpatrick. Are you sure you don't want me to stay to serve it?"

"No, thank you, Mrs. O'Leary. That won't be necessary."

"Well, then, I'll be on my way. But if you need me, just ring the bell in the yard."

Mrs. O'Leary took a few steps and then stopped. "If Mr. Shannon gets in tonight, I fixed enough food for the two of you." She proceeded down the hall, took her sweater from the kitchen, and walked out the back door toward her own little white house at the edge of the compound.

Kenna closed one of the suitcases, and left the other open for last-minute items. She walked out of the bedroom and went to check on the food in the oven.

It had been two days since Shan had left with Sunny, Jack, and Cece. She knew he'd been scheduled to go from Melbourne to Darwin, to check on the shipment of beef.

Kenna smiled in spite of herself as she thought of his apartment in Darwin, and Gregory, the superintendent. Yes, she had a lot to be grateful for when it came to Shan's generosity. But that made her sad, too. He had provided so much, without asking anything in return.

Unwilling to sit alone in the large dining room, Kenna lit the fire in the den next to the kitchen, and brought her plate to the table before the fire. She sat on the same blue plaid sofa that she had shared with Shan that night when they had both been so lonely—the night before Shan removed Miranda's portrait from the living room and replaced it with the one of his son, Dair, dressed in uniform. Later, when she noticed it, Kenna had said nothing. But what could she have said? It was Shan's house and it was none of her business what he did. Just as it was none of her business if he had chosen to spend these last two nights with Cece.

Kenna had just sat down when she heard the plane. Quickly she put on her sweater and rushed out to the sedan, parked in the driveway. By the time the plane landed, she had the car lights lined up the way Shan had showed her, to give more light to the runway at night.

He looked tired as he walked to the car. His usual exuberance was gone. And his blue eyes were unsmiling when he climbed in beside her.

"Did you have a good trip?" she asked, backing around to return to the road.

"A disappointing one," he admitted. "The Japs sank the last two ships filled with Koraburra's meat."

"I'm sorry."

"It's not my own loss that bothers me," he added. "Knowing the troops will do without is the disheartening thing. But you deserve better news than that. Jack got to Melbourne on time. And I saw Sunny to the train station."

"You've been grand with them, Shan. Thank you."

He ignored her thanks. "Have you eaten dinner yet?"

"Actually not," Kenna said, remembering the plate she'd left. "Mrs. O'Leary fixed enough for both of us. We weren't sure just when you would get in. Are you hungry?"

"Ravenous."

While Shan took his luggage to his bedroom, Kenna hurried to the kitchen with her cold plate of food. She removed Shan's share of dinner from the refrigerator and reheated hers along with his.

Hearing him walk to the kitchen, Kenna called out, "I was planning to eat in the den in front of the fire. Is that all right with you?"

"Yes. Can I help you carry anything?"

"The mugs of hot tea," she answered, pointing to the same earthenware mugs they had used once before.

During dinner, Shan was unusually silent. And Kenna, thinking his mind was still on the sunken ships, did not press him into unnecessary conversation. But once the meal was over and Kenna had refilled the mugs, Shan spoke. "Do you remember the first night we had dinner in here?"

Kenna looked slightly embarrassed. "It wasn't a night one forgets easily."

"You're planning to leave me, aren't you?"

Kenna set down her earthenware mug. "I'm planning to leave Koraburra, if that's what you mean. There's no reason to stay anymore, now that Sunny is safe again."

"But if we found another reason for you to stay…"

"Putting it off any longer will just make it more difficult, Shan. You have your life to live here. And I've been away from home far too long."

"I had hoped that by now Koraburra would seem like home to you, Kenna."

"It does, Shan. And that's the trouble."

"Trouble? For whom?"

"For me. For you, too. No, I *must* leave."

His sadness turned to anger. "Don't you think losing *one* parent is enough pain for Sunny and Jack to take at the moment?"

"What do you mean?"

"I'm afraid, Kenna, your odds of getting to America, either by ship or plane, aren't very good. The Japanese have seen to that."

Kenna looked desperate. "I'll have to take that chance, Shan, whatever the odds. If I don't leave now, I may never want to leave."

"Then, stay here, Kenna. As my wife."

She looked at Shan, and his eyes had regained the assured, mocking look she remembered when she first saw him, leaning lazily against the Cessna at Alice Springs.

She didn't want to leave. She wanted to stay—with Shan. There was nothing left for her in America except memories of Irish. He would always be a part of her, and Sunny had helped her to see that. She need never deny those memories. But he was dead, and she was alive. She needed love and warm arms around her—to calm her fears when the nightmares of war came too close, like the piercing yellow eyes of the dingoes that had haunted her in the night. And if it were too soon by society's standards, Kenna knew that Irish would understand.

"What about Cece?" she hedged.

"I think your son will take care of her. They hit it off quite well. He was the reason she wanted to go to Melbourne."

"You're a generous, loving man, Alisdair Shannon."

"Let's not bring generosity into the picture, Kenna. From the moment I took you to the train station, I planned for you to return to Korraburra with me. I was completely selfish in that."

"But you let me go. I even boarded the train."

Shan suddenly grinned. "I think I knew you better than you knew yourself, even then. You weren't going to leave Australia, with your daughter still missing. I kept saying that under my breath while I waited for you to call me back."

Kenna laughed. "If you know me so well, tell me what I'm thinking at this very moment."

"The same thoughts as mine. That we've wasted enough time denying our love for each other. Come here, darling."

Shan held out his arms. "Generous—no. But loving—yes," he whispered. His mouth claimed hers in a long, lingering kiss, while a kookaburra bird, settling down for the night, shrieked in the distance.

At Kenna's slight response to the noise, Shan lifted his head and smiled. Tenderly, he said, "I think you've already become a part of this land, Kenna. Just as you've become a part of my heart."

"I behaved rather well, didn't I?" she teased. "At least I didn't jump two feet high this time at the shriek of the bird. But, of course, my attention was diverted."

In the white Victorian mansion surrounded by the red clay hills of Korraburra, Kenna Fitzpatrick, in Alisdair Shannon's arms, found respite from the terrors of war.

Chapter 41

THE WAR IN THE PACIFIC CONTINUED, WHILE PRIORITY to supplies, planes, and men went to the European theater. The battle for Guadalcanal lasted through September, October, November, with casualties picked up by the hospital ship *Consolation.*

It wasn't until February 1943 that the U.S. forces completed the Guadalcanal campaign, destroying the Japanese hidden in the caves in the hills, where Sunny had once sought shelter.

Sunny Fitzpatrick, stationed on the *Consolation,* was a different nurse from the fun-loving one on the *Good Hope.* At times, when Benita and Wendy would bring up the subject of her island sojourn, Sunny told them little beyond Kelia and the shrunken heads, a story repeated by the nurses to each new group of injured from that same island.

Occasionally, they found her examining the contents of an old, stained waterproof pouch, but she would quickly hide it again, without revealing what it contained.

During those months, Sunny kept up her search for some small sign that Alex Ramsay might still be alive, that he might have been taken prisoner by the Japanese and, at that very moment, could even be digging coal, along with Father Waal, on one of the islands off Japan's coast.

But that small spark of hope was snuffed out by the

confidential conversation with one of her recuperating patients, Lt. Martin Reynaud, who had served on Guadalcanal
from the time of the initial invasion.

As he slowly strolled on deck with Sunny, he whispered,
"I shouldn't be telling you this. There was a giant cover-up,
and it never reached the newspapers."

"What happened, Lieutenant?" she urged.

Still hesitating to reveal the secret, Martin asked, "Did
the Red Cross ever have your friend on their official list as a
'guest' of the Japanese government?"

"No."

Martin swallowed and , making up his mind, he finally
confessed, "A thousand prisoners of war were on a Japanese
cruiser headed for Japan from the Solomons. We sank her,
Sunny, and there were no survivors. It was only later that
we found out that the men on board were our own. If your
Alex Ramsay were taken prisoner about that time, then he
was more than likely on that ship."

"No, Martin," an anguished Sunny cried.

The Japanese had the upper hand in the South Pacific
until June 1943 when Operation Cartwheel was launched,
with Rabaul as the principal target. By the next June 1944,
the U.S. Marines had invaded Saipan, shortly after the
Normandy invasion in Europe. And by June 1945, after the
war in Europe was over, the U.S. Tenth Army captured
Okinawa.

The Japanese had finally overextended themselves. One
by one, each island was retaken—at great cost—and the
Allied sights were set on Japan, herself.

"Have you heard the latest scuttlebutt, Sunny?" Wendy
inquired as they leaned over the railing and watched the sun
set.

"About Benita's retiring and going back to the States?"

"No. That's not scuttlebutt. That's fact."

"Then I haven't heard."

"It's still hush-hush, but the U.S. is supposed to have a

secret weapon, even more powerful than the German rockets."

"Did you get that from Brogdon?"

Wendy squirmed. "You know he's not supposed to tell me any military secrets."

"Then where did you hear it?"

"Let's just say from an 'unconfirmed source.' "

Sunny nodded her head. "Brogdon. He never could keep any secrets—especially from you."

Wendy turned to look over her shoulder, to see if the two were still alone.

"There's one secret he's kept. For an entire year," Sunny said. "The only reason he's done that is he knows *you'd* be booted off this ship if he didn't."

"What are you talking about?"

"Oh, come on, Wendy. I've known ever since Saipan that you two got married on leave."

A horrified Wendy said, "Not so loud, Sunny." And then she leaned closer, and asked, "Do I talk in my sleep?"

"You just make noises—ooh and aah, and little love sounds."

An indignant Wendy said, "I do not. You're teasing me, aren't you?"

"Yes. But don't worry. I'll keep your secret."

"It's hard enough to see each other every day and be so circumspect. But I think I would just die if I had to be separated from him." Then in a teasing mood of her own, Wendy spoke up. "You may not know it, but *you're* the one who talks in her sleep."

"I do?" a startled Sunny replied.

"Yes. One night, I listened while you dreamed you were at a wedding. It was the funniest thing—something about a bride wearing khaki, and the attendants, cockatoo feathers. Benita and I decided the jungle had really gotten to you."

A wary Sunny eyed her friend. "What else did I say in my sleep?"

"I've forgotten. It was only those first few weeks, anyway. And we really didn't pay much attention."

"The war has lasted a long time, hasn't it?"

"Yes. That was why I was so excited when…when the 'unconfirmed source' told me about the secret weapon. I want to go home—and have babies, Sunny, and a little white house with a picket fence. And roses in the garden. If we could use the weapon and, presto, no more war, think how many lives could be saved."

"I know."

"Have you heard from Matt lately?" Wendy asked suddenly.

"No. But I haven't written him, either."

"You two used to be so close. What happened?"

"The war, I guess."

"Moxie asked me the other day why you didn't go after Captain Singleton."

"Please tell her that I don't deliberately go after anybody. That sounds so crass."

"I think she was asking for her own benefit, not yours. And she isn't called Moxie for nothing."

"Come on. Let's go back to our quarters," Sunny suggested.

"Well, I apologize for bringing up the subject, but you're not getting any younger, you know. As I recall, you're twenty-five, the same age I am."

"My mother got married again when she was in her forties," Sunny commented.

"But that was the second time around. That's different."

The last part of the conversation with Wendy did nothing to cheer Sunny. Instead, it had the opposite effect. Everyone seemed to be pairing off, like a formal dance card. Even her brother Jack was engaged to Cece Bennigan. In the three families, Todd was the only other one left—besides herself.

Her mother had been one of the lucky ones. But for Sunny, there was no Alisdair Shannon waiting to share her grief or to help pick up the pieces of her life. If there were, she couldn't see him. Alex Ramsay was too real, even after three years. And Sunny realized the only way she could ever rid herself of his influence and accept his death was to see Alex's cousin, Malcolm, in his place as the marquess of Dalhousie. Only then could she be free.

By August, the secret weapon Wendy had mentioned was no longer a secret to the world. The atomic bomb was dropped on Japan, forcing the rising sun to set over two ravaged cities—Hiroshima and Nagasaki—and the Japanese sword of *Bushido* was surrendered to the Allies in the official ceremony aboard the U.S. battleship *Missouri.*

From the Japanese concentration camps throughout the East—from Singapore, Burma, and unpronounceable islands off the shores of Japan—the emaciated men and women, prisoners of war, British, Chinese, Australian, and American, began to be rescued.

Sunny remained in Australia as long as she could, hoping with all her heart that a miracle might occur—that Alex Ramsay would appear, as he had that day in the Java Sea after his escape from Singapore. Finally, giving up all hope, she said good-bye to her mother, Kenna, and left Koraburra. Her pilgrimage seemed more urgent than ever.

On the farthermost island off the mainland of Japan, two men in tattered garments, with the grime of coal dust clinging to their skin, emerged from the mine shaft at the end of the day.

The island was strangely silent. No Japanese guards waited to prod them back to camp with rifle butts and bayonets. After the hours of darkness in the mines, the two blinked and shielded their eyes from the glitter of sunlight.

Off the island's coast, a ship of mercy, similar to the hospital ship *Good Hope,* lay at anchor. And two destroyers, with their American flags flying high in the breeze, aimed their guns toward shore, while a motor launch sped toward the beach of volcanic rock.

Watching its progress, the first man, in a trembling voice, inquired, "Do you think the war's finally over, Alex?"

"I pray to God it is," a weak Alex Ramsay replied.

Behind them, the other prisoners emerged from the mine shaft. They, too, saw the flags and heard the sound of the launch. The twenty men still alive from the original five hundred prisoners on the island shouted in triumph and stumbled toward the beach to greet their liberators.

Unaware that Alex Ramsay was alive, Sunny Fitzpatrick arrived in Scotland. It was now November. The bluebells and heather had long since gone, and a cold grayness surrounded the land, with its mist and fog from the sea swirling over the heath. The wind carried the sound of gulls and a few flakes of snow as Sunny, holding her one piece of luggage, stepped off the country bus in front of the tavern, Tall Man's Bluff, where an attic room had been reserved for her.

"Come in to the fire, lassie," the craggy-faced man called out. "We be havin' a real blow now, to greet ye." He took her luggage inside, set it down, and waved her on to the huge fireplace of stone where the logs hissed and sang in protest to the coming storm.

Her coat, brown and blue plaid, was not only warm, but fashionable, with matching blue cap, scarf, and mittens. On her feet, she wore soft brown boots, ankle length and lined in fur. And as she removed her coat, her blue wool two-piece dress was revealed.

"Colin asked me to bring a hot mug of cider to ye," the woman coming toward her offered. "It's not often we get visitors this time of year. And I know ye be cold from the long trip on MacGillivray's bus."

"Thank you, Mrs…"

"Just call me Flossie. Everyone does."

"And I'm Amanda Fitzpatrick. But my friends call me Sunny."

"And I can see why. Your hair was kissed by the sun the

day ye were born."

Taking a sip of the hot cider, Sunny looked out the window. "Do you think the storm will be over by tomorrow?"

"Maybe yes. Maybe no. It depends on the wind and the sea."

"How far is Creaganshill from here?" Sunny asked suddenly.

"About four kilometers by road. Shorter over the moor, but ye won't be wantin' to travel that way. Are ye planning on visiting Sir Malcolm? He'll send a car for ye if ye are."

"Oh, no. I don't plan to call on him. I was told the manor house is a beautiful one And I'd like to see it. From a distance, of course."

"More like a castle," Flossie corrected. "I remember the time when his uncle owned the place. Then it passed to his son, Sir Alex. A shame that the boy had to die like that. Not that I begrudge Sir Malcolm his inheritance. Don't get me wrong. But Sir Alex was always a favorite around here. That is, the times he came home from that heathen land."

"What happened to…Sir Alex?"

"I only know what Sir Malcolm told my Mary. She works up at the house now. He was on some island when the Japanese took it. And he was never heard from again. Shot, I guess."

Flossie, seeing Sunny's face, said, "Go on and get closer to the fire. Your face is as white as a snowflake. It takes a long time for the November chill to leave ye."

Sunny did as she was told, swallowed the rest of her cider, and then asked Flossie to show her to her room.

Later, she came downstairs for tea, and then quickly retired to her room since the men were beginning to come to the tavern for their nightly ale.

By the next morning, the sun was out. Sunny, having her breakfast in her room, was glad. Although the room was small, it was comfortable, with a feather bed and a small rocking chair with tatted lace to protect the upholstered arms and back. And in the corner fireplace, a peat fire burned to chase the chill from the room. Faded wallpaper of heather design, once lavender and white with sprigs of green, was now muted by the sun, matching the glass shade on the lamp by the bed. Her few clothes hung in the small armoire across the room. The small, diamond-shaped windowpanes of colored glass cast their reflections on the ceiling as the sun shone through the room.

When Sunny had finished her breakfast and sponged her body in cold water from the pitcher, she hurriedly dressed in her warmest clothes and went downstairs.

"Ye be goin' out now?" Flossie inquired.

"Yes. I want to take a long walk. Could you please point me in the direction of Creaganshill?"

The woman stood at the door and watched until Sunny was out of sight.

Used to computing land distance in miles, Sunny translated Flossie's estimate of four kilometers by road. Six-tenths of a mile times four—a little less than two and a half miles. Not a great distance to walk compared to the mountain range and ridges on Guadalcanal that she and Alex had walked.

The narrow road began to wind with the curve of the land. Along the way an occasional crofter's cottage appeared, with smoke curling from the chimney. Then a herd of sheep, guarded by a small black collie, made its appearance around the bend. Sunny stepped to the side until the shepherd and his animals passed by.

Sunny walked slowly, aware of the sea and the majesty of Ben Lomond's snowcapped peak in the distance. The great yew trees, planted by Robert the Bruce, stood gnarled with age in the foreground.

With each step, she drank in the harsh beauty of the land and attempted to remember everything Scottish in her life so that, when she finally saw Creaganshill, she would have forged a strong bond to Alex and his heritage.

Sunny recalled her ancestor who had been murdered by MacBeth. She repeated the Selkirk grace that her first-grade teacher had used to bless her milk and crackers. And she remembered Robert Louis Stevenson, born in Edinburgh and buried at Pago Pago, where the *Good Hope* had anchored.

Then she saw it, high on the hill, bleak at first against the winter sky, its stones washed white with lime, with a fortification of walls proclaiming its age from before the days of Cromwell. She stood on the road and wept , her warm, salt-laden tears lifted from her cheeks by the wind to become a part of the mist.

She should never have come, for she found no peace looking over the land where Alex had walked, or listening to the roar of the rampaging sea in the distance, battering against the rocky crags. She wiped her tears with her glove and fled back toward the shelter of the village and the inn.

On the moor, not far from the winding road, a tall, gaunt figure of a man journeyed toward the manor house. But Sunny paid little attention to him. She was too steeped in her own misery.

For the rest of the day, Sunny remained in her room. She came downstairs for tea, and to let Colin know she would be leaving by MacGillivray's bus the next day.

"Mary will be servin' ye tonight," Colin said. "My Flossie is a bit under the weather."

"I'm sorry. Is there anything I can do? I'm a nurse, you know."

"Now, that's kind of ye. But she'll be all right."

"My mum's havin' another bairn—at her age," Mary whispered. "She won't get better for another six months."

As she sat down at the table and took the menu, Sunny forced herself to put her sadness behind her. "I understand that you work at Creaganshill," she said.

"Yes. For three months now."

"And do you like it?"

"It's all right. Sir Malcolm is nice enough to work for. And I like staying near my mum, especially right now."

Sunny gave her order, and listened to the howl of the

wind outside while she waited. Mary brought the food, piping hot—eggs and haggis, fresh bread, and hot tea. And when Sunny had finished, she went upstairs, the same as the evening before, to escape the stares of the village men coming in for their nightly mug. So Sunny did not hear the news that spread throughout the tavern—of the man who had come in that very day on MacGillivray's bus while she was out for her walk.

By morning, Mary had gone to work, and Flossie, recovered from the day before, brought breakfast to Sunny's room.

"I understand ye be leavin' today?" she said, setting the tray on the table.

"Yes. My vacation is over. I need to get back to the States. But I want to thank you and your husband for being so nice to me these past two days."

"It isn't often we get an American in, now that the war is over. And such a pretty one, too. Mary was talking about that before she left for work this morning."

After breakfast, Sunny dressed in her new brown and blue plaid coat and walked downstairs. Her fur-lined boots made no noise on the faded green carpet of the stairs. In her hands, she cradled a piece of bread left over from her breakfast.

Nodding to Colin, she said, "I'm going for a walk along the crag near the beach. I'll be back in plenty of time for MacGillivray's bus, Mr. Keith."

"Be careful of the fen, Miss Fitzpatrick. It's dangerous this time of the year."

"I'll be careful."

Following the sound of waves crashing against the rocks, Sunny made her way to the crag that overlooked the sea and the snowcapped mountains in the distance. Great gulls wheeled about in the air and called to one another. She stood close to the edge, broke off a piece of bread, and watched it tumble toward the rocks below. Halfway down, a gull swooped past with the prize in its beak, and a great cry of the other birds prompted Sunny to hurl other pieces of bread into the wind.

With the gulls echoing the lonely cry in her heart, Sunny said her final farewell to Alex's land. A bleakness, despite the morning sun, surrounded her and, unable to stand it any longer, she turned to leave.

She stopped. Below, on the beach, a figure walked purposefully with his face toward the sun. Compelled to watch him, Sunny felt the ache in her throat grow as he came closer. There was something in his walk that reminded her of Alex. But, of course, it couldn't be. Alex was dead.

Unwilling to spy on the man, Sunny threw the last bit of bread to the gulls and began to walk away.

The man below looked up, saw Sunny, and waved his arms to attract her attention. "Sunny," he shouted, his voice carrying upward by the wind to reach the cliff where she was standing. "Sunny, wait!"

It couldn't be. It couldn't be Alex, her husband. And yet, the voice—"Alex?" she called out. "Alex, is that you?"

"Yes."

She searched frantically for some way to reach him, but the cliff separated them. A piece of ground gave way as she got too near the edge, and she stepped back quickly.

"Alex, how do I get down?"

"Stay there," he shouted. "I'll come up to you."

He disappeared, but she didn't dare move. Her mind reeled like the gulls in the bleak November sky. Alex was alive. That was all she could fathom. Her husband was alive. She hugged her arms to herself to stop the shaking that was not due to the cold. The waiting seemed an eternity, yet she had waited for three long years, hoping with all her heart that he was still alive, until all hope had ceased.

"I searched everywhere for you," the voice behind her said.

She rushed toward the voice and the outstretched arms. He kissed the tears on her upturned face, and then he stepped back, still holding to her hands. "Let me look at you, darling. For three years I stayed alive by dreaming of this moment." He drank in the sight of her and he reached out to touch her hair, to trace the contours of her face, gently, lovingly, like a blind man recapturing the shape of love.

"Alex, tell me..." Her voice left her, while the cry of gulls filled the air. She tried again. "That day on Guadalcanal—I thought you had been killed."

"I was taken prisoner, instead. Father Waal and I. Your Japanese pilot, Yamuto, is to be thanked for that, although at times I felt it a dubious gift."

"And Father Waal?" She was almost afraid to ask.

"He died in the prisoner-of-war camp, but for him it was a blessing, Sunny."

Sadness and joy were both reflected in the large topaz eyes that stared unwaveringly at Alex. "You're so thin," Sunny said.

Alex's smile was gentle, bittersweet. "I remember a time when a certain nurse on a hospital ship took care of that. Would she be willing, do you think, to take on the chore again—but this time in less hazardous surroundings?"

She wiped a tear from her eyes. And with the jauntiness of that long-ago day, she said, "Would you like some ice cream, sailor?"

"I would prefer a cup of tea," he replied. "Hot."

"So would I," Sunny admitted, shivering in the cold.

"Then let's go home, Sunny—to fire and hearth."

"Oh, no. My luggage. It's probably on MacGillivray's bus right now."

"No. I asked Colin to send it up to Creaganshill."

Later that evening, in the master suite of the manor house surrounded by fortress walls, Sunny and Alex lay in each other's arms. The massive stone fireplace of the bedroom glowed with a brilliance that spread through the room.

There were so many questions to be answered; so many things still left unsaid. But somehow, it didn't seem to matter, for Sunny and Alex had an entire lifetime ahead.

"Do you remember our wedding night, when I gave you the plaited-grass ring that All-Same-Barrel had made?"

"Yes. I kept it for more than a year. It finally disintegrated, and I scattered the remains over the Coral Sea."

"I made a promise that night to give you a proper ring. So, hold out your hand, my lady."

"Alex?"

He took her left hand in his and, reaching under the pillow, he brought out an heirloom amethyst -and-diamond circlet that glittered in the glow of the fire. Placing it on her finger, he looked into her eyes. "Till death do us part."

"No, Alex," she whispered. "For all eternity." She snuggled against him. "I love you, Alex Ramsay, marquess of Dalhousie."

"My darling," he said, taking her again in his arms. Sunny had no need to translate the Gaelic he spoke. The words had become engraved in her heart on that first night at Bohorok, and again on the high ridge above the Lunga Plain of Guadalcanal.

EPILOGUE

THE FULL STORY OF AMANDA "SUNNY" FITZPATRICK AND Alex Ramsay, marquess of Dalhousie, can never be told, for in all lives, there are moments too intimate to share, even with friends.

Sunny and Alex remained in Scotland only a few months. With Sir Malcolm, Alex's cousin, left in charge of Creaganshill, the two returned to India, where Alex's heart had always been.

With Mountbatten, who was the first viceroy and later governor-general, Alex, the diplomat, worked for an India independent of British rule.

"One man cannot own another man. Only in the freedom of all can even one man be free."

The experience as a prisoner of war, and his friendship with the martyred Chuang San Chu, had left a profound mark on Alex Ramsay's soul.

§

Acknowledgments

When I had finished the third book in a series , showing two generations of the same family from World War I (*Phoenix Rising*), their lives between the two wars (*From Love's Ashes*) and the World War II novel, in the European theater (*On Wings of Fire*) , I thought the series was complete. But then my publisher asked if I would write another in the series, showing the war in the Pacific.

To Face the Sun is the fourth and last of "The Phoenix Quartet."

Much research went into the writing of this book. I joined the Military Book Club and scouted for unusual histories and books at used book sales. At one, I found the log of a hospital ship that showed its actual route on the so-called "lollipop run" to the various islands of the Pacific to pick up the wounded. And so my heroine, Sunny Fitzpatrick, was born — as a U.S. Navy nurse.

When this book was first published, it received a number of awards, including The Reviewer's Choice Award as the best WWII novel of that year.

I am happy to present this second edition of *To Face the Sun,* with the hope that the tremendous bravery of those Allies who fought in the Pacific in WWII will live on in the hearts and memories of all who cherish freedom.

Frances Patton Statham

About the Author

Frances Patton Statham is an award-winning writer, artist, musician, and lecturer. She rceived her undergraduate degree, *magna cum laude*, with a double major in voice performance and music education from Winthrop University, a Master of Fine Arts degree from the University of Georgia, with further opera study.

As a lyric-coloratura soprano, she has given recitals and lectures in such cities as Singapore, Madrid, Budapest, and Vancouver.

A resident of metro-Atlanta, she is listed in a number of biographical references, including *International Who's Who of Authors and Writers*, *International Biography*, *International Who's Who of Women*, *Personalities of the South*, and *Contemporary Authors*.